FAIRY'S TOUCH

LEGION OF ANGELS: BOOK 7

ELLA SUMMERS

FAIRY'S TOUCH

Legion of Angels: Book 7

www.ellasummers.com/fairys-touch

ISBN 978-1-0800-6590-5

BOOKS BY ELLA SUMMERS

Legion of Angels

Vampire's Kiss

Witch's Cauldron

Siren's Song

Dragon's Storm

Shifter's Shadow

Psychic's Spell

Fairy's Touch

Angel's Flight

Ghost's Whisper

Phoenix's Refrain

Immortal Legacy

Angel Fire

Angel Fury

Angel Fever

Dragon Born

Mercenary Magic

Magic Edge

Magic Games

Magic Nights

Blood Magic

Magic Kingdom

Fairy Magic

Rival Magic

Shadow World

Spirit Magic

Magic Immortal

Shadow Magic

Sorcery & Science

Sorcery & Science

Vampires & Vigilantes

And more books coming soon…

CHAPTERS

CHAPTER 1

LEGION'S LEGACY

I stepped onto the platform. Before me, the station sign read 'Crystal Falls' in embossed gold letters. Behind me, the red-and-bronze airship that had brought me to this isolated jungle island bobbed gently in the wind, preparing to depart.

I stood alone on the spotless station platform. There wasn't another soul in sight. Unsurprisingly. This wasn't a tourist getaway; it was a private island occupied by the Legion of Angels, the gods' army on Earth. The Legion used the facility here to train soldiers they believed possessed the potential to become angels.

For the next several days, I and six others would train hard and long under the guidance of the angel Colonel Dragonblood. At the end of it, we would be stronger, smarter, and that much closer to leveling up our magic.

At least that was the plan. With my luck, sea monsters would overrun the island two minutes into the training. And then we'd spend the next week fighting for our lives. Yeah, you could say my life was a nonstop blockbuster action movie with paranormal trimmings.

"The island is well-protected. There's no reason to believe anything like that will happen this time," I told myself, swinging my pack onto my back.

I followed the winding trail away from the station. As I entered the trees, a chorus of shrill bird cries welcomed me to the jungle. I looked up, scanning the tropical foliage. There were bright fuchsia flowers and more strings of trumpet-sized bluebells than I could count, but I didn't spot any creatures. Or any monsters, I noted happily.

My ringing phone interrupted the unseen birds' next war cry.

"Hi, Bella," I answered.

"You sound out of breath," my sister said.

"I'm hiking through a scorching hot jungle in one hundred percent humidity." I swiped the sweat from my brow. I didn't bother with the sweat covering the rest of my body. There wasn't any point in this weather. I'd only walked a few steps, and my tank top was already pasted to my skin.

"Oh. I thought I was interrupting...something."

I snorted. "If I were having sex with Nero, trust me, I wouldn't have answered my phone."

"I see."

I couldn't see her blush, but I'd wager my set of collectable Legion playing cards that she was as red as a cherry right now. Which meant I had to tease her further, of course. After all, what were sisters for?

"Speaking of angel lovers who make you forget all else, Harker told me you finally agreed to go out with him."

"I did no such thing," she protested.

I could picture the dignified indignation on her face as clearly as though she were standing right in front of me.

"Did you know he blindsided me on campus last week?" she said.

Bella was in her second and final year of school at the New York University of Witchcraft.

"No, I didn't know Harker visited you there," I said.

"You visit me. Calli and the girls visit me. We chat, drink tea, and have a pleasant time. Harker does *not* visit. He completely covers the campus quad and all its adjacent buildings in red roses. Thousands of red roses."

"Were they pretty?" I was trying really hard not to laugh.

"Leda!"

I coughed. "Sorry."

"Then, amidst the sea of roses, the eyes of every witch on campus trained on us, he asked me to dinner."

"What did you say?"

"I told him that his unwavering persistence was maddening. That it was enough to make any woman break down and agree to go out with him just to make him stop."

"I can see how he took that statement as an acceptance."

"You are not helping," she snapped.

Bella was usually so calm, so serene. Harker had really gotten under her skin. That's how I knew she totally liked him.

"How can I possibly help?" I asked her.

"Harker is your friend."

"He is also an angel—with all the good and bad that comes with it. To you, covering the quad in roses might seem extreme, but I promise you that he was holding back."

"There were roses everywhere. Everyone was watching. There was nothing left to hold back," she laughed weakly.

"That's not true. There could have been diamond tiaras and silk runners, elephants and unicorns, acrobats, dancers, carnival floats, and a mariachi band."

Dead silence.

"Bella?" I asked.

"You think just like them. Like an angel," she said quietly.

"You have to know 'em to beat 'em," I chuckled.

Silence again.

"What do I do about Harker?" Bella finally asked.

"What do you want to do about him?"

"I'm…not sure," she admitted. "The roses and public declarations of affection are a bit much…"

"But a part of you likes it all," I finished for her.

"Does that make me crazy?" she said quietly.

"Of course. Our whole family is crazy," I replied brightly.

It didn't matter that we weren't related by blood. We were united by love. And by a healthy dose of madness.

Bella's chuckle was soft and sweet—like a purring kitten. "Thank you."

"For explaining the ways of angels?"

"For being there. And for listening."

"Any time. You've always been there for me," I said. "And, hey, if you want to truly understand the ways of angels, I have a great book you can study."

"Thanks, but I have some actual studying to do right now for exams."

"All the important stuff in life will never be on a test."

"Your philosophy in a nutshell, Leda."

"Yep. With a few more bells and whistles added on. And a scattering of bombshells."

"I'm glad you're my sister," Bella laughed.

"Love you too." A grin spread my lips. "Now you go study and kick all those witches' asses on your exams."

"Try not to blow up anything at your training."

I stuck my tongue out at the phone screen.

"See you soon," said Bella.

"Absolutely. When I'm back in the city, there's a new bakery close to the office that we have to try. They have chocolate cheesecake. We can invite Harker too."

"Funny."

"I thought so."

I heard a bell ring on Bella's end.

"I have to get going, Leda."

"Bye."

I tucked my phone into my bag. I'd reached the entrance of the Crystal Falls training facility, a set of two formidable doors five times as tall as I was. I paused on the threshold and drew in a deep breath, inhaling the sweet and spicy jungle air. It smelled remarkably like a batch of hot cinnamon rolls fresh out of the oven.

I pushed the doors open and stepped inside. With its white stone pillars and high archways, the entrance hall resembled a cathedral more than a military training facility. Spotlit murals featured gods and angels framed in golden halos, their majestic wings spread wide. Armed with flaming swords and shimmering shields, they battled demons and monsters.

The Champions of Earth. The Saviors of Humanity. The Patrons of Magic. From the gilded city temples to the filthy street corners of the Frontier, that was the song the Pilgrims, the voice of the gods' message, sang to humanity.

Magnanimous, omnipotent, and perfectly immaculate: those were the qualities the Pilgrims told us the gods represented.

I'd met the seven ruling gods and goddesses of the gods' council, and they weren't so much magnanimous as merciless. They were certainly immensely powerful, but I wasn't sure about omnipotent. Surely, their power had limits—or at least I chose to think so. And I didn't believe for a moment that the gods were free from flaws. But they made the rules, so it was ultimately up to them to define what constituted a 'flaw'.

I'd reached the end of the hall and stopped in front of Room 126. Someone had slid a paper with my name on it into the slot on the door. Captain Leda Pierce. She sounded so dignified, so proper, so serious—so everything I was not.

I entered my room and set my backpack down on the desk beside the bed. Waiting on my mattress were a pair of shoes, shorts, and a blue tank top with this training's logo: the blue silhouette of an angel standing between the block text words 'Crystal' and 'Falls'. I changed into the gym uniform. As expected, everything fit me perfectly. The Legion knew all its soldiers' measurements from head to toe.

As I headed to the main gym, I wondered what challenges the Crystal Falls training would throw at me.

My first challenge presented itself a few minutes later. The way to the gym was barred—by a gigantic waterfall plunging down between two of the facility's buildings.

I searched for a way around the obstacle but ultimately came to the unfortunate conclusion that the only way forward was through the crashing curtain of water. And so through I went. On the plus side, I wasn't hot anymore. On the not-so-plus side, my shoes were squishy.

The waterfall now behind me, I entered the gym hall. It was massive in every direction, including in height. A whole airship could have fit inside here. But despite its docking bay dimensions, the gym wasn't raw or rough. The wood floors were glossy and bright. Framed paintings of famous angels throughout history covered every inch of the walls not occupied by ropes, ladders, bars, and other training apparatuses.

I spotted Nero's likeness up there on the wall, magic burning on his hands, lighting up his dark wings. Nyx, the First Angel, was on that wall as well. So were Nero's parents, Damiel Dragonsire and Cadence Lightbringer. I also recognized Leila Starborn of Storm Castle and Bella's suitor Harker Sunstorm. The painting of Colonel Fireswift, the brutal head of the Legion's Interrogators, seemed almost alive. His cold glare drilled into me, as though the real Colonel Fireswift were gazing across land and water to spy on me even here.

Training stations were set up all across the gym. Some contained workout benches and weights. Others featured weapons and target boards. There were bars and bands, ladders and beams, ropes and nets.

And standing at the center of the hall were six soldiers dressed in the same Crystal Falls gym uniform as I was. Except for Jace Fireswift, son of Colonel Fireswift, I didn't recognize a single one of them.

"Hello," I said with a smile, greeting the soldiers who would be my comrades for the next few days.

"So she joins us at last," said a female soldier. She wore an elaborate assortment of dark braids—and a haughty sneer on her lips. "The infamous Leda Pierce, Legion celebrity."

Well, wasn't that nice? She didn't even know me, and already she hated me.

The best way to counter that stellar welcome was with a generous serving of sugar.

"I'd hardly call myself a celebrity," I replied with a sweet smile.

"She expects she will be up there soon," a male soldier said to the others, his eyes lifting to the wall of angels.

Another soldier laughed. "I guess no one told her that wall is reserved for those with angel blood."

I glanced at the insignia on their shirts. A flower, the symbol for Fairy's Touch, was embroidered on each and every one of them. They were all level seven soldiers, one step short of being an angel.

And that wasn't even the best part. They didn't only all outrank me; they all came from established magic families. The surnames printed on their uniforms marked them as Legion brats, legacy soldiers who had an angel parent. Demonslayer. Spellsmiter. Silvertongue. Wardbreaker. Battleborn. Fireswift. There were a lot of famous angel names in there.

I was the only level six soldier here, the only one who wasn't a Legion brat. The outsider. It was no wonder they looked at me like I was a ragged, flea-infested alley cat who'd wandered into the hall uninvited, smelling of rotting garbage and humble beginnings.

"She is absolutely soaked," the soldier named Silvertongue said in horror, her eyes following the trail of puddles I'd left in my wake.

There wasn't a drop of water on the six of them. How the hell had they gotten through the waterfall without getting soaked? I didn't ask that question. They'd only mock my ignorance.

"Time to warm up," the soldier named Spellsmiter said to the others, turning his back on me to look at the equipment.

The others followed suit. Apparently, they'd already grown bored of mocking me. Thank goodness.

"Come on, Jace," Battleborn called him over to the sea of ropes hanging from the ceiling.

Jace paused, his gaze shifting between me and his fellow brats, then he joined Battleborn at the ropes. Jace and I were friends—and competitors. Like all things in my life, it was complicated. But I didn't blame him for going with the other Legion brats.

Ostensibly, the Crystal Falls training was for level six and level seven soldiers, but things were obviously different this time around. The Legion had recently lost an angel, and it was widely known that Colonel Dragonblood would create a new angel from our ranks. The pressure on the level seven soldiers to perform, to prove themselves worthy of that honor, was enormous.

I wasn't a level seven soldier, so I couldn't even win that prize. And, as I watched the positively brutal way the others were warming up, I decided things were better this way. If they were hitting their friends that hard, I didn't want to experience how hard they hit the outsider, the intruder in their sacred circle of angel blood. I'd rather traverse the plains of monsters than find myself in the crosshairs of these level sevens. From the looks of it, they would gladly kill each other in their scramble to the top, in their unfriendly competition to become an angel here.

I wandered over to an unoccupied lifting station. I picked up a barbell and began doing benchpresses. I hadn't even done twenty reps when Spellsmiter claimed the workout bench closest to mine and preceded to benchpress a barbell loaded with twice as much weight as mine. I sighed. So much for being ignored.

His message was clear: I was way out of my league here. My response was equally clear. I got up and added more weight to my barbell until mine was heavier than his. I couldn't help it. He was just asking for me to egg him on.

Spellsmiter made a derisive noise, then piled more weight on his bar.

I responded in kind. He might be the son of an angel, but I'd been trained by the archangel Nero Windstriker. Nero had special bars that could hold more weight than the Legion's regular high-capacity bars—and he'd used them extensively when torturing me with his workout routines.

Spellsmiter kept loading on more weight, and I kept countering. By now, there was so much weight on his bar that he could barely push it up. His face was red, his muscles quivering, and he was grunting like a stuck pig—but still he carried on stubbornly, determined to put me in my place.

It clearly wasn't working out as he'd planned. What could I say? When you went up against Chaos, plans fell apart.

Growling in frustration, Spellsmiter lowered the full barbell to the ground. Then he picked up a heavy medicine ball and hurled it at me. I cast a shifting spell on the ball midair, transforming it into an inflatable swimming ring. I caught the light toy around my wrist, swinging it once before tossing it to the floor.

"Cheap tricks won't get you through this training,

blondie," Spellsmiter growled and hurled another weight ball at me.

I changed it into a pink rubber ducky and tossed it down beside the swimming ring. "Perhaps not, but at least my cheap tricks will make your company more bearable."

"Snark will serve you no better."

"But it might bring a smile to your face?" I said hopefully.

He didn't favor me with a smile. He just kept throwing loaded balls at me until the rack was empty—and I was surrounded by inflatable pool toys. Making friends with Legion brats was hard. They simply didn't appreciate my sense of humor.

Sighing, I moved on to another training station. Here, I shot an arrow at a target board and hit the bullseye. Hmm, not bad.

An arrow split mine in half. I looked back to find another Legion brat. Silvertongue, the one who'd derided me for my wet clothes. Like Spellsmiter, she had followed me to my exercise station.

The Legion brats were trying to show me they were better at every single thing in every conceivable way. They were telling me in no uncertain terms that I did not deserve to be here. I was an outsider. I hadn't grown up in their world. I hadn't trained in combat and magic from the time I could walk. I was not a member of the elite, the magic legacies, the closed social circles that reached back centuries.

I walked over to the mats to stretch. Sure enough, within a minute of my arrival, a Legion brat lowered down right beside me.

"Stopped by to see who can stretch for longer?" I quipped.

"Sitting on my ass doing nothing? I don't know, Leda. I don't think that's a competition I can win."

I turned to look at Jace. He was the Legion brat who'd joined me on the mats.

Instead of an insult, he offered me a smile. "We haven't talked in a while. How have you been?"

I arched my brows. "Are you sure your friends want you talking to me?"

"They aren't my friends. You are," he replied.

"They don't think I belong here, in your world."

"No, they don't. They think you've been scraping by with a lot of luck, hiding under the coattails of greater soldiers."

I looked across the gym, watching the brats' competitions of magic, strength, and skill. They were so polished, so practiced, so perfect—in everything they did. I had to work twice as hard for half the results.

"Maybe they're right," I said. "Maybe I don't belong here."

"No, they're *not* right," Jace said. "They are powerful and clever and the top of their game in every way. But they aren't you. None of them were imprisoned by a demon. None of them survived hell. They don't know how hard you've had it. Or how strong you truly are."

"Why, Jace, is that a compliment addressed at me, your competitor?"

"It's a truth. You don't see things the same way as the rest of us. Your mind is so…"

"Twisted?" I suggested.

"Unique," he decided. "And strong, despite what they might think. That's how you survived hell. And that's why you will one day be an angel."

"Just not before you're an angel, right?"

Jace laughed.

I smiled at him.

"What?" he asked.

"You're looking better," I told him.

His sister's death last month had hit him hard. I hadn't seen a genuine smile on his face in a long time.

"I'm surviving," he said stoically. "Because that's what we must do. That is our duty. We must be strong. So that we may defend the Earth and push back the dark forces that threaten humanity."

I gave him a big hug.

Confusion flitted across his face. "What was that for?"

"You needed it."

He glanced around, his hands twitching.

"Are you nervous?" I asked him.

"Yes," he admitted.

"Don't worry. Your friends aren't watching," I teased him. "They didn't see our touching moment. They're too engrossed in their wrestling match."

"It's not them I'm worried about." Jace dropped his voice to a hushed whisper and added, "It's General Windstriker."

"Nero doesn't mind a hug between friends."

"He once threatened to kill me for looking at you," Jace said drily.

"I'm sure he didn't mean it."

"I'm sure that he did."

"Well, then it's a good thing for you that Nero is thousands of miles away right now," I said with a smile.

A gust of wind blew through the gym, throwing the doors open. That wasn't a mundane breeze. It was a gale born from formidable magic. Angel magic. Everyone stopped what they were doing to watch Colonel Dragonblood's arrival.

But Colonel Dragonblood did not step through those open doors. Another angel did, one far more powerful. And far more dangerous.

Magic uncurled from him, flooding the entire hall with unfettered power. It ignited the air like a lightning storm. Goosebumps prickled up across my skin, responding to the overwhelming force of magic.

Unbothered by the tropical heat, he wore a black leather uniform fitted perfectly to his body. I could see every dip, every curve of muscle beneath that leather skin. His body, sculpted by centuries of merciless workouts, wasn't human at all. It was divine—as divine as his glowing caramel hair, lit up in his halo, as divine as his emerald eyes, burning with magic.

"Nero." His name brushed against my lips like a lover's kiss.

"Colonel Dragonblood is unavailable," Nero declared, addressing the entire room. "As of now, I am overseeing the Crystal Falls training."

CHAPTER 2

THE BIG PRIZE

Nero started us out with a magical warmup right away.

"Pair up," he instructed us. "You are going to drill your seven basic magic skills in turn."

That meant Vampire's Kiss, Witch's Cauldron, Siren's Song, Dragon's Storm, Shifter's Shadow, Psychic's Spell, and Fairy's Touch.

"In each round, one person will be on offense, the other on defense," Nero continued. "Before a round begins, you will each pull your ability out of this." He held up a glass bowl filled with tiny slips of folded paper. "You may use your assigned ability—and *only* your assigned ability against your partner. The timer will be set to five minutes. That is five minutes for the attacker to defeat your opponent. If you succeed within the allotted time, you win. But if the defender is still standing when the bell rings, you lose. Now choose your first partner."

The six Legion brats quickly paired up. That just left me, standing here all alone. When I'd joined the Legion of Angels, I'd not anticipated how much like high school it was going to be. Except in high school, I'd at least had my sister Bella in some of my classes. And in high school, the other kids hadn't been killing machines.

Nero's eyes, as hard as green diamonds, honed in on me. "No partner, Pandora?"

"I guess I'm not one of the cool kids," I replied with a nonchalant shrug.

"Very well. You will pair with me for this round."

His tone was very official, very businesslike. So like an angel. And so unlike how Nero was with me. Something weird was going on here.

"Where is Colonel Dragonblood?" I asked him.

"Colonel Dragonblood is engaged elsewhere," he said coolly. "Now take a piece of paper, Pandora."

Thus rebuffed, I reached into the bowl and pulled out a folded slip of paper. It was so pretty, so ornately folded, that it was a shame to ruin the art. I unfolded it anyway. The calligraphic text inside read 'Defense: Vampire's Kiss'.

As soon as I'd read the words, the paper disintegrated into thin air. I knew that spell. Potions had been mixed into the paper and ink. Bella had made some of these self-destructing papers back when we were kids. It was a great way to pass notes without any evidence for the teachers to find.

In front of me, Nero was rolling back his shoulders, preparing to fight me.

"You didn't draw a piece of paper," I told him.

"I don't need to."

The starting bell chimed. Before its echo had faded from the hall, Nero had already launched two fireballs, three exploding potions, and a telekinetic blast at me. I zigzagged, scrambling to evade his spells. I was too slow. I avoided most of the spells, but his psychic blast grazed my shoulder. It barely touched me, but that tiny nudge shot me across the gym, slamming me into the wall.

It was then, as I untangled myself from a twisted mess of ropes, that I realized the spell on the paper wasn't as simple as the one I knew. It hadn't just disintegrated the material; that single touch of my fingers against the paper had blocked all my magic except for Vampire's Kiss, including any defense I'd built up against unfriendly spells. It was no wonder Nero's psychic spell only had to tap me to hurl me into the air.

Frowning, I pushed away from the wall. Without my other magic, I couldn't cheat. Not that I'd planned to—or at least not more than a teensy bit.

As Nero strode toward me, each step as soft as a feather and as powerful as an earthquake, I moved away, keeping my distance. That would give me more time to react to his attacks.

Ten seconds later, Nero had me pinned to the ground, my arms pulled painfully and awkwardly behind my back, my legs locked beneath his knees.

"That didn't go according to plan," I grunted.

Nero had slammed a continuous barrage of spell walls into me from all directions. All my strength and speed had not been enough to avoid that. Not even close. Not against an archangel.

Nero rose smoothly. I flopped over, my body throbbing with a dull, persistent ache. Nero stared down at me expectantly. He was waiting for me to stand up. I wasn't sure I could.

"It's not fair." Gritting my teeth, I rose slowly, my balance wobbly. "You got to use the whole spectrum of your magic and I didn't."

"Nothing about this training is fair. You'd best get used to it from the start."

Ever since the angel Colonel Battleborn had died in the battle at Memphis last month, things had been different. The Legion was pushing harder than ever before to level up its soldiers' magic, for more power to beat the demons' Dark Force. In my time at the Legion, I'd battled dark angels. I'd crossed the plains of monsters. I'd been kidnapped by a demon and injected with Venom. But none of that scared me as much as the look on Nero's face now. Something was really, seriously wrong.

"What happened to Colonel Dragonblood?" I asked again. I spoke my next words barely above a whisper. "Is he dead?"

His death would have rattled the Legion. Colonel Dragonblood wasn't just an angel. He trained the Legion's best mid-level soldiers, those with the potential to become angels. And angels were in short supply right now.

"Colonel Dragonblood is not dead," said Nero. "He is busy with something crucial to the Legion's future."

That sounded dangerous. And really foreboding.

"And I told you not to worry about it," Nero added. "I trust I won't have to repeat myself in the future. Today's training ends at nineteen hundred hours for everyone—except for you. You will run around the island's outer trail. Fifty miles. That should give you enough time to consider the benefits of following orders."

I frowned at him. Gods, it was like being an initiate all over again, training under Colonel Hard Ass. Except now Nero had been upgraded to General Hard Ass. I didn't say any of that aloud, however, for fear that he would make it *two* laps around the island.

Nero nodded, a hint of that delightful fire shining through the cold marble sheen of his eyes. "A wise choice."

As I moved down the line in the warmup rotation, I heard a few muted laughs from the Legion brats at my expense. Jace, my next partner, wasn't one of them. He wasn't laughing. He was, however, looking at me like I'd completely lost my mind to question Nero.

He was probably right. The Crystal Falls training was serious. These soldiers were fighting for the big prize: to become the Legion's next angel. None of them were taking it lightly. And neither could I, even though I wasn't in line to become an angel this time around.

I was working toward something more important than immortal glory and honor. I had to level up my magic, to gain the power of telepathy I needed to find my brother Zane. And I had to do it without clueing in the gods, or anyone at the Legion, as to what I really was. Because they certainly wouldn't welcome that revelation with open arms.

"Getting into trouble already, Pandora?" Jace said as we took our magic origami papers from the bowl.

Mine read 'Defense: Witch's Cauldron', his 'Offense: Psychic's Spell'.

"Trouble? Me?" I said with a shrug as our papers disintegrated. "Well, you know how I am."

"Yes, I know how you are. All too well." He said it with both admiration and admonition.

My gaze panned briefly across the five other soldiers training with us. "But I don't know who *they* are."

"Are you trying to make new friends or dissect their weaknesses?"

"Maybe a bit of both," I admitted with a smile. "Though they don't seem amenable to the idea of friendship."

"No. They are here for a single reason."

"To win. To become the Legion's next angel. And to bowl over anyone or anything in their way."

Jace nodded.

"Tell me about them," I implored him.

Instead, Jace hurled a psychic spell at me. I grabbed a pinch of powder from my potion belt and tossed it. His spell dissolved.

Jace tried again. My powder dissolved that spell too.

"How did you do that?" he demanded.

"Magic," I replied with a mysterious smile.

A calculating crinkle formed between his eyes. "That powder dissolved my spells."

"Yes, it did. Neat trick, isn't it?"

"A powder that dissolves magic. I've never heard of such a thing. That is a useful weapon."

"It is indeed," I agreed.

"How do you make it?"

He wasn't mad at me for thwarting his attacks, not like any of the other Legion brats here would have been. No, Jace was too pragmatic for pride to stand in the way of his goals. He would build up his personal arsenal of spells and knowledge in any way possible.

"Tell me about the other soldiers here, and I'll give you the recipe for this powder," I proposed.

"Agreed," he said immediately.

Jace's gaze flitted to the soldier with long bouncy black curls pushed back from her face with a headband that closely resembled a crown. She was the Legion brat who'd mocked my wet clothes.

"That's Siri Silvertongue," he said. "She's the daughter of Colonel Silvertongue, the angel who commands the eastern half of Australia."

He glanced at the dark-haired man currently battling Siri. The soldier bore a striking resemblance to his partner.

"And that's Siri's cousin Andrin Spellsmiter. His father General Spellsmiter is Colonel Silvertongue's brother. General Spellsmiter rules the western half of Australia. He also commands the Vanguard."

The Vanguard was an elite squad of Legion warriors. They were stronger and faster than other Legion soldiers. They had a reputation for being vicious fighters who never stopped moving long enough to even contemplate the idea of mercy. They cut through their foes like a wildfire across a drought-beset prairie. There was nothing soft or easy about the 'normal' Legion training, but soldiers in the Vanguard took things to a whole other level. They trained harder and longer, pushing their bodies and magic to the breaking point on a daily basis.

"Fireswift! Pierce!" Nero's voice cut across the hall like a bullet. "Less chitchatting and more dueling."

In response, Jace swung a telekinetic punch at me. My powder dissolved that too, just as it had his psychic blasts. Jace's gaze dipped to my powder pouch. He wanted that recipe badly. I could see it in his eyes.

Which was why he risked Nero's ire by continuing our conversation. Though first he checked to make sure Nero wasn't watching. Nero was at the other end of the gym, chiding another pair for their 'manic use of magic'.

"That is Arius Demonslayer," Jace said, his voice low, indicating the male soldier in the pair Nero was critiquing.

The golden-haired man was handsome in a boyishly charming sort of way. He must have been at least the Legion's minimum enlistment age of twenty-two when he'd become immortal, but he looked closer to sixteen.

Demonslayer. The name was familiar.

"Arius's father was—"

"The angel Sirius Demonslayer, killed just over twenty years ago," I said, remembering now.

"How did you know?"

"I once read a book about him."

In truth, I hadn't read any books about Sirius Demonslayer. My friend Stash had told me about the angel. Rumor had it that Sirius Demonslayer was Stash's father. The rumors were wrong. Stash's father was actually the deity Zarion, God of the Faith. Zarion had killed both his mortal lover and Sirius Demonslayer, the angel who had guarded her. No one knew that Zarion had killed them. Everyone thought they'd died in battle against dark angels.

"And who is the woman dueling Arius?" I asked Jace.

"That's Isabelle Battleborn."

Isabelle was short and slender, a lean bundle of toned muscle on a small frame. She wore her bright red hair braided back from her face; it was long in the back, reaching nearly to her waist. She moved quickly, like flames crackling on a campfire.

"The daughter of Colonel Battleborn," I realized.

"Yes," Jace said solemnly.

Jace's sister had died from the wounds she'd incurred in the same battle that had killed Colonel Battleborn and so many other Legion soldiers. Venom-laced bullets had ripped their magic apart.

"Are you all right?" I asked Jace.

He drew in a deep breath, masking his pain, his anguish. It was the face of a soldier.

"That's Delta Wardbreaker," he said, looking at the final soldier.

I didn't fail to note that Jace hadn't answered my question, but I didn't press him on it either. He needed time.

He hadn't especially liked his sister, but he had loved her. I could see that in his eyes, no matter how much he buried his feelings.

I followed his gaze to Delta, the soldier wearing an elaborate assortment of dark braids.

"Delta's father is General Osiris Wardbreaker, the archangel who lost his mind and went rogue," said Jace. "The Legion believes him to be dead, but no one has seen the body. Or knows how he died."

I knew. Nero's father Damiel, another archangel who was supposed to be dead, had found Osiris Wardbreaker in a mad, murderous rage. And Damiel had killed him.

"Delta is the oldest of us here," Jace told me. "She's been waiting over a century to be made an angel."

"Perhaps she doesn't have the right temperament," I suggested.

"Perhaps not. Delta is a bit crazy herself. And being an angel requires a certain levelheadedness." He slanted an assessing look my way.

I smiled. "I'm very levelheaded."

He snorted. "Pay up. Tell me what's in that spell-eating powder."

"The mixture includes two petals of emerald lily, a stalk of shredded thunder root, one dragon eye, and twenty strands of silver wolf hair," I rattled off. "It's a little concoction my sister Bella taught me how to make."

"And it dissolves all spells?"

"No, only psychic spells. I have different powders to dissolve the other kinds of magic."

"And how do you make those other powders?"

"Oh, no," I said with a smirk. "That wasn't part of our deal. You only asked for *this* powder's recipe. Next time, you might want to negotiate better."

Jace hit me with his silent stare.

I countered with a cheerful smile.

"As always, well played, Leda," he chuckled.

I dipped into a curtsy.

Jace's laugh was short-lived. A dark look crossed his face.

"Nero is standing behind me, isn't he?" I asked.

Jace nodded.

"Of course he is," I sighed, then turned around to face Nero. He loomed like a dragon closing in on an unsuspecting village. I shot him my most disarming smile.

He folded his arms across his chest, clearly not amused. "I told you to train against your partner. This does *not* look like training."

I kept on smiling. "Sorry?" I offered sheepishly.

"Time to split up this little dream team. Fireswift, partner with Spellsmiter."

Jace hurried over to Andrin Spellsmiter.

"You're with Wardbreaker," Nero told me.

I met Delta's feral grin and sighed. "Awesome."

I jogged across the room, stopping opposite her.

"The famous Pandora, hero of the Earth. At long last, I have the chance to test my skills against such a renown opponent," Delta sneered.

The demented gleam in her eyes was downright disturbing, like she intended to take me apart piece by piece—and then bathe in my blood.

We drew papers from the bowl. Delta got offense and Dragon's Storm, the power of elemental magic. I got defense yet again and Fairy's Touch. Well, this would be interesting. If I'd been a level seven soldier, I could have used my fairy magic to heal myself. But I wasn't a level seven soldier; I didn't have any fairy magic at all. Which left me with exactly zero magic to combat Delta Wardbreaker, the craziest soldier here.

"Fairy's Touch," Delta purred as my paper disintegrated. "It's too bad you don't possess that ability."

She wove an air spell between her hands, then shot the sparkling silver ribbon of magic at me. Nice. Delta had hardly given me a chance to read the ability off my paper before attacking. I evaded her spell—but only just barely. I was so slow without my vampire powers.

"Don't worry about me," I said, keeping my smile cheerful. "I'm pretty good at improvising."

"*Improvising*," Delta said with a saccharine smile. "Yes, I've heard all about your dirty tricks. Like a mangy dog fighting in the streets. Maybe you think you can teach us all a thing or two?"

She didn't even wait for me to answer. Instead, she set her sword on fire and swung it at my head. Well, that was just rude.

Jumping up, I grabbed one of the ropes hanging from the ceiling. I swung it like a whip, smacking the knotted end down hard on Delta's hand. Swinging the rope again, I wrapped it around her, pinning her arms to her sides.

"Teach you something?" I smiled at her. "Only if you ask nicely." I knocked the sword from her hand.

Growling, Delta set the whole rope on fire. She didn't seem to care that she was setting herself on fire too. Well, she was kind of fireproof. Unlike the rope. The fire covered it completely now. And the flames were quickly consuming the other apparatuses, spreading across the gym.

Nero came over and calmly put out the fire with a single tap of his magic. He looked from Delta, to the charred remains of the rope, to the scorch marks on the gym floor—then finally to me.

"You are not following my instructions," he told me, his tone as cold as an Arctic field after a winter storm. "I said to defend using the power you drew from the bowl. I don't remember writing 'gym equipment' on any of those papers."

Wait just one minute. Delta had almost burnt down the gym, and he was blaming *me*?

I was tempted to point out that I'd drawn a power I didn't possess—and how unfair it was. But the Legion wasn't about fairness. In a battle, you couldn't suddenly stop and cry foul and expect anyone to care. They'd just see you as a stationary target.

So I didn't complain about the unfair exercise, or even that Nero was picking on me more than he was on anyone else here. Instead, I stared at him in stony silence.

"Shoes off," he commanded.

I slid out of my shoes.

"The rest of you too."

The others did as he said, doing their best to cover their confusion.

Nero tapped his finger to his phone screen. The gym floor split apart in the middle of the room, revealing a large recessed pit the size of a running track. Smoke billowed up from the newly-emerged track. It was completely covered in red-hot coals.

"How long have you been a soldier in the Legion of Angels?" Nero asked me.

I could barely take my eyes off the red glowing embers. "Fourteen months."

The Legion brats sneered at me like I was an upstart, a troublemaker for daring to believe that I could become an angel after such a short time. I noticed they didn't look that way at Jace, even though he'd joined the Legion at the exact same time as I had. Because he was the son of an angel, a Legion brat, the heir to a legacy.

"The Legion is a team," Nero said, addressing the whole room now. "We are working toward a common goal: to uphold the gods' justice and protect the Earth and its people. We cannot afford to have any weak links. Our enemies will exploit them. We share in our victories as well as in our defeats. And we all bear the burden of our mistakes and shortcomings. To that end, you will all now run fourteen miles around the track, courtesy of Leda Pierce. One mile for every month that she should have learned the importance of following orders."

Fourteen miles on the burning hot coals track? Barefoot? Was he serious? Sure, we were all mostly fireproof now that the magic-inhibiting potions had worn off, but that didn't mean it wouldn't hurt to run over burning coals. Nero had lost his mind.

I was kicking myself for not answering with one year instead of fourteen months. One mile around the burning coal track was better than fourteen. Of course, Nero probably would have found a way to make one equal more than fourteen. One hundred miles perhaps. Angel math was creative like that.

The Legion brats had abandoned all pretense of stoicism. They were now openly glaring at me. All except for Jace. He was just shaking his head, obviously lamenting the latest trouble I'd gotten him into.

"Get running, all of you," Nero snapped. His voice tore through the hall, echoing, resounding. It seemed to come from every direction at once. "Before I add another mile. Or ten."

The others threw me a final scornful glare, then ran

onto the track. Great. Now they all hated me even more. So much for making friends.

As the hot breath of the coals kissed my feet, my mind tried to comprehend why Nero was acting this way. An unsettling possibility presented itself. Maybe the angel in the gym hall with us right now wasn't Nero at all. The First Angel had once masqueraded as Basanti, masking herself with a shifting spell. Could someone else be pretending to be Nero? And if so, what had happened to the real Nero?

CHAPTER 3

BOOT CAMP 2.0

The training facility's exterior floodlights flashed on, lighting up the night and welcoming me back to civilization. I dragged my aching, bleeding body inside. I would have kissed the ground in relief if I'd thought I could have stood up again.

I'd just finished my disciplinary run around the island. The real problem hadn't been the fifty-mile run after the insane day of nightmare training. No, it had been the fifty-mile run through the pitch-dark, monster-infested jungle after the insane day of nightmare training.

Fifty miles had *never* felt so long, not even back when I'd been mortal. It had been more like fifty miles of monster fights with a lot of running in between. The Legion of Angels Boot Camp 2.0 at Crystal Falls made my early days at the Legion seem like a distant, pleasant dream.

Only my sheer stubbornness of will had kept me going through the barefoot run over burning coals and everything that had followed—all the way up to and including my descent into the monster-infested jungle.

Back when I'd been a Legion initiate, I'd been absolutely certain that no one could be tougher than Nero Windstriker. Tough, ha! I hadn't even known the true meaning of the word until today. The new Nero wasn't just pushing us to the brink of exhaustion. He was pushing us to the brink of our own immortality. Truth be told, I wasn't feeling particularly immortal right now.

As I walked down the hall, I tried to remind myself that Nero was just trying to make me stronger. Unfortunately, my aching bones were screaming louder than the voice of reason in my head.

And what if the man training us wasn't Nero at all?

I'd had a lot of time to think during my jungle run—to analyze Nero's words, his actions. He wasn't really acting out of character. And yet, he was acting very oddly toward me. Cold and distant. Detached. Like the two of us weren't a couple at all, like we didn't share an apartment in New York. Like I wasn't his mate.

Why would someone be pretending to be Nero?

It might be Nyx again. After all, the First Angel had once impersonated Basanti, so there was precedent. Nyx might be hoping to learn more from someone here by pretending to be Nero. But the only person here who was close to Nero was me, and this 'Nero' was acting like we were near strangers. Rebuffing me certainly wasn't the best way to learn anything from me.

Perhaps it was Colonel Fireswift, off on one of his investigations. But why impersonate Nero? Colonel Fireswift had no problem torturing people in his own skin. In fact, he'd built his reputation on torture—and training that might as well have been called torture.

Maybe it was some other angel impersonating Nero,

but I didn't know many of them. So I couldn't guess what their reasons might be for this charade.

Worse yet, the person pretending to be Nero could be a god. Or even a dark angel or a demon.

There were just too many possibilities—and no proof to support any of them. Until I figured out what this 'Nero' was up to, I couldn't do more than speculate who was impersonating him. I had to watch him and see if he showed his cards.

But right now, first of all, I needed to eat. I hadn't had dinner yet. I'd gone straight from training to my deep jungle run.

So it was tired, muddy, and ravenous that I trudged into the dining and recreation corridor. And just my luck, the canteen was closed. The doors swung shut behind Siri Silvertongue and Andrin Spellsmiter as they left the canteen. The cousins—no, the *evil* cousins—passed by me, no pity in their eyes, no shred of humanity in their souls.

Hungry and dirty, I returned to my room and jumped in the shower to at least solve one of my problems. Half an hour of vigorous scrubbing later, I finally couldn't smell monster on me anymore. So I stepped out of the shower and got started on the homework Nero had given us: to read a three-hundred page book on the Legion's history and customs.

I suspected I was the only one reading tonight. The other soldiers here were the children of angels. They knew their history and customs. They knew them forward and backward, left and right, inside and out. After all, this was their world.

I had years of catching up to do. Nero had warned us that he expected us to know everything in the book tomorrow, down to the tiniest detail. That meant he was going to quiz us on it, probably right in the middle of some physically-excruciating task. If I didn't have all the right answers, tomorrow would be even worse than today.

I read for an hour, repeating the sentences aloud for better retention. By then, my stomach was rumbling so loudly that I could hardly even hear myself speak. I was also too hungry to fall asleep, assuming there was time to sleep. I wasn't sure I'd manage to finish my homework before dawn.

One thing was clear: I needed food. It didn't have to be a seven-course gourmet meal. I'd have settled for some fruit and crackers. But where was I going to find anything remotely edible at this hour? The canteen was closed for the day. I certainly wouldn't earn any plus points by breaking into the kitchen and stealing a midnight snack. Maybe I should have started a fire and roasted one of the beasts I'd killed during my fifty-mile run through the jungle.

I pushed back from my desk, standing to my feet. That was exactly what I'd do. I was going back into the jungle to catch myself a snack right now. The bizarre beasts in there hadn't looked all that appetizing, but it sure beat starving.

I grabbed a set of running clothes and shoes. Before I could put them on, however, a knock sounded on my door. What now? Were the Legion brats stopping by to play some juvenile prank on me?

I dropped my sports attire and picked up my sword. Then I opened the door.

Nero stood on the other side—or at least someone who looked like Nero. He stepped into my room without a word. The door whispered shut behind him.

He looked me up and down, his gaze darting from the

sword in my hand, to the running clothes at my feet. "Where are you going at this hour?"

"For another run. Because I don't think I repented thoroughly enough during the first one," I added with an innocent smile.

He cocked a single eyebrow at me. "Don't bullshit me, Pandora. We've been through too much."

"Have we?" I set my sword on my desk, still close enough to grab it if the need arose. I picked up my sports clothes and tossed them onto my bed. "Because today you acted like we've never met before."

An idea hit me. Nero and I were linked by magic. Which meant there was a surefire way to see if he truly was who he appeared to be, one thing no amount of magic could hide, no matter how powerful someone was. Even a deity could not fake this.

I grabbed him and bit down on his neck. As his blood filled my mouth—that delicious, fragrant, one-of-a-kind flavor—I realized it really was him. It was *my* Nero.

His blood called to me, mixing with my own blood and magic. Its seductive song was drawing me under, sending my self control spiraling through the shredder. I gripped his back, clutching him to me, craving him. All of him.

I let go abruptly, pushing away from him. My labored breaths shook my chest.

"That was some welcome." Passion, need, hunger—that and much more burned in Nero's emerald eyes. His gaze slid over my body, devouring me. He reached toward me, like he wanted to drink from me too.

Instead, he retracted his hand and tapped his fingers to his neck. As I watched him heal the wounds I'd left there, I swallowed my hunger—and along with it, the last few precious drops of his blood lingering in my mouth. My fangs retracted.

"I had to make sure you were you," I told him.

"Who else should I be?"

"An imposter. You were acting so strangely today."

"I had to act that way. I had to be detached and professional. I am in charge of this training now. I can't show favorites."

"Oh, but you *are* showing favorites," I countered. "I am obviously your favorite—to torture. You weren't here for five minutes before you punished me."

"Yes." He bit out the word. "I wasn't here for five minutes before you forced me to punish you." He closed in, his massive body casting a shadow over me. His finger brushed softly across my lower lip. "Before this mouth got you into trouble."

I caught his hand in mine, holding it to my lips. I kissed his fingers softly. Sure, I was angry at him for the hell he'd put me through today, but I'd also missed him. And I was so relieved that it was really my Nero here, not an imposter.

"Your method to ascertain my identity was somewhat extreme," he commented.

"Says the man who had us run fourteen miles over hot coals."

"That was the angel, not the man."

"Ok, then the *angel* was extreme."

"I hope you will not make a habit of biting people as a greeting."

I flashed him a smile. "Oh, no. I reserve that greeting just for you, honey."

"Good."

I chuckled.

"What would you have done if I'd not been me?" Nero asked.

"I would have promptly spat out the imposter's blood, of course."

Nero nodded. "Good," he said again.

"I'm so glad that you're you and not Nyx." I made a face. "Or Colonel Fireswift."

"Fireswift?"

"He was one of your potential imposters."

"I don't like to imagine you biting Fireswift."

"Neither do I. If his personality is any indication, he probably tastes like lighter fluid." I smiled coyly at him. "I prefer my Nero."

I threw my arms around him and hugged him to me, feeling downright giddy, even drunk. That was his blood at work. I'd only had a sip, but a sip of Nero's blood was all it took to send me to cloud nine. My lack of dinner after a day of hard labor wasn't doing much for my sanity either. And I was just so happy to see him, to have him with me once again. That, more than anything, compelled me to be bold. I leaned in to kiss his lips.

"Stop," he said, our mouths only inches apart.

"Why?" I said wickedly, my tongue tracing my lower lip.

"It's not appropriate."

I plunged my hands down his back and gave his butt a good, hard squeeze. "That's the whole point, Nero. Being appropriate isn't all that much fun."

Gold and silver magic shimmered inside his green eyes. "Those are the words of an anarchist."

"Guilty as charged." Grinning, I met his eyes. "So, the question remains, what are you going to do about it?"

"If you can still tease me, you didn't work hard enough today. And you obviously haven't repented enough."

"That's what I told you. Hence my plan to take another run around the island."

"We agreed that you would stop bullshitting me."

"No, we didn't," I laughed. "You agreed with yourself and expected me to just follow along."

"The chain of command is not a diamond necklace, Pandora. Following orders is the keystone of a functional military."

"But not of a functional relationship," I countered.

He blinked. "You're right."

"I get it—all that you're saying about not picking favorites, about being detached. Out in training, in front of everyone, you have to be as tough on me as you are on the others. Maybe even tougher. Fine. I can deal with that. But in here, when we're alone, you're not General Windstriker, an archangel in the Legion of Angels. You are just Nero. And I'm just Leda. Talk to me. Tell me what's going on. I know something is up. Something big. Why are you here instead of Colonel Dragonblood? What happened to him? Is it the demons? Did they hurt him because he is key to training the Legion's soon-to-be angels? Or is he on a mission to strike out at the demons and their forces?"

A calculating smile twisted his lips. "Tit for tat, Pandora. First, tell me why you're going out running in the middle of the night."

"It really bothers you not knowing something, doesn't it?"

"Yes."

"And if I said I just need the extra training?"

"I would agree with that statement."

I snorted. Nero firmly believed that you could never train too long or too hard.

"However," Nero continued. "It is not the reason you are headed into a monster-infested jungle again."

His singleminded stubbornness to uncover what I was up to brought me right back to the day I'd signed up to join the Legion. Nero had taken me aside and interrogated me because he'd been convinced I had some ulterior motive for joining, some secret reason that was different than what I'd stated on my application. He hadn't been able to figure out what it was, and that had *really* bothered him.

"It's stupid," I sighed.

Nero waited, watching me like a dragon watched his treasure—with unyielding patience.

"You'll laugh at me," I said.

"I will not."

"I'm hungry. No, not just hungry. Famished," I gasped. "And by the time I got back from my run around the island, the canteen was closed."

"And you believe running will take your mind off your hunger." He nodded in approval.

"No. I fear my hunger is far beyond that point. Running will only make me even hungrier. But the jungle was teeming with beasts." I gave him a sheepish look. "Some of them looked edible."

Nero laughed.

I punched him in the shoulder. "Hey! You promised you wouldn't laugh."

He quickly reformed his face into a completely neutral expression.

"Ok, now you know my big secret. It's your turn." I

folded my arms across my chest. "Spill the beans about Colonel Dragonblood."

"Colonel Dragonblood is not injured, and he's not going after the demons, dark angels, or their Dark Force. His mission is of a completely different nature."

"You said his mission was crucial to the Legion's survival."

"And it is. His wife has the Fever."

The Fever. A term that referred to the time in which a female Legion soldier was fertile. It only happened every few decades. When it did, she had a window of only a few days to become pregnant. The Legion matched angels to soldiers who were magically compatible. Colonel Dragonblood's wife was married to an angel, which meant their offspring would have a high magic potential. There was a good chance those children would later become angels themselves. Colonel Dragonblood's mission was indeed important to the Legion's survival.

"Since Colonel Dragonblood will be busy for the next week, Nyx asked me to take his place," Nero said.

That made sense. Only Colonel Dragonblood could go on his mission. But any number of angels were qualified to fill in for him at Crystal Falls, at least until he could return. Nero was high on that list of angels.

I suddenly felt very foolish for assuming some great scheme was playing out here. My life had been far too exciting lately; I was starting to see conspiracies everywhere.

"Well, I suppose I'd rather have you training us than Colonel Fireswift," I said with a coy smile.

"You *suppose*?" he repeated, looking offended.

Nero and Colonel Fireswift were rivals, each one constantly vying to best the other.

"I'm thinking of my aching muscles, Nero. Colonel Fireswift has a shitty personality, but I can ignore his derisive comments. You are actually the tougher trainer. It hurts a lot more after one of your trainings than after one of his."

"I should hope so," he said, puffing out his chest proudly.

My eyes dipped to that chest, appreciating the delicious ripples of muscle under his black leather uniform. I licked my lips.

"Pandora?" My nickname rolled off his tongue like a drop of warm honey.

"I'm suddenly finding myself suffering from a different kind of hunger."

"That would be a bad idea," he said, his chuckle low and deep in his chest.

"I know. Sooo bad." My fingers closed around the zipper of his leather vest.

He set his hands on my hips. He was so close. The deliciously masculine flavor of sex and angel seared my senses, the scent of hot spice teasing my nose. My fangs burned my gums. Lust and hunger collided, cascading through me.

I dipped my mouth to his neck. Every beat of his heart, every throb of his pulse against my lips, was a fresh lash of torture. His blood popped against my fangs, inciting me to madness. Daring me to taste him.

"Stop playing around, Pandora, and bite me," he growled in fervent command.

Who said I didn't follow orders?

My previous bite had been restrained, a mere taste to see if he really was Nero. I hadn't allowed myself to truly dive in. I did now.

I sank my fangs into his neck. His blood rushed into my

mouth, hot and sweet with just the right kick of spice. Nero's blood didn't taste like blood at all. It tasted sweeter than honey—and more potent than Nectar, the immortal food of the gods. His blood slid down my throat, a river of fire, both a cure and a curse for the reckless desire raging inside of me. Like two volatile elements, his blood and mine collided in an explosion that shook the very fabric of my being. I could hardly stand, barely breathe, and I absolutely had to have more. If I was an addict, Nero was my drug of choice.

Gripping him tightly, I pulled back just far enough to meet his eyes. I brushed my hair off my shoulder and tilted my neck, baring it to him. "Tit for tat," I said drunkenly.

Emerald fire lit up his eyes. Dual flashes of pain and pleasure pierced me as his fangs penetrated my skin. Every time he drew me into him, my body quaked, a deep, penetrating throb rocking me from head to toe, inside and out. The only thing better than biting Nero was for him to bite me back. I was drowning in fire, overdosing on euphoria—and I was two hundred percent ok with that.

Nero's hands rounded my butt, diving roughly under my skirt to relieve me of my panties. "I need you. *Now*," he growled against my neck, his voice rough, almost ragged.

Lust washed over me, leaving me feverish, dizzy. We'd only been apart for a week, but I knew exactly how he felt.

"I need you too," I said, tugging his shirt over his head.

A knock sounded on my door.

Nero abruptly dropped his hands to his sides. "It's Nyx."

"As always, the First Angel's timing is impeccable," I growled under my breath.

I brushed down my skirt, then opened the door.

Dressed in black leather armor and a long red cape, the

force of Nyx's aura filled up all the available space around her. She'd already taken over the whole hallway, and her presence pounded like a war hammer through the open door, now claiming my room as well.

Without uttering a word, Nyx entered the room. Her black hair, pulled up in a high ponytail, floated in the air, suspended as though it were floating underwater. The silver heels of her high boots snapped against the deafening silence. Only after she'd shut the door behind her did she finally speak.

Nyx's blue eyes panned down my body, snagging on my absent pantyline. "You're missing your underwear, Captain."

My cheeks flushed, I grabbed my lacy red panties from the floor and slipped them on under my skirt. I always seemed to be losing my underwear around Nero.

"And there's blood on your neck," Nyx pointed out.

I grabbed the towel off the back of my chair and wiped the blood off my neck.

Nyx's gaze shifted to Nero. "There's blood on your neck too, General."

Neither flushed nor unraveled, Nero calmly wiped down his neck. His tongue darted out to lick the blood from his lips. The sight of him licking up my blood, devouring my life force, made my heart skip a beat. Heat flushed my skin. Nero's tongue flicked across his lips once more, meeting my eyes as he licked up the final drop of my blood.

Nyx's gaze flickered between Nero and me. "When I sent you here to take over for Colonel Dragonblood, Nero, I told you to keep it professional," she sighed.

So that was why Nero had been so aloof. It hadn't been

his own idea. Nyx had instructed him to act that way. And now I'd gotten him in trouble. Again. Oops.

"Oh, don't worry," I told Nyx. "He's totally professional. He's been torturing me thoroughly all day."

Gold flashed in Nyx's blue eyes. Her dark brows lifted.

"Torturing me in training," I added hastily. "This was just a…"

"A reward for good behavior?" Nyx suggested, her eyes dancing with amusement.

Was she laughing at me?

"This was a deviation," I amended. "Totally my fault. I'm a bad influence."

"Oh, I am well aware of that. Before you, Nero walked the straight and narrow path without any trouble whatsoever." Nyx waved us toward the door. "Well, come along then. I have a little midnight surprise for everyone."

I glanced at Nero. The look on his face told me he didn't have a clue what the First Angel was up to. It seemed her arrival was as much a surprise to him as it was to me.

We followed her down the long hallway, passing into the training building. Jace and the other five Legion brats were already waiting in the gym. And at the center of the training hall, high on a raised platform, stood the seven ruling gods.

CHAPTER 4

SEVEN GODS & SEVEN ANGELS

Ten gods, dressed in the white-and-gold armor of Heaven's Army, surrounded the raised platform where the seven ruling gods stood. The warrior gods were poised like tigers—silent, unmoving, and ready to spring into action at any moment to defend the gods' council.

"Soldiers of the Legion of Angels," said Valora, the Queen Goddess, leader of the gods' council and ruler of heaven. "We have come to you at a critical junction."

Valora was the quintessential goddess: a tall, slender woman with long, perfectly-curled golden hair that looked as soft as her white silk-and-chiffon gown. Her cheeks were rosy, her lips glossy red, and her skin alight with a heavenly glow. Her hair and dress flowed gently in an airy, magical breeze that seemed to be confined solely to her body. Pearls beaded her slippers; diamonds dripped from her earrings and necklaces like tears.

"Recent events have shocked the Legion's foundations," Valora continued. "The demons have killed an angel. They have killed many other soldiers who would have become angels. They're trying to weaken the Legion. They know how important you are to the gods' presence on Earth. We cannot allow the demons to succeed in their ploys. And so the gods' council has decided that we must take an active role in bolstering the Legion, to make you ready for the inevitable confrontation."

Aleris, the God of Nature and Emperor of the Elements, spread his arms. A flock of blue butterflies burst out of the flowering vines that crisscrossed his chest and arms, woven seamlessly into his robes like a set of armor.

"And to make the Legion ready, we need a new angel to replace your fallen comrade Colonel Battleborn," Aleris said.

"Not since the dawn of the Legion, have we lost so many soldiers to the Dark Force," said Zarion, the God of Faith and Lord of the Pilgrims.

Even as far as gods went, Zarion was ostentatious. Hundreds of tiny gemstones were braided into his long platinum hair; the sparkling rubies, amethysts, and sapphires matched perfectly with the shimmering fabric of his gaudy robes.

"In these dark times, we don't just need our soldiers to be stronger than ever before," Maya began.

"We need our angels to be stronger too," Meda finished seamlessly, the twin sister goddesses perfectly in sync.

Maya, the Goddess of Healing, and Meda, the Goddess of Technology, were virtually indistinguishable. It was only their different fashion styles that allowed me to tell them apart. Maya, the patron goddess of fairies, wore a short whimsical dress, a long cape, and tiny sandals. The belt around her waist was stocked with potions and medical instruments.

As the patron Goddess of Witchcraft, Meda dressed a lot like the witches I knew. Today, she wore a red-and-black corset over a bell-sleeved white blouse with a plunging neckline. Her skirt, mini in front with a long, blossoming train in back, matched her gold top hat perfectly. Her shoes were buckled, her thigh-high stockings black, and her exposed garter belts adorned with big bows.

"That is why you are all here," said Ronan, the God of Earth's Army and Lord of the Legion of Angels. "Colonel Battleborn's death has left his territory without a leader. It is vulnerable, and therefore so is the entire Earth. Before this training is over, one of you will become an angel and take Colonel Battleborn's place. And the rest of you will be far stronger than you are now."

Ronan was the tallest man I'd ever seen. Even next to the other gods, he looked massive, the highest peak in a cluster of giant mountains. His eyes were as black as his hair—and as dark as the battle leather he now wore.

"To that end, we, the gods' council, have taken control of the Crystal Falls training, effective immediately," said Faris, the dark-haired God of Heaven's Army.

His white-and-gold armor shone so brightly, it was almost blinding. Like Ronan, he controlled an army. Except Faris's soldiers were all gods—and they fought the demons' army on every world the immortals of light clashed with the deities of darkness.

"We will determine how you shall train," Faris continued. "We will set the tasks. And we will decide who will become the next angel to join the Legion's ranks."

Excitement bubbled and popped off the other Crystal Falls training candidates. Nyx's reaction was very different. She was trying to hide it, but I could see in her eyes that she wasn't happy. Of course she wasn't. She was the First Angel. She was supposed to be running things at the Legion. She decided who would become an angel. By coming here, by taking over, the gods' were effectively stripping her of her authority.

"You will, however, find our training style to be more strenuous than anything you're accustomed to," Faris said.

Nero met his cool gaze, obviously not pleased by the assertion that his training sessions were anything but completely strenuous.

I wasn't a fan of the heavy-handed, over-the-top dramatic way the gods were taking over here. And yet... Wasn't it good that the Legion's new angel would be trained by the gods? Wasn't it important for all of us to be as strong as we could possibly be?

"Upon careful examination, we've determined that the Legion's training program, as it currently stands, is not sufficient to face the demons' Dark Force," Faris said. "Their soldiers are consistently more powerful at each magic level than our own, due to their intense training regimen—one that we must not only match, but beat. We will be implementing new standards all across the line, and we will start with the top. Seven angels will be training right along with you." Faris glanced at Nero. "And I will not tolerate them winging it."

Oh, this was getting better and better. The gods weren't just taking over at Crystal Falls; they were dragging angels back into basic training. Faris's lame joke aside—assuming the god actually had enough humor in him to make a joke—this was big. Angels commanded. They were supposed to be above the rest of us.

Apparently not anymore. Faris had just sent those angels back down to Earth.

The God of Heaven's Army waved his hand at the doors to the gym, and they swung open. Five angels strode into the room: Colonel Fireswift, Harker, Leila Starborn, and two angels I didn't know, one male, one female. The new arrivals formed a cluster to the right of me and the Legion brats.

"You too, Windstriker," Faris told Nero, his brows arching.

Nero joined the other angels, silent, expressionless. And cold. So cold I could feel a shiver trickle down my spine.

I scanned the group of angels, doing the math. Seven of us and six angels. There was still an angel missing.

Faris waved his hand at the First Angel. "They are waiting for you, Nyx. We wouldn't want you to miss out on all the fun."

Nyx was a demigod. She was above all the other angels. But right here and now, Faris was making it very clear to everyone that he didn't subscribe to that view of heaven's hierarchy. He could have summoned another angel here, but instead he'd lumped Nyx in with the others. He'd put her at the same level as the angels she commanded. If that wasn't a power play, I didn't know what was.

As Nyx joined the other angels, I could only guess at the fury burning inside of her, but the First Angel didn't betray it. In fact, each and every angel was doing their best to keep any hint of expression off their face—even though they must have been shocked that Nyx was training with them, she who had trained with gods.

"Now that you're all sorted, let's begin," declared Faris.

Zarion's gaze zeroed in on me. "Wait one moment. This training session is for angels and angel candidates only. *She* doesn't belong here," he hissed, contempt dripping off every syllable.

Zarion glared at me like I was a gatecrasher, as though I were the dirtiest, vilest *thing* ever to crawl the Earth for even daring to come here. I wasn't surprised. Zarion was a stickler for the rules, including ones he and the other gods had only made up five minutes ago. Or maybe *especially* the rules he and the other gods had only made up five minutes ago.

When I'd arrived at Crystal Falls, I had qualified for the training. It was supposed to be for level six and level seven soldiers. It wasn't my fault the name of the game had changed mid-play. They couldn't punish me for failing to predict that the gods would change their minds...or could they?

Oh, gods, Zarion was going to make a fuss until the other gods agreed to kick me out of here. Despite the inevitable strike of lightning to the ass on the way out, getting kicked out of here might just be the luckiest thing to happen to me all day. I didn't know what the gods' had planned for this training, but I was pretty sure it was going to hurt like a rusty razor blade to the eye. Suddenly, running several miles barefoot over burning coals and trekking through a monster-infested jungle sounded like bliss.

On the other hand, if I got kicked out of Crystal Falls, I couldn't watch Nero's back. I didn't want to leave Nero here under the gods' kind and caring tutelage. Sure, Harker and Leila would look out for him. And maybe Nyx would too. I wasn't so sure about the other angels, though. Angels had a reputation for being cutthroat. And that reputation was well-earned. Colonel Fireswift sure wouldn't be looking out for Nero's well-being here. On the contrary, he'd be looking for any sign of weakness in Nero's armor.

Sure, I wasn't as powerful as anyone in this room, but I couldn't help but want to stay by Nero's side. Perhaps it was hubris to think I could make a lick of difference when it came to protecting him against angels and gods, but I didn't care. As far as sins went, I'd committed worse ones to do the right thing.

"Indeed she does not belong here," Faris said to Zarion.

That must have been the first time in millennia that the two brothers had agreed on anything. They were always standing at opposing ends of the cannon fire.

But Zarion's self-satisfied smirk faded at his brother's next words.

"However, that problem is easily remedied." A hard smile twisted Faris's lips. "Congratulations, Leda Pierce. You're being promoted." A bottle of Nectar appeared in his hands. "Step up to the stage."

CHAPTER 5

FAIRY'S TOUCH

I felt my legs moving me along toward the gods' stage. My mind, however, was still stuck back where I'd stood a few moments before. Faris was promoting me. My mind struggled to digest that.

After all, I hadn't yet trained the power Fairy's Touch, the magic of healing. I'd just gotten here, to this training that was supposed to make me stronger, to prime my magic and prepare me for the next level. And now I was skipping all of that, jumping to the front of the line. Or, as I now feared, I was being pushed in front of the firing squad.

What the hell was Faris up to? Did he not care if the Nectar killed me? Or was he really that confident that I could absorb the Nectar and gain the gods' next gift, the power of healing? After all, he had instructed Harker to feed me pure Nectar, the immortal elixir that created archangels, just weeks after I'd joined the Legion.

I didn't think Faris wanted to kill me. Not that he cared about my life. But he did want to level me up to a second-tier angel so he could use my connection to my brother Zane to find him—and then add Zane to his collection of powerful telepaths.

Faris couldn't level me up if I was dead. On the other hand, he also couldn't level me up if I didn't drink the Nectar. Maybe this was his way of shortcutting the leveling game, of changing the rules, of pushing me up faster than the Legion's bureaucracy generally allowed. By being here at Crystal Falls, by training under the gods, I could be playing right into his hand. I cringed. All these machinations were making my head hurt. My life had been simpler before gods and angels had entered into the equation.

Though, considering what I was, gods and angels had always been part of the equation. And demons too. Past, present, and future. There was no avoiding them. This was my life.

I stopped in front of Faris, my gaze dipping to the glass bottle in his hands. As you moved up the Legion, the Nectar grew brighter, shinier, less diluted. Pure Nectar looked like liquid diamonds, the fluid so bright it was almost blinding. The Nectar Faris held now, the Nectar to make me a level seven soldier, wasn't that white yet. It was white-silver in color with occasional pale gold streaks swirled into the mixture.

Faris uncapped the bottle. No one said a thing, not even Zarion to protest that my filthy transgression was being rewarded by leveling me up. As the God of Faith, he probably figured if I wasn't worthy, I'd just die and that would settle that.

Faris poured the Nectar into a goblet. The drink was thick and silky, like hot liquid metal.

My heart hiccuped. I didn't feel ready. Not yet. This had happened so suddenly. I wasn't prepared.

You are prepared, Nero's reassuring voice spoke in my

mind, even as a panicking part of me was preparing to bolt out of here.

I sent him a silent thank-you for being here. Even though he wasn't standing beside me, he was always right there with me, lending me his strength and love.

Most Legion leveling-up ceremonies were characterized by long, flowery speeches brimming with jingoistic fervor. Everyone was dressed to impress for the ceremony and the wild party that followed. But Faris wasn't saying a thing. And besides some of the gods, no one was dressed in formal attire. I also seriously doubted there would be a party to follow this ceremony.

Faris set the goblet in my hands. All eyes were on me, and I was sure at least some of the people here hoped I wouldn't survive. I lifted the goblet to my lips and drank.

Fire and ice exploded inside my mouth. Lightning flashed through my veins, igniting my blood. Dizzy with magic and delirium, I stumbled back. I steadied my steps, regaining my balance before I fell off the stage. Waves of euphoria pounded into me like a hammer. It felt so good—and hurt so much. I hiccuped. Something was wrong.

"You are now a soldier of the seventh level," Faris declared.

No, it was wrong. It was all very wrong.

The whole room was spinning around me like I was caught inside a vortex. I stepped off the stage, almost falling flat on my face. As my feet hit the gym floor, vibrations pulsed through my legs. Vertigo swallowed me. I rushed past everyone, their faces a blur. I hurried on shaky steps to the nearby bathroom.

An earthquake shook the bathroom. White tiles poured down the walls like a stone waterfall, covering the floor, burying the toilet stalls.

I blinked, and the tiles were back on the walls.

I rushed to the sink. My shaking hands fumbled with the faucet.

"What the hell was in that Nectar?" I coughed, splashing my face with water.

I looked in the mirror above the sink, but everything was blurry. My eyes couldn't focus. They kept jumping around erratically, seeing things that I was pretty sure weren't there. Carnivorous vines grew out of the toilets, stretching out their poison-tipped tentacles toward me. Fire wolves crashed through the bathroom door, their breath setting everything ablaze. The demon Sonja burst through the mirror, her fist reaching for my throat.

I scrambled backward, tripping over my own feet. My chin banged against the sink. As I lay curled up on the floor, hugging myself, the wildfire raging inside of me slowly settled into a steady burn. My dizziness subsided. I gripped the edge of the sink and pulled myself back up. When I looked into the mirror now, I didn't see a demon. I saw my own reflection.

Behind me, the bathroom door swung open. I turned around to find Nero standing there.

"What happened?" His gaze dipped to my bruised chin.

"I slipped and fell."

"Something is wrong."

"Yes." I sashayed up to him. "Very wrong." Gods, he really was sexy. I looped my arms over his shoulders.

"Leda…"

A hysterical laugh burst out of my lips.

"You are drunk," he said.

"Yes. That cup of Nectar packed a potent punch."

"Stop."

I looked down to see my hands were at his belt. Gods, I'd lost my mind. I didn't even remember doing that.

He set his hands on my cheeks, meeting my eyes. "What happened?"

"Something went wrong," I laughed shakily. The dizziness had returned with a vengeance. I crashed into Nero. "The Nectar was wrong. All very wrong."

I blacked out. When I came to, I was on the floor, my head on Nero's lap. My fangs pierced his wrist, my mouth sucking in his blood in long, deep draws. His other hand gently stroked through my hair. Nero's blood tasted like heaven, sweet and spicy and oh-so-delicious. But it also tasted like love, stability, balance. It didn't throw me for a loop like the Nectar at the ceremony had.

My mind was clearing. The jumbled flash of fractured hallucinations had petered out.

I separated my mouth from his wrist. "What happened?"

"You tried to attack me," he said calmly. "Or tried to have your way with me. It was unclear to me. And to you, it seemed."

I gaped at him.

"You don't remember?"

"No." I swallowed the hard lump in my throat. "How long was I delirious?"

"For about ten minutes."

Ten minutes? I'd been a raging lunatic for ten whole minutes, trying to hurt the person I loved—and I didn't remember a single moment of it.

"Nero, I'm sorry. Something happened when I drank the Nectar. There was something wrong with it." I shook my head. "No, that's not it." Now that my head had cleared, I could look back without any madness to taint my mind. "The Nectar was fine. Something is wrong with *me*. When I drank the Nectar, my body went all whacky." My hands fidgeted nervously with the hem of my shirt. "Why did I react that way? What's the matter with me?"

"It appears your body rejected the Nectar."

Usually that meant instant death. You either absorbed the magic of the Nectar, or it killed you. That was simply how things worked. There was no magical limbo, no place between dying and leveling up, no way around the laws of magic.

"Why am I still alive?" I asked Nero.

He shook his head. "I don't know."

My heart thumped in panic. "Nero."

Reacting to my anxiety, he cupped my hands inside his.

"I'm alive. But the Nectar didn't ignite my magic." I drew in a deep breath. "I don't have the power of Fairy's Touch."

"That shouldn't be possible. It's never happened to anyone before, not once in the history of the Legion."

"This is because of my unusual origin," I said quietly.

"Perhaps. But we can't be sure at this point. We'll figure it out. Somehow."

If this had never happened before, how would we figure it out? There was no precedent.

"We just will," he said, responding to my unspoken panic attack. "In the meantime, you can't tell *anyone*."

"I won't."

"I'm serious, Pandora. No one must know, no matter how much you think you can trust them. Don't say it. Don't even think it. Even more than angels, gods are a victim of their own intelligence, of the wealth of their immortal experiences. They believe they perfectly understand the natural order of the universe. When confronted with something they don't understand, they don't trust it. And they respond according."

Swiftly and without mercy. And not bothering to ask any questions first.

Nero was right. I was going to be stuck for days—or even weeks, for all I knew—with a bunch of telepathic angels and gods. I couldn't think about what had just happened here. In fact, I had to block my thoughts completely. I'd never blocked so many telepaths for so long.

"They are going to find out, Nero. Sooner or later, they will. I will be under close observation in this training. My *magic* will be under close observation."

"Fake it.

"This isn't something I can just fake. I can't pretend I have a power I do not possess. What if I'm supposed to heal someone? How do I fake that?"

"I have every confidence in your ability to improvise."

I snorted. "Funny statement coming from you."

I'd been doing nothing but improvising since I'd joined the Legion—which had gotten me into heaps of trouble. Nero had chastised me about my unorthodox methods many times before. In the Legion, you weren't supposed to make things up as you went along; you were supposed to toe the line, to keep to the straight and narrow path, as determined by the Legion's handbook.

"You're not just any Legion soldier," Nero said, his fingers caressing my cheek softly. "Are you ready?"

"Ready to face my doom?" I laughed weakly.

He intertwined his fingers with mine, squeezing them.

"Nero?" I said quietly.

"Yes?"

"Why would my body reject something it always craved before? Something that it thrived on?"

"I don't know. Something was different this time."

I looked at the door with dread. "I really have to go back out there, don't I?"

"Yes. If you don't, they will come in here eventually."

"Ok." I rose to my feet. "Let's go."

He rose with me. "They will have questions."

"Then it's a good thing I have all the answers," I said, putting on a bright smile.

Just as soon as I think of them, I added silently as we stepped out of the bathroom.

CHAPTER 6

PALACE OF THE GODS

Everyone's eyes tracked me and Nero as we reentered the gym hall. There were a few whispers from the Legion brats about my flushed cheeks, elevated heart rate, and eyes dilated with magic. Siri Silvertongue was even brazen enough to suggest that Nero and I had run off to the bathroom for a quickie.

I did not correct her misconceptions. It was better for them to assume that we'd had sex because I'd been so completely drunk on Nectar that I couldn't control myself, than for anyone to realize what had really happened. That I was broken, a threat to the Legion's established leveling system.

It was supposed to be so clearcut, so black and white. You leveled up, or you died. That was how it had always been. There wasn't supposed to be anything in-between. I was an anomaly that should not have existed.

I breathed in and out, slow and even, Back in the bathroom, Nero had said to keep calm, to not let anyone know that anything was wrong. I was trying. And failing. No, I sure as hell wasn't calm. And not just because of what would happen if the gods found out that I had neither leveled up nor died, that I had derailed their whole system, the foundation, the very building blocks of Earth's army, the do-or-die duality upon which the Legion of Angels was built.

What shook me hardest was the very real possibility that I was staring at the end of my journey. If I couldn't level up my magic anymore, if I couldn't gain the power of Ghost's Whisper, then how would I ever be able to perform the magic to find my brother Zane?

No, I had to push those thoughts aside and worry about them another time. I would find a way to fix this. Somehow.

But right now, I had to focus on this training—and on not letting anyone know that something was really wrong with me.

"The new Crystal Falls training will now begin," Faris declared. "But first, a change of venue is required." Like a crack of lightning, his hands clapped together once.

A ring of magic flared up around us, and then we weren't in the gym anymore. We now stood in a grand hall basking in soft, ethereal light. I recognized the place, even though it had looked a bit different the last time I'd visited. This hall was the audience chamber in the palace of the gods. We weren't on Earth anymore. We were in heaven.

"The symbols on the floor of the Crystal Falls gym are a gateway to this world between worlds," Nero commented beside me.

Seven open arches dominated one side of the hall. Waterfalls and water worlds, mountains and deserts, plains and forests—a different magnificent view was visible through each archway. Looking closely, I realized the archways were not open. Each one contained a mirror. The scenes looked so lifelike, like they were right in front of me, like I could simply reach out and grab them. Like I could grasp the sand between my fingers, feel the cold against my skin, smell the sweet floral blossoms. But those places weren't here at all. They were inside the mirrors.

"Each magic mirror is a gateway to another world," Nero explained as the scenes inside the mirrors changed, cycling to a set of seven new worlds.

Across the room, facing the archways, the seven gods took their seven thrones.

Made of crystals and gems, the Queen Goddess's throne sparkled with as much beauty as she did. Zarion's throne, made of gold rather than gems, was equally ornate. Like a burning sun, blinding light pulsed from its shimmery surface.

Ronan's throne wasn't formed from precious stones or gold. It was made of beautifully-crafted dark metals. It had the mark of a weapon smith, not a jeweler. Such smooth and perfect lines—such balance, such fierce beauty. Soft light reflected off the throne, making it appear almost liquid, like a molten river of metals flowing in perfect harmony, in constant, fluid motion.

Faris's throne was blacker than a starless night. The material didn't reflect the light. It absorbed it all, sucking it in. Spikes jutted out of the throne's top, exactly the sort you'd expect to find bodies impaled upon. Based on what I knew of Faris's personality, it was a fitting detail.

Aleris sat on a living tree, its thick roots sinking deep into the marble floor. Pink flowers sprouted from the branches, expelling a fragrant floral perfume. Yellow butterflies rested on the blossoms, softly pumping their wings.

The sister goddesses were perched on thrones woven from strands of precious metals. Meda's contained mostly bronze, Maya's an even mix of gold and silver. Delicate metal flowers with tiny gem centers adorned Maya's fairytale throne.

"Listen closely," Faris's voice echoed through the hall, drawing all eyes to him. "I will now outline the perimeters of this training."

Faris was dominating the gods' dialogue right now. They must have put him in the director's chair. Earlier, Faris had claimed the gods were here to push the Legion to higher standards. So why wasn't Ronan taking charge? He was the Lord of the Legion.

"Your task is to obtain several important items," Faris continued. "A scavenger hunt, if you will."

Somehow, I doubted this would be the kind of scavenger hunt with cute riddles, fun challenges, and a bundle of heart balloons at the end of it all.

"There will be seven teams," said Faris. "Each team will consist of an angel and a level seven soldier. Obtaining the items will not be easy."

The darkly delighted look on Faris's face said it would be damn near impossible to get those items.

"We will be watching all of you. Closely. Don't ever forget that this is a competition, not a party. The level seven soldier whose performance we find most worthy will be promoted to an angel. And we will bestow a special gift of magic on the top-performing angel."

I could almost hear the cracking knuckles and revving magic rippling through the hall. Oh, boy. Angels and their offspring were highly competitive. Losing wasn't in their vocabulary, and their egos didn't leave any room for failure. They'd be pushing themselves two hundred percent all the way.

"Before you get too excited, you should know that *I* will be choosing the groups." Faris's cool gaze slid over our ranks. "Andrin Spellsmiter, you're with Colonel Desiree Silvertongue. Siri Silvertongue is with General Kiros Spellsmiter."

Andrin and Siri each went to stand beside their angel partner.

"Isabelle Battleborn, your angel teammate is Harker Sunstorm."

Isabelle joined Harker, giving him a scathing look. I'd never seen a Legion brat glare at an angel like that. They respected them far too much to feel any disdain for them, let alone show it.

"And Jace Firestorm goes to Leila Starborn."

Unlike Isabelle, Jace looked relieved. Leila, who commanded Storm Castle, had the most powerful elemental magic of any angel on Earth. She was a kickass warrior and an all-round nice person—not two qualities you often found in combination inside angels.

"Then we have Arius Demonslayer and Nyx. And Delta Wardbreaker and Nero Windstriker."

Shit. Faris was pairing me with Colonel Fireswift. I didn't need to count to fourteen to know that we were the only two people left. I knew what was coming, but Faris's next words were like the final nail in my very dead corpse. Because his words made this real. They made it more than just a bad dream.

"And finally, Leda Pierce, you're with Colonel Fireswift."

Numbly, I went to stand beside Colonel Fireswift. It

was a partnership made in hell. I couldn't imagine a partner less compatible with me. From the sour look pinching Colonel Fireswift's cheeks, he was, for once, in complete agreement with me. And he was looking at me like this whole thing was *my* fault.

Gods, Faris really must have hated me to pair me up with the sadistic head of the Legion's Interrogators.

"For the remainder of this training, this person is your partner," Faris told us. "Let this be a reminder that as a soldier in the Legion of Angels, you sometimes fight alongside friends—and sometimes alongside people you do not like."

'Not like' did not even begin to describe the nature of my relationship with Colonel Fireswift. He positively loathed me.

"Your feelings are irrelevant," Faris told us. "You serve the greater good. Your duty is to the Legion and to the gods. Don't swaddle yourselves in love and misguided sentimentality. A time may come when you must fight against your friends and family *for the greater good*."

His final words rang loud and long, like a bell echoing in the hall. And as he spoke, his eyes were completely locked on Nero. Long ago, the Legion had assigned Nero's mother the task of killing his father. As far as the gods' council knew, both of them were now dead.

"In case you're tempted to help someone on another team, clear your mind of that madness." Faris's gaze slid from Nero to me. "The consequences of breaking the rules will be severe."

Most of the Legion brats no longer looked so excited about this training. Of course they weren't. Faris was making it clear that it was no mistake he'd pitted us against those we loved. In fact, pitting us against those we loved was the whole point of this exercise. I didn't have any idea what the consequences of helping our friends would be, but I could make a decent guess. The world of gods was devoid of mercy. It was a place without happy endings or second chances.

The gods watched our growing unease with mild but detached amusement, just as you'd expect from an all-powerful deity. Faris had basically handed the gods a reality television setup of epic proportions. And we were the unwilling participants.

"Each team will have a patron god. That god will provide you with instructions, which you must obey without question or delay."

Though Faris's gaze didn't pan to me, I could have sworn he was glaring right at me. Or more like right *through* me. Yeah, I was definitely on Faris's shit list. I'd been there ever since I'd thwarted his plans to publicly—and very explosively—expose his brother Zarion's misdeeds.

Faris assigned each team to a god. Andrin and Desiree Silvertongue went to Aleris, Jace and Leila to Valora. Zarion got Arius and Nyx. Delta and Nero were assigned to Maya. Maya's sister Meda took Siri and Kiros Spellsmiter. That left Ronan with Isabelle and Harker—and Faris with me and Colonel Fireswift.

That decision made me wonder. Had Faris made himself my patron god because he was trying to manipulate the challenges so that I won? That would give him the excuse he needed to level me up, to bring me one step closer to the power I needed to find Zane. I knew Faris planned to be right there when I did find him.

But if he was trying to level me up, the joke was on him. Right now, I couldn't even level up. I was just stuck.

Not that he knew that. And he couldn't find out. I closed off my mind, keeping my thoughts in—and every telepath around me out.

"This training will consist of seven challenges," Faris declared. "Seven challenges, seven items. You see, you will all be competing to steal the gods' most prized possessions."

CHAPTER 7

THE GAMES OF GODS

Stealing the most prized possessions of the seven ruling gods did not sound easy at all. In fact, it sounded downright impossible. And the gods did not look happy about it.

"This is not what we discussed, Faris," Zarion protested. "We were not to be part of this spectacle."

He and the other gods had been quite content to watch this 'spectacle' just a few moments ago. The irony of Zarion's words was laughable, but I kept my face blank and my internal chuckles to myself.

"You all agreed to give me full control over this training," Faris replied coolly.

Just as I'd thought. Faris was the one running the show —which meant he could manipulate the show. The reminder that the cold and calculating God of Heaven's Army was controlling us all knocked the amusement right out of me.

"We agreed to give you some leeway, Faris," said Meda. "But not like *this*."

"Indeed," Maya agreed. "I do not wish for these earthly

soldiers to rummage through my underwear drawer in search of treasure."

Zarion's platinum brows rose, a sharp smile cutting his lips. "Just what do you keep in there, Maya?"

She flashed her teeth at him. "You shall never know."

Meda snickered. Maybe Zarion had hit on Maya before and she'd rejected him.

"Faris is right. We agreed to give him full control over this training," Aleris said. "And so we must follow through. Our word is gospel. It rings true and real from every world in our domain. It is constant, unbreakable."

I wasn't surprised by Aleris's words. He was a real stickler for the rules. More than anything, I'd taken that knowledge from my few brief encounters with him. He was fair and balanced, never making a decision in haste or out of emotion.

"We did indeed agree to hand Faris the reins in this matter." Valora gave the God of Heaven's Army a sharp look. "But tread lightly, Faris. The gods' council will not be made a mockery of."

"I wouldn't dream of it." Faris turned to address me and the other Legion soldiers once more. "As I said, the seven teams will attempt to steal each god's most prized possession. But beware. These items are well-protected."

"Exactly how will you determine each god's most prized possession?" Meda asked.

"With magic." Faris flicked his hand, and the doors to the hall swung open.

A man entered the gods' audience chamber. He looked like he'd stepped straight out of a fairytale—a dark and gritty fairytale. He wore a sweeping crimson cloak over a ruffled pirate shirt made of dark satin, and a pair of knee-high boots over black leather pants. His pale blond hair, styled into dozens of long braids, was like a bright full moon over his outfit's black night backdrop. His amber eyes glowed like liquid butterscotch, always shifting, always in motion. As he met my gaze, I looked away. There was something very disturbing boiling deep inside those eyes. Something I'd never seen before. I didn't know what it was, but it scared me.

Everyone in the room seemed to recognize the stranger —everyone except for me. The gods prided themselves on being omniscient, but his arrival had shocked even them. The stranger must have been someone special if his mere presence had stunned the gods to silence.

"First we dine," Faris declared. "Then the fun will begin."

He waved his hand, and his godly soldiers ushered servers into the room. Each one carried a platter of food, which they set on buffet tables that had materialized out of nowhere.

Faris had warned us about conspiring with our friends on opposing teams, so I followed Nero to the cheese table under the pretense of hunger. It wasn't a difficult role to play. I hadn't consumed anything but blood and Nectar since lunchtime. I was absolutely famished.

Nero lifted the knife and sliced a piece off a particularly potent cheese block. My nose crinkled. If he ate that, I would not be kissing him later. Which was probably a good thing. Smoochies with an opposing team member probably fell into Faris's definition of 'conspiring'.

"What do you think of Faris's team assignments?" I asked Nero.

"Faris does have a point," he replied. "And it's perfectly in line with the Legion's mantra. To be disconnected, detached, so you can do your duty." He spread the cheese over a cracker. "But I suspect that is merely the icing on the cake."

"A shiny layer to hide what truly lies inside," I said.

"Yes. Nothing about this training is random. Nothing is coincidental. Faris carefully planned each and every detail, the team assignments included. He paired up enemies for a reason, something beyond the usual Legion platitudes. The question is what his true motive is."

"What does Isabelle Battleborn have against Harker?" I asked him. "Do they have a history?"

"Up until a month ago, they were friends."

"What happened a month ago…" Then it hit me. "The battle at Memphis. Colonel Battleborn died there."

"But Harker did not," said Nero. "Isabelle blames Harker for her father's death. For not saving him. And for surviving when Colonel Battleborn did not."

"Their team isn't the only one built out of discord," I said, glancing at Siri.

She stood with General Spellsmiter, but her eyes focused intently on her mother, like she was silently asking Colonel Silvertongue to tell her what she should do.

"Desiree Silvertongue and Kiros Spellsmiter are locked in a century-long family feud," Nero explained. "They are engaged in a vicious competition to see whose child will become an angel first. Siri or Andrin."

Jace had mentioned this competition.

"By pairing Colonel Silvertongue with Andrin Spellsmiter and General Spellsmiter with Siri Silvertongue, Faris created a massive conflict of interest," I said. "The two angels want to win the gods' prize, but in doing so, they are each hurting their own child's chances of becoming an angel before their cousin."

"Exactly."

"And then there's my team. Colonel Fireswift and I can't stand each other." I frowned. "Faris made himself my team's patron god. That's not an accident either."

"No, it is not," agreed Nero. "You will have to be very diligent to keep your secrets sealed and your mind closed. Both Faris and Colonel Fireswift excel at exposing secrets."

Secrets like how I hadn't leveled up. What had seemed difficult to hide before, had now been promoted to impossible. I would be working closely with Faris and Colonel Fireswift. How was I supposed to keep that secret from the head of the Interrogators and the God of Sirens? Every day of their immortal lives, they lived and breathed compulsion and control. And they excelled at exposing secrets.

I watched the fairytale stranger across the room. He stood alone, separate, leaning casually against a wall, his eerie amber eyes drinking everything in. "Who's the mystery man?"

"I don't know who he is, but there's no hiding *what* he is," replied Nero. "He is an Everlasting."

He said the word like it meant something. I just didn't know what.

"A descendant of the original immortals," he explained, responding to my apparent confusion. "The Everlasting are telepaths, the most powerful in all the worlds."

"Like a ghost?" I asked. Ghosts weren't the cloaked spirits of the dead who popped out to say 'boo!' on Halloween. No, they were living beings with telepathic magic. The Legion ability 'Ghost's Whisper', the power I needed to find my brother, referred to telepathic magic.

"Even the powerful ghosts on Earth are nothing compared to the telepathic power the Everlasting wield," Nero told me. "Telepathy was a native ability of the original immortals, one passed on to their Everlasting descendants. The power is not native to gods or demons; they gained telepathy by breeding it into their magic line."

"So what is a descendent of the original immortals doing here?" I wondered.

"That is a mystery. The Everlasting stay out of the gods' and demons' conflicts. They keep to themselves. I have no idea how Faris convinced one of them to come here, let alone to use his magic to unearth the identity of the gods' most prized possessions."

With that said, Nero walked back to his partner Delta Wardbreaker, carrying his plate of cheese and crackers. I grabbed a few final morsels, then left the buffet table too. There was only so long we could pretend to collect food. Faris was already watching me suspiciously.

And he wasn't the only one.

"What were you discussing with Windstriker?" Colonel Fireswift demanded as I stopped beside him.

"Oh, you know, we were exchanging the usual threats and battle banter," I replied pleasantly, eating a piece of mango.

Colonel Fireswift's nose scrunched up in irritation. He was clearly not amused. "Do not consort with the enemy."

"It's just a game, Colonel."

"You stupid little girl. Of course it's a game, but the games of gods are very real." His hand clamped down on my wrist. "Don't give the gods a reason to punish you. Because when you turn their wrath on you, *I* will share in the punishment." His voice dropped to a searing hiss. "That's what it means to be on the same team. You weren't listening to Faris at all, were you? We share our triumphs *and* our failures. And I will not go down because of a dirty little vagrant like you."

His grip hurt like a bear trap, but I just kept smiling.

"Has anyone ever told you how charming you are, Colonel?"

"No," he growled. "They all know that no amount of flattery will save them from the fate they deserve."

Gods, he was grim. Faris could not have paired me with a less compatible partner. Across the room, Nero was talking to his own partner. He and Delta seemed to know each other. More than that, they seemed to like each other. Even the warring cousins and their angel parents were getting along—and they'd been competing for years.

Years. Years that everyone here had known one another. Everyone except *me*. I was the only non-Legion brat in my training group, the only one who didn't hail from the elite inner circle, and I'd been paired with the most prejudiced, old school, snobbish, mean angel of them all. If the competition didn't kill me, my teammate just might.

Sure, I could have focused on that, but I decided to concentrate on eating instead. That was something I could do as well as anyone here. *Better* even. I'd devoured the contents of three very full plates, much to Colonel Fireswift's disgust, when Faris rose from his throne once more.

"The first challenge will soon begin," Faris announced. "We shall begin with Aleris." He glanced at the Everlasting.

"Aleris's most prized possession is an ancient pair of opera glasses," the Everlasting said. "They are rose gold in color. On their handle, there's a painting of the moon and stars of the night sky."

As the Everlasting spoke, Aleris listened with mild curiosity. The ever-calm God of Nature didn't even look concerned that fourteen Legion soldiers would soon be fighting tooth and nail to steal his most prized possession."

"The glasses are kept in Aleris's home castle," the Everlasting finished, then took a step back to lean against the wall once more.

"Each team will now go to their apartment to await their patron god's arrival. There you will be briefed on your mission." Faris waved at his soldiers. Seven godly warriors in shiny armor moved forward in perfect unison. "My soldiers will show you to your chambers, where you will stay for the duration of this training. Your bags have been brought over from Crystal Falls. They are already in your rooms. Now prepare yourselves for the first challenge."

The gods' council remained planted regally on their thrones, watching us leave the audience chamber like we were dramatic players running backstage to prepare for the next act. Faris's soldiers led us up a long, winding staircase. At each floor, a godly warrior ushered one of the teams to their room. Finally, it was just me, Colonel Fireswift, and a poker-faced female soldier with a shaved scalp.

"We get the penthouse suite?" I asked her brightly.

Her response was to shove me toward the old wooden door.

I looked over my shoulder at her. "So what's your name?"

"You talk too much," she told me, lifting her arms.

Before the muscle goddess could push me again, I turned the handle to open the door and ducked inside. My backpack was already waiting there, as were Colonel Fireswift's five bags.

"Not really a light packer, are you?" I asked him as he opened his bags, presumably to check that the contents were still all there.

Every single bag was filled with weapons—and some scary-looking instruments I could only assume were used for torturing people. Oh, boy. This was going to be a long few days.

"Faris's soldier is right," Colonel Fireswift snapped. "You talk too much."

I merely shrugged, turning my back on the battle chests, and moved further into the room. It was enormous, easily large enough to comfortably sleep twenty soldiers. And yet there was only one bed.

"Faris, you are sick," I cursed under my breath. Then I spun around to face Colonel Fireswift. "Shall we flip for the bed?"

He coolly considered the gold coin I'd pulled out of my bag. "That is unnecessary. I outrank you, so I must clearly take the bed."

"What ever happened to chivalry?" I muttered as he set his armory of bags on the mattress.

"If you wanted to be treated like a lady, you should have taken up employment at a brothel, not the Legion of Angels," he declared, his hard blue eyes cutting through me like a knife. "In the gods' service, there is no special treatment for anyone. You are either strong and survive, or you are weak and perish."

I had to give it to Colonel Fireswift. Twisted as he was, he at least believed in equality of the sexes. Not equality of heritage, mind you. I was still a dirty street urchin in his eyes—and I always would be.

I wondered what he would think of me if he'd known what I really was, if he found out about my divine blood. He'd probably call me an unnatural anomaly of magic. Best not to think about it, lest he picked up on my thoughts. I grabbed my backpack and tossed it onto the sofa.

As I exchanged my skirt, tank top, and slip-on shoes for leather armor and boots, Colonel Fireswift kept his eyes firmly on me. A gentleman would have turned his back, but as we'd just established, Colonel Fireswift was devoid of chivalrous aspirations. He wasn't gawking at me, at least. His face was cold, detached. He'd probably seen a lot of naked bodies—both living and dead ones. A shiver rippled down my spine.

"The gods sure do like to stir the pot, don't they?" I commented. "Pitting you against Jace, and me against Nero."

His blond brows drew together. "Why are you talking to me?"

To fill the silence? To connect to my teammate? Colonel Fireswift didn't look like he'd appreciate either answer.

"The gods do as they see fit, and we obey," he told me. "That is the way of things. It is not our place to question it. There's no room for emotion or speculation."

No room for emotion? My mind flickered back to his face as his daughter died, her body poisoned, her magic torn apart by Venom. He hadn't been logical or cold then. There was a real person inside of Colonel Fireswift. Maybe not a good person, but someone who had feelings. Someone who experienced pain and joy and all those other pesky human emotions he tried to pretend were not a part of him.

"The gods command the angels, and the angels command the Legion." Colonel Fireswift's voice was as hard as a diamond drill. "When we get out there in the field, I will command. And you will obey. There is no room for anything else. You will not question me. You will not take matters into your own hands. And you will most certainly not antagonize the gods. You will act with the dignity expected of a Legion soldier. If you do not, I will use your body as a shield on the battlefield and let our competitors kill you for me. Do you understand?"

I considered my response carefully. Angels demanded obedience, but they respected strength. If I let Colonel Fireswift walk all over me, I'd act obedient but appear weak. He'd respect me even less than he already did, which meant he'd only abuse me more. On the other hand, if I talked back, I'd demonstrate strength but be guilty of insubordination. Talk about an impossible choice.

A sharp knock cut through the heavy silence before I could mark my doom one way or the other. I slipped past Colonel Fireswift and opened the door.

"Make way for Faris, God of Heaven's Army, King of Sirens, Slayer of Demons," the bald soldier declared, every title ringing off her tongue like a blade clashing against another.

The soldier drew back, and Faris glided silkily into our room, the base of his cloak slithering across the floor behind him. A breath of magic clicked the door shut. His gaze panned across the room.

"What a cozy chamber. So romantic," he commented.

I nearly gagged. Faris and Colonel Fireswift were neck-in-neck in the race to each prove himself the universe's biggest asshole.

"You will soon go to Aleris's castle," Faris told us. Thankfully, he made no further comments about the 'romantic' room. If he had, I might have vomited all over his fancy boots. "It is on the world Harmony."

"How do we get to another world?" I asked.

"Heaven is a crossroads, a gateway to other worlds," Faris explained. "From here, you can travel to our kingdoms and many other places."

"A gateway. Those were the doors on the other side of

the audience chamber. The mirrors are those gateways to other worlds," I realized.

Faris's gaze slid over Colonel Fireswift's stockpile of weapons. "For this challenge, you are not permitted to bring weapons with you to Harmony. It is solely about magic. The team assigned to Aleris will join his castle guards to defend the glasses."

Aleris's team. That meant Colonel Silvertongue and Andrin Spellsmiter.

"Aleris's defenders will have use of both their magic and weapons to protect the glasses," Faris continued. "You will be outnumbered and unarmed. But you have something the other teams do not."

"A sense of humor in the face of certain doom?" I suggested, meeting Colonel Fireswift's deadpan face.

"Time," said Faris. "Five minutes time, to be exact. The gods drew numbers, and I pulled number one. Team two will arrive five minutes after you, then another team every five minutes after that until you're all there."

Five minutes wasn't much time to a mortal, but a Legion soldier could move fast, so a lot could happen in five minutes. A lot of good or a lot of bad. I'd like to think that depended entirely on us, but I had a feeling the gods had stacked the odds decidedly against us. After all, easy games didn't make for good entertainment.

"Now, return to the audience chamber," Faris commanded us. "And whatever you do, don't die. The gods have taken out bets on this little contest, and if I lose, I'll be *very* annoyed."

CHAPTER 8

THE SEER'S OPERA GLASSES

That's all we really were to the gods: curiosities, amusements to pass the long centuries, pawns in their immortal game for power and dominance.

"If we are to win this, you must understand our opponents," Colonel Fireswift told me as we stood alone in the now-empty audience chamber.

We were waiting in front of one of seven mirrors. A golden glow covered the bottom edge of the mirror's frame. When that glow covered the entire frame, we would pass through the magic glass to enter Aleris's domain.

"Desiree Silvertongue is a mistress of compulsion," Colonel Fireswift said. "She can talk her way into or out of anything. She is very strong and fast, but her other magical skills aren't very powerful for an angel. Her brother Kiros Spellsmiter is also an excellent physical fighter, even stronger than she is. His siren magic is almost on par with hers. But he has the same weaknesses as she does, a consequence of their family's faulty breeding practices."

Their breeding couldn't be all that bad if both brother and sister had become angels. And if breeding were truly everything, then no one who didn't come from a Legion legacy family could ever become an angel. Hard work and determination counted for a lot—much more than Colonel Fireswift's magic equation allowed for.

"They pushed too hard for siren and vampire magic at the expense of the other magical traits." Colonel Fireswift turned up his nose, like his family would never have made such a novice mistake. It seemed that, even amongst Legion legacy families, a hierarchy existed. And Colonel Fireswift considered himself right at the top of it.

"It's the same story, the same weaknesses, in their offspring: Andrin Spellsmiter and Siri Silvertongue. Use distance attacks against them. Don't let any of the four of them get close enough to grab you or compel you," said Colonel Fireswift. "And we can play them off one another, using their family rivalry to keep them busy."

There was no doubt that Colonel Fireswift was an incurable asshole, but that didn't mean he wasn't intelligent.

"Harker Sunstorm is strong but he's a new angel. He's still unsure of himself." He gave me an assessing look. "We can use his indecision to our advantage."

"Harker is my friend."

Colonel Fireswift nodded. "Yes, we can use that to our advantage as well. Sunstorm concerns himself overly much with friendship."

"Whereas you do not concern yourself with such things at all."

"Of course not," he said, as though that were the only answer, the only way. "If you were listening at all to Faris's words, you would realize the gods are testing our ability to rise above human weaknesses, above the chains of friendship."

"The *chains* of friendship?" As though friends trapped and weakened you.

"The gods do not concern themselves with anything as whimsical as friendship," he replied. "And they expect the same discipline from us."

"I think the gods are more human than you realize."

He scowled at me. "Keep your blasphemous thoughts to yourself. The gods are watching. Always watching."

"Are they?" I countered. "Are we all so important that the gods do nothing else but watch us day in and day out? I ask you, Colonel: which is the greater sin: hubris or blasphemy?"

His scowl deepened. Ha! He didn't have an answer to that. I used to do the same thing back home to the Pilgrims, the priests who spread the gods' message. They happened to spread that message by cornering unsuspecting sinners on the street. When they'd cornered me, I'd twisted their logic into knots and then left them to untangle it.

A veteran angel, Colonel Fireswift was not so easily baffled. "Isabelle Battleborn is well-balanced, like her father," he said, continuing his run-through of our opponents' strengths and weaknesses. "She's a good all-rounder, a product of well-implemented selective breeding. But she has been unhinged by Colonel Battleborn's death. We can exploit that."

I frowned at him. "You want to use Isabelle's grief to beat her at a game?"

"I told you already. This isn't just a game. Pay attention. I don't enjoy repeating myself," he snapped.

I wondered how many times he'd told that to his interrogation victims. On second thought, no, I really didn't want to know.

"Don't bother yourself with moral conundrums, Leda Pierce. Such superficial ponderation is best left to the meandering minds of philosophers."

Don't bother yourself with moral conundrums. That was Colonel Fireswift's moral code in a nutshell.

"Isabelle Battleborn might look like an innocent young kitten, but she is a man-eating tiger inside," he said. "As she should be. If we are to win these challenges, we must use any and every weakness to do so. Isabelle would do the same to us."

"That doesn't make it right."

"Being *right* is what this whole thing is all about," he replied. "The *right* move. The *right* strategy to win this game. We must play to our strengths and their weaknesses. Only an idiot plays to their opponent's strengths. Windstriker should have taught you that. He should have beaten the humanity out of you by now."

And Colonel Fireswift did mean 'beaten' both figuratively and literally. Just as he had mercilessly trained his children. I'd once run into Jace after he'd been training with his father; I'd seen torture victims in better shape.

"Nero and I don't have that kind of relationship," I told Colonel Fireswift. "He does not feel the need to beat anything out of me."

"If he cares about you, he won't go easy on you. He will do everything in his power to make you strong enough to survive whatever may come."

A shadow darkened Colonel Fireswift face. He was thinking back to his daughter. I could see it in his harrowed eyes. He was reliving her death. The angel in him thought he could have prevented her death by just training her harder, making her stronger, more resilient.

He was wrong. It would have only accelerated her

demise. The weapons in that battle, those that had killed so many, had been born from hell. They'd eaten away at the Legion soldiers' light magic. The more light magic someone had, the more resilient they were, the more they'd leveled up—the faster the poison had torn through their body, unraveling their magic until there was nothing left.

Damn it. I didn't like Colonel Fireswift. Still, I couldn't help but feel sorry for him and all that he'd lost.

I set my hand on his shoulder. "What happened to your daughter was not your fault."

He shrugged off my hand, fury burning in his eyes. "I don't need your pity." Then he continued the strategy session, as though he found solace in this routine. "Leila Starborn is a powerful elemental, an accomplished healer, and her telepathic and psychic magics are strong. Her weaknesses are Shifter's Shadow, Vampire's Kiss, Siren's Song, and Witch's Cauldron."

I wondered if the Legion's angels who trained together, working toward a common goal, knew they would someday be using their inside knowledge of their colleagues against them. Probably. They were angels, after all. The Legion's doctrine instructed them to make themselves islands, beings beyond the complications of emotional entanglements.

Today was that *someday*, the day the floodgates had been blown wide open. The day they'd use all that they'd collected on their fellow angels over the centuries.

"As for the First Angel," Colonel Fireswift pressed on, unhindered by moral complications. "Nyx trained with gods, is stronger than any angel, and she doesn't have any magic weaknesses. Our best bet against her is to exploit her partner's weaknesses. That's Arius Demonslayer. He has been in the Legion longer than most of you, but not nearly long enough. He is currently stuck at a volatile stage, more experienced and powerful than his peers, but not yet an angel. His pride makes him reckless. He already thinks he's won, that he will be the next angel. That he is above the rest of you. His overconfidence is his weakness. He doesn't understand his own limits and failings. He takes risks he shouldn't and that will be his downfall here."

"You seem to know a lot about everyone here," I said.

"That's my job."

"But what about your son? What about Jace? What are his weaknesses?" I braided my fingers together. "You might as well be thorough."

Colonel Fireswift hesitated.

"Perhaps the chains of friendship hold power over you after all?" I suggested.

He bristled at my statement. "No, they most certainly do not," he snapped. "Jace's weakness is the desperate need to prove himself, to be worthy in my eyes. And also in yours."

"Mine?"

"His friendship with you makes him too human. He has grown too concerned with the feelings of others. You have the same effect on Windstriker. It's an agitating trait, but perhaps we can exploit it."

"You are *not* going to use Nero's feelings for me to hurt him."

A savage smile twisted his mouth. "Do you want to win, or don't you?"

I ignored that statement. "And Delta? What's her profile?"

"Delta Wardbreaker has been around a long time, even longer than Arius Demonslayer. She is well-trained, disciplined, and confident. She tends to favor the more aggressive, more explosive and showy side of the magical spectrum."

"So vampire, shifter, elemental, and psychic?"

Colonel Fireswift nodded. "Yes. She is a wrecking ball that the Legion points at obstacles. She is not subtle. She has no appreciation for the nuances of magic."

"So you don't think she is the strongest contender of the level sevens?" I asked him.

"She is," he replied. "She has so much raw power and so many years of experience. But others here would make a better angel."

"Like Jace?" I didn't bother asking him about myself. I knew his opinion of me all too well. He'd never been shy about sharing it.

"Time will tell. These challenges will show exactly what kind of soldier everyone is." He looked at me like he already knew exactly what kind of soldier I was—and he'd found me lacking on all fronts. He didn't even see any use for me as a mindless wrecking ball like Delta.

"Windstriker was in the Legion for two hundred years before he met you." A frown furrowed Colonel Fireswift's perfect angel face.

"Meaning?"

"Meaning, Windstriker is no fool. He knows your weaknesses. He won't sit on that information. He will tell his partner."

"What do I care what he tells Delta?" I laughed.

"You might care to know that he and Delta Wardbreaker were once romantically involved."

I blinked.

"You didn't know that. And it bothers you," he observed, watching me closely.

No, I hadn't known that. And, admittedly, it did

bother me. But I wasn't going to throw fuel on Colonel Fireswift's fire.

"Perhaps this is just the situation they need to rekindle their relationship," he suggested.

I slanted a seething look his way. "Stop trying to manipulate me and turn me against Nero."

"You are already against each other by being on opposing sides."

"Only on the battlefield. Only in the games of gods. Not in real life."

"This *is* your life now. You are just too stubborn to admit it."

A flash of light pulsed off the magic mirror's frame. It was time. Colonel Fireswift stepped through the glass and disappeared. I followed.

Another world waited on the other side, a beautiful, violent world. We stood atop a high open tower, inside a ring of burning torches. Ice stretched its bitter-cold fingers across the stone floor, climbing the torch stands, eating away at the flames, the only things keeping this place warm. Above us, red fire bled across the stormy sky, turning the clouds to ash. Far below the tower, every few seconds lightning pounded against a cracked and charred earth. And feral vines had almost completely swallowed the sea beyond the blackened plains. This world shouldn't have been named Harmony. It was discord through and through.

"Water hurting Fire. Fire hurting Sky. Sky hurting Earth. And Earth hurting Water. This whole place is like one giant four-way elemental game of rock-paper-scissors," I commented.

"Why are you rambling on about a children's game?" Colonel Fireswift demanded in disgust.

I jumped, narrowly avoiding being struck by lightning. "Something isn't right here." When one of the feral vines shot out of the sea like a rocket and tried to land on my head, I gave it a taste of my lightning magic. It slithered away. "The whole world is trying to kill us."

"It's a challenge. It's not meant to be easy," Colonel Fireswift said pragmatically.

"The *challenge*," I muttered. "That is the challenge: turning discord into harmony."

"Explain."

"What do we know about Aleris? That he controls the elements. He keeps them in balance." I pointed at the hellish war of the elements raging around us. "Nothing here is in balance."

"We have to put the magic elements back in balance," Colonel Fireswift realized. "That will win the challenge. That will reveal Aleris's treasure."

He said it like this had been his idea all along. So much for sharing in our victories.

"The question is how to put the elements back in balance," I said.

"There." Colonel Fireswift pointed at a thick stone mountain jutting up from the center of the tower platform. Eight giant granite slabs, each one marked with a rune, covered it. "It's a puzzle. We must use our magic to move the slabs into the right order."

He'd no sooner spoken the words, when a soldier in red armor materialized on the platform. She immediately charged at us, swinging her enormous battle axe.

Colonel Fireswift blasted her away with an explosive bundle of telekinetic magic. "I will hold her off. You solve that puzzle."

I approached the stone mountain, glancing up at the eight granite slabs. The runes on them looked familiar.

There was another flash. Andrin Spellsmiter and Colonel Silvertongue, Aleris's team, were now on the tower too. They rushed me, trying to drive me away from the puzzle. Colonel Fireswift cut them off, snapping at them with the lightning whip he'd conjured with his magic.

I stared at the runes. I was sure I'd seen them before. But where?

Another soldier appeared on the tower. Colonel Fireswift wove spell after spell and sent them at our attackers, but he was slowly losing ground. He wouldn't be able to hold them off much longer.

I tilted my head and squinted at the chiseled runes. From the side, one of them bore a striking resemblance to a flame. And if flipped vertically, another looked just like a snowflake. And there was a lightning bolt too. A whiff of smoke, a dewdrop, a cloud, a tree, a lump of metal. These eight symbols *were* the elements. I just had to put them where they belonged and harmony would return to Harmony.

Another flash of magic delivered Jace and Leila to the tower. Time was running out. Aleris's soldiers were popping up every minute. The competing Legion teams arrived every five minutes. This tower was filling up fast. Before long, we'd be completely overrun.

I wrapped my telekinetic magic around the flame slab, moving it into the bright red corner of the mountain. That had to represent the element of Fire. I next moved the lightning bolt. As it clicked into the indigo-and-gold Sky corner, a flaming potion bottle shot over my shoulder, missing me by mere inches. It smashed into the stone puzzle and exploded. The mountain was unbothered by the thunderous explosion. Thankfully. I couldn't imagine Aleris would appreciate us blowing up his tower.

The puzzle was still in one piece, but that explosion was a jolting reminder that the other soldiers were nearly upon me. I hastily rearranged the marble slabs into their respective elemental corners. The whiff of smoke settled into place beside the flame under Fire. The cloud joined the lightning bolt in the Sky corner.

By now, sweat lathered my skin from crown to heel. Maneuvering those marble slabs around the board was straining my telekinetic magic in a way mere psychic blasts did not. I kept going. The tree and lump of metal went to Earth. That just left Water's snowflake and dewdrop.

Something hard pounded into the back of my head, knocking me to the ground. My head spinning, my vision blurry, I pushed up.

I was too late.

Jace stood in front of the puzzle. And he'd just locked the final two pieces into place. There was a soft click, followed by a thunderous roar. The mountain split down the middle to reveal a pair of gold opera glasses with a painted handle. Jace grabbed them.

The warring elements stopped clashing—and so did the warring people on the tower. As Aleris's soldiers took the staircase down into the castle, Colonel Fireswift closed in beside me. He didn't look happy.

"The Seer's Opera Glasses," Leila said, looking at the glasses in Jace's hands. "They're an ancient relic. An immortal artifact."

"What do they do?" Jace asked her.

"I don't know, but right now they've won us this challenge," Leila said, winking at Colonel Fireswift.

His scowl deepened. Wow, he really did not like losing.

He looked even more upset than Colonel Silvertongue and Andrin, and they'd lost the item they were supposed to be guarding for Aleris.

"Congratulations." I slapped Jace on the back. "You bested us."

"Yes, we did," he replied, his gaze shifting to Colonel Fireswift. I'd never seen him look at his father with such excitement.

The magic mirror reappeared on the tower platform. The six of us stepped through. A moment later, we were back in the gods' audience chamber. The other four teams were still waiting to go through.

"Sorry you missed the party," Leila teased Harker.

It had all happened so fast. The other teams had not even made it to the challenge on the tower.

"Your son is looking pretty triumphant," I told Colonel Fireswift, noting that Leila wasn't the only one looking mighty smug right now.

"You are not taking this seriously," he snapped.

"Look at them." I pointed out the other losers' glum faces. "They are all taking it seriously."

"Might you learn from their example."

"They are miserable, Colonel. Because they *are* taking this game seriously. And they lost today."

"*We* lost today too," he ground out.

I arched my brows. "Did we?"

"What did you do?" he said slowly, suspicion dripping from every syllable.

I smiled. "Nothing."

"You will tell me now."

"Later. Back in the apartment." Which happened to be completely sound proof, impervious to the super hearing of even angels and gods.

His eyes drilled into me. I could feel his magic testing me, trying to peel back my mental defenses.

"That won't work," I told him. "I've had a lot of practice blocking angels."

"I am not Windstriker."

"No, you're not," I agreed. "He is an archangel. You are not."

Across the room, Nero snorted.

Colonel Fireswift glared at me like he was contemplating setting me on fire. It was a good thing I was fireproof.

The gods dismissed us from the hall. When we were back in our assigned apartment, the door securely sealed, Colonel Fireswift turned his Interrogator stare on me once more.

"Explain yourself. What have you done?" he demanded.

I pulled Aleris's opera glasses out of my jacket.

Surprise flashed in Colonel Fireswift's eyes. "How did they find their way into your possession?"

"I don't know. It happened around the same time they fell out of Jace's possession."

"You picked his pockets."

I shrugged.

"You *cheated*."

"Did I? Where do the rules state I cannot take the item from another team?" I asked.

He stewed that over in silence for a few moments. "It's implied."

"No, it's not. It's just your interpretation of the rules. What gives you the right to interpret the will of the gods?"

His face turned bright red. He looked like he was going to pop a blood vessel.

I merely smiled at him.

He took a step forward, but he froze at the sound of a godly knock on our door.

"Hide the glasses." His words were a growled, rasped whisper. "We can still return them before anyone notices your disgraceful behavior."

"Disgraceful behavior? I think you mean my winning strategy."

"Are you going to steal the item from every team in every challenge?" he snarled between his teeth.

"No, of course not. I'm depending on your battlefield prowess to win us at least one artifact the good old-fashioned way," I said sweetly.

"You are absurd."

"I'm touched, Colonel. That might just be the nicest thing you've ever said to me."

Another knock thumped against the door, more impatient this time. More godly.

"Stop fooling around and hide the damn thing," Colonel Fireswift hissed at me.

"Where should I hide it? Under my pillow? Thanks to you, I don't even have one."

His hand reached for his sword.

"Fine," I sighed, stuffing the opera glasses into my underwear drawer.

Colonel Fireswift was already at the door. He bowed deeply to Faris.

"What took so long?" demanded the God of Heaven's Army. The hallway behind him was empty. None of his warriors were with him this time.

"The Colonel was just trying to burn me to ashes," I said flippantly. "But that can wait."

Faris's nose twitched, probably out of disgust. He liked

me even less than Colonel Fireswift did, if that was even possible.

"Aleris's opera glasses were stolen," Faris declared, walking into our apartment like he owned the place.

"Yes, we know. We were there on Aleris's tower when Jace and Leila stole them." I smiled at him. "Try talking to them."

If looks could kill, Colonel Fireswift would have murdered me in twenty different ways by now.

Faris's expression didn't flicker; it remained as cold as it had been since he'd arrived. "They were stolen *again*."

"That's unfortunate," I said.

"I *know* you did it." Faris's words were as smooth as silk, and his eyes as hard as granite. "Show me the glasses."

I went over to my dresser and pulled out the glasses. I handed them to Faris without a word.

His nose twitched again. "They smell like lavender."

"That's my potpourri," I told him helpfully.

"Your what?"

"Potpourri." I just kept smiling. "The scented little bundles that girls keep in their underwear drawers to make their lingerie smell nice."

"I know what potpourri is."

"You do? I didn't know gods used potpourri."

His eyes narrowed to slits. "Are you always so irreverent?"

"Yes," Colonel Fireswift declared, glaring at me. He bowed to Faris. "I humbly request a new teammate."

I was surprised the word humble was even in Colonel Fireswift's vocabulary. I wasn't at all surprised, however, that he wanted a new teammate.

"Why do you want a new partner when your current one put your team in the lead?" Faris asked him.

"What?"

"You have Aleris's artifact. You're winning," Faris told him.

"But she cheated."

"The rules of this challenge as I laid them out do not explicitly forbid taking the item from another team," Faris replied.

Ha! The look on Colonel Fireswift's face was priceless. I was sorely tempted to pull out my phone and snap a photo.

"In fact, there will be a lot more of that before this is done," Faris continued. "All teams must keep their acquired artifacts on them at all times."

"So the other teams have a chance at stealing them?" I asked.

"Or reclaiming them. That should keep you on your toes."

And make it interesting for the gods to watch.

"Now get some sleep," Faris ordered us. "You will report to the audience chamber tomorrow morning at five for your next challenge." Then he left our apartment.

"See?" I grinned at Colonel Fireswift. "I told you that we're winning."

"This training is so…undignified. So chaotic."

"Then it's a good thing you ended up with the Misfit of Chaos on your team," I laughed, slapping him hard on the back. "Now, how about some dinner? I'm starving. Do you think room service delivers pizza?"

CHAPTER 9

SHADOW DREAMS

It turned out that room service, which consisted of two godly soldiers wearing gold armor and steely expressions, did not deliver pizza. Apparently, pizza wasn't highbrow enough for heaven. Instead, I was offered the choice of various bizarre dead creatures that looked an awful like monsters but were supposedly gourmet dishes.

My other option was a protein shake made of pureed meat and raw vegetables. When I pointed out that it looked like sludge, the soldiers informed me it was a nutritious meal replacement designed to optimize my performance. Yeah, there was nothing more delicious than optimizing my performance. I ended up eating some bread, cheese, and fruit from the snack platter sitting on the table in the apartment's living room.

After eating, I fell asleep on the sofa. It was much prettier than it was comfortable, but it sure beat sleeping on the hard ground in the woods. At least there were no roots or branches poking me in the back. Or bugs crawling all over my skin.

In my dreams, soldiers chased me through the dark

halls of a nightmare castle. My lungs burning, I ran as fast as my legs would carry me. It wasn't fast enough. *I* wasn't fast enough. They surrounded me. I couldn't see their faces; their whole bodies were cloaked in shadow. They raised their swords and—

I jolted awake, heaving in air. My body was bathed in sweat, my pounding heart rattling my chest. Colonel Fireswift's hands were on my arms, shaking me awake.

"Get up," he said in a gruff, impatient tone. "We are due in the audience chamber in five minutes. And I will not allow you to make me late for a meeting with the gods."

I tucked Aleris's glasses inside my jacket. My hands shook as I pulled on my battle gear. The dream had felt so real. I'd really thought I was in grave danger.

And I *was* in danger. My mind sure had a fun way of processing the perilous game of gods I was trapped in.

My tummy rumbled. I would have suggested a bite of breakfast, but Colonel Fireswift's searing glare was somewhat of a deterrent. And besides, there probably wasn't anything more appetizing than performance-optimizing shakes on the menu.

We hurried to the audience chamber, where the gods waited, poised regally on their thrones. The other teams were already there, all except for Jace and Leila. Valora's team. That meant we were going after the Queen Goddess's item this time. And Jace and Leila would try to stop us.

"The second challenge will soon begin," Faris declared, then looked at the Everlasting man.

"Valora's most prized possession is a crown, kept in her private chambers inside her castle," said the immortal telepath.

Those sure were specific directions. But I didn't believe for a second that this would be easy.

Congratulations on your theft of the Seer's Opera Glasses, Nero's voice spoke in my mind.

I met his approving eyes across the room. He didn't always agree with my wild ways, but he did appreciate that my out-of-the-box thinking often produced results where traditional means failed.

Nero wasn't the only one watching me. Nyx's eyes were following me closely, like she too was assessing me.

"For the last challenge, you were not permitted to bring your own weapons. The same rule will apply to the second challenge as well," Faris told us. "In addition, each team will be allowed the use of only one magic ability, the specialty of their patron god. Your other abilities will be neutralized for the duration of this challenge."

Faris's soldiers dispensed the magic-neutralizing serums. I was still reeling from the potion's effects when two soldiers pushed me and Colonel Fireswift through one of the magic mirrors. At the same time, soldiers all across the audience chamber pushed our competitors through the other mirrors.

Colonel Fireswift and I popped up in the middle of a castle courtyard, completely surrounded by Valora's soldiers. The other teams were scattered throughout the courtyard. Spells and arrows shot at us from every direction. I pulled Colonel Fireswift behind a pegasus statue. A blast of Isabelle Battleborn's psychic magic whizzed past us. A second later, and it would have smacked right into our backs. And since we didn't have any psychic resistance to speak of right now, that would have knocked us out in an instant.

"It is cowardly to hide," Colonel Fireswift growled.

"And it's stupid to die," I countered. "We have only our siren magic right now. We have no weapons, and our defenses against most magic are nonexistent. Before we fight, we need a plan."

I glanced at the twenty or so soldiers in white uniforms, Valora's Guard. They were armed to the teeth—and shooting spells like there was no tomorrow.

"To get into the castle, we have to make it past them," I muttered.

Colonel Fireswift's eyes panned across the army, like he was trying to decide what to do. Without weapons or most of his magic, indecision had seized him. He wasn't sure how to win.

"This isn't about magic or weapons or martial prowess, Colonel," I told him.

His gaze shifted from the battlefield to me.

"It's about this." I tapped my finger to my head. "It's about your mind. You're an angel. You're the head of the Interrogators. You're supposed to be smart, right?"

He stiffened, looking offended that I would even dare to ask the question. "I *am* smart."

"You were trained since you could lift up your head. To fight. To assess a battle scene. To strategize." I pointed at the battle raging on beyond our barrier. "So how do we get through that?"

He just watched the battle. For once, he was actually speechless.

I didn't have any idea how we were going to win either. There were just so many guards. And we had to worry about the other teams too, some of whom still possessed the power to bombard us with explosive offensive spells. I didn't even have anything to hit them back with.

Wait a minute…that wasn't entirely true. We still had

our siren magic. And unlike Valora's soldiers, right now our competitors had zero resistance to Siren's Song.

"We have to make our opponents fight for us. We have to compel them," I told Colonel Fireswift. "They are our weapons against the other teams—and against Valora's Guard. Divide and conquer."

Colonel Firestorm looked at me, an unfamiliar gleam in his eyes. "You are smarter than you appear." He looked like every word of that admission burned his tongue.

I flashed him a grin. "See? I knew all we needed was a little time together for you to warm up to me."

He glowered at me, the threat apparent in his eyes. "Don't confuse repugnance with affection."

"Was that a joke?" I snorted. "Why, Colonel, I never realized you had a sense of humor."

His glower went supernova.

Snickering, I glanced across the battlefield. "The Spellsmiters and Silvertongues are closest. Let's have some fun with them."

"Fun? I am sure what you meant to say is, let us unleash our carefully-planned attacks on them."

I shrugged. "Ok, sure. If saying it that way makes you feel better."

"You turn Andrin Spellsmiter against Desiree Silvertongue," he instructed me coolly. "I will handle Siri Silvertongue and Kiros Spellsmiter."

It was a good starting point. Both teams were already conflicted. The gods had seen to that. Breaking those teams apart would be simpler, require less magic and finesse, than breaking apart friends.

I aimed my siren magic at Colonel Silvertongue and Andrin. The spell came easily, shooting out of me almost before I'd finished composing it inside my mind. It was like what Ronan had explained to me recently, how cutting out some magical abilities allowed my remaining magic to burn brighter. It felt so natural, so easy. So right.

Andrin and his aunt spun around, unleashing elemental spells on each other, even as Siri and her uncle began hurling explosive potion bottles back and forth. It appeared Colonel Fireswift's siren spell had been successful as well.

"Compel Isabelle Battleborn," he instructed me as we emerged from our hiding spot to run across the courtyard, his eyes honing in on Harker's teammate.

I barely had to touch Isabelle's magic to ignite her wrath. Her anger, which had been boiling below the surface for so long, finally exploded.

"You!" she screamed, shooting a telekinetic blast at Harker. "Why didn't you save him?" She shot her magic at him again. Her rage was burning so hot that I hardly had to compel her. "Why did you come back when he died there on that battlefield?"

One of Isabelle's spells intended for Harker slammed into a castle tower, slicing the top right off.

"Sorry," I said to him, cringing. I'd known Isabelle was angry, but I hadn't realized her grief so completely consumed her.

"We are competitors, Pandora," replied Harker. "You're not supposed to be sorry for using the weapons at your disposal."

Colonel Fireswift grabbed my arm, yanking me roughly toward the stairs that led into the castle. Harker was too busy holding off Isabelle's attacks to stop us. But Nyx and Arius Demonslayer were already ahead of us—

and, thanks to their vampire magic, they were moving much faster than we could. I shot a siren spell at them, but they evaded easily. They were too fast to hit.

I muttered a preemptive 'sorry' to Harker, then I clamped my siren magic down on him. He spun around, a psychic spell bursting from his hand. It slammed into Nyx and Arius, blasting them back down into the courtyard. I gave Isabelle another nudge of my magic, and she added her spells to Harker's barrage. Nyx and Arius were caught inside a storm of psychic energy. They wouldn't be going anywhere.

As Colonel Fireswift and I entered the castle hall, he compelled Harker to blast the steps with his magic, destroying them so no one could follow us inside.

"You fight dirty after all, Colonel," I laughed.

We started our ascent of the winding stairwell that would lead us to the top of Valora's tower. The gilded rails and trail of decorative crown motifs were like a giant flashing arrow pointing to her private chamber.

"Dirty?" Colonel Fireswift sneered. "That was a perfectly dignified maneuver."

I grinned. "The difference between dignified and dirty isn't as great as you think."

His brows drew together. "It's a wonder you've made it as far as you have in the Legion with that impudent attitude."

"Actually, that impudent attitude is the reason that I've made it this far."

The staircase we were running up seemed to go on forever. And without my vampire magic, I felt as weak as a Legion initiate.

"We must be almost there by now," I puffed out.

"Apparently, your impudent attitude isn't helping you now," he noted coolly.

"Why aren't you out of breath? You don't have any vampiric endurance right now either."

"When I was a child, my father bound weights to my ankles and wrists, and he commanded me to run up and down our estate's stairs. Over and over again. Only when I collapsed from exhaustion did he pull me off the ground. Then he added more weights and made me go again. I didn't have the benefit of magic back then either."

"That is so cruel."

"That is how angels are made," he countered proudly. "That is how the Legion endures. It is how my father made me stronger, and it is how I made my children stronger. If by some fluke of fate, you one day become an angel and have children of your own, you will do the same to them."

"I will most certainly *not*," I huffed in indignation.

"The world is cruel and merciless. It is best your children learn that from you than they get a nasty shock later, when it's already too late. When you can't protect them anymore."

Colonel Fireswift went quiet. He must have been thinking of his daughter Kendra again. Her years of hard training hadn't saved her life. Her magic, the gods' gifts, hadn't saved her. They'd only made her easy to kill.

I didn't mention Kendra's cruel fate. Colonel Fireswift was a supreme asshole on the best of days, but no one deserved to lose a child like that. Or to be reminded of the pain of that loss.

"I didn't see Wardbreaker and Windstriker down below," Colonel Fireswift commented, his face blank once more.

"They might have taken another way up."

We'd finally reached the top of the tower, Valora's chamber. Neither Nero nor Delta were here. But Jace and Leila were waiting for us.

Valora's team moved quickly. Jace hardly waited for me to enter the room before he threw a spell at me. The telekinetic blast slammed me hard into the wall. My back hit the stone wall.

"You don't play nice, Jace." As I pulled myself off the floor, my bones groaned in protest.

Jace was already swinging his sword at me. Flames flared up on the blade, hot and hungry. I jumped back. I'd forgotten how hot magic fire was—and how much it sucked to not have any resistance to it.

I grabbed a shield from the wall, throwing it up to block Jace's next sword swing. He tossed a potion at me instead. The flask smashed against my shield, the bubbling liquid dissolving the metal. My shield crumbled to pieces in my hands. I threw down the worthless scrap of rapidly-dissolving metal. What little was left of it shattered upon impact. Tiny pieces of metal rolled across the floor.

Jace didn't give me a chance to catch my breath. I jumped back from his flaming sword. I looked around for something I could use as a weapon, but there wasn't anything within reach.

My gaze flickered to Colonel Fireswift. The fight wasn't going well for him either. Leila had him trapped in an elemental web of magic, and she was slowly tightening the screws.

Jace swung his sword at me. I darted to the side, grabbing the long curtain hanging in the window. I wrapped it around Jace's flaming sword. He heaved, trying to free his blade. It didn't budge. Instead, the flames jumped to the curtain, setting the heavy fabric on fire. I snatched the curtain's tassel, thumping its fat knotted end against Jace's forehead. He froze for a moment—whether from surprise or the impact of the knot, I didn't know. And I couldn't afford to contemplate.

I grabbed the untouched edge of the burning curtain and wrapped Jace up in it. Sure, he was resistant to fire, but untangling himself would keep him busy for a while.

While he concentrated on freeing himself, I slammed my siren magic into him, crushing his will with my mind. Then I turned him on Leila. Colonel Fireswift had told me Leila's vampire magic was weak, so I sent Jace charging at her. His thick arms wrapped around her torso, pinning her arms to her sides.

"Jace, what are you—"

I trapped her mind inside my siren's song. She stopped struggling. Jace dropped his arms. They both just stood there, waiting for me to tell them what to do.

Colonel Fireswift closed in beside me. "They are resistant to siren magic. How did you do that?"

"Magic." I winked. Then I looked at Jace. "Tell me where Valora's crown is."

His lips drew back to speak. Growling, he pulled them closed again.

"Tell me where Valora's crown is," I repeated, with more siren magic this time.

"In the bowl." His mouth spoke the words, but his eyes burned with defiance.

I walked toward the bowl on Valora's coffee table. It was filled with red-yellow apples. There wasn't a crown in there.

"I see only apples," I told Jace.

He just stared at me.

"Valora shifted the crown's shape," Leila said. She was fighting my magic a lot less than Jace was.

"So one of these apples is the crown?" I asked.

Leila nodded.

I stared down into the apple bowl. All of them looked the same. Which one was the crown?

CHAPTER 10

THE KING'S CROWN

I considered the bowl of apples. Which of the dozen apples in there was Valora's crown? Which one had the goddess used her shifting magic to disguise? With Shifter's Shadow currently locked out of my magical toolbox, I couldn't see past the illusion.

Colonel Fireswift joined me beside the bowl. "That one." He pointed at one of the apples. "That is the crown."

"How can you tell?"

"It's too perfect." He plucked the apple from the bowl, turning it over in his hand. "This apple is a work of art, not a random, imperfect fluke of nature."

"Even without your shifting magic, you recognize the spell. You can penetrate the illusion without being able to see through it. How?"

"It's obvious."

And yet I hadn't seen it. He was critiquing my reasoning skills. Nice. I'd complimented him, and he'd replied with an insult.

"You really are an asshole of the highest order," I told him.

"That's my job," he replied, pride reverberating from every syllable.

I didn't know how much more of Colonel Fireswift I could take. The end of the gods' game couldn't come soon enough.

I snatched the apple out of his hands and gave it to Leila. "The demons are attacking. This crown is our only hope to defeat them," I said softly, wrapping my siren magic around her.

Leila pushed the apple away.

"That strategy will never work," Colonel Fireswift told me. "She is fighting your compulsion. She knows there are no demons. She knows this is a game and we are her enemies."

"We've been fighting. Her adrenaline is up. All we need to do is nudge her in the right direction," I countered. "What is more logical, I ask you: that the Legion is engaged in a civil war, or demons are attacking?"

He opened his mouth, then it clicked shut, like he didn't know how to respond to my twisted logic. Finally, he settled on, "You are unbelievable."

"And I suppose you want to break her with brute force?"

"Whereas you prefer to woe your enemy with flowers and chocolates."

"No, but it's easier to manipulate someone's mind with magic when you understand their psychology. Leila is a defender, a champion of the Legion. This drive is burned into her very being," I said. "And don't be so medieval, Colonel." I returned my attention to Leila. "The Earth is in danger. You can save it. But to do that, we need to turn this apple back into a crown."

When I handed the apple to Leila this time, she took it.

"I don't believe it." Colonel Fireswift's brow crinkled. "It's working. You're winning her over."

"You attract more bees with honey than with vinegar, Colonel," I replied brightly. "You might want to try that sometime."

He responded with a steely glower.

"No, not like that," I sighed. "Aim for cheerful, not murderous. Practice your smile in front of a mirror. It will help."

"Watch that tongue, Leda Pierce. Or I will cut it out while you sleep."

"What happened to not being medieval?"

Shaking my head, I turned back to Leila, who had just completed the spell to shift the apple back into its true form. And it was beautiful. Alternating rubies and sapphires topped the crown's gold spires, sparkling in the sunset rays streaming in from the balcony.

I was just about to hand the crown to Colonel Fireswift when every window in the room broke at once. Nero and Delta burst through the waterfall of shattering glass, landing in a crouch before us. A thick putrid cloud of magic shot out of Nero's hands. A curse. As it hit me, my body locked up. I hit the floor like a stiff plank.

That was the other, not-so-pretty side of Fairy's Touch, the power that could either heal or infect. Plagues and curses were created and cured at a fairy's whim. Nero's curse wasn't of the excruciating variety, but it had paralyzed me and my teammate from head to toe.

Delta reached down and snatched the crown from my frozen fingers. And I was completely powerless to stop her. She stole Aleris's glasses from me next, her smile haughty, her eyes triumphant. To top it all off, the way she was looking at Nero was downright indecent.

"You waited," I said to Nero, ignoring Delta and the bedroom eyes she was giving him. "You let us do the work for you. And now you have both gods' items. This was your plan all along."

"I had every confidence that you would succeed in obtaining Valora's crown," Nero replied. "You are very persuasive."

He'd known I'd figure out that I could use my siren magic to force others to fight for me—and to make Jace and Leila give me the crown.

"You lingered here too long, Pandora," Nero said. "You should have gotten out as soon as you had the crown. You could have shifted it later, when your magic returned. Curiosity got the better of you."

I glared up into his smug eyes. "Thanks for the lesson."

Being paralyzed really sucked. Not only could I not fight back, my throat was so tight I could barely talk—and only kind of roll my eyes at him. I couldn't use my magic either; it was frozen along with the rest of me.

"She shouldn't even be able to talk," Delta said. "You went too easy on her, Nero. Your spell wasn't at full potency. If we're going to win this, we need to hit the competition with everything we've got. The gods are watching us. And judging us."

Damn, she sure was taking this game seriously. Faris should have partnered Colonel Fireswift with her instead of me.

"She's down, unable to fight. That's all that matters," Nero told her. "Wasting your energy on being vicious serves no strategical purpose. It simply divides your attention."

Delta slammed a second paralyzing spell into me, far more potent than Nero's. Now I *really* couldn't move, and I couldn't talk either. I was completely frozen.

"Actually, it served a very important purpose," Delta said, sneering down at me. "It shut her up."

Anger popped inside my paralyzed body. I was going to get her back for this. Somewhere, somehow.

"Enough." Nero took the crown from Delta. "We need to get out of here."

He turned to leave—but then he just stopped. A strange reflection flickered across the milky lenses of the opera glasses. Nero had seen it too. That's what had stopped him. Carefully, he turned the glasses over in his hands, like he suspected sabotage. The glasses were now sparkling like a glitter shower.

"They're reacting to something." Nero glanced at the crown. "They are reacting to this. To the crown's magic."

"Both are immortal artifacts," Delta said.

Nero waved the glasses in front of the crown. Streams of light burst out of the crown, projecting an image over the room.

A man wearing Valora's crown threw open the balcony doors.

"That's Mercer, the old king of the gods' council," Delta said. "Valora's father."

Mercer stepped onto the balcony and looked down on the demon army pounding at his castle gates. Thousands of soldiers covered the land like a black blanket.

"This is the Battle of Illusion." Nero watched the god on the balcony. "The day the demons attacked Mercer's castle here on the world of Illusion, hoping to claim the King God's world as their own."

"The gods' armies pushed them back," said Delta. "But

a small team of demons had already infiltrated the castle in secret. Even as what remained of the demon army retreated, they were making their way through the castle. To the king."

The sound of clashing blades and gunfire sounded from the hallway beyond Mercer's chamber.

"The demons killed Mercer and then tried to flee," Delta said. "But they never made it out alive again."

Mercer turned, grabbing a sword as the doors to his chamber burst open. The godly soldiers in the hall were all dead.

Two demon warriors rushed inside, each one brandishing a glowing gun. Immortal weapons. Deity killers. Mercer lifted his sword, preparing to fight the demons.

But the warriors never made it to him. Arrows pierced their bodies. They fell on their faces, revealing Valora behind them. She held a glowing bow in her hands. Mercer looked down at the two demon warriors. Silver poison spread through their veins. Valora's arrows had been shot from an immortal weapon. Soon the demons would be dead.

"There might be more of them," Mercer said to his daughter. "We must be ready." He grabbed a shield from his weapons closet.

A shot went off.

Mercer fell, clutching his chest. Silver poison was quickly spreading through his veins. A bullet had pierced his chest—a bullet shot from one of the demons' guns.

"Why?" Mercer gasped, his surprised eyes flickering from the dead demons on the floor, to the gun in his daughter's hand.

"You have failed us, Father," Valora declared as he fell dead to the floor. She looked down on him, her face cold. "You have failed me," she rasped, her voice breaking.

Tossing the gun to the ground, she stepped onto the balcony. As she watched the demons' army retreat, a single teardrop fell from her eye. Killing her father had hurt Valora. She loved him.

And yet she'd killed him anyway. Why? What was the failure she'd spoken of, I wondered as the memory faded out.

Nero looked down at the crown in his hands. "We always thought demons had killed Mercer. But it was Valora all along. She killed her father. She killed the king."

CHAPTER 11

EXPOSED

The revelation hung heavy in the air. Valora had killed her father, the former king of the gods. Neither Nero nor Delta said a word. I supposed they didn't know what to say to that.

Nero and Delta departed the castle through a magic mirror, Aleris's glasses and Valora's crown securely in their possession. Still paralyzed beneath the weight of their magic curses, I was powerless to stop them.

The moment they left Valora's world, I could move again. The curse had lifted. Beside me, Colonel Fireswift was also rising to his feet.

"What did we just see?" I could speak again too.

"It is not our place to think about it," said Colonel Fireswift.

"Not think about it? That was murder."

"The Legion is the instrument of the gods' justice. We perform that justice on humans." He slanted a hard look my way. "Not on gods."

"But—"

"He's right, Leda," Leila told me. "This is a mess you

don't want to get tangled up in. You want to stay as far away from all this as you can." She glanced down at her unmoving body. "And you want to release us now."

Leila and Jace's minds were free, but their bodies were still locked down inside my siren spell. I tore apart the spell's remaining threads, releasing them. Strange that some part of my compulsion spell had held when I'd been paralyzed.

"You stole from me," Jace said to me as the four of us walked toward the magic mirror. "Twice."

I shrugged.

"And then General Windstriker stole from you." Jace looked tickled about that. He clearly liked the idea of me getting a taste of my own medicine—or being a victim of my own dirty fighting.

"Oh, don't you worry about that," I said. "I'll get the artifacts back from him just fine."

Colonel Fireswift glowered at me. "The Legion did not engage in such cheap trickery and thievery before you."

"What can I say? I'm a bad influence." I winked at him.

Leila laughed.

Colonel Fireswift shot her an incredulous look. "You are an angel, Colonel Starborn. Do try to act with some semblance of dignity."

Leila quickly put on a more subdued expression. Apparently, even other angels feared the head of the Interrogators.

We passed through the mirror and returned to the gods' audience chamber. It was like stepping into the middle of a thunderstorm.

"Your crown, your palace, your place on the council—everything you have you bought with blood. Your father's blood," Meda snapped angrily at Valora, her voice booming like thunder.

The gods really were watching our every move. They'd seen the memories the glasses' magic had exposed off the crown, like chemicals exposing an old filmstrip.

"Mercer ruled well," said Maya. "He had a formidable army. When you killed him, you left that army without a leader to rally them, to command them to great victories against the demons. And so the demons gained ground in those years following his death. Because of you, Valora."

Zarion rose, turning on the sister goddesses. "You benefitted from Mercer's rule, Maya. You and Meda were always his favorites, parroting whatever he said, voting with him no matter what."

Meda's eyes pierced like a spear. "Don't tell me you're still bitter that we and Mercer didn't back your extravagant pyramid project, Zarion."

An irritated crinkle formed between his eyes. "That pyramid was to be the base from which we launched our campaign to claim back the wilderness, to wash the plains of monsters from the Earth. It was a beacon of hope, a base of opportunity."

"It was garish," Meda countered. "Nothing more than a shrine to your own self-importance."

"I wouldn't expect *you* to understand. You spend too much time tinkering, inventing walls and generators and all these things we wouldn't even need if we concentrated on what's really important: the magic of the people's faith. And how that magic is great enough to crush armies and topple enemy strongholds. That faith should be fostered. That should be our focus, not the latest technical doodad your demented mind can think up."

"Funny how fostering that faith means you get a big

shrine where the people pray to you," Maya said, her laugh sardonic. "That boosts *your* power, Zarion. Not ours."

He folded his silken-sleeved arms over his chest. "A win for me is a win for you. For all of us."

"He wasn't saying that when you wanted a new hospital, Maya," Meda pointed out.

Her sister snorted.

The gods were bickering like a pack of politicians—or high school students.

"As amusing as this little spat is, it's beside the point," Faris told Zarion and the twin goddesses.

"Indeed," agreed Aleris. "Neither pyramids nor hospitals have anything to do with this new revelation."

Their words did little to quell the fires of fury. The gods hurled accusations back and forth. Some defended Valora, others condemned her.

"Like I said, you really want to stay out of this," Leila whispered to me.

"Apparently," I said, watching Meda set her dagger on fire and turn it on Valora.

As the Queen Goddess drew her crossbow, Nero came to stand beside me. "How are you?"

"Delta was right. You didn't hit me hard enough. I'm still walking. And plotting my next move." I smirked at him. "Which is bad for you."

"Unless I've already anticipated your next move. Again." His face remained perfectly calm and controlled. My words had obviously not ruffled him in the slightest.

"Not this time," I told him.

"We shall see." His eyes lit up. "Have dinner with me tonight."

"We are *all* having dinner together as soon as the other

teams get back. Assuming the gods don't destroy the hall," I added as a nearby table exploded.

"You misunderstand." His voice dipped lower. Each syllable was a caress and a command, silk and steel wrapped up in one. "I wish for you to have dinner with me *alone*."

"I'm not sure Colonel Fireswift would approve of me fraternizing with the enemy," I teased.

"To hell with Colonel Fireswift. You're not his. You're mine." Conviction rang in Nero's voice.

"He told me about you and Delta. That you were *the* hot couple."

"That was over a century ago. And we were not a couple."

"You just slept together."

"Does that bother you?"

"No, Nero, that doesn't bother me. Delta bothers me. She's nuts. And she is making it obvious to everyone with eyes that she's trying to get you back."

"Ignore her. She's just trying to rile you up."

"So you claim Delta doesn't want to sleep with you?"

"No, she does. But she can want until she's blue in the face, and it won't do her any good. I told you that you're mine. And I'm yours." He set his hands on my cheeks and kissed my lips softly. "Don't ever forget that."

I leaned into him. "When you kiss me like that, it's easy to forget a lot of things."

Chuckling softly, Nero kissed me once more, then he stepped back, putting a respectable distance between us. "Also, don't forget who Colonel Fireswift is and why he told you what he did. He's trying to get in your head. That's what he does. It's his job, and he's damn good at it."

"But Colonel Fireswift and I are supposed to be on the

same team. So why would he do that, besides the obvious high he gets out of messing with me?"

"Once he knocks you off center, you are vulnerable to attack. He wants something from you," Nero said darkly. "Maybe to kill you, use you, or just weaken you so that his son beats you. Or maybe he wants to crack your secret."

My heart stammered. "Which one?" I laughed.

"Be careful, Leda. Colonel Fireswift didn't get to be the head of the Interrogators by playing nice."

"He is watching us now," I whispered.

I glanced at Colonel Fireswift, who stood across the room, talking to Faris. The God of Heaven's Army was staying out of the conflict that had consumed most of the other gods. Colonel Fireswift bowed to Faris, then started walking our way.

Tonight at midnight, Nero spoke in my mind. *Meet me beside the siren statue in the red tulip garden.*

There was a flash of magic, then the remaining teams were back here in the gods' hall, back from Illusion. Nyx froze, listening to the gods' arguments. Fury flashed in her blue eyes. Nyx marched toward Valora, reaching for her sword.

Ronan's hand caught hers before she could draw her weapon. "This is neither the time nor the place to go to war."

Nyx's mouth tightened. Magic flared in her eyes. The First Angel looked completely, uncharacteristically out of control.

"Mercer is Nyx's father," Nero told me.

"That makes her Valora's half-sister."

"Yes, but Nyx and Valora have never gotten along," Nero said. "Valora has always hated Nyx. She sees her as a symbol of her father straying, of his affair with a mortal.

And Mercer really loved Nyx. He invited her to train with the gods. Valora hated that even more. She made Nyx's life difficult during those years."

Faris flicked his hand. His godly soldiers surrounded me and the other Legion soldiers, pushing us toward the exit. For a moment, Nyx looked like she was going to stay and fight, but she allowed the soldiers to lead her out of the hall as well. I only hoped she didn't sneak in later and try to kill Valora. We did not need to be here when all hell broke loose in heaven.

We ascended the staircase, a Legion team departing at each floor. Soon Colonel Fireswift and I were at the top. I glanced back at our escort—but she wasn't there. Faris stood in her place. I wasn't sure if I should be honored or worried that the God of Heaven's Army had personally accompanied us. Inside the apartment, platters of food already lay on the table. Wow, the gods sure worked fast.

I smiled at Faris. "You're missing the battle."

Colonel Fireswift looked at me like I'd completely lost my mind to try my jokes on a god.

"That is no battle," said Faris, cool and unconcerned. "It is no more than a squabble."

"Wars often begin with a squabble," I pointed out.

"Perhaps on Earth. In heaven, we are more civilized."

"Meda tried to bring down a chandelier on Valora's head. You call that civilized?"

"Do you always ask so many questions?" Faris said impatiently.

"Yes," I replied, grinning. "Asking so many questions is how I got to be so smart."

Colonel Fireswift's gaze flitted around the room, like he was looking for a sock to stuff in my mouth—or a heavy object to hit me over the head with.

Faris regarded me coolly. He obviously had no sense of humor.

"I will see to it she is punished for her impudence, my lord," Colonel Fireswift promised him.

Faris's gaze flickered briefly to me. "No, Colonel. I need her in one piece. I need you two to win this game."

"The gods are on the brink of civil war, and all you care about is winning this silly game?" I gasped.

Faris considered me like I was an insect who'd snuck inside uninvited. "We are not on the brink of civil war. We've gone through this song and dance countless times before. Secrets come out. Some gods are annoyed, others applaud. Alliances shift. Then the smoke clears, and we go back to business as usual. After this many millennia, you accumulate quite a few skeletons in your closet."

I blinked, his cold indifference spurring my surprise. "Just how many skeletons do you have stuffed in there?"

He bristled. "That is not a prudent question to pose a god."

"If all everyone ever did was ask prudent questions, we'd never get anywhere. We'd never grow. We'd never evolve."

"Are you quite sure you don't want me to punish her, my lord?" Colonel Fireswift said. "I would be happy to do it."

I didn't doubt it.

Faris seemed to consider it for a moment. "No, don't harm her. Your team must win," he reiterated. "When all this is said and done, I really do want to win my bet with Ronan. The consequences of failure would be unpalatable."

He said it like he was critiquing the food at some high-end restaurant—and not finding it up to snuff.

"Now eat and get rested for tomorrow's challenge," Faris commanded us.

Colonel Fireswift bowed to Faris as the god departed. When the Colonel and I were alone again, he turned his hard glare on me.

"It's against the rules to kill your teammate," I reminded him, popping a grape into my mouth.

Silver flickered across Colonel Fireswift's blue irises. "I don't find your flippant remarks amusing."

"Funny." I flashed him a grin. "Most people find them charming."

"Nor did Faris find them amusing," Colonel Fireswift continued as though I hadn't spoken at all.

"Well, Faris has the personality of a battle axe."

Colonel Fireswift glowered.

"Oh, don't get your panties in a twist, Colonel. Faris would take that statement as a compliment. As would you." I yawned. "Now, if you would excuse me. I need to get my beauty sleep."

He grabbed my arm as I turned toward the sofa. "We need to talk about the battle on Illusion today."

I flashed him an irritated look. "Why don't you just write up all the things I did wrong, along with any colorful, disparaging remarks about my corrupt moral character?" I peeled his hand off my arm. "I'll read it in the morning."

I really needed to get some rest if I was going to be awake for my dinner date with Nero tonight. The last two days had completely sucked. I was not going to miss a chance for a few pleasant moments before the next terrible day began.

"The battle uncovered more than Valora's secret," said

Colonel Fireswift. "It uncovered something about you too."

I bit my lip. Nero had warned me that Colonel Fireswift excelled at uncovering people's secrets. My sword was on the dresser. I could get to it in under a second. The question was whether I could get to it before Colonel Fireswift got to me.

"Your magic is more powerful than I thought," he said.

"Huh?"

"You were able to maintain a compulsion spell even when you were paralyzed. Your siren magic is powerful."

"But?" I supplied for him. I just knew that 'but' was on the tip of his tongue.

"There is no 'but' this time," he said. "The potency of your magic is unexpected."

"It was boosted, focused, by the potion that blocked my other powers."

Just as Ronan's potion had once boosted my psychic magic, allowing it to bubble to the surface.

"No potion can boost your power that much." Colonel Fireswift looked suspicious, even thoughtful. Like I was a puzzle to solve. Or dissect.

I buried that unsettling thought beneath a smile. "Colonel Fireswift, I'm flattered that you like my magic so much. I feel like we're finally getting along. My good influence must be wearing off on you."

"Do not mock me, Major Pierce."

"Wouldn't dream of it. And call me Leda."

His scowl deepened.

"And your name is?" Until now, I'd never even wondered what his first name was.

"Colonel Fireswift."

"Your first name is 'Colonel'?" I chuckled. "Your

parents were really thinking ahead, weren't they? But what if you get promoted? General Colonel Fireswift." I made a face. "That just sounds clunky."

"Stop being ridiculous. Of course my first name is not Colonel," he snapped.

"Then why did you say it is?" I asked, putting on my most innocent face.

His knuckles cracked.

"And on that happy note, I'm getting some sleep," I said brightly. "We're not going to win this thing if we're sleepwalking through it, are we?"

"Your dedication to duty is suspicious."

"Not at all. That's your angelic influence rubbing off on me."

Then I plopped down on the sofa, pulled my blanket over my body, and closed my eyes, hoping tomorrow was better than today.

CHAPTER 12

TEMPLE OF THE NIGHT

This time, I didn't dream I was being chased. I didn't dream of shadows and fear, nor of masked menaces and hidden threats. I dreamt of Nero. We fought over a cookie. It broke in half. Then we licked the melted chocolate chips off each other. It was a good dream.

And like all good things, it was over far too soon. Unfortunately, I didn't get to see what happened once the cookie was gone.

I awoke abruptly. The clock on the wall told me it was shortly before midnight. And Faris's disapproving face scowling down on me told me there was trouble in my near future.

"Your next challenge will soon begin," the god said, his arms crossed.

So much for my date with Nero. I jumped up, putting my battle leather on over my camisole and hot pants.

"I thought the next challenge wasn't starting until morning," I said groggily.

At least that's what we'd been told.

"War is unpredictable," replied Faris.

Kind of like the gods who were inventing these wars.

"Do we get to bring our weapons this time?" I asked.

"Each soldier may bring one weapon," he replied.

I grabbed my knife from the dresser. It wasn't the biggest, baddest weapon in town, but the slender silver blade was enchanted. It could cut through almost any spell. After my recent experience with that paralyzing curse, I intended to be prepared.

We followed Faris to the gods' audience chamber. The gods sat on their thrones in silence, their expressions perfectly masked. They must have finally gotten all the fire and fury out of their system. The other Legion teams were also here—all except for Nyx and Arius. Zarion's team was missing. That meant they were defending this time around.

"For your third challenge, you will need to steal from Zarion," Faris declared.

The Everlasting telepath stood beside him. "Zarion's secret vault in the Temple of the Night contains his most treasured possession."

I really, really hoped it wasn't a corpse. That seemed like the sort of thing Zarion might keep around. That or maybe a mirror so he could admire his own reflection.

"The rules of the third challenge are as follows," Faris said. "One weapon per person. Every soldier will have access to one power: the magic of vampires. But beware. That power comes with the vampire's hunger too. And with your other magic blocked, that hunger is greatly magnified. If you don't manage to control it, it could cost you far more than this challenge."

Of course our hunger would be magnified. The gods weren't interested in a dull show. In fact, after the revelation of Valora's secret—and the bickering that followed—I bet they were eager to shift the focus back to us.

After we all drank a potion that blocked everything but Vampire's Kiss, we walked through our designated mirrors to enter Zarion's domain. Colonel Fireswift and I popped up on a busy city street. Along the smooth paved road, flashing magic lights projected images onto tall skyscrapers, rotating between the gods' holy message and ads for makeup, clothing, and cars. Sprinkled between the retail shops, spas, and hair stylists were numerous temples and shrines.

The largest temple of them all was a sparkling pyramid that appeared to be entirely covered in diamonds. Stone gods and angels lined the very long walkway that led to the temple, fighting monsters, pushing away the darkness. They were the champions of light and right. They were the shields that protected the weak, the swords that banished all evil. That was the story Zarion's temple was selling.

"That's the place," I said. "That's where we'll find Zarion's artifact."

The building had to be Zarion's. It had to be the Temple of the Night. It totally fit his personality. Zarion might as well have painted his name all across the outside of the building. Oh, wait. He had. A gold plaque was stuck to a pillar in front of the building. Its text read 'Temple of the Night, Temple of Zarion, God of Faith, Lord of Pilgrims, and King of Vampires'.

"Follow behind me," Colonel Fireswift instructed me, leading the way to the temple.

He opened the door, and we stepped through it. Instead of entering Zarion's temple, however, we ended up right back where we'd started: outside the temple, staring at the now-closed door.

Frowning, Colonel Fireswift opened the door, and we tried again. The result was no different. We circled around the temple, trying every door we found. Nothing worked. We could not enter the temple.

I stopped a man who was passing by. "How do we enter Zarion's temple?" I asked him.

"Only the faithful, the true believers at heart, those loyal to the god Zarion, can enter the temple," he declared, then continued on his way.

"Well, that wasn't cryptic at all," I muttered.

"The message is as clear as the gods' bell tolling over an open prairie," Colonel Fireswift told me. "Only the faithful may enter. That excludes *you*." He pointed at the patch of sidewalk I was standing on. "Stay here."

This time, he approached the temple door alone and tried to enter without me. A moment later, he popped up behind me.

I glanced back at him. "Apparently, you aren't as true of heart as you thought, Colonel," I said, trying really hard not to laugh.

"This is impossible," he growled. "I am an angel. There is no truer believer in all the gods' worlds, no one more faithful to the gods, no one who better serves their will than an angel."

I arched my brows at him. "And yet the temple judged you and found you unworthy."

"It's still sensing your presence," he snapped at me. "Step back further."

"I could step back to the edge of the city. I could fall off the edge of the world. And it wouldn't make a bit of difference. The temple still wouldn't let you in. Because this isn't about faith. There's a trick to it."

Irked by my suggestion, he growled something about street urchins and dirty tricks. I was already turning away, so I didn't quite catch it. I scanned the city block. Nestled between the temples and retail shops were bars. Of course there were bars. Where there were people, there were always bars. Any world, any time. It was one of the constants in the universe.

Here at the epicenter of civilization, the alcohol was likely better than the moonshine lighter fluid they sold back in my Frontier hometown of Purgatory. Still, though the drinks and denizens changed, human nature did not.

I headed for the bar adjacent to the temple.

"What are you doing?" Colonel Fireswift demanded, heading me off.

"Going inside, of course."

He shot the bar a scornful look. "Now is not the time to visit a bar."

"That's where you're wrong," I told him. "Now is *exactly* the time to visit this bar."

He looked at me like I was a drunk degenerate for going into a bar while on duty. He just didn't get it.

I pointed to the sign hanging over the bar's entrance. It read 'Faithful'.

"This is the way into Zarion's temple," I said.

Colonel Fireswift gave me a dubious look, but he followed me inside anyway. Maybe he was starting to trust me. Or maybe he was just hoping I'd dig my own grave—and then all he'd have to do was push me in.

"Really, Colonel, in your line of work, you should know that bars are an excellent source of information," I said. "Copious amounts of alcohol lead to loose tongues."

"So do copious amounts of torture."

I stopped and pivoted around to look him in the eye. His face was dead serious.

"You are very disturbing," I told him.

His nod was as crisp as his response. "Good."

Shaking my head, I pushed through the swinging door to enter the bar.

"I will do the talking," Colonel Fireswift said, passing in front of me as we approached the counter. "You just stay out of the way."

Three men in tight leather pants and flashy dress shirts sat at the bar, singing drinking songs. The first man's shirt was a checker pattern of gold and black. The second's was as red as freshly-spilled blood. And the third man's white shirt was as shiny as Zarion's temple.

"Care for a triple shot?" the man in the white shirt asked the other two.

"Of course," replied Gold-and-Black.

"There's nothing like a good jolt to the body at seven in the morning. Wakes you right up," said Red Shirt.

The three men waved over three starry-eyed women in minidresses seated around a table at the edge of the room. The women sashayed over to the bar, swaying their hips as they wobbled drunkenly on their stilettos. Three identical grins curled the men's lips. In a flash of inhuman speed, they grabbed the women and bit down on their necks.

Vampires.

"We require passage into Zarion's temple," Colonel Fireswift told them in his sharp, commanding voice.

The vampires kept drinking, unmoved by his words or tone. He couldn't even compel them, at least not without his siren magic to back up his words. That must have been really frustrating. Forcing people to do things they didn't want to do was pretty much the gist of Colonel Fireswift's job.

"I am an angel, a divine soldier chosen by the gods, sworn to uphold their justice," Colonel Fireswift pressed on stubbornly. "Our mission requires entrance into Zarion's temple. You will tell me how to enter it."

The vampires continued to ignore him, not even looking up. The three women they were feeding from should have been drained dry by now, but they appeared unaffected by the blood loss. In fact, they didn't even seem to realize there were vampires attached to their necks.

Colonel Fireswift took another step toward the vampires, drawing his sword.

The vampires *did* react to that. They pulled away from the women, blood dripping from their fangs. Then they jumped off their barstools and charged forward. Colonel Fireswift pushed back all three vampires as the women ran screaming to the edge of the room. I watched.

Colonel Fireswift punched Sparkling White in the face, his eyes flickering to me just long enough to shoot a scathing look my way. "Why are you just standing there?" he demanded.

"I am staying out of the way." I fluttered my eyelashes. "Just as you commanded, Colonel."

A scowl etched into his face, he sidestepped Gold-and-Black, then caught the vampire's arm, pulling back hard on his shoulder. A sickening crunch followed, and Gold-and-Black fell. Red Shirt jumped on Colonel Fireswift's back, locking his arms around his throat.

"Windstriker and Sunstorm are too soft," Colonel Fireswift said, his voice strained, his breathing labored. "If you'd been under *my* command, I'd have long since had you shot for insubordination."

He was trying to throw off the red shirt vampire without success. As he struggled, Sparkling White swung a punch at his face. Colonel Fireswift stumbled back, the vampire attached to his back throwing off his balance. He narrowly missed a fist to the face.

He didn't seem to be in any real peril. This was a bar brawl, not a battle.

"Insubordination?" I repeated. "For following your orders? Forgive me, I'm just a boorish, uncultured street urchin, but isn't following orders the opposite of insubordination?"

"Don't be cute with me," he growled. "Just get this blasted vampire off of me."

"As you command," I said with a bow.

I grabbed the red shirt vampire attached to Colonel Fireswift's back and threw him over the counter. He smashed into the mirror behind the bar and fell down, along with a bunch of liquor bottles.

Colonel Fireswift was still busy with the other two vampires. I grabbed a dishtowel from the bar and set it on the counter. I emptied the contents of a liquor bottle all over the towel, drenching it thoroughly. Then I threw the sopping wet towel at Gold-and-Black. It landed over his head. As he tried to peel it off, I slid over the counter and grabbed a lighter out of a drawer. I flicked the flame at the towel, setting it on fire. The gold-and-black vampire ran off screaming and zigzagging as he tried to push off the towel and pat out the fire at the same time.

Colonel Fireswift spun around, knocking Sparkling White unconscious to the floor. Red Shirt, the vampire I'd tossed earlier, had crawled back over the counter, and he was sneaking up on Colonel Fireswift. I threw a liquor bottle at him. He caught it. I threw another. He caught that with his other hand.

"You need to learn some new tricks," he laughed. "You won't be setting me on fire, missy."

"That's not even my plan," I replied with a smile.

I launched bottle after bottle at him, faster than he could deflect them. One of the bottles smashed into his forehead, his hard skull shattering it. Alcohol poured all over him. Snarling, the vampire took a step toward me—and slipped on the pool of alcohol under his feet. He fell over, his back slapping the floor. As he struggled to sit up, I cuffed one of his hands to the bar.

"This won't hold me," he growled, spittle flinging off his fangs as he tried to free himself.

"Sure it will," I said calmly, even as he grabbed for me. "See those sparkly swirls in the steel bar you're handcuffed to? The metal has obviously been reinforced by magic. It could hold a vampire much bigger and tougher than you, pinky."

"*Pinky*?" he barked. "This shirt is *red*."

"Not anymore." I pointed out the pink streaks covering most of his shirt.

"Alcohol does not do that."

I grinned. "But bleach does. I might have dug into the cleaning supplies behind the counter."

Growling, the vampire jumped at me, forgetting the handcuffs. They pulled him back down. The more he pushed and struggled, the more his feet slipped on the wet floor.

Colonel Fireswift closed in beside me, his eyes panning from the screaming vampire running back and forth across the bar with a flaming towel over his head—to the thrashing, handcuffed, bleach-soaked vampire slipping continuously on the floor as he tried to free himself.

"How do you always manage to create such a circus?" Colonel Fireswift demanded.

"It's a talent. And you're welcome, by the way," I added.

He merely glared at me.

"You know, for rescuing you," I said. "You were in such distress."

"An angel is *never* in distress."

"Your voice was a tad squeaky."

"It's still not too late to shoot you, Pierce."

"You didn't bring a gun along," I pointed out, nodding at his sword.

"I'm patient. And this training will be long."

The look on his face promised he would shoot me in my sleep before this was all over. I shook off the shiver cutting down my spine. Well, I'd certainly not be sleeping well.

The sparkling white vampire Colonel Fireswift had knocked out was awake again. And he was tickled as pink as his companion's newly-bleached shirt.

"For partners, you two sure don't get along very well," he laughed.

"We are not partners. I am her superior." *In every way,* the look on Colonel Fireswift's face screamed loud and clear.

"Honey, I think you're on the wrong side," Sparkling White told me. "How about you join us?"

"Well, you boys seem like a lot of fun, but I'm afraid I have to pass." I shrugged. "I already swore my undying allegiance to the Legion."

"Too bad. Well, if you change your mind, you know where to find us." The vampire chuckled. "You know, I like you…what was your name?"

"Leda," I told him. "But my friends call me Pandora."

"Pandora, the Legion's infamous Mistress of Chaos?"

"That's me."

"Fantastic." He grinned like he wholeheartedly approved. "You're cool, Pandora. And so I'm going to help you out. Let's talk about how to get you into Zarion's temple."

CHAPTER 13

THE WARRIOR'S HAIRBRUSH

The vampire with the sparkling white shirt gestured toward the bar. "Please sit down."

The gold-and-black vampire had finally freed himself from the burning towel, and the red-shirted vampire was no longer handcuffed to the bar.

I took a seat on the barstools between them, but Colonel Fireswift remained standing. He probably thought sitting while on duty was a mortal sin.

Sparkling White looked at him, amusement dancing in his eyes. "That's ok. Sitting isn't necessary. Drinking is. You see, we're going to play a little game, and if you win, you'll gain entry into Zarion's temple."

Colonel Fireswift's cool gaze panned across the shot glasses lined up on the counter. "A drinking game," he said, turning up his nose.

The vampire flashed him teeth as white as his sparkling shirt. "Yes."

"That won't be a problem." Colonel Fireswift picked up one of the shot glasses.

I was surprised he even knew about such common

things. Way up high in his ivory angel tower, far away from us ruffians, he'd certainly not engage in anything as pedestrian as a drinking game. Then again, he *had* just engaged in a bar brawl with three vampires. So maybe there was more to Colonel Fireswift once you got past the evil overlord facade.

Sparkling White glanced down at the shot glass in Colonel Fireswift's hand and laughed. "Oh, it's not going to be that easy. We're drinking straight from the source."

Colonel Fireswift's gaze first shifted to the wall of alcohol bottles behind the counter—before finally settling on the three humans and the bite marks in their throats.

Straight from the source? Surely, the vampire didn't expect us to drink from these humans.

My thoughts must have shown on my face because the vampire laughed again. "No, not them. You'll be sampling something a bit more exotic."

A door on the back wall whispered open, and a man with long dark hair strode into the room and positioned himself behind the bar. The bartender. And yet his blue tunic, accented with gold threads, looked too fancy to be a bartender's uniform.

"The rules are simple," Sparkling White told me and Colonel Fireswift. "For every question that either of you asks of us, you must both drink from our friend here."

Something inside of me warned me to tread carefully. There was more to this sparkly-shirted vampire than met the eye.

"You're a priest of Zarion's Temple of the Night," I realized.

"I am," Sparkling White confirmed, smiling. "And now you must drink, for I have answered your question."

"That wasn't a question. It was a statement."

"A question inside a statement costume still remains a question," countered the vampire priest.

"I don't think—"

"You shouldn't think," Colonel Fireswift told me. "Your thinking only leads to trouble. As we've just seen."

I frowned at him. No, I'd been right about him the first time. He really was only an evil overlord, through and through. That was no facade.

Colonel Fireswift grabbed the bartender by the collar and bit him. The angel pulled away immediately, his blue eyes swirling with silver.

"What's wrong?" I asked him.

"His blood tastes like Nectar," Colonel Fireswift said, his voice teetering.

If I hadn't seen it with my own eyes, I wouldn't have believed it. Colonel Fireswift—leader of the Legion's Interrogators, champion of self-discipline at the expense of all fun—was sinking under the weight of his own bloodlust, sparked by the bartender's blood, which apparently tasted like Nectar.

Faris had warned us all that our bloodlust would be stronger than usual. That would make winning this challenge hard. Hell, it would make just getting through this drinking game hard.

Sparkling White looked at me expectantly. Ah, he was waiting for me to drink too.

I sighed. So much for treading carefully.

I allowed my fangs to descend, sinking them into the bartender's neck. I tried to keep it short, to swallow only a single mouthful. But the taste of his blood exploded on my tongue, igniting my hunger. His blood really *did* taste like Nectar. It was a taste unlike anyone else's blood.

Except for Nero. Nero's blood tasted like Nectar too. In

fact, Nero's blood tasted even better, even more like Nectar, than the bartender's blood. But why? Why did their blood taste so different than other people's blood?

That burning question churning in my head anchored my mind. It kept me from drowning in my own bloodlust. Having drunk Nero's blood helped even more. I had resisted Nero's sweet blood before; I could resist this man's blood too. I stepped back, releasing my grip on the bartender.

Beside me, Colonel Fireswift stared at him, mesmerized, tracking every pop of his pulsing neck.

"What are you?" Colonel Fireswift asked in awe.

I elbowed him. Now *he* was the one wasting questions.

Colonel Fireswift had just realized that too. An annoyed expression flashed across his face—and for once it wasn't directed at me. It was aimed solely at himself.

"That is Kanja, a priest of Zarion," said Sparkling White.

It was neither a complete nor a good answer, but I didn't argue the point. That might lead to more accusations of questions masquerading as other things, which would then lead to more drinks from Kanja. Right now, we had to concentrate on getting into Zarion's temple, not ponder curiosities like why only Kanja's and Nero's blood tasted like Nectar. So I filed this mystery away for the future.

The vampire was looking at us expectantly. It was time to pay up and drink. Colonel Fireswift looked like he really wanted to drink from Kanja again. And yet, at the same time, he looked like he really didn't want to do it, like another sip might just push him over the edge, sending him spiraling into full-out bloodlust.

So I went first this time. I kept it quick, resisting the urge to lick up the tasty drop of Kanja's blood that fell on my lips. Instead, I wiped it off with a napkin. Then I shot Colonel Fireswift a challenging look.

Bristling, he grabbed Kanja and drank. His muscles twitched, his veins pulsed, but he pulled back after a single sip—just as I'd known he would. He would never allow himself to lose a battle of willpower with a dirty street urchin. That drive to prove he was more civilized than a heathen like me was powerful enough to keep his bloodlust in check.

"What is the way into Zarion's temple?" I asked Sparkling White.

Disappointment crinkled his brow. I could tell he'd been hoping that my mind wouldn't remain sane enough to remember the purpose of this game.

"You aren't like the others," he told me.

I smiled. "That's what all my enemies say."

Laughing, he pulled on a series of beer taps at the bar. The mirrored wall at the back of the bar slid open to reveal a passage.

Now it was time to pay the price one final time. I drank from Kanja, then Colonel Fireswift did the same. His body was shaking so hard by now that I doubted he could hold a weapon. In fact, he appeared to be having trouble just standing there. I nudged him toward the secret door.

"It was fun, boys," I told the three vampires and the mysterious bartender with the Nectar blood. "We'll have to do it again the next time I'm in your corner of the cosmos."

Then I pulled Colonel Fireswift through the door after me. It closed right behind us. Beyond the wall, I could already hear the vampires singing drinking songs again.

Colonel Fireswift and I followed the hallway. His spasming muscles had already quieted down. He even managed to walk in a straight line now. He was fighting off the last lingering effects of Kanja's blood. Not falling on your face was a pretty essential skill in battle. Our chances of making it through this challenge had just skyrocketed from 'no way in hell' to 'maybe possible'.

The passageway was dark except for some glowing crystals on the walls, positioned like lamps. The magic light reflected off the glossy black marble floor, the surface as slick as a sheet of black ice. Ten bodies lay strewn all across the floor.

"Our competitors," I commented.

Colonel Fireswift's gaze slid over the soldiers. "Nyx and Arius took them down."

I bent down beside Nero, feeling his neck for a pulse. He was still alive. In theory, we weren't supposed to kill the other teams, but Nyx had looked oddly psychotic last night.

"What are you doing?" Colonel Fireswift demanded.

I pilfered several pieces of jewelry from unconscious Delta's body.

Colonel Fireswift's brows lifted. "Scavenging from the fallen?"

"Haha." I plucked a metallic piece off her necklace, combining it with pieces I snapped off her ring and her dagger. I handed the finished item to him. "Look familiar?"

He blinked in surprise. "These are Aleris's glasses."

"Bingo. Delta broke them into pieces and attached them to her jewelry to hide them."

It was a mundane solution to a magical problem, a trick most angels wouldn't have thought to consider. It turned out Delta was pretty clever and resourceful. Too bad she was such a bitch, or she and I might have been friends.

Colonel Fireswift tucked the glasses into his jacket. “And Valora’s crown?”

“It’s not on either Nero or Delta. Maybe one of the other teams stole it,” I suggested.

We quickly checked the other soldiers, but none of them had the crown either—not even in a disassembled form as Delta had stored the glasses.

“We will continue along this passage,” Colonel Fireswift decided. “Zarion’s treasure is this way. His team might now also hold the crown.”

We ran down the hall. It dead-ended at a vault door.

“Where are Nyx and Arius?” I asked, yawning.

They weren’t anywhere in sight, but it felt like they were lurking right over my shoulder. When I looked all around, however, I didn’t see them.

“I do not know.”

I yawned again. “Do you feel tired?” My legs felt like lead.

“It’s the blood,” he said. “It’s disrupted our equilibrium.”

“No, it’s something different.”

I glanced down at my feet. The marble floor looked… almost liquid. Like it was made of a thick flowing goo. I blinked. It *was* flowing. It slid over our feet, swallowing our legs. And then the floor just stopped moving. It was solid again—and our legs were encased in marble.

“A shifting spell.” Colonel Fireswift slid his hand over our marble bindings. “This is Nyx’s magic. No angel can wield Shifter’s Shadow quite like her.”

I thought back to the time Nyx had masqueraded as my friend Basanti. She’d fooled everyone. None of us had even suspected her. The goddess Valora's specialty was also shifting magic. The two of them shared magic and a father. They had a lot in common, and still they hated each other. Hatred was such a useless emotion.

Nyx and Arius emerged from the shadows, their eyes panning over all the opponents they'd defeated. Some of the unconscious soldiers stirred—and so did the marble sea. It snapped over their wrists and ankles, pinning them to the floor.

An ornate gold hairbrush sparkled in Nyx's hand. Either the First Angel had been hit with the sudden urge to brush her hair, or that hairbrush was Zarion's artifact. I was banking on the latter, even though it did look like a lady's brush. After all, Zarion did have all that long blond hair to brush through. And he liked bright and shiny objects.

As Nyx closed in on us, Colonel Fireswift pulled the glasses out of his jacket. Unless he wanted to toss them at her, I wasn't sure what he hoped to accomplish by that. He waved the glasses around. Magic glitter sprinkled off the lenses. It looked like crushed diamonds. The diamond glitter floated through the air, sticking to the hairbrush in Nyx's hand. Magic flashed. An image poured out of the hairbrush, projecting over the room.

A memory. The glasses had pulled a memory out of Zarion's hairbrush, just as they'd done to Valora's crown.

No, not just one memory. A series of fragmented memories and Zarion's thoughts poured out of the hairbrush, playing out so fast that without my vampiric senses, I couldn't have processed them at all.

I saw Zarion battling the angel Sirius Demonslayer.

The angel put up a good fight, but he was no match for a god. Zarion's magic blade tore through him. The traitor Demonslayer, who'd betrayed his calling to hide away his stolen lover, was dead. Zarion plunged his blade through the angel again, just to be sure he really was dead. Zarion took especial pleasure in ending the life of Eveline's new lover.

Then, with her final line of defense shattered, Zarion turned his sword on Eveline. Scarred from an early age, the leader of the Chicago werewolf pack was not beautiful, but she was a fierce warrior. And Zarion loved her as he'd never loved another. That love had spurred him into temporary insanity. Zarion glanced at Eveline's round belly. The baby inside of her —Zarion's child—wasn't just a problem. It was a catastrophe.

Mercer had only gotten away with fathering a demigod because he'd been king of the gods. If the other gods found out about Zarion's child, his alliances would fall apart. He had so many sensitive things in play right now. There was too much at stake. He needed those alliances. He needed the other gods' support. He could not allow all that he'd been working toward to crumble to pieces, not when he was so close to fulfilling his destiny.

Zarion attacked Eveline. She fought valiantly, as she always did, but it wasn't long before she too fell to the god's blade.

He knelt beside her dead body, his hand brushing lightly over her forehead. "I will not forget your sacrifice."

He held her in his arms for a few final moments, stroking her hair. Then he rose and took the golden hairbrush from the dresser. It had been Zarion's gift to her, a symbol of their love. Now he was taking it back, a memento to remind him of the woman he'd loved. She and their unborn child had died for the greater good. The world would be a better place because of their sacrifice.

As Zarion left the destroyed town behind him, the hairbrush firmly in his hand, another memory washed his body away. The color of the images pouring out of the hairbrush shifted, a blue overcast replacing the red. This time, the memory wasn't Zarion's. It was Nyx's.

Nyx stood on the Black Plains beside Leda Pierce, magically cloaked in the form of Basanti Somerset. Nero and Harker watched Stash closely. Stash was a shifter who'd defied all laws of magic and suddenly become an angel. To make matters worse, he currently commanded a supernatural army that was threatening to take over the world—and when they were done with that, they'd take on the gods.

"Stash is the child of a shifter mother," said the witch Constantine Wildman, currently under Stash's spell. "Her name was Eveline. She was a Chicago werewolf pack leader. Leader of the strongest shifter pack in the city."

"Twenty years ago, my mother fell in love with the god," Stash said. "But matings between gods and mortals are frowned upon. Gods guilty of such matings lose face with the other gods. When my father found out she was pregnant, he tried to kill her."

Stash wasn't just a shifter. He was a demigod. Just like Nyx. And here she'd thought she was the only one.

"My mother barely escaped with her life," Stash said. "She made a deal with a witch coven who had recently grown very powerful. It was said they could perform miracles. They cast a spell on her. The next time my father came for her, he stabbed her in the belly, and she died. He thought he'd killed me too, but I lived, protected inside a magic shell in her womb."

The memory flickered, jolting us into a dilapidated shack. I remembered the place. It was located on the Black Plains, where Nyx had brought us after she'd cast off her Basanti disguise.

"I will help you learn to control your power, Stash," Nyx told him.

The memory shot us further into the future. I saw Nyx

and Ronan train Stash. With each exercise, his magic grew stronger; with each battle, they molded him into a warrior of their own design.

The final frame of the final memory froze, then the projection puffed out, the remnants of the spell fluttering away on the wind like a flock of butterflies.

Sometime during the flood of memories, the marble floor had released us. Everyone was awake again. Nero and I stood side-by-side, exchanging loaded looks. This wasn't good. Not good at all.

Nyx's teammate Arius Demonslayer paced up and down the hall. "Dark angels killed my father," he muttered. "Everyone knows that. Its engraved on the plaque with his name on it that hangs in every Legion office."

His mind was clearly still trying to make sense of what he'd just seen. His father had been the lover of Zarion's mistress. And Sirius Demonslayer had died to protect her and her unborn child. Zarion had killed him.

Nyx grabbed Arius, and they disappeared through the magic mirror with Zarion's hairbrush.

Colonel Fireswift's eyes locked onto me and Nero. "Of course you two were in the middle of this mess."

"I'd hardly say we were 'in the middle of it'," I countered. "We just happened to be there. By chance. We had nothing to do with it."

"And yet you always happen to be there whenever something explodes. Chaos orbits around you, Leda Pierce."

"We only stumbled across the secret because Faris was manipulating the sirens, us, and anyone within shooting distance," I countered. "He tried to use us to expose Zarion's secret."

Colonel Fireswift shot me a look that told me I wasn't

helping my case. In his mind, all of this was entirely my fault.

"As far as the Legion's disaster statistics go, Fireswift, you still hold the record," Nero told him. "You ride on the heels of chaos."

Colonel Fireswift turned his glare on Nero. "I'm the head of the Interrogators. Its my job to chase down chaos and put an end to it. What's your excuse, Windstriker?"

Nero winked at me. "My excellent taste in women."

I grinned at him. I'd never loved him more than at this very moment.

Colonel Fireswift was clearly not amused. "Sentimentalism does not suit an angel."

"Then it's a good thing I'm an archangel."

The reminder that Nero outranked him silenced Colonel Fireswift. Scowling, he pivoted around and walked off toward the magic mirror exit.

"It would be totally inappropriate if I kissed you right now, wouldn't it?" I whispered to Nero as we made our way to the mirror too.

"Yes, it would," Nero said in a low voice. "But if you don't kiss me, I will kiss you."

The other soldiers were in front of us. No one was watching—well, except for the gods. But they were apparently always watching. If I worried about whether their eyes were on me, I'd never have any fun. I leaned in and kissed Nero on the lips.

"I'm dying to know, Nero," I said, lingering close to him.

His brows arched.

"Where did you hide Valora's crown?"

"I thought that was you feeling me up as I lay unconscious on the ground."

I smirked at him. "Oh, please. I only feel you up if you're at least half-conscious."

Nero's chuckle was as decadent as dark chocolate. "As soon as we got the crown, I shifted it into a sock."

"You are wearing Valora's prized artifact...on your foot?" I was nearly bursting at the seams with suppressed giggles.

"It's the last place anyone would look."

I snorted. One of those suppressed giggles exploded from my mouth. Indeed, no one would think to look for Valora's crown on Nero's foot. It was even more clever than Delta's hiding place.

"It's weird that Nyx didn't see through the spell," I commented.

"It was a thorough spell," he said. "But, yes, that was surprising. Honestly, it's hard to fool her with a shifting spell. I wasn't sure my plan would work. I can only guess it's because the First Angel has been distracted lately."

First, the gods had thrown her into the training with the rest of us. Then she'd learned that her half-sister had killed their father. With everything going on, it was no wonder Nyx was distracted.

"There's one thing that doesn't make sense," I said. "The hairbrush is Zarion's. His memories were imprinted on it. But how did Nyx's memories get in there too?"

"I recognize the brush," replied Nero. "Once, when Ronan and Zarion were at odds, Ronan stole it from him."

"Why?"

Nero shrugged. "He knew it was somehow very important to Zarion, and he wanted to annoy him. It worked, especially when Zarion learned that Ronan had gifted the brush to Nyx."

I laughed.

"Eventually, Nyx traded it back to Zarion in exchange for the Surefire Bow, another immortal artifact," Nero said, then we stepped through the magic mirror.

We were the last to return to the gods' hall. Zarion's challenge had jolted new life into the thunderstorm raging there. And this time it was Zarion and his secret caught in the crossfire. Ronan and Nyx weren't getting off easily either. The other gods were incensed that they'd hidden a demigod from them.

Nero drew me to the side of the room. "Let's get some air."

We ducked out of the gods' audience chamber. No one even noticed.

"This is a mess," I commented as we walked through the flower gardens outside. "I'm getting the feeling that this training isn't about angels, at least not entirely."

"It's about the gods," Nero agreed. "Someone is trying to expose their secrets."

"But why? And who?"

"Someone is coming." Nero's arms folded around me, and he pulled us into a hidden garden.

"Where are Aleris's glasses?" Faris's voice demanded beyond the high hedge. "I still need them."

"I have them," replied Colonel Fireswift. "I took them from Major Pierce." He spoke my name with utter disdain.

Faris picked up on that too. "I still need her too. Do not kill her, Colonel. Tempting as it may be."

The God of Heaven's Army sounded like he was speaking from personal experience. Well, Faris didn't hide how he felt about me, how he only saw me as a tool to be manipulated—and later discarded when he was done with me. I'd imagine he thought I was too much trouble to keep around any longer than absolutely necessary.

"As you wish, my lord," Colonel Fireswift said. "I will refrain from killing the street urchin."

"Hold on to the glasses, Colonel. When you reach Maya's item in the next challenge, you must be the one holding the glasses so you can reveal the memories stored there. Just as you exposed Zarion's secret."

I looked at Nero. So it seemed Faris had given Colonel Fireswift the task to use the glasses on Zarion's hairbrush, to finally expose his brother's secret. Back on the Black Plains, Faris had tried and failed to manipulate us into revealing Zarion's son to the gods.

Obviously, he hadn't given up. In fact, he'd only upped his game. First, Valora's secret, now Zarion's and next Maya's. Faris had manipulated this whole training. He'd orchestrated the challenges to reveal the other gods' secrets. That's why we'd stolen Aleris's glasses first. They had the power to expose memories from the gods' other objects.

Faris was on a mission to divide and conquer the gods' council, and I wasn't sure there was anything we could do to stop him.

CHAPTER 14

EVERLASTING

Faris and Colonel Fireswift left the lily garden, their voices fading as they walked away.

"Colonel Fireswift is such a hypocrite," I said to Nero. "He had the nerve to lecture me for being at the center of chaos, when all along he was helping Faris air the other gods' dirty laundry."

"If Faris is manipulating the other gods, turning them against one another, we must be careful," Nero replied. 'He is very powerful. And right now, he is busily stacking the cards in his favor, while the other gods still haven't even realized what the game is."

My fists clenched. I might have fought dirty, but Faris fought immorally.

"We have to do something," I said.

But what? Tell the other gods? That would lead to counterattacks. And then Faris would find out that Nero and I had exposed his plot. We'd be caught in the gods' crossfire.

"We don't know enough. We need to see where this is leading. Where Faris is taking this," Nero said. "This isn't just about exposing the gods' secrets. He has another move in mind, something to take advantage of the unrest in the gods' council. We need to watch Faris and Colonel Fireswift. They are your team. Keep them close. Figure out what they are planning."

He started walking back to the gods' hall. "I'll go first. You wait a few moments before you follow. We don't want anyone to think we're conspiring together."

Which we totally were. But, to be fair, so was everyone else.

I squeezed his hand. "Be careful."

"You too."

His fingers slipped through mine. I counted out a minute in my head after he'd entered the building, then I started down the path myself. I wasn't even halfway there when Colonel Fireswift found me.

"Where have you been?" he demanded.

Definitely not conspiring with the God of Heaven's Army to expose the other gods' secret. Unlike you.

"I was just getting some fresh air," I said.

He looked around, like the trees would start talking and declare me a liar. When they did not oblige, he turned his hard glare on me, probably hoping to compel me into submission.

"Oh, look. I'm not the only one getting some fresh air." I watched Nyx walk down a path parallel to ours.

Colonel Fireswift made a beeline for the First Angel, as though he'd been seeking her all along. Did this have to do with Faris's plan? What more had he told Colonel Fireswift after they'd walked out of earshot?

"First Angel, I require a moment of your time," he said, bowing before her.

"This is not a good idea, Colonel. They are watching." Nyx looked around. The 'they' obviously meant the gods.

Colonel Fireswift was undeterred. "It's about her." He shot me a stern look.

Oh goody. This was going to be fun.

"You are not allowed to kill your teammate," Nyx said.

"Everyone keeps telling him that," I laughed.

Neither angel laughed with me. Instead they looked at me like I was nuts.

"I want her magic tested," Colonel Fireswift continued. "The test results will indicate that she belongs in my division."

Now that was a shock. He'd commented on my siren magic before, surprised that it was strong. I never expected he'd try to recruit me into the Interrogators.

"You can't stand me," I gasped, still in shock. "And yet you want me in your division?"

"Personal like or dislike has nothing to do with doing our job," he said coolly. "You are a tool, Leda Pierce. And your siren magic is a tool—a tool I could make use of." He bowed again to Nyx. "Give me a few months with her, First Angel, and I will turn her into a proper Interrogator."

"And what if I don't want to be an Interrogator?" I demanded.

"Your wishes are irrelevant." He gave his hand a dismissive wave. "You left your freewill at the door the day you joined the Legion of Angels." He looked at Nyx again.

"Her magic will be tested," Nyx agreed. "But only *after* this train wreck masquerading as a training is behind us."

Victory gleamed in Colonel Fireswift's eyes, as though he'd already won this battle I didn't even know I was fighting. For someone who hated me so much, he sure was eager to recruit me. Maybe he just liked the idea of torturing me, training me, stripping me of my freewill in an attempt to completely and totally break me.

Yes, I decided, he *would* enjoy breaking me, stripping me of my humanity so he could shape me into a weapon of his own design. That was his job, and he loved it. And now he wanted to turn me into that kind of person too. No. I wouldn't let him.

"But I can't guarantee she will end up in your division after the magic tests," Nyx said to Colonel Fireswift. "General Spellsmiter has also asked for her."

Wait, what? I hadn't said two words to General Spellsmiter since the training had started. So why would he want to recruit me?

"She's clearly siren magic dominant," Colonel Fireswift argued. "That makes her mine."

Siren-magic-dominant soldiers often went to the Interrogators; the more siren magic you had, the easier it was to compel someone to give up all the secrets they had no intention of giving up. But siren magic or not, I was *not* his. Not by a long shot.

"Based on her performance in the last challenge, General Spellsmiter claims she is vampire magic dominant," said Nyx.

Was I? Sure, I'd handled the bloodlust all right, even sipping from the man with the Nectar blood. But that was because I was stubborn. I'd never demonstrated powerful vampire qualities, at least not any more than others had.

Except… Well, I had drunk from Nero about two seconds after the gods' first gift of Vampire's Kiss. If anything, that meant I had the vampires' desires, their lust for blood. Ravenous hunger—wow, what an awesome power to have.

Colonel Fireswift scoffed at the suggestion that I

belonged in General Spellsmiter's division. "She does not have the constitution for an Elite Warrior."

As leader of the Vanguard, General Spellsmiter commanded the strongest, fastest, most resilient fighters in the Legion. Even by Legion standards, the Elite Warriors were legends.

"He's right," I told Nyx. "I'm not an Elite Warrior. But I'm not an Interrogator either."

"That is not for you to decide," Nyx said sharply. "Nor for General Spellsmiter or you, Colonel Fireswift. We'll run the magic tests after the training is over. Then *I* will decide where she goes."

Nyx words were short and tight, like her patience was stretched thin. More than that, she sounded worried. And I had a good idea why. Faris was determined to blow open the gods' secrets, and he'd already shown he was more than able to do so. Maybe Nyx didn't know Faris was behind all of this, but she had to realize that someone was manipulating the challenges.

Her and Ronan's involvement with Stash had already incurred the gods' fury. Hiding and training him wasn't their only secret. I knew of a few others, and I was sure there were many more I didn't know about. As Faris had told me, after so many millennia, you accumulated quite a few skeletons in your closet.

Colonel Fireswift and I followed Nyx back to the gods' audience chamber.

"Your lover and his old lover are missing," Colonel Fireswift whispered to me as Nyx left us.

He said it like he wanted me to draw all sorts of conclusions. The wrong sort.

"Do you mind checking all the closets for me?" I said drily.

His brows drew together. "If you are to be an Interrogator, you need to be less trusting."

"Then it's a good thing I'm not going to be an Interrogator."

"We shall see."

I did my best to push away my worries. I ignored the image in my head of me as an Elite Warrior in the Vanguard, standing at the forefront of every bloody battle. I tried to forget the vision of me as an Interrogator, feared and hated, forced to hunt down and torture the people I loved.

And the magic tests. Those scared me even more. Would they reveal what I really was? At the very least, they would show I was not really a level seven soldier as I pretended to be—that the Nectar had neither killed me nor leveled me up. That discovery would lead to questions. And a jail cell. Or possibly the execution block.

Nyx was right. This was not the time to think about magic tests. I had to focus on the current crisis. That was life at the Legion in a nutshell: rushing to put out one fire after the other, never having a moment to breathe and prepare for the big fire you could see coming from a mile away.

Nero and Delta had just entered the room. They were talking, but my attempt to read their lips was thwarted by someone hissing at me.

I spun around to face Colonel Fireswift. "What did you say?"

"I said nothing." His eyes narrowed with suspicion.

So it was just the voices in my head speaking to me. Great. I really didn't need everyone to think I was going mad.

"Never mind," I told him. "There are so many people

in this room. I must have overheard someone else's conversation."

Or I really *was* crazy. No matter what I'd told Colonel Fireswift, no, I hadn't overheard someone else. The hissed voice had come from his direction.

Someone screamed.

I zeroed in on Colonel Fireswift's jacket. The scream had come from his pocket. I was sure of it.

Short, panted gasps followed. So Colonel Fireswift's pocket was panicking now? This was getting weirder and weirder.

Heavy footsteps thumped against a hard ground. Cobbled. It sounded like a cobbled road. I blinked, and for one terrifying moment, I saw shadow soldiers all around me, closing in.

This was the nightmare I'd had two nights ago. Except I wasn't sleeping anymore.

That's when it hit me. This wasn't a nightmare. It was a memory, just like the ones stored inside Valora's crown and Zarion's hairbrush. And it was the glasses that had exposed those memories, the glasses that were currently tucked inside Faris's pocket.

But what were the voices I was hearing now? Were the crown and hairbrush close enough for the glasses to be siphoning more memories from them? After all, Nero had the crown with him, and he'd just entered the hall.

But I'd had this nightmare *before* anyone had stolen any of the other artifacts.

"You look troubled."

I turned around. Colonel Fireswift had gone off while I'd been contemplating my own sanity. It was the Everlasting telepath who now stood beside me.

"I'm fine," I told him, smiling.

"No, you're not."

"What's your name?" I asked him.

"Athan."

"Well, Athan, I'm exhausted but otherwise fine."

"It's about the glasses." He glanced at Colonel Fireswift across the room, the one who held the glasses.

"How did you know?" I asked.

"I can read thoughts."

I frowned. I'd thought I had been masking my thoughts well.

"You have," Athan told me. "Your defenses are formidable. They are enough to keep the gods and angels from reading your thoughts, for as long as you remain focused. But my telepathic magic is not as diluted as theirs."

So he could read everything inside my head? Like literally everything? Shit. I started humming inside my head, hoping to bury my secrets.

"I have no interest in your secrets, Leda Pierce," the telepath chuckled. "And I won't expose them." He glanced at the gods sitting on their thrones. "I don't answer to *them*."

"And yet here you are in the gods' hall."

"I am merely paying back a debt. To that end, I was tasked to use my magic to find each god's most prized possession. No more and no less."

"Which god do you owe a favor? Is it Faris?" I asked him.

He merely smiled. Yeah, of course he wasn't going to tell me anything.

"Aleris's glasses reveal memories imprinted on objects," I said.

"The glasses reveal the memories imprinted on other

immortal artifacts. Normal objects, even normal magic objects, do not possess enough magic to hold memories."

"So the glasses are an immortal artifact," I concluded. "And they react with other immortal artifacts."

"Among other things."

"Things? What things?" I asked. "You said only immortal artifacts have enough magic."

"I said regular items do not have enough magic to store the memories," he replied. "But there are things that aren't really things, which *do* possess enough magic to store memories."

"Things that aren't really things?" I repeated, shaking my head. "You're not making any sense."

"It will all become clear very soon."

"Soon? Like during this next challenge?" I asked. Faris had told Colonel Fireswift to use the glasses on Maya's item next. "What will happen? What are we stealing?" I resisted the urge to grab him by the collar and shake the answers out of him.

Athan spread his empty hands. "I cannot say."

"Faris already knows what all the gods' possessions are, doesn't he?"

Athan smiled. "I must be going now."

The gods' bell rang through the hall.

Valora rose from her throne. "Faris, send your godly soldiers to apprehend Zarion's son," her crystal-clear voice commanded. "A demigod is too powerful to be left unchecked on Earth, to be trained outside the gods' supervision. *All* the gods' supervision," she added, slanting a severe look Ronan's way.

Faris waved at a group of his godly soldiers. "They will find the demigod," he assured Valora.

His soldiers marched out of the hall, their shining armor sparkling as brightly as the sun.

"When they return with the demigod, we shall see what he has to say for himself," Valora said. "And we will learn how deep this betrayal goes."

"Surely not as deep as killing the king of the gods," Maya whispered to her sister Meda.

Meda coughed. Valora's nostrils flared in agitation. She glared at Nyx like this was all her fault, like her half-sister was the root of everything that had ever gone wrong in her life.

Ronan took Nyx's hand in an obvious sign of solidarity. Lines were already being drawn in the sand. This was just what Faris wanted. This was his plan. But how was he going to capitalize on the fracturing alliances?

"Now, soldiers of the Legion," Faris declared. "It is time for your next challenge."

CHAPTER 15

THE INFINITY ROOM

The time between the gods' challenges was shrinking. And I had a hunch that this too was all part of Faris's plan.

"For your next challenge, you will all compete to obtain something Maya treasures," the God of Heaven's Army announced.

I noticed that Nero and Delta had once more disappeared. They were Maya's team, so they'd be on defense for this challenge.

"The name of the game is curses and counter curses," Faris continued. "You will have access to only that field of magic."

Curses and counter curses—that meant Fairy's Touch, the ability I had failed to acquire at my last leveling-up ceremony. The optimist in me said getting through this challenge without exposing myself would be problematic. The pessimist in me was bracing for an all-out catastrophe.

After a sip of the gods' magic-destroying potion, Colonel Fireswift and I stepped through the magic mirror.

We popped out inside what appeared to be a palace parlor room, which I assumed was located on Maya's world.

The room was massive, so long that I couldn't even see the other end. And nearly everything inside it was red. The sofas were red. The wallpaper was red, accented with gold and tiny gems. I brushed my hand across the satin surface. Were those real diamonds inside the wallpaper?

The carpet was red. The paintings on the wall featured the color red like it was holy: a wine glass filled with red wine, a warrior in a red cape caught in the breeze; his sword was raised high in the air, blood dripping from the blade.

There were even tiny red dishes with even tinier red candies inside. I drew in a deep breath. The sharp bite of cinnamon hung in the air, mixed with the soft creamy aroma of roses.

"This way," Colonel Fireswift said and began walking down the very long room. Or hall. Whatever this place was supposed to be.

He moved like he knew precisely where he was going. Faris had probably given him a map straight to Maya's vault. There was no small amount of irony in the fact that the high and holy head of the Interrogators, hunter of sinners and traitors, was not above cheating to win this challenge. He probably justified it to himself with the assertion that he was following a god's orders.

As I walked beside him, I tried to puzzle out what Faris was up to—and how much Colonel Fireswift knew about it all.

"I wonder how far this room goes," I said. We'd already walked for over a minute, and I still didn't see the end of it.

"It goes as far as there are enemies to fight," replied Colonel Fireswift.

"That sounds like a curse," I joked.

His face was devoid of amusement—or any other emotion for that matter. Actually, he looked rather constipated.

"Prepare yourself for battle," he replied stiffly.

Prepare myself for my non-existent resistance to curses? And prepare my own equally non-existent curses? Done and done.

But I didn't say a thing. Chatting with Colonel Fireswift never ended well. It turned out that walking in silence wasn't any better, however. Colonel Fireswift watched me like he was dissecting me with his eyes.

Just when I was about to break the silence, certain that talking to him could not possibly be worse than the creepy look he was giving me, he spoke, "Tell me where you come from."

"I'm a mutt, straight off the streets of Purgatory," I said with a smile. "I'm sure you haven't forgotten, Colonel. You never let me forget it."

"Who were your parents?"

"I never knew them," I said cautiously. This conversation was going places, none of them good.

"And your magic before you joined the Legion?"

He looked analytical, not sympathetic. He wasn't making small talk; he was acting like this was an interrogation. Hell, it probably was. Ok, I'd changed my mind. The silence had been so much better than this.

"What magic did you possess before joining the Legion?" he prompted me again.

"I didn't have any."

"General Spellsmiter believes you are vampire dominant. I know you are siren dominant. It is unusual for someone to possess two dominant magic powers. That is a trait seen only in the offspring of angels."

"I am not the offspring of an angel."

"Obviously." His nose pinched up, like he could still smell the dirty street scent on me from my years of living there. As far as he was concerned, the stench was permanently imprinted there. "But you are...*something*."

"Something," I repeated with a nonchalant shrug. "That's a step up from nothing."

"Why must you constantly make jokes?"

"It lightens the mood. Makes things more fun."

"Fun." He said it like he'd never experienced the feeling before—and wouldn't care to. Like it was an infectious disease that would strip him of his magic and holiness.

After that, Colonel Fireswift didn't say anything more. Neither did I. My mind was still looping his words, his promise that he would break me and turn me into an Interrogator.

Trying to break free of that mental loop, I turned my attention to the decor. That was when I saw that the room looked different in this section. It wasn't red; it was orange. I looked behind me, trying to figure out when the color had changed. I couldn't tell. The room seemed to go on forever in front of us. And to extend forever behind us. I couldn't even see where we'd entered.

I looked up. Everything was limitless in this infinity room, even the ceiling.

Glowing beams of light shot out from the side walls, blinding me. I blinked rapidly, trying to clear my vision. A moment ago, we'd been all alone, but now Jace and Leila were standing right in front of us.

"One soldier from each team shall fight," a voice

boomed from every direction. It sounded like a god, but I couldn't tell which one.

One of the glowing light beams slid over me, encasing my body. I reached out to touch the beam—and received a nasty jolt. Leila stood trapped inside another magic ray of light. And thus began the first round of this challenge, sparing me any more quality alone time with Colonel Fireswift.

He and Jace were already hurling curses at each other as fast as they could weave them. Finally, Jace was hit, unable to avoid his father's brutal barrage of spells any longer. As Jace fell to the floor, Colonel Fireswift slammed another five curses into him for good measure. Gods, he was ruthless, even to his son. No, *especially* to his son.

That is how the Legion endures, Colonel Fireswift had told me a few days ago. *It is how my father made me stronger, and it is how I made my children stronger.*

There had to be another way.

Jace and Leila disappeared before my eyes. The beam that had trapped me during the battle dropped. I could move again.

"That was over fast," I commented as we continued walking.

"Yes," Colonel Fireswift said, his voice at the same time arrogant and irked.

Apparently, Jace hadn't performed up to his father's angelic standards. I didn't dare hope Colonel Fireswift wouldn't take it out on him the next time they trained; I knew that he would. As Colonel Fireswift had proudly declared, this was how he made his children stronger.

The infinity room's color palette had shifted once again. Everything in this section was pink. The decor consisted of pristine antiques. Between the pink-striped walls and vases of spring flowers, it looked like the sort of place where you'd sit down for tea and cake. It was certainly unlike any fighting arena I'd ever seen.

Magic light flashed, and Nyx and Arius were suddenly in front of us. Two glowing beams swallowed the two angels. Great. That meant I had to pit my fairy magic against Arius's. This battle would be even shorter than the last one.

"Nyx and Arius have both already fought a battle in this challenge," Colonel Fireswift said to me. "You can see it in their eyes. They are fatigued. Do not hesitate. Arius won't."

Yeah, good advice, minus the fact that I couldn't wield any fairy spells. I needed a plan, and I needed one fast. Flying by the seat of your pants was all well and good—until your pants caught on fire.

Arius unleashed a reeking miasma of sparkling black particles. I didn't recognize the curse, but I was pretty sure it wasn't a cure for acne. I jumped out of the black cloud's path. It slammed against the wall behind me, the wallpaper wilting out from the impact point.

"Why are you running away, little girl?" Arius taunted. "Stand and fight!"

Little girl? Ha! I wasn't the one who looked sixteen.

As Arius unleashed his next curse, a putrid green fog, I wondered how I was going to get myself out of this mess this time. How could I win this battle of fairy magic without using any fairy magic?

Arius was coughing out curses faster than I could sneeze. My eyes flickered from the magic beams of light encasing Nyx and Colonel Fireswift, to the projectors on the walls.

Arius continued shooting curses at me nonstop. Surely,

he had to run out of stamina eventually. I was sure tired of dodging his spells.

I ran to the side, kicked off a pastel-pink sofa, and yanked one of the projectors off the wall. As Arius angled another curse my way, I turned the beam on him. He flitted away too quickly. The magic beam missed him, but his curse grazed my side. It felt like someone had kicked me in the ribs. I didn't want to imagine how much it would have hurt if the curse had hit me full on.

I turned the projector with Arius, tracking him as he ran a tight circle around me. His eyes widened, his sense overruling his arrogance, and he evaded. As he jumped out of the way, the magic beam skid across his chest. The hit wasn't direct enough to trap him, but it did throw him to the floor. Before he could jump up, I thumped the heavy projector over his head, knocking him out. I reached down and swiped Valora's hairbrush off of Arius as he and Nyx faded away.

The magic beam released Colonel Fireswift, and we advanced deeper into the infinity room.

"There is no dignity in the way you fight," Colonel Fireswift said gruffly.

"Dignity doesn't win battles."

"Warn me before the next time you extort such blasphemy, so I can step a safe distance away from you in case the gods decide to smite you."

I wiped the sweat off my forehead with the back of my hand. "The more time we spend together, the more I come to appreciate your sense of humor." I smirked at him. "We'll be braiding each other's hair before you know it."

"I am an angel."

I snorted. "Yeah, I'd noticed."

"You do not treat me with the necessary reverence of

an angel in my position."

"How should I treat you?"

"You should fear me."

"There's no strategic advantage to being afraid of you."

"No strategic advantage." He repeated my words like he couldn't believe I'd uttered them.

"In other words, it doesn't help me to be afraid of you."

"I know what it means," he snapped.

"Of course you do. You're smart. Like me." I smiled as hard as I could. Sure, it hurt my face, but it was worth it to see the puzzled expression on his face.

"This is Windstriker's influence. He coached you on how to mess with me."

He looked more sure now, more settled, now that he had an explanation for my sensible words. An angel had told me what to say; that was way better than admitting I could rub more than two brain cells together. I could never throw him for a whirl. Of course not. No, I was just a dirty street dog who'd learned a trick, taught to me by an angel. An angel was a worthy adversary, unlike me.

"Yeah, sure thing," I laughed. "Nero told me how to mess with you. Believe that if it makes you feel better."

His mouth was a hard line, his eyes an Arctic wasteland of cold fury. "I don't like you."

"So you've already told me a thousand times. I know. I've got it. I'm smart, remember?"

"I will enjoy breaking you."

"And I will enjoy continuing to flabbergast you. If you think you can break me, then ask yourself one question: which of us is more stubborn?"

His brows drew together in annoyance.

"Don't frown, Colonel, or eventually your face will freeze like that," I told him.

He didn't have a chance to retort. We'd finally reached the end of the infinity room: the bronze door to Maya's vault. Colonel Fireswift grabbed the lever and started turning.

Nero and Delta attacked us from behind. Where the hell had they come from? Each of them held one of the magic projectors. They turned them on me. Oh, shit.

I tried to run, but they caught me in their magic crossfire. Twin beams swallowed me up, locking me in. Nero countered my glare with a sly smile.

Yes, Mr. Smartypants. You used my own trick against me. Again.

I contemplated pounding my fists against my magic prison in fury—but decided against it. If the gods launched us straight into the next challenge, it might help to actually be conscious.

Nero and Delta had caught Colonel Fireswift inside a light beam. Another second, and he'd have had the treasure. The vault door was already halfway open.

Delta saw that too. She stepped toward the vault, something within catching her eyes. Pulling back the door the rest of the way, she hurried inside.

I gasped when I saw the contents of Maya's vault. There were no precious metals or gems, no paintings or artifacts. There was no treasure at all. There was only one thing inside the vault—and indeed, just as Athan had said, it was not a thing at all. It was a dead body.

"That is General Wardbreaker," Colonel Fireswift said, his eyes widening in surprise.

General Wardbreaker, Delta's father, was the archangel who'd died last year. Damiel had killed him. But how had Maya ended up with him? And why did the goddess have a dead angel's body stashed away in her vault?

CHAPTER 16

THE GODDESS'S LOVER

How had Maya ended up with the body of the archangel General Wardbreaker? The same question obviously burned inside of Delta. And she wasn't waiting for answers.

She lifted the magic projector over her head, then smashed it against the ground. The spell binding Colonel Fireswift dissolved. Before he could move, Delta grabbed Aleris's glasses from his hands. She shot her magic through the lenses, directing the sparkling stream at General Wardbreaker. A montage of images rose from her father's body and projected over the infinity room.

"I should go." Osiris Wardbreaker turned over in bed, his disheveled dark hair falling over his lover's face as he kissed her cheek. "Nyx has summoned me to Los Angeles."

"The First Angel can wait. I cannot."

The woman turned to face him. It was Maya. She wasn't wearing a thread of clothing, nothing but a diamond-studded flower necklace around her neck.

"Or do you dare defy the gods?" demanded the Goddess of Fairies.

He watched her hand glide slowly up her side, wetting his lips. "I know only one goddess."

When Maya giggled, she didn't sound like an immortal, all-powerful god; she sounded like a young woman in love. In love? Was it possible the goddess was in love with an angel?

Osiris took Maya's hand, kissing her fingers as they stared into each others' eyes. Yes, she was in love. And she wasn't the only one. Osiris didn't just love her; he worshipped her beyond mere piety or duty. He'd said he knew only one goddess. Every glance, every move that he made, betrayed his immortal love.

Osiris began to rise from the bed, but she caught his hand.

"I have already lingered too long, my love," he said, his thumb massaging deep circles into her palm. "If the other gods found out I was here with you in heaven—"

"They won't." But Maya promptly released his hand.

"They would turn on you." Osiris leaned down and stroked her cheek. "I am not strong enough."

"I won't allow any harm to come to you," Maya promised him.

"I am not strong enough," he repeated. "But I will be. Soon."

The scene flickered out, the ethereal light of heaven dissolving under the weight of blood and grit.

Osiris lay on the floor in a partially destroyed city apartment building, debris strewn all around him. He flipped over, his mad, wild eyes looking up at the massive hole in the ceiling as he rose to his feet. Blood dripped from his body, splattering the ground.

Damiel Dragonsire, Nero's father, shot through the ceiling, his wings tightly angled as he dove at Osiris. The two archangels collided in an explosion of magic, muscle, and feathers.

"Why have you risen from the dead, Dragonsire?" Osiris growled, insanity saturating his voice.

He hadn't sounded like this when he'd spoken to Maya. Oddly enough, the goddess seemed to bring out the humanity in him.

"I was never dead," Damiel said.

Osiris sneered. "You will be when the Legion finds out you survived."

"You won't be telling them. You abandoned the Legion of Angels, Osiris. Or don't you remember?"

Osiris blinked in confusion.

Fire erupted on Damiel's blade. "You massacred over a hundred children."

Osiris's roar shattered the remaining threads of his sanity. He surged forward, magic exploding out of him, slamming Damiel against the wall. Several of Damiel's ribs were now broken, but the archangel didn't seem to care.

"It's too late for you, Osiris."

Damiel lifted his sword, and this time his opponent didn't bombard him with magic. In fact, the glowing aura had completely faded from his body. Osiris's mindless fury had faded too. His eyes darted around the room, unfocused, confused. What had happened to him?

"Damiel," Osiris croaked. "I don't remember…"

Damiel shook his head. "I can't fix this. All I can do is end it."

His blade plunged through Osiris's chest, pulsing blue. Then Osiris dropped to the ground. That sword had to be an immortal weapon. Nothing else could bring down an angel that quickly.

"What happened to you, Osiris?" Damiel lifted the dying archangel over his shoulder.

The final, fading taps of Damiel's boots echoed as the

building disappeared. New images shot out of the General's dead body.

"Wardbreaker lost his mind," Damiel said, setting Osiris to the ground at Ronan's feet.

Osiris was still alive—barely—but he was fading fast.

Ronan's leather vest creaked as the god folded his arms across his chest. "What was the cause?"

"I don't know," Damiel said. "But something about his magic isn't right. Do you want me to investigate?"

"No," Nyx replied. "We have something more pressing for you to do."

Osiris choked out a final dying breath.

As the final scene dissolved like smoke, Delta tucked the opera glasses into her jacket. Her eyes quivering, she lifted up her father's body and carried it through the magic mirror on the wall.

"I KNEW YOU TWO WERE PLOTTING SOMETHING," Valora's voice boomed like thunder as the Legion teams returned to the gods' audience chamber. She glared at Nyx and Ronan—but mostly just at Nyx. "First, you hide a demigod from us, and now an archangel."

Meda glanced at Maya. From the look in her eyes, she was just as surprised by Maya's affair as the other gods. Maya hadn't even told her own sister about Osiris.

"Gods sleeping with mortals. Goddesses sleeping with angels. Gods sleeping with demigods." Valora slanted a searing look Nyx's way. "These Earthly relations have gone too far."

"Agreed," said Aleris. "No good has ever come of mixing heaven and Earth."

"Nor has any good ever come of overreacting," Faris declared. "Let us table these discussions for a later date."

So Faris wanted the gods to stew in their anger, hoping it would explode.

"Which brings us back to the challenges." Faris walked away from his throne, stopping in front of Delta. "I'm afraid General Wardbreaker's body is too impractical to carry around." He unclasped the diamond flower necklace from the archangel's neck, the very same one Maya had worn in the vision. "We will hold Wardbreaker's body in storage for the duration of these challenges. This necklace will serve as its replacement."

Delta glowered at Nero. His father had killed her father. But she couldn't possibly be blaming him for that, could she?

Well, she wasn't alone. At least half the people in this hall couldn't stand each other. Yes, Faris's plan was certainly working out nicely for him. And I still had no idea what that plan even was. Once the gods' alliances fell, what would he do next? If Faris tried to attack, they would immediately unite again to fight off a common enemy.

Faris waved his hand, and the archangel's body vanished. When Faris handed Maya's necklace to Nero rather than Delta, her glower intensified. Faris wasn't just sowing discord between the gods; he was cracking apart the Legion while he was at it too.

As the God of Heaven's Army took his throne, I glanced hungrily at the buffet tables. Nowadays, meals and rest were few and far between, so I was going to seize the opportunity while I still could. I avoided the performance-optimizing shakes, instead opting for the cheese-and-tomato baguette slices. With a little bit of imagination, they almost tasted like pizza.

"Leda Pierce."

I stuffed the rest of my baguette slice into my mouth and turned around to face the Everlasting telepath. "The memories were inside a body. That's what you meant by an item that was not an item."

"Yes."

"So memories can be stored inside corpses."

"Only in immortal bodies with enough magic," Athan said.

"Like that of an archangel?"

He nodded. "Immortal bodies can store memories long after death. Have you ever wondered why immortal artifacts can store memories too? And why they are called immortal artifacts?"

Then he walked away, leaving me to decipher what the hell he meant by that. Speaking in riddles seemed to be the unifying feature of all immortals.

"We're losing."

I jumped at Colonel Fireswift's sudden appearance behind me.

"For now," I said, meeting his agitated eyes.

"You have a plan."

"Am I allowed to have a plan?" I asked innocently. "I thought you were in charge, that I was to follow your lead and basically do everything you say. You make the plans. I'm just the tool supposed to obediently follow them."

He ground his teeth. "This isn't a typical situation."

I smiled at him.

"You are going to make me say it," he growled.

"Well, I know how much you enjoy hearing yourself speak. And how much you enjoy my undivided attention. Well, Colonel, right now you have it."

His fists clenched up.

"Ok. I'll just be over there by the strawberry cake when you're ready." I turned to leave.

He caught my wrist.

I looked back at him, arching my brows.

"Your methods are undignified and repulsive," he told me.

"But?"

There was *definitely* a 'but' this time.

"But you are persistent against a superior enemy and without any resources at your disposal. You're scrappy. Like a cockroach. So how do we win this?"

"A cockroach?" I repeated, my nose scrunching up. "Did you woo your wife with those flowery words?"

"There was no wooing. The Legion found our magic to be compatible, that we had a high chance of producing children with the potential to become angels. So the Legion ordered us to marry."

"Of course."

My stomach flopped. Magic testing. That was what Nyx wanted to do to me. Being turned into an Interrogator or an Elite Warrior in the Vanguard bothered me—but not as much as what else that magic testing meant. It meant the Legion would look closely at my magic. Even if that did not reveal my origins, they would use my magic test results to pair me up with someone 'compatible'.

I was with Nero. I didn't want to be assigned a spouse just so we could produce children with the potential to become angels.

Maybe I could delay the testing, at least long enough for me to gain the magic I needed to find Zane. Then Nero and I would run away. The Legion would chase us, of course. We'd spend the rest of our lives on the run, hiding, forced to stay far away from our friends and family. I'd have to take them with us, uprooting them from their lives. What if they didn't want to go?

And what if Nero didn't want to go? Hell, I didn't want to go. I had friends at the Legion. And past all the angels' and gods' bullshit, I actually liked what I did. I liked helping people. I liked making the world safer, and I wanted to keep doing that. It was just…the thought of the Legion pairing me and Nero off to other people made me sick to my stomach.

Colonel Fireswift was watching me closely. Smiling, I did a quick check of my mental shields. The gods were telepathic, and so were most of the angels here. I didn't want any of them to overhear me plotting treason—least of all the head of the Interrogators, whose job it was to root out treason from within the Legion's ranks.

"I'm not sure what the plan is," I told Colonel Fireswift. "I'm still thinking of how we'll win. Let's just wing it for a while until an opportunity presents itself."

"Wing it for a while until an opportunity presents itself?" he repeated in disgust.

"It usually does."

"*This* is how you outmaneuvered so many enemies? By *winging it*?"

"What did you expect? Flow charts and color-coded maps?"

"I expected something. Some order. Some planning."

"Order and planning? From me?" I snorted. "I'm flattered that you think so much of me, Colonel. Really, I am."

Magic crackled in his eyes. "You are messing with me."

"Yes. And no." He was such an easy target that I couldn't help kicking the hornet's nest a little. "I really don't have a plan yet. I'll know what to do when the time comes."

"How can you be sure?"

I shrugged. "I always do."

"This is not how one plans a military campaign," he protested.

"Oh, most definitely not. But your proper planning obviously isn't getting us anywhere, is it? We don't have any idea what our next challenge will be, nor how the gods will handicap us. Hence the need to wing it."

"I don't wing it."

"Then don't think of it as winging it. Let's call it something else," I suggested. "How about the Wait-and-Adjust Strategy?

"Dressing it up with a garish name doesn't change its underlying principle. It's a terrible plan, and I don't like it."

"I know you don't, but try breaking out of your comfort zone once in a while. Embrace the exciting uncertainty of life. Breathe in the chaos."

"You are breathing in enough chaos for the both of us."

And he'd clearly had all he could take of that chaos for the moment. He went to the buffet table, his eyes honing in immediately on the disgusting performance-optimizing shakes. I wasn't surprised. I was sure there was nothing as appealing to Colonel Fireswift as optimizing his performance.

I met Nero's eyes. He was watching me from across the room. I started to walk toward him, but Colonel Silvertongue intercepted me.

The angel didn't waste time. She cut right to the chase, opening with, "Both General Spellsmiter and Colonel Fireswift are dead-set on having you in their division. Why? What is so special about you?"

Her gaze drilled into me, her eyes swirling with magic, like a funnel dragging a boat at sea under the water. Warning bells tolled in my head, keeping me above water.

"I'm not special at all," I told her. "I'm not sure why they want me. Perhaps you should ask them?"

"I'm asking *you*, Leda Pierce. Half the angels in this room can't stand you; the other half of them adore you. Why?"

I felt an itch in my nose, like a sneeze was coming on. "I'm a very polarizing person," I said brightly.

Colonel Silvertongue's eyes narrowed into slits. "Your lips are moving, but you are not saying anything I want to hear."

"I'm sorry?"

Colonel Silvertongue expelled an impatient breath, then walked away.

My nose finally stopped itching. That's when I realized I wasn't suffering from an impending sneeze at all.

"I believe Colonel Silvertongue just tried to compel me," I told Nero as I grabbed a grape off the buffet table beside him.

"Yes." He dropped his voice. "You're making waves."

There was a hint of reproach in his voice. And a hint of pride too.

"I'm not doing it on purpose, you know," I told him.

"You are certainly torturing Colonel Fireswift quite thoroughly."

There wasn't even a hint of reproach in his voice this time.

"Ok, *that* I did on purpose," I admitted. "But only because he completely deserves it."

"Yes."

Smirking, I said, "He asked me to come up with a plan

to win, you know. I told him I was just going to wing it. I think he nearly had a heart attack on the spot."

Gold and silver lightning flashed across Nero's green irises. "Colonel Fireswift isn't wrong about your skills. You would make a terrific Interrogator. You hone right in to someone's greatest weakness—and exploit it."

He lifted his hand to my ponytail, brushing it off my shoulder. Soft and teasing, his touch jolted my heart. My pulse jumped, revving up like a truck growling to life. My head was feverish, flushed.

"So, do you want to skip the rest of this little party?" I asked.

"More than anything." Hot and silky, his words kissed my neck.

His magic rippled across my body like a lover's whisper. My nipples hardened.

"But our absence would be noticed," he laughed, low and deep.

I pouted out my lips. "You're a terrible tease, Nero."

"So what is your plan?" His hand stroked up my side.

"What?" I gasped, distracted.

"Your plan to win the challenges? What is it?"

"I told you already. I'm going to wing it."

"I know what you told Colonel Fireswift," Nero said, his hot breath caressing my neck. "I want to hear the truth." His teeth nibbled on the thick, pulsing vein on my throat.

"I don't have one yet," I said breathlessly.

"Are you quite sure?" His fangs extended, their sharp tips teasing my neck.

My blood was burning, my whole body quivering with raw sexual need. "Yes, I'm sure." My nails dug into his back, drawing him in closer, willing him to bite me. I turned my neck and presented it to him.

"Good." He pulled away, his back slipping past my fingers.

It seemed I wasn't the only one who knew knew how to exploit weaknesses.

"You were digging for information," I said, my heart hammering so hard I could hardly hear myself speak.

"One must always know their enemy, inside and out," he said with a scorching look that burned away all thoughts save one: sex.

I slid my hand over the table. It would do nicely once all the food was cleared. Or leave it on. I wasn't sure I was patient enough to clean up first. A distant voice inside of me reminded me that it wasn't prudent to throw my panties at an angel in the presence of the gods. It was getting easier to ignore that voice with every passing second.

"You play as dirty as I do, General Windstriker," I hissed in a low whisper.

"No, Pandora." His hands closed around my waist. "No one plays as dirty as you do."

"Let's find out." I grabbed his hands and pulled him out of the room.

We found a secluded spot in the gardens. There, surrounded by roses and peonies, I slunk up to him and kissed him softly on the cheek.

His eyes slid down the length of my body. "Leda."

I turned his face toward mine. "Nero," I whispered against his lips.

His hands clutched me tightly, his mouth coming down hard on mine as he dipped my head back. His tongue slipped past my lips, pillaging the inside of my mouth with savage hunger. I tore at his clothes, peeling back his jacket.

Nero's hands locked around my wrists. "Leda." My name was both a growl and a laugh on his lips.

He forced my clenched fist open, reclaiming the necklace I'd dug out of his jacket.

"Maya's necklace," he said, shaking his head. "So you did have a plan after all."

"You can't blame me for trying. You are hogging the artifacts."

"Competence is not a crime, Pandora."

"Very funny." Biting my lip coyly, I fluttered my eyelashes at him.

"I've just caught you redhanded, and you're already trying again?"

"You can't blame me for wanting to touch you. You are hot, Nero."

"Just how far were you going to take this little game?" he chuckled.

"Until I had your three godly possessions and we were both thoroughly satiated," I replied solemnly.

"And if Delta had been in possession of the artifacts? Would you have tried your charms on her?"

"Hmm, I don't know. She's not really my type. So I'd probably have sent Colonel Fireswift to seduce her."

A sexy grin twisted Nero's mouth. Unable to resist, I leaned in and caught his lower lip between my teeth, giving it a nip. A drop of blood popped the surface of his lips. I licked it up, and sweet ecstasy exploded in my mouth.

His lips dipped to my throat. Pain and pleasure—intertwined, inseparable—pierced me as his fangs penetrated my skin. A hard, agonizing throb pulsed deep inside of me, steadily building into an explosive crescendo. His magic swallowed me whole, turning the world inside out. I couldn't see anything but him.

He captured both my hands as they plunged down his back. "Later," he hissed in my ear. "After this competition is over and I know you don't want me for my priceless immortal artifacts."

I watched him walk away, my heart pounding, my body flushed. "Is that a promise?"

"Absolutely."

Still shaking, I returned to the gods' hall. The moment I stepped through the door, Colonel Fireswift was at my side.

"You shouldn't leave the hall until the gods dismiss you," he chastised me.

"Sorry. I was on a mission."

"Sleeping with General Windstriker will not help us win this competition."

"Well, we won't know that until we try, will we?"

He glowered at me.

"I didn't sleep with him." Unfortunately.

"There's blood on your mouth."

I slid my tongue over my lips, licking up the precious drop of Nero's blood.

"Nothing you do surprises me at this point, but Windstriker..." Colonel Fireswift shook his head in stern disapproval. "An angel should know better than to fraternize with the enemy."

"Nero and I aren't enemies."

"He marked you again. Did you realize that?"

I lifted up my arm and gave it a sniff, inhaling the spicy, deliciously masculine scent of sex and angel. I sniffed my hand next. Colonel Fireswift was right. My whole body smelled like Nero's magic.

Nero was good. Really good. I didn't think it possible, but he'd managed to mark me using only a few drops of his blood.

I looked at Colonel Fireswift, snorting. "Nero is feeling a tad possessive, you know, with all the quality time you and I have been spending together lately."

He looked like he'd just bitten down on a spoiled orange. "He didn't only leave a magic mark. He left a notable physical one as well. I can see *precisely* where he sucked on your neck."

I brushed my fingers across my throat, feeling the uneven lumps Nero's fangs had left there. An angel hickey. How embarrassing. He'd forgotten to heal me.

No, not forgotten, I realized. Nero didn't do anything without a reason. He'd left them there for Colonel Fireswift to see.

"Aren't you going to heal that?" Colonel Fireswift demanded, impatience staining his words.

Heal it? How? My brain clicked back on. He expected me to heal the marks with my fairy magic—the fairy magic I was supposed to possess. Shit. Nero's need to prove a point to Colonel Fireswift was going to get me into trouble.

I could use a potion to heal the marks. They weren't that bad. But then Colonel Fireswift would wonder why I was going through all the ordeal of mixing and using a potion when I could simply tap my finger to my neck and heal the marks in two seconds with Fairy's Touch.

Colonel Fireswift's eyes narrowed. "Well?"

"I think I'll leave it," I said, smiling. "I like keeping a piece of Nero with me at all times."

I was aiming for sweet and lovestruck, but Colonel Fireswift looked at me like I was some sort of weird sexual deviant who got off on bite marks. I supposed that was better than him realizing I wasn't using my fairy magic because I didn't have any. This was really starting to become a problem, and I'd only been hiding my weird experience with leveling up—or *not* leveling up, as it were —for a few days. I needed to get this sorted out stat. Before I was exposed.

And I needed to change the subject. I reached into my jacket and pulled a plump red grape out of my sleeve.

"What are you doing?" Colonel Fireswift demanded as I waved my hand over the grape.

"You'll see."

Magic rippled across the grape, shifting it into Maya's necklace. Colonel Fireswift's jaw dropped. He gaped at me. He was completely speechless.

"What is it?" I flashed him a grin. "Do I have something in my teeth?"

"You stole the necklace from Windstriker."

"Of course. I told you I was on a mission. So I turned my grape into a replica of the necklace and swapped it with the real necklace."

When Nero had caught my hand, I'd already slid the real necklace—in the shape of a grape—up my sleeve. Nero got the grape in the shape of a necklace. Too bad he'd caught my hand before I could swap his other two artifacts.

Across the room, Nero was watching me. He held a grape in his hand, and he looked really sour about it. Dangling the necklace between my fingers, I blew him a kiss.

"You are even more cunning than I'd thought,"

Colonel Fireswift said. "Your underhanded skills could be pruned and polished to serve the Interrogators well."

"Have you ever thought that my methods work because they are neither pruned nor polished?"

"I have just the assignment for you lined up," he continued, as though I hadn't spoken at all.

I didn't bother pointing out that I wasn't an Interrogator—or that I still had time to get out of becoming one. He was too busy planning my bleak future to listen.

"Soldiers of the Legion," Faris's voice pierced the chatter of the hall. "Your next challenge is about to begin."

CHAPTER 17

THE DREAMER'S MIRROR

I hadn't even caught my breath after the last challenge, and now it was time for the next one? When this was over, I was treating myself to a week-long nap.

"The challenge will be different this time," Faris told everyone. "It will be a game. I know you are all familiar with the game of Legion."

Legion was a card game its makers had marketed as a faithful representation of the Legion of Angels. Featured on the playing cards were every kind of supernatural—and every Legion rank from lowly initiate to archangel. The angel cards featured actual angels. Whoever had illustrated Nero's card had given him a body almost as good as the real thing; and a ridiculously long sword that no one could wield, no matter how much magic they possessed.

"This is a game of wits, not magic. It will show who you really are inside." Faris's words were downright foreboding. "Let's see what you're made of."

He gestured toward the only glowing mirror in the hall. The other frames were dormant right now. For the first time, all seven teams passed through the same mirror together.

It transported us to a posh lounge, a room full of rare and expensive collectables. Several cozy fireplaces were cut into the four walls, and a vibrant rainbow fire burned inside each of them. In front of the largest fireplace, a big beastly cat slept, snoring lazily. The cat was a very appropriate pet for the Goddess of Witchcraft.

The other players gave the beast cat a suspicious look and a wide berth, except for me. I moved in closer. Sure, the cat looked like a monster, but it didn't act like a monster. It was so calm and gentle, even docile. I petted it softly on the head. It blinked its blue eyes and purred like a house cat a fraction of its size.

Beyond the cat, Athan the Everlasting stood beside a great round table with fourteen chairs.

"Place the gods' items that are in your possession onto the table now," he said. "The winning team of each round will claim one artifact."

So much for my cunning play to steal Nero's item. I shouldn't have even bothered. We were all relinquishing our artifacts now anyway.

Colonel Fireswift placed Maya's necklace and Zarion's hairbrush on the table. Nero set down Aleris's glasses and Valora's crown next to them. Finally, General Spellsmiter slipped a slim silver mirror out of his jacket and added it to the other four items. That must have been Meda's object.

"You will be playing the partner variation of the Legion card game," said Athan. "Your teammate is your partner. To prevent cheating, all telepathic angels in the room will now drink a potion that blocks your ability to read thoughts."

Six shot glasses with dark liquid waited on the table.

All the angels except Harker took a shot glass. He was the newest angel, the only one here who hadn't yet gained the power of Ghost's Whisper.

I'd been feeling like an outsider this whole training. At this moment, I realized that I wasn't the only one. Like me, Harker was not from a Legion legacy family. And like me, his magic level was lower than his peers. I wondered how he felt about that. Did he feel as out of place, as out of his league, as I did? I couldn't tell from his expression. He had the stony angel face down pat.

"You now have five minutes alone with your partner to plan your strategy," Athan said once the six angels had emptied their glasses.

Seven doors, each one positioned between two fireplaces, whispered open. Each team walked through one of them.

FIVE MINUTES OF FURIOUSLY-PACED STRATEGY planning later, Colonel Fireswift and I returned to the room of many magic fireplaces and took our seats across from each other at the fancy round table. The six other teams did the same. Harker sat on my right side, Jace to my left. Considering all the psychopaths sitting around the table, I could have fared much worse. At least I liked the two of them. And neither one wanted to kill me.

Granted, Harker had once tried to give me pure Nectar that I likely wouldn't have survived; and Jace might still succumb to his upbringing and push me under the bus to win the honor of becoming an angel first. But other than all that, we were the best of friends.

Still standing, Athan dealt out cards to each of the

fourteen players around the table. "There will be five rounds. Each round, you will be competing for one of the gods' possessions." He set five cards in front of himself. He flipped over one of them. "The first prize is Maya's necklace." He tapped his finger on the illustrated card face; the drawing was a very faithful representation of the real necklace.

The first move was Colonel Fireswift's. He played a witch coven leader card, a solid mid-level card, powerful enough to spark our opponents' interest but not strong enough to ward off their attacks. Just as we'd discussed in our five-minute strategy session.

"You have an angel in your hand," Colonel Silvertongue told him.

Colonel Fireswift's face remained inscrutable—up until Leila's tentacle plant monster card hit the table. Then he just looked annoyed. The plant monster card couldn't win the round, but it could keep him busy for the next eight turns as his witch fought off its tentacles.

The hint of a smile twitched Colonel Silvertongue's lower lip. "That didn't work out as you'd planned."

"Oh, shut up," he snapped.

Colonel Silvertongue played the Sea Dragon card, one of the Legion's most powerful elementals.

"I think your face is broken, Fireswift. There's something resembling an expression on it." General Spellsmiter's Fire Dragon subdued his sister's Sea Dragon.

General Spellsmiter and Colonel Silvertongue will go for an aggressive opening, a show of force, Colonel Fireswift had said during our strategy session. *They are very competitive with each other. If we can keep them focused on fighting each other, they won't last long. They'll be locked into this cycle of escalation, not realizing there are other threats before it's too late.*

And so far it was working exactly as Colonel Fireswift had planned. Kiros Spellsmiter and Desiree Silvertongue were coming out so strong that they didn't realize Colonel Fireswift was playing them, right down to his sour face. They should have known better than to believe the cold, unfeeling Interrogator was having a tantrum because they were poking fun at him. Only I had the talent for annoying people that much.

Nero, on the other hand, was clearly not fooled. He played a lowly Legion initiate, the weakest card in the deck. Even Leila's plant monster was more useful. The initiate card's sole purpose was to annoy the other players —or maybe to throw it at a landmine if someone played one of those.

Nyx glanced at the growing pile of cards. Then she played an angel card. Colonel Fireswift had been right about her too. She was playing aggressively. This whole training had threatened her power and credibility as First Angel. She had to reestablish both.

The next players' turns were rather bland. It was clear who had won this round—at least it was to everyone here except Delta. She countered Nyx's angel with one of her own. Arius added his angel to Nyx's, and the two of them annihilated Delta.

"That was a stupid move," Nero told Delta coolly. "Stick to the plan."

Delta watched Nyx claim the necklace, her eyes quivering. She wasn't thinking with her head right now. She wasn't thinking at all. She was reacting instinctively. She'd forgotten all else but claiming the necklace that represented her father's body. Colonel Fireswift had predicted that as well. The angel's ability to deconstruct people was eerily accurate.

Athan flipped over the second of his five cards to uncover the next round's prize: Zarion's hairbrush.

Jace considered the cards in his hands carefully.

"Staring at them won't suddenly turn them into better cards," I teased him.

"I don't know about that. Maybe with a little magic."

I glanced down at the pink fairy card he'd just played. "You were just waiting to get that card off your hands."

He scowled at me.

"I can't imagine why. She has such a great outfit. It's just so pink." I winked at him.

Jace pretended to be fascinated by the card Andrin Spellsmiter had just played.

I snorted. "You might be a superstar in the Legion, Jace, but you really suck at the card game."

"His father always forbade him from playing 'such a ridiculous mockery of the real thing'," Siri said, making her move.

"You all talk too much." Delta narrowed her eyes at me. "Especially you."

"At least I can talk and play at the same time." My gaze fell over the card she'd just played. "Unlike some people."

Nero's face was distinctly blank. He obviously wasn't impressed with Delta's move either.

When it was Colonel Fireswift's turn, he played a two-handed flaming sword, an angel's weapon.

"What are you plotting, Xerxes?" said Colonel Silvertongue.

"Xerxes?" I repeated. "*That* is your name?"

"That's Colonel Fireswift to you," he snapped at me.

His gaze slid over to Colonel Silvertongue. "And deciphering my so-called plot will cost you."

Colonel Silvertongue flipped over an angel card. General Spellsmiter followed that up with an angel of his own. He didn't seem able to help himself; he was almost compelled to counter every move his sister made.

Nero overpowered them both with his own angel card. "My thanks, Fireswift," he declared, sliding the sword card toward his own card. "For the sword." He showed Colonel Fireswift the angel card with his face on it. "And for the helping hand."

Nero had defeated Colonel Fireswift with his own card. A laugh buzzed on my lips, threatening to burst out of my mouth. I resisted, a feat made damn near impossible by the sour expression on Colonel Fireswift's face. He wasn't faking his annoyance this time.

He and Nero glared across the table at each other for two more turns. That was when I slapped my angel card down. It featured a very muscular Nero Windstriker carrying a very long sword—and he wasn't wearing many clothes either. It was almost a shame to give him up, but the real Nero's expression made it all worth it.

"Pandora." His deep voice reverberated somewhere between a purr and a growl. "You did not just defeat me with my own card."

My heart skipped a beat. "Why, yes I did," I replied brightly. "And I got this cool sword too." Meeting his smoldering eyes, I grabbed the pile of played cards—and the prize from the middle of the table.

"There will be consequences," Nero warned me.

"I look forward to it."

Magic crackled between us, ricocheting off the pile of

gods' artifacts. My whole body pulsed, completely in tune with whatever Nero's magic was doing to me right now.

"It's your turn," Harker said, nudging me.

That was when I realized the third round had already begun. I looked at the big pile of cards on the table. In fact, the round was almost over. I met Nero's smug gaze. Despite his angelic halo and heavenly decorum, he truly did fight as dirty as I did. No wonder I was completely under his spell.

I looked over the cards that people had already played. I had a Legion major in my hand that beat every one of them, but there was still one player to go: Jace. Did he hold a card in his hand that could beat mine?

"What's the first thing you'll do when you become an angel?" I asked him.

"What?" he said, the question throwing him off guard. His eyes dipped to the Nero card at the top of my winning stack.

"Never mind. Think about it. And tell me later."

I played my major card. It was the strongest major in the deck. An angel was the only card that could beat it, and Jace didn't have one. If he'd held an angel, his gaze would have dipped to the angel card in his hand, not my Nero card which was further from him.

Jace set a card down. A potion? What the hell? My gaze snagged on the demon mark on the potion's label. Venom. Oh, shit. Jace slid the card over to my major, poisoning her. That put me out of the fight. Leila's captain, the next highest card on the table, won the battle.

"That wasn't nice," I told Jace, frowning as Leila claimed Valora's crown. "And you're supposed to be a terrible Legion player. Where did you learn a move like that?"

"Morrows has been giving me lessons," Jace admitted, his face almost sheepish.

Delta kicked off the fourth round of Legion, playing a card whose sole purpose was obviously to annoy Nero.

Her actions will be driven more by emotion than logical reasoning, Colonel Fireswift had said of Delta.

He wasn't wrong about that. Learning that Nero's father had killed hers had completely turned her against him. She wanted to see him suffer—and she didn't care if she crashed down with him.

"Morrows? As in, Alec Morrows?" I asked Jace. "How did you convince him to give you Legion lessons?"

"I got him into Heaven."

He meant the Legion club in New York, not the hall of the gods. Only Legion soldiers level five and above—and their guests—were allowed inside.

"And what did you two do there?" I asked him.

"Morrows got high on Nectar and made out with several women."

"At the same time?"

"It varied."

"And you?" I asked.

Colonel Fireswift watched us closely, even as he set down his card. It was a major, one almost as powerful as the one I'd played last round.

Jace's eyes flickered to his father, then back again twice as fast. "I behaved with the dignity befitting a Legion soldier of my rank and blood."

"Ah. Right." I winked at him.

"Stop trying to get me into trouble, Leda."

"Why? Half the fun is getting into trouble. The other half is getting away with it."

No one could beat Colonel Fireswift's card—until Nyx. She played the second strongest major in the deck.

"You can't beat that," Harker told me.

"Neither can you."

"No." He looked at his partner across the table. "But I was never going to win a partner game."

He was right. And Isabelle's blinding hatred for him was the culprit. The gods liked to make flowery speeches about shedding your personal feelings to do your duty, but that was easier said than done. Just look at how well the gods were following their own advice.

"I think you'll find that I have a few more tricks up my sleeves," I said, playing my card.

Jace's eyes widened when he saw the Nectar bottle on the card face. "No way."

"Yes, way." I slid the card over Colonel Fireswift's. "I think it's time to level up this major, don't you?"

For the first time ever, Colonel Fireswift looked at me as though he didn't completely despise me. I claimed Aleris's glasses, then tried to decide which of my cards I'd play in this final round.

Colonel Fireswift was giving me the signal to play a fairy. Unfortunately, I didn't have one. I flicked my ponytail over my shoulder, indicating that. He repositioned two of the cards in his hand. That was the signal for vampire. I didn't have one of those either. Colonel Fireswift's lips drew into a hard line. It looked like he was already back to despising me.

"Your plan will never work."

"It already has."

I blinked at the other thirteen players sitting around the table. No one had said a word.

"You can't hold me here forever."

"I don't have to hold you forever. I only need to hold you long enough."

If the other players weren't speaking, where were those voices coming from? Were Aleris's glasses even now picking up memories stored in the other gods' objects? But if these were memories projected by the magic glasses, then why wasn't anyone else acting like they'd heard them?

"The Legion's trials will soon begin. After they are over, it won't matter anymore."

The voice sounded distant. Distorted. And like it belonged to a god. A god had hunted down and imprisoned this person…this *innocent* person. She was innocent. I knew it. I could feel it, just as I could feel that she was a she. She was in trouble. And scared. I could feel my fear pumping through my veins as though it were my own fear. I had to help her. But how was I supposed to find her?

Harker nudged me. Apparently, it was my turn. I played my witch card. It wasn't a fairy or a vampire like Colonel Fireswift wanted, but it was the closest I had to either. Colonel Fireswift's scowl deepened. I supposed when this was all over, he wouldn't be patting me on the back for a job well done after all.

Jace and Leila won the final round. Everyone's eyes tracked Leila's hands as they closed around Meda's mirror. By now, there wasn't a person here who didn't know what was coming next.

We were all wrong. Aleris's glasses didn't spark the mirror's magic and lift the memories imprinted there. No secrets came pouring out. Nothing happened at all.

"We will return to the gods' hall," Nyx declared, moving toward a stained glass window situated between two fireplaces. She stepped through a picture of seven gods posed regally on seven thrones.

"That was anticlimactic," Leila commented beside me.

"Like waiting for an explosion that never happened," I agreed.

"There's something not right about this training."

"Only *one* thing?" I laughed.

Leila and I passed through the stained glass window. The magic of the transporting mirror rippled through the glasses in my hand and hit the mirror in hers. As we materialized in the gods' audience chamber, so did the mirror's memories.

Meda sat on a plump cushion in front of an ivory vanity, arranging her hair into an elaborate collection of braids. She pinned them down with sparkling pins and feathered clips.

"I need more of the serum," said the Goddess of Witchcraft and Technology, looking into the mirror propped up against the vanity.

"I gave you twenty vials just last week." The voice came from the mirror, but the glass showed no one but Meda.

"They go fast. There are a lot of monsters," she replied, applying pink glittery gloss to her lips.

"And have your experiments yielded results?" asked the mystery voice beyond the mirror.

"I've combined your Life serum with other magical ingredients to create a potion of my own design. The monsters are responding to it. Their magic has grown stronger, and I've managed to gain control over half the tested beast species. With some further tweaking of the formula, I expect I'll soon be able to control them all."

Life. I'd seen the silver liquid in one of my visions of Cadence, Nero's mother. Life was the serum the Guardians used to balance people's magic, giving them control over the full spectrum of light and dark powers. Like Nectar and Venom, Life was given gradually over time, in increasingly more potent doses.

Meda was experimenting with Life to control the monsters that the gods and demons had lost control over centuries ago, the feral beasts that now reigned over larger parts of the world. Suddenly, the docile cat monster in the room of fireplaces made a lot of sense.

As far as I knew, only the Guardians had the knowledge and power to make the Life serum. Which meant the person on the other side of the mirror was a Guardian—and Meda was working with him.

I wasn't the only one in the gods' audience chamber who'd come to that conclusion.

"Treachery," hissed Zarion. "You have allied yourself with the Guardians."

"I have done no such thing," Meda said with a flick of her hand.

Valora rose smoothly from her throne, her stance stiff. "Explain yourself, Meda."

"I needed the Life serum for my experiments on monsters."

"Experiments you did not clear with the gods' council," Aleris said, braiding his fingers together.

"Just to have Meda's work tied up in committees for centuries?" Maya scoffed. "The demons are gaining ground. We need an advantage, a weapon against them. And we need it now. Meda's work is that solution. With the monsters once more under our control, the demons will fall quickly."

"But at what price?" Ronan shook his head. "You're just trading the demon problem for the Guardian problem."

Meda laughed. "I am *not* allying with them. I simply need their Life serum for my potion."

Ronan arched a single dark brow. "Which they provided to you out of the goodness of their hearts?"

"They have not asked for anything in return. So I expect they plan to steal my complete potion formula once I have perfected it." A vicious smile curled her lips. "They will not succeed."

"Once we're done with the demons, we will send the monsters to take out the Guardians. Then we will rule the cosmos," Maya said.

A deep frown furrowed Zarion's brow. "There's no point in wondering whether you knew of Meda's scheme."

"I stand with my sister." Maya took Meda's hand. "Always."

The memory frozen in front of us rippled, melting into another scene.

Meda stood behind a table, a vial of silver liquid in her hand. The Life serum. She uncorked the vial and poured it into a small pot. Meda stirred the potion until it had absorbed the silver strands of Life. Then she filled a syringe with the potion and brought it into a curtained room.

Inside, someone lay chained to a medical bed. As Meda neared, he stirred, pushing against his restraints.

"Now, now, there's no need for that," Meda said. "I'm here with your medicine."

"Medicine?" a dry, cracked voice said. It sounded familiar. "You mean poison."

"Perfection takes time. You knew that when we set off down this path. Your discomfort will soon pass. And then you will not only be more powerful than any angel who has ever lived; you will be in the league of gods."

"Very well. Proceed."

Meda leaned over to inject him with the syringe, her movement revealing his face. It was Osiris Wardbreaker.

"It won't be long now," Meda said in a coaxing voice.

The archangel closed his eyes, his mouth hardening as the needle pierced his skin. His muscles went from tense, to quivering, to all-out spasming. He thrashed frantically on the table, roaring in agony. Curses poured out of his mouth. The chains bit into his skin. Thin streams of blood trickled down his body, dripping onto the white tiled floor.

"Still not right," Meda muttered, making notes on her pad. "The magic boost is fighting the magic-balancing agent." She coolly regarded the screaming archangel on the bed. "I'll need to tweak the formula further."

At her words, Osiris Wardbreaker heaved hard against the chains, snapping one of them. Meda wove a spell to replace the broken chain. He glared at her, red fire burning in his eyes.

The vision faded away, absorbing back into the mirror in Leila's hand. Silence, as cold and foreboding as an imminent blizzard, hung over the gods' hall. Meda hadn't just experimented on monsters. She'd experimented on an angel. That was why Osiris Wardbreaker had gone mad. That was why he'd gone off on a killing spree that had ended with his death.

CHAPTER 18

THE ORIGIN OF CHAOS

Maya dropped her sister's hand. She'd grown oddly still. She wasn't even breathing.

"I did not kill Osiris Wardbreaker, sister," Meda said. "Damiel Dragonsire did."

"You might not have killed him with your own two hands, but your obsession with balancing light and dark magic, your experiments to create a new breed of warrior, signed his death warrant," Maya replied, her words clipped. "You made him lose his mind. And when an angel loses his mind, he must be put down."

"I didn't know about you two." Meda reached out.

Maya shot her sister's hand a scathing look. "I don't believe you. Osiris insisted he would find a way for us to be together. You promised him that way. You told him he would be a god. You knew about us. And you exploited him."

Anger piled on top of Maya's heartbreak. It seemed that like angels, gods had those same pesky human emotions at their core.

"You cannot simply experiment on my angels, Meda,"

Ronan told her, a fair share of anger smoldering in his eyes too.

"Or make deals with the so-called Guardians, those self-appointed usurpers," Zarion snapped.

Self-appointed usurpers? What did Zarion mean by that? What was the history between the gods and the Guardians?

Magic brushed against my shoulder. I glanced back. Nero stood across the room, his back against the wall, his eyes beckoning me to him. I quietly slipped past Leila and Jace. They hardly seemed to notice. Nor did anyone else. Their eyes were all locked on the gods.

"The gods' council is coming apart at the seams," I whispered, leaning against the wall beside Nero. "Except for Aleris and Faris. They're the only ones this training hasn't exposed."

"I noticed that as well."

We'd already determined that Faris was behind this. But Aleris?

"Aleris must be Faris's ally," Nero said. "He has helped him expose the other gods' secrets."

"But why would Aleris ally himself with Faris?"

Nero shook his head. "I do not know. They are unlikely allies."

"Let's find out."

I located Athan near the door and walked toward him, Nero by my side.

"Which god do you owe a favor?" I asked the Everlasting telepath.

He said nothing.

"It's Aleris, isn't it?"

It had to be Aleris. Faris needed a powerful telepath to tell him where the objects that contained the gods' greatest secrets were kept. So he had enlisted Aleris's help because an Everlasting telepath owed the God of Nature a favor. That was it. I was sure of it. Otherwise, Faris would have had no use for Aleris. He would have exposed the other gods' secrets alone, Aleris's included.

"You are very observant," Athan noted. "But do you see everything that is going on here?"

"See what? What's going on?"

His gaze dipped to the glasses poking out of my jacket. "Hold on to the Seer's Opera Glasses. You will need them."

"Need them for what? To expose the gods' greatest dirty secrets? That's what Faris and Aleris want, isn't it? That's why we had to get Aleris's glasses first, why that was the first challenge. So we could use them to expose the other gods' secrets. Aleris didn't have his secrets blown right open. And neither will Faris, assuming we ever get to his artifact. Assuming the other gods haven't exploded into civil war by then, effectively ending this training."

I had it all figured out. Except…there was still something that didn't make sense.

"I get why Faris would ally with Aleris. He needed your help, and you owe Aleris a favor," I said to Athan. "But why would Aleris team up with Faris?"

"Aleris's distaste for delinquency is well known," Nero pointed out.

"In other words, he doesn't like naughty behavior?"

"No, he most decidedly does not," said Nero. "Zarion plays the self-righteous god of piety, but it's Aleris who is really the strict, straight-and-narrow god. And he expects all the other gods to behave in the same manner."

I frowned. "So he teams up with Faris, the biggest sinner of them all?"

"Aleris didn't learn the other gods' secrets on his own.

He isn't a plotter and schemer. He isn't a sin scavenger hunter," replied Nero. "Faris probably came to him with a list of the other gods' sins, along with this fun little game they could play to expose them, to air them all out in the open. He naturally would have left his own deviations out of the conversation."

"Interesting theory," Athan commented.

I considered him closely. "You said I'll need the glasses. Why?"

"You'll find out."

"Why are you even telling us anything?" I asked in exasperation.

"I have told you nothing."

"You just implied."

The telepath smiled.

"You are a telepath." I bit my lip. "But you are also something else. You understand so much about the magical workings of the immortal artifacts."

I recalled something he'd said about the immortal artifacts during our last conversation. He'd asked me why they were called immortal artifacts—and why they could store memories when other magical objects could not.

"The immortal artifacts hold immortal souls, don't they?" I said. "The souls of the original immortals. Immortals with a capital 'I'. That's why the immortal artifacts are so powerful."

Athan dipped his chin in acknowledgement.

It was a slightly different story than the one told to me by the magic smith at Storm Castle, but myths changed with each telling. And Athan just might have been around long enough to know what had really happened.

"Why would an Immortal agree to be put inside an artifact?" I asked.

"You ask a lot of questions."

And I would keep asking them. "How does that even work, putting an Immortal's soul into an artifact?"

"With great difficulty."

"You can make immortal artifacts, can't you?" I realized. "And you can manipulate the artifacts' magic."

"That art was lost long ago."

"And yet here we are."

He didn't smile this time. "Your mind doesn't work like theirs." Athan said, his face reflective. His eyes panned across the room of gods, angels, and would-be angels.

"I am not like them," I told him.

"Yes. And no. You are more human than they will ever be. And yet, at the same time, less human," he said. "General Spellsmiter and Colonel Fireswift are both right about you. You would make a good Interrogator and a good warrior in the Vanguard."

"What does that have to do with anything?"

"It has to do with *everything*," he said. "Have you ever wondered why that is?"

"Why what is?"

"Have you ever wondered why you would be a good Interrogator and a good Elite Warrior."

"Because I'm just so talented?" I quipped impatiently.

"Because of your history."

He meant my divine origin. My father was a god, my mother a demon. Which made me an abnormality that shouldn't exist.

At least Athan hadn't gone straight out and said it in heaven's halls. He was speaking in code because anyone could be listening. Considering that he had no qualms about blowing up everyone else's secrets, I supposed I should have been grateful he wasn't announcing mine to everyone here.

"Exposing you to all the gods is not part of the deal," he said, responding to my unspoken thoughts.

All the gods? Did that mean that *one* of the gods knew what I was?

"Some gods. Not all." Again, he'd read my thoughts, as though my mental shield were made of tissue paper.

I cringed. If just one god knew about me, that was one too many. And he'd said 'gods'. As in, plural, more than one.

"You're overthinking this," he told me.

But I wasn't letting him throw me off course. "Which gods know about me?"

"Your father by now."

I swallowed the hard lump in my throat. "Anyone else?"

Athan smiled coyly. He clearly wasn't going to answer that question.

My heart hammered in my chest. "Who is my father?"

"Patience."

"Is about as much fun as a squirt of lemon juice in the eye," I finished for him.

"Your magic is light and dark, perfectly balanced."

Like Meda had achieved with some of the monsters—and had tried to achieve with an angel. Except I had been born this way.

"But though your light and dark magic are balanced, your magic *powers* are not in balance," Athan continued. "You have strengths, powers that come more easily to you, inherited from your parents."

Fairy magic was obviously not one of those powers.

Otherwise, I'd not have failed to level up at the last ceremony.

"We'll get around to your problem later," Athan said.

Did that mean he knew why I had neither leveled up nor died?

"Of course I know," he said. "It's actually pretty obvious if you think about it."

He really did have all the answers.

"If you live well enough for long enough, you learn a few things about the nature of the magical universe," he said. "But back to your magical strengths. What is a good Interrogator in the most basic sense, at its core?"

"A bad person?" I suggested.

He sighed. "Conversations with you are exhausting, Leda Pierce."

"That's what all my friends tell me. And my enemies." I grinned at him.

"What is a good Interrogator in the most basic sense, at its core?" he said again. "What magical ability do they tap into the most?"

"Siren's Song."

"Yes, the magic to compel people. It is the Interrogators' most valuable tool, one they use to great effect." Athan paused. "But their siren magic doesn't hold a candle to yours. When you use the entire siren magical spectrum, light and dark, you have more power than someone who only taps into either light or dark, who can only ever use half of the power. Angels cannot compel you. Colonel Silvertongue tried and failed. By now, you've grown powerful enough that even gods and demons cannot compel you either."

He might be right about that. Last month, Faris had

tried to break my mind. I'd held out—barely. It had hurt like hell, but I hadn't spilled my secrets to him.

"And what is a good warrior in the Legion's Vanguard in the most basic sense, at its core?" Athan asked me.

I thought about that. Elite Warriors needed spells like the rest of us, but mostly they just needed raw strength and speed. They were the battering rams of the Legion, the soldiers on the front line who broke through the enemy's defenses—and held ours.

"Vampire magic," I said. "The Vanguard's warriors need the physical strength, speed, and stamina of vampires."

Athan nodded. "And so you have your answer."

I frowned. "Answer to what?"

As soon as I said the words, I knew. I had the answer to my origin. I possessed both light and dark magic because I was the daughter of a god and a demon. And I possessed both the vampire and siren magical strengths because of which god was my father and which demon was my mother.

"Your vampire and siren magic, two powers so potent that they even broke through the magic-neutralizing effect of your light and dark magic," Athan told me.

Uh, what? My light and dark magic had neutralized my magic, leaving me without any, at least until I'd joined the Legion of Angels and had my first sip of Nectar.

"What do you mean *potent*?" I said. "I didn't have any magic before I joined the Legion."

"But you did," he countered. "You possessed the magical strengths of your father and your mother."

Except I'd had neither vampire nor siren magic before joining the Legion.

"They were expressed in a very unusual way," he told me.

The demon Sonja had said the same thing about my magic. But what did it mean? I couldn't remember possessing any magic back then. Sure, I'd been slightly faster and stronger than regular humans, but so was anyone with a little supernatural blood in them. That tiny boost certainly hadn't put me in the same league as supernaturals—or allowed me to fight them without trickery. That was why I'd relied on dirty fighting for all those years. I'd had to make up for my lack of magic in a supernatural world. I'd had to develop a way to level the playing field.

So what inherent siren magic and vampire magic was Athan referring to? I hadn't been able to compel anyone. I'd managed to sweet-talk my marks as a bounty hunter, to lure them in, but not any better than any other woman with breasts could.

"I said the magic manifested in a very unusual way," Athan reminded me. "So unusual that you wouldn't even be able to identify it as vampire or siren magic. But that unique ability of yours was both powers intertwined. You never understood why it happened to you, a phenomenon you had neither seen nor heard of before."

I finally realized what he was talking about, what Sonja had been referring to as well.

My hair. Sometimes, it glowed. In my pre-Legion days, the glow had mesmerized vampires, compelling them to bite me. My hair was the manifestation of siren and vampire magic in one, allowing me to mesmerize vampires—and *only* vampires. All that time, my hair had been the answer to my magic's origin. The origin of Pandora. The origin of chaos.

"Magic always finds a way to be seen," Athan commented.

I hardly heard him. My mind was racing ever faster,

backtracking now, trying to sort through everything I'd just learned. And as my mind rewound through the long meandering conversation, it snagged on two things: vampire and siren magic. I'd gotten one of those powers from my father, a god. That meant my father was either Faris or Zarion.

CHAPTER 19

WAR BY PROXY

My godly father was either Faris or Zarion. Yuck.

Zarion, God of the Faith, God of Vampires, had killed his mortal lover and tried to kill their unborn child. He was very holy in words but not in actions. Zarion had already broken the rules by conceiving a child with a mortal. Chances were that he'd strayed from his holy path more than once.

And then there was Zarion's brother Faris, the God of Heaven's Army. Within a few weeks of my joining the Legion, Faris had tried to have me killed. He'd instructed Harker to give me pure Nectar that would level up my magic just long enough to find my telepathic brother—and then I'd die an excruciating death.

Also, Faris was manipulating this training and everyone here, weakening the other gods' alliances to fuel his rise to the top. He didn't care how many innocents were caught in the crossfire, or how many friendships he shattered along the way.

Both gods had the personality of a spiked mace coated

in poison. It was just a matter of picking your poison. Except *I* couldn't pick anything. My past was already set in stone.

Athan's immortal eyes met mine once more, then he turned and walked away. Though I'd just learned a lot about myself, I dreaded ever talking to him again, fearing what other terrible bombshells from my past I would pick up along the trail of our conversation. I had a sinking feeling I would be talking to him again soon. This wasn't the end. Not by a long shot.

Athan knew about me. He knew my origin and my secrets. In fact, he knew more about me than I knew about myself. Ignorance might very well be bliss, but I had to know about my past. My secrets put me in danger, especially when others knew secrets I didn't even know that I had. If I didn't know about them, I couldn't prepare. I wouldn't be ready.

Ready for what, Leda? I asked myself.

I shuddered to consider the possibilities—the hazards that lay before me, the landmines that lay buried in my past, ready for me to stumble upon them.

Why was Faris keeping me close right now? Had he put me on his team because he believed I was his daughter? Or because he knew that Zarion was my father and keeping me close might offer him an opportunity to expose his brother—and me in the process. Just as he'd exposed his brother's other child.

Was that why he'd instructed Colonel Fireswift to hold on to the glasses? Could the glasses expose my secret? If so, it was only a matter of time. Faris had told Colonel Fireswift that he still needed me. I'd thought he only needed me to find Zane, but what if he had more plans for me? What if my very existence was the key to unraveling what was left of Zarion's support in the gods' council?

I clenched my fists, trying to quiet my muscle tremors. I couldn't process what I'd just learned. I just couldn't.

After I'd escaped Sonja's fortress, I'd decided I had to uncover my origin's full story, to find out who my parents were. I'd never expected joyous family reunions. I just had to know. Perhaps, that hadn't been the best idea. No good ever came from digging into the past. It was like kicking a nest of hornets. That's what my foster mother Calli had always said.

Brushing off those metaphorical hornets, I pushed all thoughts of my past to the sidelines. I had to focus on something else. I had to keep my mind off the terrible truth that either Zarion or Faris was my father. They both despised me. Zarion wanted me dead. And Faris was even worse. He wanted to use me as a tool, then discard me like trash on the side of the highway.

I tried to think about the upcoming challenges, but they all seemed to lead back to me. To exposing me.

No, I needed something else. I needed a mission, a purpose, something that had nothing to do with my own past. And I knew just the thing.

"I've been having nightmares," I told Nero.

"That's understandable." His hand took mine, his thumb tracing soothing circles into the underside of my wrist. "You're under a lot of stress."

"In those nightmares, a woman is running away. Soldiers are chasing her. They catch her and imprison her."

"Your mind is trying to process everything that's happening to you."

"I don't think they're dreams," I said. "I think they're memories. The woman is being held by one of the gods."

"Which god?" he asked me.

"I don't know. I never saw the god's face. During the final round of the Legion card game in our last challenge, I heard her speaking to the god who holds her prisoner."

"So that's why you were so distracted at the end."

"Yes."

"What could you tell from the god's voice?"

"Very little," I said. "The god's voice was distorted, magnified like they do when they're trying to intimidate us. It was working. The woman was very frightened."

"Who is this woman?"

"I don't know. I couldn't see her face. I couldn't see much of anything. The memories were shrouded in shadows. I know one thing: the memory is recent. The god mentioned the Legion trials would soon begin."

"You want to rescue this woman."

"She is suffering."

"The gods hold many prisoners," he told me. "They are all suffering."

"I know. But this one is different. I know she is."

"Where is she being held?"

"I don't know."

His face was hard.

"You think I'm crazy to want to rescue her."

"Of course you're crazy. That's one of your finest qualities," he said, his laugh a deep purr. He set his hands on my shoulders. "But we should put the rescue mission on hold until we have a bit more to go on."

Nero was right. Admitting that didn't help to quell my burning urge to rescue the woman and put an end to her suffering. When I'd experienced those memories, it had felt as though I were living through them myself. I might not have seen much, but I'd *felt* everything: her fear, her panic, her despair.

"Ok, we'll wait," I agreed. It simply wouldn't do to go blindly breaking into all the gods' castles, looking for the woman.

The irony was, that was exactly what we were expected to do in this training: break into all the gods' castles.

I looked across the audience chamber of bickering gods. It was hardly the scene of tranquility everyone imagined the gods' haven to be.

"So what now?" I asked Nero.

"The next challenge starts in the morning. Get changed and meet me in the gym in half an hour."

"For what?"

His green eyes sparkled. "Training."

"You aren't in charge of the Crystal Falls training anymore," I teased him, smirking.

"This isn't the Crystal Falls training, Leda. It has become something else entirely."

"The gods' battleground," I said. "Their war by proxy."

"Yes. The gods' alliances come and go with the tide and the shifting wind. When they leave, when they return to their castles, we remain in the wreckage of their immortal spats. And we have to keep on living. We have to survive in a world that they have left worse for wear. In order to do that, to survive, we need to train and we need to grow. We need to be ready for whatever comes next. Because if we don't grow stronger, we just might not survive their next altercation."

My brows peaked. "Train hard and train long?"

"Always," Nero said with a crisp nod.

Well, I'd been searching for something to take my mind off the million things plaguing me. Who was my father? What would the other gods do when they found out what I was? What would the next challenge be? Whose secrets would be exposed next? Which godly alliances would splinter? What was the significance of the woman one of the gods was holding prisoner? And how much longer could I hide that I had neither leveled up nor died? Colonel Fireswift was watching my every move. He might already suspect it.

"Ok, let's do it," I told Nero, washing all those worries from my mind. "Let's train." I winked at him. "But I won't go easy on you."

A savage smile broke through his civilized facade. "Good. Only a fool holds back when battling an angel. And I never took you for a fool, Leda Pierce."

"Just a troublemaker." I looped my arms over his shoulders.

"Always and forever," he said against my mouth.

His words fell heavy against my lips—with the weight of finality. Of the eternity that lay before us.

Or did it? A flash of fresh panic pulsed through me. Nyx had said she would be testing my magic when this training was over. The Legion would use those magic tests to try to pair me off with another soldier. That was what they did. What if it was not Nero? I couldn't stand the thought.

Maybe I was worrying for nothing. My magic was so weird that it was unlikely anyone was magically compatible with me.

I pushed those worries down with all the other turmoil bubbling in my stomach, all those things I was ignoring because there was not a damn thing I could do about any of them right now.

A second emotion pulsed through my veins. Hope,

sparked by the fact that Nero was by my side. We'd faced dark angels and demons. We'd survived immortal plots. And we'd done it all together. So we would get through all of this together too.

There was something linking us, something bigger than all of this: love. And destiny. I truly did believe that Nero and I were destined to be together, the wars of gods and demons be damned.

I moved in to kiss Nero, but an arm caught me, pulling me back. My gaze slid sideways to Colonel Fireswift.

"Consorting with the enemy," he growled as his hand clamped down harder on my arm, leading me across the room. "Have you no shame?"

"The enemy?" I laughed. "You are my enemy more than Nero is."

You could have bounced diamonds off Colonel Fireswift's hard face. "Not right now."

Nero started moving toward us, rage burning in the inferno of his eyes. If I didn't stop him now, he was going to kill Colonel Fireswift. And then the gods would kill him.

I met Nero's eyes, shaking my head once. Then I freed myself from Colonel Fireswift's grip.

I'm all right, I broadcast to Nero.

He stopped walking toward us. *If he hurts you again, he won't be all right.*

You can't kill another angel. The gods forbid it.

The gods won't ever know. There won't be anything left of Fireswift to find.

A shiver trickled down my spine. I wasn't sure if it was born from horror or delight. And that scared me more than anything.

"You are taking this entirely too seriously," I told

Colonel Fireswift. "It's a game. And right now, the gods are too busy fighting themselves to smite us."

"This is nothing but a minor skirmish," he replied. "It will soon be resolved. The gods have been switching alliances for millennia. They will not allow their mutual dislike to override their judgment."

"It's still a game."

"The games of gods play out upon the backbones of mortals. They have dire stakes beyond mere life or death. You either play by their rules, or you face the consequences." His cold eyes snapped to Nero, then back to me. "As Windstriker very well knows. And so should you by now. When you break the rules, you might be able to dodge it for a short while, but the gods' justice always catches up to you in the end."

The doors to the audience chamber flew open, heralding in a wave of godly soldiers. Buried inside their perfect rows, shackled at the wrists and ankles, walked Damiel and Stash. The sight of them captured and chained up like this threw ice-cold fear on the fire of hope burning inside of me. My optimistic insistence that everything would work out—that it just *had* to work out—petered out, like air bursting out of a punctured tire.

"It seems today is that day of reckoning for your lover's father," Colonel Fireswift said, glancing at Nero. Then his gaze locked on to me, like a hawk spotting his prey. "And for your friend."

CHAPTER 20

THE GODS' JUSTICE

All discussions and arguments in the gods' hall promptly died a swift death. Every eye in the room tracked Damiel and Stash as Faris's soldiers brought them before the gods' thrones.

"Enter the traitors and rebels," Valora declared, her voice as clear as a bell. "The insurgents. The evaders of the gods' justice."

She certainly was laying on the drama thick.

"And one of them is sitting on her father's throne," a voice pierced the hall.

Valora's eyes darted around, trying to figure out who had spoken against her. They fell on Meda.

Zarion glowered at Meda. "Says she who betrayed us to the Guardians."

"Be silent, Zarion. This mess is all your fault," Meda snapped at him. "You and your lust."

"Lust comes in many forms, Meda. Including your lust for power. For control. That is the root of your abominable experiments on monsters." Zarion's eyes flickered to Maya. "And on angels. You tortured your poor sister's lover."

"Shut up, Zarion," Maya snapped. "I don't need your help. Or your sympathy."

"Nor do you have either," he growled. "Your weak heart and your sister's thirst for power lost us an angel. Wardbreaker would have been better off if you'd killed him the moment you realized you had feelings for him."

"I am not you," Maya growled between clenched teeth. She drew her sword.

Flames flared to life on Zarion's hands. Meda aimed a gun at his head. Maya drew a second sword and pointed it at her sister. A coil of hissing blue magic formed in Valora's hands. Aleris had summoned a flock of wild red bats out of thin air. They spiraled around him like a spinning cyclone. Ronan watched them all, his arms folded across his chest, psychic magic pulsing out from him like a drum's heavy war beat.

"Do you still think this is just a minor skirmish between the gods, soon to be resolved?" I asked Colonel Fireswift as Zarion shot a fireball at Meda's head.

Colonel Fireswift's eyes darted between the gods, his jaw clenching up. He looked like his world, everything he knew to be proper and dignified and orderly, was crumbling to pieces before his eyes.

"The gods' justice will prevail," he said stubbornly.

"Enough," Faris's voice boomed over the bickering gods.

The walls shook—and everyone just stopped. I could feel his siren magic rippling over me and everyone else in this room. It hadn't compelled the gods, but it had made them stop and listen.

"That's better." Faris waved Damiel and Stash toward him. "Come forward, prisoners."

Faris's godly soldiers nudged Damiel and Stash forward

with their weapons. The silver-tipped spears shone like immortal weapons. Damiel and Stash sure moved away from the spears like the weapons had the power to hurt—or even kill—an immortal.

"General Damiel Dragonsire," Faris began. "You stand accused—"

"The Legion of Angels is my domain, Faris," Ronan cut in, stepping forward. "I will determine how it is run. And I will decide how traitors are dealt with," he added, his words etched in ice.

"Yes, we all see how you dealt with this traitor," Faris laughed. "By hiding him away from us." He turned to face the other gods.

They were nodding in agreement, their eyes narrowing in annoyance when they looked upon Ronan. The gods were arrogant by nature. They didn't enjoy being fooled. It was a hit to their self-proclaimed omnipotence.

And yet they were always keeping secrets from the other gods, big ones at that. As this training continued to demonstrate.

"General Dragonsire was convicted in a different era," said Ronan. "Back then, we were overly zealous, seeing threats that were not there. We'd just lost several angels to the demons, who'd corrupted their minds and magic, turning them against us."

"And you saw that same corruption in General Dragonsire's magic," Faris said. "You saw that his magic was going dark."

Nyx stepped forward, joining Ronan. "An angel doesn't slowly go dark, Faris. That's not how magic works. We all have a little light and a little dark magic in us."

"Perhaps that is true of you, Nyx. But not of us." Faris

glanced haughtily at the other gods, who looked offended by the notion that their magic was not pure light magic.

"Angels are not gods, as you've never let me forget," replied Nyx, anger cracking her cool facade.

Nyx had trained alongside the gods under Faris's rule. He must have made every day of her life miserable.

"When the Dark Force turns an angel into a dark angel, they flip their magic entirely. They transfuse it, replacing light magic with dark. We didn't understand that well enough back then," Nyx said, steadying her voice. "A dark angel no longer has his light magic powers. General Dragonsire's magic was not turned dark. His powers are still light magic, powers given to him by the gods."

"You have tested this?" Meda asked.

"Yes," replied Nyx. "The results clearly show that while his native magic contains more dark than we typically see in soldiers who survive the gods' gifts to become an angel, his powers are powered by light magic. The source of his magic is the Nectar we gave him. He is not a dark angel."

"You are simplifying things, Nyx. Apparently, an angel can be infused with dark magic while keeping his light magic, as my sweet sister has recently shown," Maya said, her words dripping with venom, her eyes full of scorn for her sister.

"If you'd seen the state of General Wardbreaker in person, you wouldn't attest that an angel can be infused with dark magic while keeping his light magic," Damiel said. "He had retained precious little of anything. And he had completely lost his mind. His magic was fragmented, broken. It shifted with his unstable moods, going from insanely powerful to completely mortal in the blink of an eye as his light and dark magics fought each other. Meda's procedure didn't work."

"It is a work in progress," Meda said.

"A work that stops now," Maya told her angrily. "Grafting dark magic onto light magic—it's obscene."

"The demons are growing stronger," said Meda. "We need something to counter them. We need soldiers who can resist dark magic. It is too easy to kill an angel with a Venom bullet. As we saw last month."

Isabelle Battleborn cringed at the reminder of her dead father.

"It's even easier to kill an angel with a poison syringe in the name of science," Maya retorted.

"He volunteered," Meda said. "He was doing his duty."

Maya spun around to face Ronan. "Doing his duty? You knew about this?"

"No," Ronan said coolly.

"So you didn't know about Meda's experiments. You just knew that the traitor Damiel Dragonsire had killed Osiris." Maya hurled the words in his face. "And you didn't just protect Dragonsire; you allied with him. You worked with someone whose magic is as black as his soul."

"As I said, General Dragonsire's magic isn't dark. And this proves it." Nyx snapped her fingers, and a slim yellow folder appeared in each of the seven gods' hands. I hadn't known she could make objects appear out of thin air like the gods could.

"This is all irrelevant," Zarion said as the gods looked through their folders. "We are not discussing General Dragonsire's magic. We are discussing his treachery and deceit. Wardbreaker is not the only angel he killed. He killed another angel, Colonel Cadence Lightbringer. Then he faked his own death and left the Legion of Angels he had sworn to serve."

Damiel hadn't killed Cadence. He and Cadence had

staged the whole thing to make it look as though they'd both died—that Damiel had killed Cadence and that Nero had killed Damiel. I didn't volunteer that information. Telling the gods that Nero's mother was still alive would just blow open yet another secret, one I didn't think Faris knew yet. And I intended to keep it that way.

"Damiel left because the Legion's Interrogators were chasing him," I said, stepping forward. "They were trying to kill him."

"You will be silent," Zarion snapped at me. "No one cares about your opinion."

Gods, I really hoped Zarion wasn't my father. I could just imagine family dinner night. He'd probably cut out my tongue for daring to ask him to pass the potatoes.

"Don't throw stones in the hall of gods, brother," Faris told Zarion. "We will soon get to your own transgressions." Faris's gaze flickered to Stash.

Not that Faris was a better candidate for a father figure. Last year, he'd tried to use me to expose Zarion's secret, and he hadn't given up when that had failed. He'd found another opportunity in these challenges. And this time, he'd upped his game to include exposing the other gods' secrets as well while he was at it. He was still using me, under the guise of being my patron god. He was even using Aleris to strike at the other gods.

"We are dealing with General Dragonsire's treachery for the moment," Valora said. "And Ronan's."

"Treachery seems to be contagious, doesn't it?" Ronan said coolly. "Even our esteemed king, your father, fell victim to it."

Valora's lips pursed together. She didn't look happy that he was throwing her secret in her face. "It's never so simple."

"And neither is General Dragonsire's situation," Nyx said.

Valora didn't even look at her. "Very well, Ronan. General Dragonsire is your angel. He is yours to punish as you see fit."

"Ronan has already shown himself to be biased in this matter," Aleris protested. "He has been sheltering General Dragonsire."

"Enough." The word popped off her lips like a bomb. "We are moving on."

Aleris's scowl deepened. He looked pretty upset about her glossing over Damiel's betrayal. He really was obsessed with maintaining the perfect order and punishing transgressions, just as Nero had said. Colonel Fireswift should have thrown his lot in with Aleris, not Faris. Aleris was more his style.

"We now move on to the case of the demigod Stash." Valora's voice dipped to a blistering hiss, even as she shot Zarion a withering look. "And Zarion's indiscretion."

The air crackled with Zarion's irritation. He was always so righteous. It must have been a big blow to his ego to be caught as the perpetrator of this scandal.

"Romantic entanglements with mortals are prohibited, Zarion," Valora said. "You knew that."

"So did your father."

Valora's lips hardened into a thin line. "Your behavior was obscene. This act demands a response."

"Will that response be swift and decisive, Valora? Or will you scheme for years, waiting for the right moment to stab me in the back?"

Like you did to your father.

Zarion didn't say those words, but they were implied. Everyone here knew it.

Valora's eyes pulsed with pure loathing as her gaze fell upon Stash. She looked at him like she looked at Nyx, like he represented all that went wrong when the gods were seduced by mortals and led off their holy, heavenly path.

"What to do with him..."

Valora paused. She looked like she was cooking up a juicy punishment, one that involved every terrible thing she wished she could do to Nyx. Her father had protected Nyx all those years, and now Ronan did. So Valora was redirecting her anger on Stash, who didn't have a god to watch his back.

Well, I wasn't going to have it. Zarion had tried to kill Stash when he'd still been inside his mother's womb, so the god wouldn't stick out his neck for his son now. Zarion clearly didn't care what happened to Stash. He was a problem, an embarrassment, a threat to his holiness. Something to be annihilated, not protected.

Ronan stood by Nyx because he loved her, but he and Nyx were training Stash because he possessed powerful magic that they could use. They weren't his friends. They didn't care about him as a person.

But I did. Stash was my friend, and I was not going to allow him to be tortured and executed because Zarion couldn't keep his libido in check. I moved to stand beside Stash.

"What are you doing, child?" Valora demanded.

"I'm protecting Stash."

Faris looked mildly amused, like I was nothing more than an ant standing up to the dragon that would crush it. "From whom?"

"From anyone who would do him harm," I said. "Stash didn't do anything wrong, and he doesn't deserve to be punished."

"A weed doesn't do anything wrong in isolation," Aleris told me serenely. "It is living its life, growing where it has always grown. But then, pop, you kill it. Why do you think that is?"

I frowned. "Because you decided to put a flower garden there, and the weed is in your way."

"You need to look at the big picture," said Aleris. "The weed is wild, out of control. If you allow a weed to exist, it will continue to spread. It will outgrow all the roses and carnations, all the lilies and peonies. It will wrap its spiky, ugly vines around the pretty flowers and choke the life out of them. It will block out the sun and destroy all that is right and orderly and beautiful in the world. The weed is, at its very core, chaotic."

That was the gods' worldview to a T: preserve their own order and stomp everything else into oblivion.

"Why would you protect the weed and allow the roses to die?" Aleris asked me.

"Oh, I don't know. I guess you could say I have a certain affinity for weeds. They are nature's underdogs."

Nero stared at me, silently willing me not to pour any more gas on the fire. Damiel, on the other hand, snickered.

"It's not too late to punish you, Dragonsire," Ronan warned him.

Aleris's eyes considered Stash with dispassionate appraisal. "Now we just need to decide what to do with this weed." His gaze shifted to Zarion. "And the one who planted it."

"Stash has god's blood. Powerful magic," Ronan said. "And right now, we need all the magic we can get to fight the demons. That's why we were training him."

"In secret," Valora noted.

"Because we knew exactly how you would all react to the news of his existence," Nyx told her.

Valora's nose crinkled up, as though Nyx's words stank like rotting cabbage.

"What would you have us do, Nyx?" Meda asked her. "We cannot allow indiscretions to go unpunished."

Nyx's dark brows arched. "If anyone who has erred is going on the chopping block, you all have a lot to answer for."

Anger flared in Valora's eyes. "How dare you speak to us like that, you—"

"Choose your next words wisely, Valora," Ronan said, stepping in front of Nyx.

"Indeed," Aleris agreed. "Handing out punishments is all well and good, but there's no reason to lower ourselves and allow savage emotions to get in the way of reason."

The problem with Aleris was that he was merciless in his reasoning. He wouldn't laugh at you, insult you, or snarl at you—but he would kill you just the same if he found you in violation of his perfect garden of order.

"Zarion should choose Stash's fate," Faris suggested. "After all, this mess is his. Just as General Dragonsire is Ronan's mess."

"Agreed," said Valora.

But Faris wasn't done yet. "Choose your son's fate, brother," he told Zarion. "For you will share in it."

Oh, clever. If Zarion was too harsh on Stash, then he suffered. If he went too easy on him, the other gods would determine he was just saving his own skin. And then they would punish Zarion in ways I didn't even want to imagine.

Zarion turned to the other gods for support, but they now looked even more enthusiastic about him choosing his son's punishment. They were lapping up his anxiety. The gods didn't just play games with mortals and supernaturals. They played games with the other gods. If this training had taught me anything, that was it. It had given me a rare look into the ways of gods, beyond all their glamor and magic.

"The demigod Stash will submit to hard training in Heaven's Army for a period of one month, to commence at the conclusion of this Legion training," Zarion finally said after a long pause.

A delighted smile curled Faris's lips. "You realize what this means, don't you, brother?"

"That I share in his fate. Yes, I am well aware."

"You will train with young gods. Like a child." Faris was practically snickering.

"Maybe I'll teach you a thing or two."

"Maybe. Or maybe I'll break you."

"You can certainly try," Zarion said, fire in his eyes.

"Oh, I will," Faris replied, smirking. "I will."

Zarion looked at Valora, the unspoken question in his eyes. He was waiting for her to approve.

"The punishment is acceptable," she decided.

"If Stash performs adequately, he will join Heaven's Army," Faris said.

The gods nodded in agreement, much to the apparent dismay of Ronan and Nyx. In fact, they looked even unhappier than Zarion, who was sharing in Stash's punishment. Zarion simply looked resigned—and a tad defiant.

Faris would be recruiting Stash into his army. I was sure of it, just as I was sure he'd planned all along to steal him from Nyx and Ronan. Faris had been winning a lot lately. It left a bitter taste in my mouth.

I did wonder why, out of all the possible punishments, Zarion had chosen this one. During that month of training, Faris wouldn't pass up any chance to humiliate his brother. One month might have been the blink of an eye to an immortal, but Faris would find ways to make it feel like an eternity. I knew that he would. He and his brother didn't just simply not get along; they despised each other.

Jace walked up beside me. "Intense," he commented as Faris's soldiers escorted Damiel and Stash out of the hall.

"Not as intense as the last challenge." I smirked at him. "In particular, I enjoyed watching your face during our last game of Legion as I leveled up Colonel Fireswift's soldier into an angel."

He chuckled. "Not as much as I enjoyed watching your face when you realized I could actually play the game of Legion."

"So you can play now. If that wasn't cheating, I don't know what is."

"You're slipping, Pandora." He clicked his tongue at me. "You'll never beat me at this rate."

"I still have two of the artifacts," I pointed out.

"Not for long."

"I take it from the giddy expression on your face that you are scheming something."

"Always." His smile faded. "And I'm not giddy."

I bobbed my head up and down. "Like a kid in a candy store."

He scowled at me.

"You are oddly focused on this game, considering all else that's going on," I said.

"I won't allow myself to be distracted by popcorn drama." Jace's expression was brazen, but he spoke the words quietly. He was probably afraid to loudly proclaim the clashing gods were mere popcorn drama. "If you lose sight of the goal, you will never achieve it."

"The goal to become an angel," I muttered.

He stood a little taller.

"It's too early to celebrate, Fireswift. You aren't there yet."

"But I will be. The other teams have allowed themselves to be swept up into the drama, one by one turning against their own teammate."

"It didn't take any drama to turn your father against me," I told him. "He's hated me from the get-go."

"And yet you work so well together. In fact, you two are the biggest threat standing in my way."

"I'll count myself lucky if your father doesn't try to poison me before this is all over. Or shoot me in the back."

"You certainly look oddly unconcerned about winning this." His brows drew together in suspicion. "And about becoming an angel."

I couldn't even become an angel, at least not until I figured out why the Nectar hadn't leveled me up last time. Athan claimed to know, but he hadn't clued me in.

But that was not even why I wasn't so focused on becoming an angel at the moment. There was something bigger going on here. The exodus of secrets from the gods' vaults felt like merely an appetizer, a prologue leading up to one explosive finale. Who could worry about becoming an angel when all this was going on?

"Don't confuse my relaxed confidence for apathy, Fireswift," I told Jace. "I *will* beat you."

He expelled an amused grunt, then walked away.

The buffet tables were covered in food once more, so I went to check out what they had to offer. I grabbed a bowl of fruit and cheese. I was on my way back across the room when I noticed Colonel Fireswift and General Spellsmiter were both headed my way, from opposite sides of the hall. The angels looked like they were on a warpath—and that I stood between their clashing swords. They were going to fight over getting me in their division, like dogs battling over a bone. Worse yet, a bone they each found unpalatable, even vile. And Colonel Silvertongue was watching the two angels closely; she was dead set on figuring out why they both wanted to recruit me.

So I grabbed my food, hurried through the nearest door, and disappeared into the hallway. I felt like an awkward high school teenager running out of the cafeteria to eat her lunch alone outside.

I rushed toward the exit, in desperate need of some fresh air. Instead, I encountered the overly sweet scent of inflated egos. The murmur of arguing voices stopped me in my tracks. I recognized those voices. They belonged to Faris and Zarion. I ducked behind a stone column.

"...are you plotting?" Faris demanded.

"Wouldn't you like to know?" Zarion replied. "You prance around, exposing everyone's deepest, darkest secrets. I know it was you who set this up, Faris. You and Aleris. How did you convince him to roll around in the muck with you? He abhors getting his hands dirty."

Faris smiled cryptically.

"Well, the joke is on you, Faris," Zarion hissed. "Nothing came of your scheme to ruin me."

"It's not over yet, brother."

"Yes, yes. My sentence of one month at your mercy," Zarion said mockingly. "I've survived worse. You won't break me. You won't pull any more secrets out of me."

Faris laughed. "You still don't get it. I already know all your secrets, including your biggest *indiscretion*. And unlike your tangent with that werewolf, this one wasn't an accident. Before long, the other gods will know it as well."

"You're bluffing." But Zarion's face had paled.

"We shall see. In good time."

Faris walked right past the column I was using as a hiding spot, but he didn't stop. He didn't even seem to notice me. He merely continued down the hallway and entered the main hall.

Zarion stood there in the hallway for a while, looking genuinely concerned. Then he gathered up his scattered emotions, stuck on a hard face, and walked down the hallway in the same direction as Faris had gone. He didn't spot me either.

I just stood there, thinking over what the two gods had said. *Indiscretion*. That was the word Faris had spoken, the same word Valora had used to describe Zarion's mortal affair. I didn't think that was an accident.

Was Faris referring to another of Zarion's affairs, perhaps an affair with a demon, the one that had created me? Faris seemed hellbent on exposing his brother's secret. If I was right about that *indiscretion*, I would soon find myself drowning in a sea of trouble.

CHAPTER 21

IMPRISONED

I walked down the hall, trying to clear my reeling mind. There were telepaths everywhere. I couldn't afford to let my turbulent thoughts bubble to the surface.

Crazy as it sounded, the very real possibility that Zarion might be my father wasn't actually the problem. No, as far as the gods were concerned, the real problem was my demonic mother. I wouldn't escape with a mere slap on the wrist if the gods found out about that. I wouldn't be sentenced to a month of hard training under Faris. I wouldn't even get away with a whole year of training under him.

Faris *knew*. I just knew that he knew. And before this was all over, he was going to expose me.

Trying not to allow my panic to bubble to the surface, I ran outside on dizzy steps, disappearing into the gardens. I couldn't be in a room with all those angels and gods right now. I needed space, breathing room, a chance for my racing heart to quiet—and for everything to stop spinning.

I moved slowly through the gardens, breathing in the

sweet aromas, allowing the quiet serenity of my surroundings to seep into me. I was just trying to think straight again. Hell, I'd settle for seeing straight for now. Everything was blurred. Faris's promise to Zarion that he would expose his indiscretion was playing in constant repeat inside my head, the weight of my impending doom crushing me.

I heard voices. There must have been other people out here in the gardens. I veered away from the voices. I really needed some space right now.

But no matter which way I turned, the voices didn't grow quieter or more distant. They only grew louder with every passing second, closing in on me from all sides, building up to an explosive crescendo.

"Someone, please help. I don't belong here."

I recognized that voice. It didn't belong to anyone here. It belonged to the woman from my visions.

"Let me go!"

For the first time, I saw her unobscured by shadows. She stood inside a tight prison cell, her dirty hands gripping the thick iron bars. As she shook them, trying futilely to break free, strands of her dark hair fell out of her ponytail, sticking to her smudged, sweaty face. Her clothes were ripped, likely from catching on things as she'd tried to escape the warriors hunting her. Her purple eyes were wide with fear.

The god who'd imprisoned her didn't make an appearance this time, and now that I finally saw the woman's face, I didn't recognize her either. Of course I didn't. She was just one person out of countless souls on countless worlds.

Whoever the woman was, she wasn't any stronger than a human, nor did she appear to have any spells at her disposal. She looked so weak, so helpless. She hadn't even fought back when the soldiers had chased her. But that didn't make any sense. Why would a god imprison someone without any magic whatsoever?

A quake snapped me out of the vision. I blinked. The ground wasn't trembling; *I* was. Nero's hands were on my shoulders, shaking me.

"Nero?"

"You were just standing there," he told me. "Not moving. As though you were hypnotized."

"I had another vision. I saw the woman that one of the gods is holding prisoner."

"Did you see anything that would help us rescue her?"

"No." I frowned. "Just her face. But I have this weird feeling… Do you remember the visions I had last year in the Lost City?"

"Visions of the past," he said. "Your proximity to the weapons of heaven and hell triggered them."

"I saw memories stored in those immortal artifacts, just like the gods' memories stored inside their immortal artifacts. I think it takes a very strong emotion to imprint a memory on an immortal artifact." I chewed on my lower lip, thinking it through. "The glasses exposed the gods' memories stored in those artifacts. But I didn't have the glasses last year when I saw those memories in the Lost City. And why am I seeing this woman's memories now when the rest of you are not?"

"I do not know. But your magic is unique."

I didn't want to think about my magic right now.

"Why did Zarion chose the punishment that he did, to train under Faris?" I asked. "Considering his relationship with his brother, I'd expect that to be the last thing he'd choose."

"I've thought about it." Nero didn't even comment on

my abrupt change of topic. "Zarion's chosen punishment will hurt his pride more than his body."

"Which is why this doesn't make sense. Zarion is all about pride."

"Whatever reason he has for doing this, it is greater than his pride."

"That reason would have to be one monumental task," I said. "Like hurting Faris."

"Exactly. Think about it. Zarion got himself into his brother's kingdom, into his castle, up close and personal with Faris's army—for a whole month. There's a lot he can do in one month. A lot of snooping. A lot of scheming. And, when the time is right, a lot of damage. Plus, he got his son in there with him."

"But Stash hates him," I said. "Zarion killed his mother. And he tried to kill Stash too."

"To cover up his secret," Nero reminded me. "Now that the secret is out in the open, Zarion has no need to kill Stash. But he *will* try to use him. Stash is a demigod, a powerful being. Zarion would be a fool not to at least try to sway him to his side. I bet Zarion has it all worked out. Faris will train Stash with the other gods, making him stronger. Faris already said he will take Stash into Heaven's Army if he does well. Which means Zarion will have eyes in Faris's domain, a spy in his brother's army. He'll be able to keep track of what Faris is up to."

"Zarion is assuming Stash will suddenly and completely abandon his hatred for him and just do whatever daddy dearest says," I said.

"Zarion and Stash will be united in their punishment," replied Nero. "And in suffering under the same god: Faris. For a whole month. That united suffering will forge a bond between them."

I shook my head. "I don't believe it. I don't think two people can go from enemies to allies in just one month."

"You and Colonel Fireswift are allies," Nero pointed out.

I snorted. "Colonel Fireswift still hates me. And I'm not overly fond of him either."

"But you have come to an understanding. You're united in a goal, a purpose. This sort of thing starts out as a necessary alliance, but it grows into more. If this training continued for a month, you might even come to like Colonel Fireswift."

"If this training continued for a month, I think I'd be contemplating desertion," I laughed. "Assuming Colonel Fireswift didn't kill me first."

"It's only been a few days since you were teamed up. You'd be surprised how unifying a common goal is. You might come to change your mind about him," Nero said. "And this training is nothing compared to the suffering Faris will inflict on Stash. Zarion will be right there to help Stash, to share in his suffering and soothe his pain. By the end of the month, Stash will come to trust Zarion."

"It's just so hard to believe."

"Zarion didn't pick that punishment by accident," Nero said. "He realized that having Stash's loyalty—and even love—was worth a temporary blow to his ego."

Nero sounded so sure that I couldn't help but believe him. Maybe he was right. He'd seen a lot in his long tenure at the Legion. Zarion certainly was arrogant enough to believe that he could succeed in gaining Stash's loyalty.

I took a deep breath. Avoiding my problem felt better than thinking about it, but that wouldn't make it go away. I needed Nero's help. He'd have an idea of what to do.

"We have another problem," I told him. "Faris."

"Faris is always a problem."

"More so right now than ever before. I overheard him and Zarion bickering in the corridor. Faris mentioned another secret Zarion has." I looked around to see if anyone was close.

"We are alone," Nero assured me.

I'd thought so, but I couldn't help but feel like someone was always watching. Probably because, during this training, someone really was always watching. It had made me paranoid.

"When taunting his brother, Faris used the word *indiscretion*," I continued. "I think he means Zarion had another affair. And another child."

"You believe he means you."

"I don't want to believe it, but it seems I have no choice in the matter." My fake smile, the bandage I'd pasted over my tumultuous soul, wobbled. "I guess we'll find out soon enough. Faris promised Zarion he would expose all his secrets. I guess that makes me collateral damage." My tongue felt as dry and rough as sandpaper—no, a sandstorm.

Nero wrapped his arms around me, hugging me to him. "We'll take care of it."

It wasn't an actual plan, but it was all I needed to hear right now. I allowed myself to sink into him. It felt so good when he was holding me. I just knew we would work this out. Together.

"So far, Faris has exposed the other gods' secrets in the exact same way," Nero said.

"By using the glasses."

Nero kissed the top of my head, then he pulled back and met my eyes. "Hand me the glasses."

I looked at his open hand, palm extended up. "No way I'm falling for that one," I chuckled weakly.

"I'm not going to steal them, Leda. I'm going to destroy them."

I met his eyes. "You're serious."

"Dead serious."

Paranoia gripping me once more, I glanced around for anyone who might be eavesdropping. "They belong to a god," I whispered when I found no one around.

"They *belonged* to a god," he countered. "They belong to you now."

"We both know that's merely a technicality, Nero. This rule-twisting is my bad influence on you."

"I happen to enjoy your bad influence on me."

The way he said it made my magic purr in appreciation. I was moving toward him before I knew it, my lips meeting his.

"The glasses still belong to Aleris," I said between rushed, rough kisses. "He and Faris won't be happy if we break them. They are using them to air the gods' dirty laundry."

"I won't tell if you won't." The way he said it was so deliciously naughty.

I wanted to do more than just kiss him, but he held me back. He extended his open palm to me again. I handed over the glasses.

Nero set them on the ground, stepped back a few paces, then hit them with a storm of elemental spells. Nothing happened. He tried telekinetic blasts and corrosive powders. He tried breaking them with his hands and crushing them beneath his feet. He even tried shifting them into something brittle and breaking that. Nothing worked.

I slouched. "I don't think anything we have can put a dent in those glasses. They're an immortal artifact."

"Everything can be destroyed, given the right weapon," he said with unwavering confidence. "We just need another immortal artifact to do it."

I handed him Zarion's hairbrush. He slammed it against the glasses. Sparks flew, but neither immortal artifact appeared worse for wear.

"We need an immortal artifact that's an actual weapon," he decided, returning the hairbrush and glasses to me.

I tucked them into my jacket. "You didn't happen to bring along the weapons of heaven and hell, did you?"

"Unfortunately, no. They didn't fit inside my backpack."

I laughed at the joke, but it was a short and puffed laugh, strained nearly to the breaking point. And I was breaking right along with that laugh. The remaining secrets —including my own—would be revealed any time now. And without any way to break Aleris's glasses, I feared we could not stop the deluge.

Nero set his hands on my shoulders and met my eyes. "We will find a way. I won't let Faris expose you."

The conviction and passion in his eyes was so hard, so true, that I couldn't help myself. All my fear and anger and pain collided, exploding into a passion that consumed me. I threw myself at him.

"Pandora." He caught my wandering hands. "We need to focus on the glasses."

"Forget the stupid glasses. Everything is falling apart, Nero. And I don't know if we will get out of it this time. I want to feel a single moment of happiness—now, before it all comes crashing down."

"We will find a way." His lips brushed against mine. "We always find a way."

His fingers stroked through my hair, freeing it from the tight ponytail. With wicked, excruciating slowness, he brushed away the smooth locks. Fervent impatience gripped me. I tilted my head and presented my throat to him, offering him my blood, my body, everything I had. Ruthless and sensual, his emerald gaze slid over me like liquid lightning.

His hands gripped my back, holding me so tightly that I couldn't move. I could barely breathe. There was only the pounding, persistent ache of my own denied desire. His mouth dipped lower, closing over my throbbing vein.

His fangs penetrated my skin, and a pulse of white-hot pleasure shot through my entire body. My knees were weakening, my pulse racing faster with every delectable draw of his mouth. Groaning, he drank me in with insatiable hunger. Ribbons of savage, searing desire cut me deep and hard, spiraling me out of control.

He drew back.

"Don't stop," I panted.

"I'm taking too much."

"I am immortal."

"Immortal or not, losing too much blood will weaken you," he said sensibly.

To hell with sensibility.

"That's all part of your plan, right?" I moaned, breathing heavily. "The only way you have a chance of beating me at these challenges."

"Every time I drink from you, you taste better, Leda," Nero whispered against my neck. His tongue traced the marks he'd left there. "Sweeter. Riper."

My pulse popped against his mouth, inviting him to

devour me. His mouth closed over mine, kissing me savagely. Then he pulled away roughly, gripping my hand.

"Come with me," he spoke against my lips.

"Where?"

"To my room. It's too busy here."

I vaguely heard the voices of other people in the gardens, but I couldn't focus on them. Not when Nero looked at me like that.

"Come with me." His voice had grown thick, heavy.

I bit my lip coyly. "Why?"

"Very well. Have it your way," he laughed, grabbing my butt. "We can stay here. But your screams might draw attention."

My face was flushed, my nipples on fire, and the inside of my thighs slick. "You're awfully sure of yourself, General."

"Lots of practice, Pandora."

His words were like a splash of white-hot pleasure against my skin.

"Practice at being sure of yourself or at making women scream?"

"Enough talk." He bit my lip, drawing a drop of blood. "Enough insubordination."

"So if I don't go with you to have sex in your room, that's insubordination?" I laughed.

"Yes," he replied, perfectly serious.

"Your room, you say? Won't Delta mind?" I asked wickedly.

"Delta is off hating me for my father's deeds. And I will bar the door. If she tries to interrupt us, I will kill her."

I couldn't tell if he was serious or if it was just a figure of speech. And, honestly, right now I was finding it hard to care.

So I allowed Nero to lead me to the stairs, our hands linked, our gazes locked. Thankfully, his room was on the first level up. I wasn't sure I could have held out any longer than that.

We slipped into his room. Nero did, in fact, bar the door very securely. I'd never seen that many locks and deadbolts on a door, but even that wasn't enough for Nero. He piled on a few magic wards of his own.

Then, with that done, he turned around to face me, his eyes burning with magic. His wings spread out from his body, a stunning dark tapestry of glossy black, blue, and green feathers. His wings were humming to me, their sweet, seductive serenade slowly parting me from all rational thought. The world and all its problems were just background noise now, distant and muffled. I knew only Nero.

He closed the distance between us in a fraction of a second. Before I could exhale, his hands were on me. My leather jacket hit the floor. My tank top followed. I peeled off his clothes one-by-one, worshipping his body with my eyes and hands.

"Nero," I said, my gaze sliding down his naked body.

"Leda," he replied smoothly.

There wasn't a shred of clothing on either of us.

"From the moment I walked into the Crystal Falls training hall and saw you there, I've wanted you," he said, his voice thick with lust. "I'm not waiting a moment longer."

A deep horn bellowed through the castle, resounding off the thick walls. Its call was an unwelcome jolt back to hard, cruel reality. The gods were summoning everyone back to their audience chamber.

CHAPTER 22

DARK WORLD

I dropped my head to Nero's chest. "Maybe they're just announcing dessert."

The gods' horn roared again. The noise penetrated the thick walls of the great castle. It sounded like it had been blown inside this room, right in front of me.

Unburying my face from Nero's chest, I looked up at him. "Yeah, I know," I sighed. "I don't believe it either."

Begrudgingly, I started gathering my clothes. They were scattered all across the room.

"Why do you think the gods are summoning us all to the hall?" I asked Nero as I plucked my bra out of a fruit bowl. "Maybe they're sending everyone home so they can fight it out without an audience?"

He chuckled. "You are a splash of refreshing optimism in this den of deceit."

"Yeah, well, someone has to counter all the omnipresent doom and gloom."

I felt better now, after spending some time alone with Nero. Fear no longer gripped me. United, together as a team, Nero and I could face anything.

If only our time together hadn't been cut short. In this training, we'd been forced onto different teams, fighting against each other rather than with each other. The gods probably thought it was the funniest thing ever to pit us against those we loved—and to pair us with those we despised. They thought they could dissolve our friendships and love.

Well, the joke was on them. Fighting against Nero had only made me appreciate how great it felt to be on the same team with him.

I located my underwear dangling from the ceiling fan. How the hell had they ended up all the way up there? The fan was too high up to reach, so I had to poke the lacy garment with my telekinetic magic to nudge it off. Surely, the gods would have been absolutely ecstatic to learn that this was how their gifts of magic were being used.

"You know, I am tempted to leave them up there for Delta to find," I said, pulling on my underpants.

"I have no objections."

"To my lack of underwear?" I chuckled. "Noted."

"To your leaving your underwear here. Or your other clothes as well."

"That would be a funny sight, wouldn't it? If I were to walk naked into the gods' hall, everything out there for everyone to see?"

"Let them see." His chest was pressed hard against my back, each word buzzing against my skin. "Let them all know that you're mine. And only mine." His hands closed over my hips.

"Feeling rather frisky, are you, General?"

"We've already established that when it comes to you, Pandora, I cannot control myself."

"If only we had more time," I sighed wistfully.

When I turned around and saw he already had all his clothes on, I couldn't help but frown in disappointment. "You and I have very different ideas of what no self-control means, Nero."

He'd had enough control to put his clothes on in record time. His efficiency transcended battlefields and training halls. And I was standing here in nothing but my underwear…because a part of me was still hoping that Nero would throw me down on the bed, gods' summons be damned.

But that wouldn't be prudent. Gods, I really hated being prudent. It was even less fun than being punctual.

"Don't confuse multitasking with disinterest, Pandora," Nero told me. "I can dress myself and undress you with my mind at the same time."

True to his angel nature, he did mean his words quite literally. Even as I put on my bra and tank top, I felt his telekinetic magic tugging at my clothes. He was indeed undressing me with his mind. Nero's magic brushed against my skin, sliding my tank top's strap off my shoulder. The hot, caressing breath of his magic kiss trickled down my body.

I shivered. "It isn't nice to tease, Nero," I chided him, my words cracking. I rose to my tiptoes, leaning into him.

"Who's teasing?" he asked silkily. The white-hot brand of his magic's touch burned my body.

"You are most certainly teasing," I gasped. "You have no intention of following through. You know we don't have time."

"Multitasking, Pandora."

He slid my leather jacket over me. Then he zipped my pants closed. His hands were professional, efficient. His magic, on the other hand, was a whole other story. It was feeling me up and down, penetrating me deep to my wanton, wicked core, stoking my desire until every part of me from head to toe trembled.

I was fully dressed. He was fully dressed. The gods were waiting for us. And I just didn't care.

"Nero," I gasped.

He opened the door for me. I stepped into the hallway, barely seeing where I was going. Nero's magic continued to touch me, to tease and torture me. A sweat broke out on my brow. A single irrefutable thought rang loud and clear in my mind: if I didn't have him right now, I was going to die. A whimper blossomed on my lips.

"Control, Pandora," he whispered.

I struggled to gather up the tattered remains of my higher brain functions. There were other people in the hallway. Like Faris's soldiers. I couldn't slam Nero against the nearest wall and have my way with him, no matter what his misbehaving magic was doing to me.

I gritted my teeth and glared at him. "You are an evil, depraved angel," I snapped at him when we were alone in the hallway once more.

Nero leaned in and growled against my lips, "So evil and depraved that you want to drag me back to my room."

My hands clutched the back of his head, drawing him closer. "Yes, please."

His hand slowly stroked down my face, tracing my neck, my shoulder, all the way down my side, grazing my breast. I squirmed.

"As long as we're enemies, I don't think that would be appropriate," he declared, a devious spark in his eyes.

"I will get you back for this, General." My voice ground like crushed gravel.

He bowed, his gaze never leaving mine. "I'm thoroughly looking forward to it."

Shooting me an easy smile, he walked through the door and entered the gods' audience chamber. I took a moment to catch my breath, to calm myself, to reel in my raging libido. Then I followed him into the chamber. A quick visual scan of the room told me I was the last to arrive. All the gods, angels, and Legion soldiers were already here. Not that I was surprised. After all, I'd had to find my underwear first.

"The next challenge is about to begin," Faris declared.

"They are changing the plan," I whispered to Nero. "It wasn't supposed to be until tomorrow."

"I'd imagine the gods are eager to learn all the other gods' secrets, and then put this whole thing behind them."

"If Faris has anything to say about it, they won't be putting it behind them any time soon." I met Colonel Fireswift's glare, his silent command to join him. Oh, goody. "Duty calls, honey." I kissed Nero's cheek. "The gods are watching. Please don't kill Colonel Fireswift, even though he's an asshole."

Nero grunted. I took that as an agreement. Nero wasn't foolish enough to attack another angel in front of the gods.

"We've all been waiting for over five minutes," Colonel Fireswift snapped as soon as I was standing beside him. "What took you so long to answer the gods' summons?"

"I was just getting some air."

"It's hard to get air with your mouth glued to Windstriker's."

"Were you spying on me?"

"I don't need to. Your face is flushed. And there's blood on your neck. I can see where he bit you."

I flashed him a grin. "Jealous?"

Colonel Fireswift glared at me like he was contemplating whether setting me on fire or poisoning me was the better punishment. I shrugged it off and just kept smiling.

"You're not even trying to be discreet about it." His words cut like a whip. His eyes zeroed in on the bite marks on my neck.

I was worried he'd demand once more that I heal myself with the fairy magic I did not possess, but he didn't say another word. He just shook his head with detached disapproval.

"The next god you will need to steal from is Faris," Athan declared, glancing at the god standing beside him.

Faris looked relaxed, *too* relaxed considering all the godly secrets that the challenges had thus far revealed. Of course, he *had* orchestrated this whole thing. Likely, his item would merely allow him to expose the other gods' secrets. Just like the glasses of his ally Aleris had done.

The seven ruling gods summoned their teams of two forward.

"You two will go through first, before the other teams," Faris declared when we were standing in front of his magic mirror. "Come with me."

Colonel Fireswift and I followed him through the mirror. A dark world waited for us on the other side—and a massive black castle of spires and spikes. We stood on the castle's highest balcony. In one direction, a sea of tall red grass spread out from the castle, stretching to the horizon; in another, dense forests blanketed the ground around the castle.

Pink lightning flashed through the dark storm clouds swirling overhead, rumbling like a giant's empty belly screaming for food. I was hit with the unsettling notion that the clouds were, in fact, hungry—and that they planned to eat us to satiate that hunger.

"What is this place?" I asked, looking around. Yes, Faris's world was frightening, but it was also wondrous, albeit in a formidable, military-might sort of way.

"This is one of my castles," the god replied.

"*One* of your castles?"

"I have many," Faris declared smugly. "This is my stronghold on Gravite, one of my worlds."

Wow. Many castles on many worlds. With all the hair-pulling and bickering, I'd admittedly begun to think of the gods like they were people too. But Faris's words reminded me that I couldn't be more wrong. His statement had put this all in the cosmic scale. He controlled many castles and many worlds. His power and influence spanned planets and galaxies. The gods weren't people. Not at all. The universe was their playground, and I and everyone else were just props to be manipulated and moved around to suit their aspirations.

"Here on Gravite, we are at the outskirts of the gods' influence," Faris said. "It is a distant place, far from the eyes of the other gods."

I wondered what exactly Faris was plotting here, 'far from the eyes of the other gods'.

But asking that would be pretty cheeky, even for me. So instead I said, "What is it that we need to protect in this challenge?"

Faris turned, his long cloak swishing around him as he moved. The cloak was black on the outside, so dark that no light got through, and blood red on the inside. As the god moved, the sanguine material flowed silkily behind him, as though it had been woven from the hot, freshly-spilled blood of his enemies.

We followed him into the building. The chamber inside resembled a war room more than a bedroom. Rows of weapons hung from every wall. Between the knives and swords and spears, a thick black brush had painted strange symbols on the red walls. Those symbols felt familiar somehow, but no matter how long I squinted at them, I couldn't read them.

They're magical, I realized.

The symbols hummed to me like musical notes, an ancient language lost to this world. Each word practically bursted off the wall with powerful magic. If only I knew what they were saying to me.

Beside me, Colonel Fireswift didn't stare overly long at the symbols. Unlike me, he clearly couldn't hear them singing. So I kept moving, resisting the urge to stop and analyze the symbols, to decrypt their secrets.

Faris had stopped in front of a tall cabinet as high as the ceiling. It looked like a wardrobe. More of those ancient symbols were painted over the cabinet's dark wooden doors. I struggled not to stare at them, even as their singing grew louder inside my head.

Faris's dispassionate gaze slid from me to Colonel Fireswift. "This is what the other teams will try to steal from me. This is what you must protect." He waved his hand, and the doors to the wardrobe parted, revealing an impressive display of weapons.

We didn't merely have one item to protect. We had many. It was a whole set of weapons. I took a closer look at them. I recognized those immortal artifacts. They were the weapons of heaven and hell, which Nero and I had recovered from the Lost City last year.

CHAPTER 23

DOOMED TO FAIL

My eyes panned over the weapons of heaven and hell. The set of silver armor. The shield and sword. And the gun that had given me the scar in my abdomen. They were supposed to be locked up inside Nero's vault. How had they gotten all the way out here, on some distant world so far from Earth?

"You recognize these artifacts." Faris gauged my reaction.

"Yes."

"You have seen them."

I hadn't just seen them. I'd used them. Of course I didn't volunteer that information. I didn't say anything at all.

"Those are the weapons of heaven and hell," Colonel Fireswift said. "Ancient, rumored immortal artifacts of great power. No one has seen them in centuries."

"Your teammate recovered them from the Lost City last year," Faris said as he locked the cabinet with a spell.

Colonel Fireswift looked at me, his eyes narrowing. "I knew you were up to something in that city."

I ignored him, turning to Faris instead. "How did you get them?"

"You shall soon find out."

"Along with the other gods, angels, and anyone else nearby," I commented.

However this had come to be, however he'd gotten his hands on the weapons of heaven and hell, I was pretty certain the tale didn't implicate him. Instead, it would expose one of the other gods.

Like Zarion. Just a few hours ago, Faris had threatened to expose his indiscretion. That meant exposing me. I was connected to the weapons of heaven and hell. Somehow. They'd spoken to me, shown me lost memories. And I'd been able to control them without even touching them. But what was my connection to the weapons?

"Whose secret lies at the end of this challenge?" I asked Faris.

"You are more skilled than you appear," he replied coolly. "It's a shame that your lack of civility and discipline has confined you to this sad, purposeless existence."

Colonel Fireswift nodded in agreement. He'd been saying the same thing—for basically forever.

Faris was certainly one to lecture me about my apparent lack of civility. I wasn't the one who'd exposed the gods' secrets for the sole purpose of sowing discord. I didn't push everyone down, so I could rise to the top.

That was all this training had been about: Faris's proxy war against the other gods. He'd used it to strike out at them, to turn them against one another.

And Colonel Fireswift was helping him. I had to wonder what Faris had promised him as a reward. Colonel Fireswift was loyal—to the gods. To entice him to throw his lot in with Faris specifically, the god would have had to offer him a tantalizing prize. Colonel Fireswift wasn't stupid; he'd negotiate a good deal for himself to counter the very real risk of incurring the other gods' wrath.

Admittedly, right now it looked like there wasn't much risk. Colonel Fireswift had apparently picked the winning team. Faris was on a roll, weakening one god after another by exposing their most guarded secrets.

But to what end? I had to figure out what Faris's end game was. What was his grand finale?

If I'd thought Faris would answer the question outright, I'd have asked him. But from what I knew of him, a straight answer was a very unlikely outcome to that conversation. Rather than answering my question, he'd probably just kill me.

"Where will the other teams appear on this world?" I asked instead. I had to concentrate on the task at hand—and not the possibility that this challenge would expose me. Maybe this wasn't even about me. "Will the Legion teams appear inside the castle or out there?" I pointed down at the massive forest and open red prairie which surrounded the castle.

"I can't tell you that," replied Faris.

"Because you don't know, or because you don't want to tell us?"

Faris smiled. It was the smile of a hawk who'd spotted its prey.

I sighed. This was just awesome.

"How many of your soldiers protect the castle?" Colonel Fireswift asked him.

"A dozen."

"Only a dozen?" Colonel Fireswift's eyes widened. "For a castle of this size?"

"Most of the soldiers stationed at this castle are

currently otherwise occupied with important matters. I reassigned them for the time being."

"At the exact moment your most prized possession is in danger," I said. "Very clever."

It was then, as I met Faris's unconcerned eyes, that I realized he fully intended for us to fail in our task. He was setting us up. I wanted to scream at him for putting me in danger so he could expose another god's deepest secrets, but I said nothing.

"You're catching on," Faris commented.

I didn't know if he'd read my thoughts and realized that I'd figured out his plan, or if he was commending me for finally shutting up. From the look Colonel Fireswift was giving me, the angel was clearly in the latter camp.

When I turned back to Faris, he was gone. He'd simply vanished. As if it weren't already abundantly clear, the God of Heaven's Army wasn't going to help us any further. Not that he'd been of any real help so far. Quite the contrary. He'd only doomed us to fail.

"We need to set up the defenses," Colonel Fireswift told me.

"How are the two of us supposed to defend a whole castle?"

"We have twelve of Faris's soldiers."

"Who have probably been instructed to stand by and do nothing," I pointed out.

After all, Faris wanted the secret inside the weapons of heaven and hell to be revealed. He was making it all too easy for the invaders.

"We can't depend on Faris's soldiers," I said.

"So that leaves just the two of us."

Colonel Fireswift looked determined and ready to defend Faris's possessions. That made me wonder how much in the loop about everything the god was actually keeping him. Faris probably had to make this farce of a challenge appear convincing to the other gods. He had to convince them that he really was trying to defend his possession, that he was afraid the memories inside of it would expose him. That was his game: to attack the other gods without them ever realizing he was behind it all.

I stepped out onto the balcony after Colonel Fireswift. He was visually scanning the castle's exterior defenses.

"The other teams could very well pop up right inside the castle," I said.

In fact, they probably would. Anything to make it easier for them to get to the weapons of heaven and hell.

"The odds are stacked against us," I added.

Purposefully and by our own patron god, I added silently to myself.

"But you have an idea."

"What makes you think that?" I asked him.

"You always have an idea." He crinkled his nose. "Something underhanded. Something dirty."

"Well, you know how we cockroaches are, all dirty and underhanded. So unbecoming of a Legion soldier," I said. "So the question is: how badly do you want to win?"

"We must not fail," he declared, answering my earlier question. Ok, so Faris hadn't told him he intended us to fail at defending his artifacts.

I nodded. "And we won't fail."

He waited. I didn't say anything more.

"You certainly do like to put on a show," he said with a steely glare.

I snorted. "Hello, pot. Meet kettle."

He narrowed his eyes at me.

"You are an angel. You live and breathe drama," I told him.

"I will never understand you, Leda Pierce," he grumbled. "Never. Not even if you defy all odds, surviving your own foolishness to live a long, immortal life. I will still fail to piece together some semblance of sense to your existence."

"Good. If you don't understand me, that makes it harder for you to defeat me."

He glowered at me. "We are on the same team."

"You might want to remind yourself of that little fact time and again, Colonel."

He scowled at me. Obviously, my critique was unwelcome. "Do you even have a plan?" he demanded.

"That depends."

"On?"

"On whether your unique angel powers allow you to be in multiple places at once. Preferably a few hundred places at once."

"No."

"Hmm."

"Hmm? That's it?" he demanded. "See how easily your plans crumble when they are built on hot air?"

"Hey, it's not my fault your magic is lacking," I shot back.

Fire burned in his eyes. He looked like he was going to explode.

"Well, what is *your* ingenious plan?" I asked him.

His scowl deepened.

"I thought so," I said. "You don't have one. You're so used to fighting when you have all the magic and power and numbers in your favor. You don't know what to do when everything goes to shit."

Magic flashed behind me, then Jace and Leila were standing with us on the balcony. Damn that Faris. He was making this all too easy for the other teams.

"Well, it looks like our time just ran out," I told Colonel Fireswift.

"Truer words have never been spoken," said Jace.

"I'm sure we can handle the two of you," I countered, smirking.

I was less confident about warding off all the other teams at once. Magic flashed again. And again. And again. One by one, the other teams popped up all around us. The gigantic balcony suddenly felt very tiny.

I considered the situation. The other teams had to get through us to win Faris's artifacts. But they had to get through one another as well. They were all competitors in this. That would divide their attention. I wasn't sure how much that would help, but maybe I could do something with it.

I was thinking up a way to use my siren magic to make all the teams focus on fighting one another, when a ripple of magic shook the ground below, rustling the grass and leaves. I glanced down in horror as an army of dark deities emerged from the forest. Hell had belched and spat out a demonic army. There were so many of them, a seemingly endless sea of demons swarming the grounds around the castle, preparing to strike.

"I don't think this was part of Faris's plan," I muttered.

CHAPTER 24

WEAPONS OF HEAVEN AND HELL

Faris had sent away his soldiers, leaving his castle exposed. And he'd done it all to lay a trap, to make it easy for the other gods' teams to steal the weapons of heaven and hell from him.

Well, that ingenious plan had backfired big time. The demons had seen his castle was vulnerable and moved in to attack. Faris hadn't just made this challenge too easy for our competing Legion teams; he'd made it too easy for the demons too.

Down below, the demons were hurling spells at the castle. The castle's magic was holding them off—for now—but without Faris's soldiers to fortify the defenses, this wouldn't last long. The magic shield would fall, and the demonic army would swarm the castle. They'd claim the weapons of heaven and hell, and that might finally give them the power they needed to return to Earth. The resulting war between gods and demons would tear my world apart.

"The demons are trying to break through the castle's

defenses," I said to the other Legion teams on the balcony. "We need to stop them."

"This is merely part of the challenge," Colonel Silvertongue argued. "We must stay on target."

"You can stay on target to your own destruction," I told her. "I am going to force out the demons' army."

"By yourself?" General Spellsmiter scoffed.

"Of course not." I grinned. "You are all going to assist me."

"Assist," Colonel Silvertongue hissed, her nostrils flaring in agitation. "You forget your place."

"The gods will send soldiers to defend this world," General Spellsmiter said. "They will not allow it to fall to the demons."

"Wake up." I snapped my fingers. "The gods are watching. If they were going to send in soldiers, they would have done it as soon as the demons crossed into this world."

"The demons have disrupted the magic of the mirrors that allow the gods to gaze into this world." Nyx pointed out the windows between the balcony and chamber inside.

The glass was clouded over, milky and foggy, not clear. If the gods really used those mirrors to gaze into other worlds, right now they'd see nothing of this one.

"But if the gods can't see into this world, they will know something is wrong and come here." I looked to Nyx for confirmation. "Right?"

"The members of the gods' council will not come here themselves," the First Angel said. "They won't risk their own lives by stepping into an unknown, dangerous situation. Not without some idea of what's going on here. They will send in Heaven's Army first."

Heaven's Army. That meant Faris's very well-dressed soldiers.

"How long will that take?" I asked.

"Ronan has been keeping an eye on Faris's soldiers' movements," Nyx said. "He told me the soldiers departed this world yesterday. Faris sent them into battle against the demons' forces on Samaran. There is a terrible battle waging there. At the moment, Faris has the upper hand. He cannot afford to divert those soldiers back here just yet, or the battle will be lost."

So that was where Faris's soldiers had gone. He hadn't sent them away to make this challenge easy for the other gods' teams—or at least not *only* to make it easy.

"How much longer will the battle on Samaran continue?" I asked.

"At least the rest of the day," Nyx told me. "Last I heard, Faris's forces were nearly through the demons' stronghold, but many demon soldiers remain."

"In other words, we are on our own here," I sighed. "It's up to us to drive back the demons' army."

"Yes."

I tallied up what we had: seven angels, seven other Legion soldiers, and twelve godly soldiers. That wasn't a lot, not against a few hundred demons. Hopeless wasn't a word in my vocabulary, but if it had been, I'd have been lathering the word generously into my sentences right now.

Instead, I said, "We need to reinforce the castle's defenses."

Nyx's gaze slid over the fading spell barrier that protected the castle. The demon's magic barrage had already punched more than a few holes in it. Their dark magic was eating the barrier alive. I didn't think it would last much longer than a few more minutes. It needed Faris's soldiers to reinforce its magic.

"I will gather the soldiers still here and have them

fortify the magic defenses," Nyx decided. "Many of them know me from my days of training with the gods."

Most of the other Legion soldiers joined her. Only Nero, Harker, Jace, and I remained on the balcony.

"I bet when you came here, you didn't expect to be facing a demon army," I said to Jace.

"No," he replied. "When I came here, I expected to kick your ass and make off with the artifacts you've collected."

"Don't flirt with Leda," Harker told him.

"But I wasn't..." Jace's gaze shifted between Harker's amused eyes and Nero's cold glare. He took a step away from me. "What do you want to bet that the demons are carrying those Venom weapons?" His voice was serious, all banter and fun drained from his tone.

"Likely," Nero agreed. "After they proved so effective in Memphis, they would want to try them on a larger scale."

The defense barrier broke like a mirror dropped off a high tower. The dark army rushed toward the castle. Some of the soldiers were demons or dark angels, which meant that with the magic shield down, they could fly right into the castle. We didn't have much time.

I ran inside and rushed over to the weapons' wardrobe. I reached for the handle, drawing back when Faris's protection spell snapped at my hand.

"What are you doing?"

I looked back to find Jace standing behind me. "I'm using the best weapons at our disposal to push back the demons."

I caught the threads of Faris's spell around my fingers and pulled them apart like I was unraveling a ball of yarn. The spell popped like a birthday balloon.

"You broke a god's spell," Jace said, his eyes wide.

"I'll apologize to Faris later," I promised. "*After* we've saved his castle."

Jace was shaking his head. "This is impossible."

"No, not impossible. Apologizing is easy. Gaining Faris's forgiveness is...well, I'll worry about that later."

"No, I mean, it's impossible that you could break a god's spell. And impossible that you can wield those weapons," he added as I grabbed the armor from the cabinet.

The silver armor pieces shifted shape to match my size, just as they'd changed in the Lost City to alternately fit me and fit Valiant the Pilgrim. I secured the sword and gun to my armored body. This was how I would protect the weapons of heaven and hell from the demons—by wearing them. And with their immortal power, I would push back the dark force attacking us.

I tried not to dwell on the fact that the last person to wield these armor pieces had been crushed by them. *I* had done that. Somehow, I'd controlled the armor, manipulating them into killing the man who'd tried to use them to kill Nero and Damiel and me.

It had been an impressive trick, but I hadn't been able to repeat the feat since. Controlling the weapons of heaven and hell was not as easy as it looked. Valiant had tried to wield them, but he hadn't been able to tap into their true magic, the power to kill an immortal.

I had. With the armor's power, I'd killed Valiant, a Pilgrim the gods had made immortal.

And now I had to wield them again to push back the demons' army. There was no room for doubt. I just had to do it.

"Ok," I said, gripping my shield as the castle walls quaked. "Let's greet the demons' army."

Nero and Harker were fighting back the group of demons who'd flown up to the castle. Jace and I ran onto the balcony. I aimed my gun and fired three shots, hitting three demons. They went down, but they didn't die. The gun wasn't killing them like an immortal weapon should.

A demon fired at Nero. I jumped in front of him. The dark bullet, swirling with Venom magic, hit my silver armor and dissolved into harmless smoke. At least the magic-nullifying power of the armor was working.

I fired at the demons until I ran out of bullets, then I drew my sword. The flaming blade hurt the dark soldiers, but it didn't kill them either. Why weren't the weapons of heaven and hell working for me? Why couldn't I tap into their full power?

A demon leapt onto my back, pulling me down. I jumped up, but the demon was faster. Much faster. Even before my feet hit the ground, his blade slashed across my cheek. He struck again, plunging his sword through my boot. Piercing, burning pain exploded inside my foot, shooting up my leg.

Jace caught me as I fell. "Heal yourself," he said. "I'll cover you."

The demons had the two of us surrounded, and they were closing in. Jace couldn't hold them off alone, and I wasn't much help in this condition. It was a matter of life or death. There was no time for games. I reached into my potions pouch, pulled out a slim vial, and drank it. Instantly, a comforting warmth washed over me, mending my wounds.

"Fairy's Touch is quicker," Jace said. "Why didn't you use it?"

"I can't," I admitted.

Understanding flashed in his eyes. "You don't have that power."

I swung my flaming sword, pushing back the demons.

Jace fought beside me. "You never leveled up. And you didn't die."

"Don't tell anyone."

He shook his head. "That shouldn't be possible."

"Especially don't tell your father."

"I won't say anything to anyone," Jace agreed. "Because we're friends. But if I'm going to keep secrets like this for you, Leda, I expect you to tell me what the hell is going on with you."

I could not agree to that, not entirely. *Everything* included telling him what I really was.

"We will talk later," I said.

He nodded, then turned to parry a demon's blade. Beyond him, I saw that the balcony windows had gone clear again. The milky fog obscuring them had faded. That single quick peek cost me. A demon knocked the sword from my hand. Another demon pushed me down and pinned me to the ground. I struggled, pushing against his grip in an attempt to free myself.

The first demon was reaching for my fallen sword. I hadn't been able to tap into the immortal weapon's power, but he was a deity. If he could wield it, none of us would make it off this balcony alive.

Jace realized the threat too. He knocked the demon back with a psychic blast, then grabbed the sword off the ground. He swung it. The demon staggered back, wounded but not dead. It seemed that Jace wasn't able to wield the power either.

The other demons nearby saw the sword in Jace's hand, and they recognized it. All at once, they abandoned their battles with Nero and Harker. They charged at Jace, going for the prize. He tried to fend them off, but there were too many of them. And they were coming at him too fast. He was being overrun.

Fear clutched me, fear for my friend's life. My magic sparked, igniting the sword's magic. Silver flames burst up across the blade, swallowing the weaker magic fire that had burned there just a moment ago. Jace looked at the blade, his eyes going wide. He swung it at a demon in a dark helmet. The demon fell to the ground, dead.

The other demon soldiers backed up, their frightened eyes locked on the sword of silver flames in Jace's hand. Right now, their fear of the power that they believed Jace to wield had frozen them, but their shock wouldn't last long. They would soon regroup, and then they would steal the sword from him. Even with the demon-slaying silver flames burning on his blade, Jace wouldn't be able to fight off so many demons.

Magic flashed from the windows, then an army of gods flew out of the enchanted glass, Ronan and Faris at the head of them all. The godly warriors grabbed the demons on the balcony and tossed them over the edge. Then they swooped down on the army below. The gods fought with grace and power, every moment a melody of magical notes. Outnumbered, the demons' army retreated, hundreds of soldiers as beautiful and deadly as the gods themselves.

"There are so many of them," I commented as we watched the demons disappear before our eyes. They were departing this world.

"There are many more on many other worlds," Ronan said.

I'd never felt so small in all my life. So insignificant.

Ronan turned as Nyx stepped onto the balcony, the relief apparent in his eyes.

"There were no casualties on our side." Her eyes fell upon the dead demon on the floor. "And only one on theirs."

"Uneventful, as far as battles go," Faris said, looking almost bored. Was he actually disappointed that more blood hadn't been spilled?

The other five ruling gods stepped through the mirror. This balcony had been crowded before, with seven angels and seven other Legion soldiers on it. And now I felt like I couldn't even breathe without running into someone's aura.

"You have wielded an immortal weapon to kill a demon," Valora praised Jace. "A great accomplishment, worthy of your legacy."

Though he looked wiped out from the battle, Jace stood a little taller in response to the Queen Goddess's words.

Valora glanced at me, but there was no praise in her eyes. "You're wearing something that doesn't belong to you."

She didn't realize it had been *my* magic that ignited the sword—and killed the demon. The gods thought it was Jace's doing. It was just as well. I wasn't from a Legion legacy family. If they knew I'd been the one to power the sword, they would investigate.

As I removed the pieces of silver armor, I tried to piece together how I'd been able to wield the weapons of heaven and hell again. The first time, I'd turned them against Valiant to save Nero and Damiel in the Lost City. And just now, I'd used them to protect Jace from being killed by demons. It seemed that it was my need to protect those I cared about which allowed me to tap into the magic I needed to control the artifacts.

I handed the weapons of heaven and hell back to Faris.

"None of this ever would have happened if you'd not left your castle undefended," Valora criticized Faris as he placed the artifacts in his closet.

"If I'd not sent my soldiers to Samaran, our forces would not have been victorious there against the demons," Faris countered. "We never would have pushed the demons off another world. So it was worth it."

"It was a terrible risk to take, Faris." But from the look on Ronan's face, he would have taken the risk too.

"If we are to finally win this war, risks must be taken," Faris said.

Valora's gaze panned over the collection of artifacts in the closet. "How did the famed weapons of heaven and hell come to be here in your castle?"

"Simple. I took them from Ronan and Nyx." Faris smiled coolly at them.

Nero glowered at Ronan and Nyx.

"Who it appears took them from Nero Windstriker," Faris continued.

So there were two secrets Faris had wanted to expose in this challenge. Firstly, that Ronan and Nyx had stolen the weapons from Nero. And, secondly, that Nero had possessed them to begin with. Faris wasn't just targeting the gods' alliances with one another. He was trying to break their bonds with angels. He wanted to turn Nero against Ronan and Nyx.

We couldn't fall into Faris's trap. United we were all stronger, a force to threaten him. Divided, fractured, with the right army and weapons, he could just pick us off one by one. Was that his plan to follow up this discord? Did he have more soldiers than we knew about? Did he possess powerful secret weapons?

I refused to allow Faris to manipulate us to break our alliances. On the other hand, could we really trust Nyx and Ronan after they'd stolen something precious right out from under our noses? Unity was born from trust, a trust that had now evaporated.

I glanced at Faris. The look on his face told me he'd gotten exactly what he wanted out of this challenge.

And he wasn't done yet. He had more in store for all of us—more alliances to break, more secrets to expose, mine included.

CHAPTER 25

THE WARRIOR'S PENDANT

"What are we to make of this challenge?" Maya said when we were all back in the gods' audience chamber.

"The challenge is over. My team defended my treasure," Faris declared, taking his throne. "It's time to move on."

"It is not over," a voice echoed through the hall.

The words had come from Aleris. He stood in front of his throne.

"Our Everlasting guest has told me that the weapons of heaven and hell are not Faris's most prized possession," Aleris said. "That possession lies on Faris's person. It is the pendant he wears around his neck."

Surprise flashed in Faris's eyes, followed very quickly by anger. "What are you doing, Aleris?" he growled.

"You thought you could escape judgment?" Aleris's brows arched as he shot Faris a pitiless look. "You who have sinned greater than those you plotted to expose?"

The other gods jumped off their thrones, furious accusations flying out of their mouths. So much for Faris plotting from the shadows to expose the gods' most-guarded secrets, all the while escaping their wrath.

Aleris looked on as the other gods all turned on Faris. So Aleris had double-crossed him. Faris certainly hadn't seen that coming. I would have applauded the move, but it meant that Aleris was far more dangerous than I'd realized. He was devious enough to outmaneuver Faris, the king of machinations.

"Calm down," Faris said to the angry gods. "You are getting entirely too carried away."

"Calm down?" Meda repeated in disgust. "Those words fall easily from the mouth of someone who's not had his secrets ripped open and laid out for all to see, like a carcass hanging at a meat market on a scorching hot day, the rotting flesh growing more rancid by the hour, poisoning those most dear to you, turning them against you." Meda glanced at her sister.

Maya huffed and turned away in anger.

"And all this discord and unrest to momentarily satiate the ambition of the God of Heaven's Army," Meda continued. "A moment of satisfaction at the expanse of millennia of love."

Meda was still looking at her sister, but Maya adamantly refused to meet her gaze.

"Your deeds, the reasons you have all turned against one another, were of your own making," Faris said calmly. "I did not force your hand. I did not make you err, betray, and lie."

"You simply ripped open all our old scars," Zarion snarled. "Well, Faris, immortality is a long time to accumulate sins. And you are far from blameless. What will we find when we poke at your scars, I wonder?"

Zarion reached for the pendant around Faris's neck.

For the first time, I watched something akin to panic flash across his face. Faris tried to get away, but the gods grabbed him, vengeance burning hot in their eyes. For this one moment, they were united in their pursuit of a common enemy, just as I'd known would happen if they found out what he'd done to them.

Valora snatched the pendant from around Faris's neck. Magic rippled across my body, and the glasses I'd tucked inside my jacket were suddenly gone. Ronan held them inside his clenched fist. He'd used his telekinetic powers to steal them from me.

Then, before anyone could blink, Ronan punched his magic through the glasses. He angled the glittering stream at the pendant, exposing the memories hidden within.

Strands of sparkling magic curled around the room, forming shapes. The disjointed picture slowly coalesced.

Faris stood in a room with weapons hanging on the walls, much like his castle on Gravite. There was a certain hardness to the martial decor, devoid of trinkets and baubles. Like this world too sat at the far edge of the gods' territory, a place where there were still battles to be fought and won against the demons' armies.

Faris wore a sharply-angled tunic and pants made of midnight-blue silk. Despite the soft fabric, it looked like a suit made for battle. He'd accented his battlefield-in-the-ballroom outfit with a gold pendant.

It was the very same pendant Aleris had declared to be Faris's most prized possession.

Constellations of glowing dots, drawn and projected with magic, swirled in the air around Faris. Each pulsing point was either blue or silver. Faris waved his hand through the projection, unveiling new layers. New maps. Some of the blue dots turned silver, some of the silver ones turned blue. Back and forth, the colors cycled as the history of the immortal cosmic war between gods and demons played back at many times normal speed.

Faris watched the battles play out, his eyes constantly flickering from one map to the next, like he was searching for something. Perhaps he sought a strategy to beat the demons. As the God of Heaven's Army, it was his job to lead the gods to victory in battle.

He watched for only a few seconds before he growled in annoyance and waved his hand, dismissing the maps. They dissolved into wisps of smoke.

"Temper, temper."

Faris pivoted around to find a woman leaning against his desk. Tall and slender with long pale hair, she wore a blue gauzy dress of soft chiffon that billowed in the hot breeze whispering in from the open balcony door. Gold bands adorned her upper arms, and bracelets jingled from her wrists. On her forehead, she wore a gold headband set with a single tiny blue stone. The gem had a familiar gleam to it.

"Grace," Faris said.

The woman pushed off the desk, extending her arms into the air in a very graceful pose. "In the flesh."

"What are you doing here, demon?"

The gem on her headband…it was the exact same color as the blue dots that represented the demons' forces on Faris's maps.

Grace stepped up to a miniature apple tree made of gold and plucked an apple off a branch. She glanced at the fruit in her hand, then at Faris. "I've come to parley."

"Parley," Faris repeated, his eyes narrowing. "This isn't the first time you've come with that word on your lips. As I recall, it never ends well."

Grace smiled. "That depends entirely on whom you ask."

"The first time you came to parley, I ended up impaled on a spear," Faris said drily.

"Only for a few days." Her smile widened.

"And it only went downhill from there," Faris added.

Grace's sigh was as soft as rose petals falling over a serene pond. "Really, Faris. You're such a spoilsport."

"I'm too busy for your games today, Grace."

"Ava giving you trouble again, is she?"

He glowered at her. "The Demon of Hell's Army is almost as much trouble as you are."

Grace sat down behind his desk. "And yet only half as much trouble as you are." She leaned her elbows on the tabletop, balancing her chin on her hands. "Let's talk about your little secret project."

"I have many secret projects, none of them little, and all of them none of your damn business."

"Oh, really, Faris. Let's not be petty." Grace plopped her feet up on the tabletop. The demon wore gold sandals studded with diamonds.

He blasted her with a psychic spell that knocked her pretty feet off his desk. "I don't engage in smalltalk about my projects with demons."

"Or with the other gods, apparently."

"Nor do you tell the other demons everything you're up to," he shot back.

"Of course not," Grace laughed silkily.

She sat there in silence, matching his stare.

"Why are you here?" he finally said.

"You really are dense sometimes, Faris. It's no wonder that my sister's forces are kicking your ass. I already told you why I'm here. I'm here to parley."

"To what end?"

"I'm bored, the moons are full, and I just came fresh from

a fight." She rose slowly from the chair, tugging on the closure of her dress. The layers of chiffon came tumbling down, leaving her naked. "Unless you can't spare a moment from your busy schedule of glaring at battle maps." She arched her glitter-dusted brows.

"If only you wouldn't talk, that would make this parleying all a little more tolerable," he growled.

Grace smirked at him. "I promise to shut up if you will."

Faris grabbed her wrist, pulling her through an arched doorway into the bedroom. The curtains of the canopy bed whisked shut around them.

The memory froze, then faded into the next.

Faris stood in the room of martial decor, flipping through the cosmic maps. Outside his window, winter had covered the lands in a thick blanket of snow.

Grace popped up beside Faris. "Sonja knows."

Faris brushed the battle maps away, then turned to her. Bundled up in a fur-trimmed red velvet cloak, white fur hat, and elbow-high gloves, she looked like a winter wonderland princess.

"What does Sonja know?" Faris asked her.

Grace flicked her hand, and her cloak flew off, carried away on a gust of magic wind. A round belly stretched out her red gown.

Faris's gaze dropped to her baby bump. "When did this happen?"

"Don't play coy, Faris. You were there."

"Six months ago. You sure waited a long time to tell me," he said. "Besides your sister, who else knows?"

"No one. I have been in solitude for the past several months, engaged in the Magic of the Faith rituals. Sonja showed up unannounced at the temple and barged into the Room of Solitude. She saw the fruit of our labor." Grace's hand

slid over her belly. "Some of the priests were close enough to see inside the room. Sonja killed them so they couldn't spread the word."

"How kind of her to protect your secret," Faris said drily.

"Sonja wants the child for herself," Grace snapped. "There has never been a child conceived with demon and god magic. Sonja wants to weaponize the child."

"Sonja cannot be allowed to wield such a weapon, to groom it, train it, control it."

"Agreed. But I'm not giving you such a weapon either, Faris."

A twisted smile curled his lips. "You already have."

He grabbed for her, but Grace was quicker. She vanished in a cloud of black smoke.

The final memory faded from the gods' hall, leaving me with a single terrifying realization. I'd thought Zarion was my father, but he wasn't. No, it was Faris. It had been Faris all along.

CHAPTER 26

SUBTERFUGE

The gods' eyes were watching Faris, disgust marring their immortally beautiful faces. More than any of the other exposed secrets, this revelation had rattled them.

"Demon." Valora bit out the word. "You had an affair with a demon."

"You *procreated* with a demon," Zarion added in a low hiss.

"What became of the child?" Maya asked.

"Grace hid it away from me. From Sonja. From everyone." Faris appeared surprisingly calm and collected considering that all his plans for cosmic domination had just gone down the drain.

"A weapon is out there, a weapon that threatens us. One that *you* created, Faris." Valora poked her finger against his chest. "And you don't even know where it is!"

"Believe me, losing it wasn't part of the plan."

Valora's jaw dropped. "You actually *planned* to create this weapon?"

"We weren't making any headway in our war with the

demons. Someone had to do something to change that. As the God of Heaven's Army, *I* had to do something. Something that worked." He shot a sidelong glance at Meda. "Infusing a light magic soldier with dark magic is only a graft, an artificial hack. To have full power over the entire magic spectrum, the soldier must be forged with light and dark magic from the start."

As the gods argued, dizziness washed over me. I struggled to make sense of the thoughts swimming through my head.

I'd been created to be a weapon. Faris's weapon.

Faris was my father, not Zarion.

But then what was Zarion's secret that Faris was trying to expose? I shuddered to consider the possibilities. Each new secret that had come out seemed even worse than the last.

"I have not betrayed the other gods. Everything I've done has been to win this war. Unlike you," Faris said to Zarion.

"My affair with Eveline was a moment of weakness. In no way did it betray the gods," Zarion shot back.

"Oh, but I'm not referring to Eveline." Faris's smile was savage. "I speak of another affair."

Zarion's fists clenched.

"I swore I would expose your sins, brother. And I will," Faris declared. He raised his voice, addressing all the gods now, his voice penetrating their bickering. "Zarion is Valora's lover. He helped her kill Mercer. He made sure the demon soldiers found their way into the king's castle, so Valora could shoot her father with the demons' weapon and pin it all on them."

That was Zarion's other great secret? He had plotted with Valora to kill the old king of the gods. If Zarion and

Valora were lovers, that explained why she'd been so angry with him when his affair with Stash's mother had come to light. She felt betrayed by the man who'd helped her betray her father.

Well, that answered two questions. Only about a million more to go.

Zarion's face turned red with anger. He didn't bother with words. He went straight to shooting magic at his brother. Faris looked down at the piece of his throne that Zarion had blasted off. Glowering, he returned fire.

I ran toward the door. I so did not need to die right now.

"Are you all right?" Nero asked, closing in beside me.

"Not really," I laughed, my voice cracking.

I headed into the cactus garden. People tended to avoid it. I supposed they got pricked enough on the battlefield.

"The gods don't know who Faris's child is," Nero said, facing me.

"Faris knows."

He took my hands. "You can't be sure of that."

"He knows. Athan says he knows. Before this training began, Faris suspected who I am. But now he *knows*." I dropped my voice. "This training wasn't just about exposing the other gods' secrets. It was about testing me and my magic to figure out if I was his long-lost weapon."

A realization hit me like a brick wall to the face at two hundred miles an hour.

"Faris gave me the Nectar for Fairy's Touch," I said. "That was the moment he knew. It was a test. He guessed I wouldn't level up." I began pacing, working it through. "This is what Athan was hinting at. The Legion has leveled up my light magic several times. And last month, Sonja leveled up my dark magic. She put light and dark in perfect sync, completely balanced, completely equal. That's why the Nectar didn't level me up this time." It was all coming together. "My magic has reached a tipping point. Nectar alone will no longer level me up. Sonja must have realized that. When you rescued me from her fortress, she was about to give me a combined Nectar-Venom injection."

"Because your magic can only be leveled up dually now," Nero said. "Both light and dark at the same time."

I nodded bleakly. "Faris must have realized that too. He was testing me. And I exposed myself."

"You couldn't have known."

"I should have seen it." My shoulders slouched under the weight of my own stupidity. "And now it's too late."

"It's not too late," Nero told me. "Faris might know who you are, but the other gods do not. We're going to keep it that way. We're going to act as though nothing has changed."

"What do we do about Faris?"

"We wait. If Faris was going to expose you, he would have done so already."

"He won't expose me. He's keeping me for himself. This isn't just about using me to find Zane anymore. It's about using me as his ultimate weapon."

I shuddered. Faris was not a loving father. He didn't understand empathy or compassion, at least not beyond how he could exploit those qualities in others to achieve his goals.

"We just need to grow your magic so that when he finally does come knocking, he won't be a match for you," Nero told me, his confidence never faltering.

"He is a god," I pointed out.

"So are you, Leda. But you are more than god or

demon. More powerful, more complete—or at least you will be by the time we ignite the rest of your magic. Gods and demons might come to use or kill you, but they will flee in horror when they see what you can do."

He sounded so sure. I folded myself in his words, in his certainty, embracing his strength.

"You need to stay in the Legion, " Nero told me. "Leveling up your magic isn't just about finding your brother now. It's about your survival. You need to be strong, to be able to fight them if they find out."

And sooner or later, the gods would find out. As the last few days had shown very clearly, secrets didn't stay buried. It was likely already too late. Athan had hinted that another god already knew about me. Which one? And why hadn't that god exposed me?

"What about the Venom?" I asked Nero. "I need both Nectar and Venom to grow my magic. How do we get the Venom?"

"I will find a way."

Angels could get Nectar, but they didn't have access to Venom. Still, Nero appeared so completely confident he could get it, that I didn't even entertain the possibility that was impossible. I'd learned to trust him.

"We should head back to the gods' audience chamber," he said.

I took a moment to settle my uneven emotions, then we returned down the path that would bring us to the gods' hall. Nyx and Ronan were waiting right outside the building. As soon as they saw us, they moved to intercept. Nero walked around them, not saying a word.

Nyx blocked him. "Nero, we need to talk."

"I have nothing to say. And I have no interest in hearing lies." He kept moving.

"General Windstriker." The command rang in Ronan's voice.

Nero turned around.

"You told me the weapons of heaven and hell had been destroyed," Nyx said. "That was a lie. But I never lied to you, Nero."

"No," he bit out. "You only stole from me."

"I could have ordered you to hand them over," she said.

"And yet you didn't."

"You would have denied that they'd survived."

"Yes," Nero agreed.

"Protecting your precious Pandora is clouding your judgment," Ronan told him. "This is war, and in the right hands, those weapons can kill an immortal."

"Yes, they are a weapon, but not just against the demons. Against the gods as well," replied Nero. "And now, because you stole them from me, because you didn't keep them well hidden, Faris found out about them and stole them from you. You allowed Faris to get his hands on weapons that can kill a god—or all the gods. So, tell me, did this honestly work out the way you'd planned?"

"No, it did not," Ronan admitted. "But Faris is right about one thing: there is no gain without risk. I had to figure out how to best use the weapons of heaven and hell."

I blinked in surprise. "You mean, you can't wield them?"

"No, he cannot. Nor can I," Nyx said.

That was weird. Gods and demons were deities, and deities could wield immortal artifacts.

"The weapons of heaven and hell are different than other immortal artifacts," said Nyx. "Their magic is complex. However, we've had a recent breakthrough."

My eyes narrowed in suspicion. "How recent?"

"The battle today," Ronan told me.

"Jace did a great job wielding the sword," I said lightly, my heart pounding in fear.

"He might have swung the sword, but his magic did not power it up." Ronan watched me closely. "Yours did."

"The weapons of heaven and hell responded to your magic," Nyx added. "Because like the weapons, your magic is born from light and dark."

Steel sang. In a flash, Nero's sword was pressed against Nyx's throat. Ronan was just as fast. His blade was at Nero's neck. They both looked more than ready to strike.

"She is Faris's weapon," Ronan said to Nero.

Well, that answered the question of which other god knew about me.

"She is not a weapon. She is a person," Nero growled. "And she's the woman I love."

His eyes flickered between Nyx and Ronan, as though he were trying to figure out how to strike them down before either could get to me. Like he would risk himself to take out these foes, just to save me. It was both incredibly romantic and totally pigheaded all at once.

"This is ridiculous," I said, my brain racing, trying to get us out of this situation.

"She didn't strike down the demon. She didn't kill him," Nero told Ronan and Nyx. "Jace Fireswift did."

I frowned at him. I wasn't going to let him set up Jace to be killed. Jace was my friend, and he was a good friend. He was keeping my secret about not leveling up at the last ceremony. I would not betray him. And I definitely would not frame him.

But Nyx wasn't fooled by his ploy anyway. "Nice try, Nero," she said. "But we both know that Leda charged the sword, priming it with her magic. Jace Fireswift only swung the tool."

"Luckily for her, the other gods don't realize that," Ronan added. "And they don't know that the true power of the weapons of heaven and hell can only be unlocked by a deity with light and dark magic."

"The gods all think Jace killed the demon. They are all celebrating his success," Nyx said. "Except for Faris. He knows the truth."

"As do we," Ronan said darkly.

"What do you want?" Defiance and resignation clashed inside of me. "Because that's what this is coming down to, isn't it? You will keep my secret if I do something for you. You rub my back, so I have to rub yours."

That 'rub' felt an awful lot like a stab in the back.

A small smile touched Nyx's lips. "Good girl."

"At some point, Faris will find the weapons of heaven and hell taking leave of his possession," Ronan told me.

"And find their way into yours," I finished for him.

"You will wield them for us," he said.

"I should point out that there's a major flaw in your plan," I replied. "Most of the time, the weapons of heaven and hell don't work for me either."

"They are very powerful artifacts, but the ability to wield them is inside of you," Nyx said. "It is simply a matter of control, of properly directing your magic. So far, it was bursts of emotion that charged the artifacts, but in time you will learn to wield them even when calm and controlled."

"We will help you realize that power inside of you," Ronan said.

"You want to turn her into a weapon, just like Faris and Sonja do," Nero growled.

"She is already a weapon, Nero," Ronan replied calmly. "We simply wish to channel her power into something productive, for the greater good."

A lot of atrocities had been committed in the name of the 'greater good'. Because good and evil were all a matter of perspective.

"You expect us to trust you after you've already betrayed us?" Nero demanded.

"We stole from you, but you lied to us about the weapons, Damiel, and Leda's origin," Nyx said. "You are hardly blameless, Nero."

"My personal life is none of your business. I'm allowed to keep it to myself," I told her.

"Unfortunately, your personal life is not entirely yours," said Nyx. "It is entangled in this immortal war. The gods scored a victory today against the demons on Samaran, but that does not make up for our recent heavy losses. Right now, we are losing this war, Leda. We need you to help us turn things around. We need you to wield the weapons of heaven and hell and stand against the demons that would tear the Earth you love to pieces. The demons' magic cannot kill you, but your magic can kill them."

"It doesn't sound like we have a choice," I said drily.

"No, you really don't," Nyx agreed. "If the other gods find out about you, you will become a weapon. Your existence will be only that—until this war is over, or you are dead. If you ally with us, however, we will keep your secret. We will train you and protect you. Your life will otherwise be as it is now—a life rich with friends and family, surrounded by those you love."

"And Faris?" I asked.

"We will deal with Faris," Ronan assured me.

I arched a skeptical brow at him. "So far, it seems like he is dealing with you. *All* of you."

"No longer," Nyx said. "Aleris tossed him on the chopping block today."

Ronan shook his head slowly. "Faris should have known better than to trust Aleris. He is so righteous. He is convinced that the only way we can beat the demons is by shedding our own sins. Aleris would never allow Faris to escape with his own sins intact. He had to unravel them on the floor along with everyone else's."

"And you're next," I said.

There was only one challenge left, and one artifact remaining to steal: Ronan's.

"Faris and Aleris have already exposed our secrets. Save one." Nyx dipped her chin at me. "That we know about your parentage. Faris won't expose that secret, I can assure you. And if Aleris was going to do it, he would have done so when he exposed Faris. He doesn't know about you, Leda."

I choked out a strangled laugh. "Unless Aleris is building up to one killer finale."

"If that is true, we are all screwed anyway," Nyx declared.

It was such a human expression. It reminded me of the First Angel's duality, that she was in fact half human.

"What do you say, Leda Pierce? Do we have a deal?" Nyx said.

"It seems I don't have any choice."

"No good one," Nyx agreed. She glanced at Ronan. "Lower your weapon."

"You too, Nero," I sighed.

Nero and Ronan sheathed their swords.

"We will be seeing you," Nyx said as she and Ronan stepped inside the building.

This time, Nyx wasn't using a human expression. There was hidden meaning inside her words. She was warning me that she and Ronan would be watching me closely.

Beside me, Nero's eyes were hard, his face unreadable.

"You think I gave in too quickly," I said.

"No. They cornered you. There was no good way out. But things change."

He was clearly already trying to think up a way to get me out of the deal I'd just made with Nyx and Ronan. I wasn't sure there was a way, but if there was, we would find it.

"I'd rather be beholden to Nyx and Ronan than to Faris or Zarion or any of the other gods," I said.

"But?"

I grinned at him. "But if they think they have me, they haven't been paying attention at all this past year."

Laughing, Nero set his hands on my cheeks. His lips softly kissed my forehead. "I do love you."

"Oh, I'm just getting started, baby." I kissed him back, quick and rough and full on the lips.

Magic flashed in his eyes. "Keep practicing."

"Practicing what?" I asked, confused.

"Sounding like an angel. You're almost there. You just need to exude a little less humility and a little more arrogance."

I snorted. "Less humility? I didn't realize I was wearing that color today."

"Hold on to your humanity, Leda. It is your strength. It allows you to care and feel and to see things as most immortals cannot. But keep it inside of you. On the outside, you must be hard and unyielding. Wrap yourself in your magic, in your absolute certainty of your own superiority. You must always be in control, always confident, always unwavering. That's the only way you will survive going toe-to-toe with angels and gods. You see how quickly and ferociously they jump on one another at the slightest hint of weakness."

Yeah, like starved sharks who'd scented a single drop of spilled blood.

The bell in the gods' hall rang.

"The final challenge?" I guessed.

"Likely."

We entered the hall, splitting up to each join our partner.

"You were with Windstriker," Colonel Fireswift said by way of greeting. "Again."

"You say that like it's a bad thing."

Colonel Fireswift looked at me like he was regretting not killing me earlier.

"This training has been long and intense." I smirked at him. "You can't blame a girl for catching a quickie between rounds."

"As always, your irreverence clashes terribly with the decor."

"Dare I hope that was a joke, Colonel?"

He ignored my question. "You were not 'catching a quickie'. You don't smell like sex. In fact, you're reeking of lust. You smell like you have not had sex in a very long time."

"Have you been analyzing my scents?" I said, aghast. That was exactly what I did *not* need right now.

"They require no analyzing. Your scents are as crass and blunt as your words."

Ew. Time to start wearing really strong perfume whenever I met with the head of the Interrogators.

"Come with me," Faris told me and Colonel Fireswift, waving for us to follow him.

There was no finesse, no pizazz nor flourish. Not this time. The gods seemed to be as completely done with this training as the rest of us. I suspected the only reason they hadn't put an end to it was they all thought they had no secrets left to expose—and they wanted to see what the other gods were hiding.

Faris led us through one of the magic mirrors. It brought us to a dark underground cavern. Torches hung on lumpy rock walls. A thick blanket of dust covered the ground.

"The final challenge will begin here," Faris told us.

"The final challenge will begin here? But it won't end here, will it?" I asked.

"No, it will not."

If he was impressed that I'd picked up that hint in his wording, he didn't show it. He didn't look at me any differently than he ever had. He certainly didn't look at me like I was his daughter, or that he felt anything whatsoever—not even fear that my discovery would cause more trouble for him.

The gods hadn't punished Faris for his transgression. Yet. They were so caught up in fighting one another, that they couldn't agree on anything, even on how to punish the other gods. That certainly hadn't worked out as Aleris had planned. He'd not set out to create strife like Faris had. He'd exposed the gods' secrets so they could be punished for them.

Faris had to know I was his daughter. He'd tested me

with the Nectar. He'd put me on his team to keep an eye on me.

Or was I really his daughter? Dare I hope that another god had had an affair with a demon and that had created me? The gods certainly weren't keeping their noses clean.

But would it really be any better to have another god as a father?

I frowned. I would drive myself mad trying to sort this all out.

A blinding flash of magic lit up the dark cavern. When my overloaded eyes could focus again, I saw all the other teams were standing with us in a circle. Faris was gone, and in his place, at the middle of the room, equal distance from every team, was an ornate magic key. Reaching it was our next challenge.

CHAPTER 27

THE KEY

The other soldiers' eyes flickered between their competitors and the glowing key at the center of the room. That had to be Ronan's artifact. This challenge was so simple on the outside, so straightforward. The gods had not given us potions to block our magic or stripped us of our weapons. At face value, the challenge seemed to be as simple and straightforward as getting to the key before anyone else did.

But I never took anything at face value.

Isabelle Battleborn made the first move. She hurled a telekinetic spell at the key, obviously trying to pull the artifact to her. Her spell rippled through the circle of her competitors, but the key remained exactly where it was, unmoved. It seemed immune to this kind of magic.

Isabelle's spell backfired off the key and knocked her to the ground. A glowing red translucent shell swallowed up her unconscious body, sheathing it like a cocoon. She'd made the wrong move, and now she was out of the game. Just like that.

This challenge wasn't just not at all straightforward; it

was completely unforgiving. One mistake, and you were out. One mistake, and your chance at winning the artifact was over.

Her face haughty, Colonel Silvertongue glanced down at Isabelle's cocooned body. "Ronan is the god of psychics. Any artifact of his would surely be immune to telekinetic magic."

"Besides, that would have been too easy," General Spellsmiter added.

The brother and sister angels were watching the key like they were trying to unravel its secrets.

"The question is, does *any* magic work on the artifact?" Harker said.

Andrin performed an elemental spell born from air magic. The key didn't budge, but his own spell bounced back at him. He cast a shield of magic to ward it off, but the ricocheted spell tore right through it.

His teammate Colonel Silvertongue cast a dozen magic shields in front of him, woven from holy angel magic, sparkling like diamonds. The rebounded spell pierced the diamond shields one by one, swelling to swallow up Andrin and Colonel Silvertongue. Their cocooned bodies hit the ground.

"The key might be immune to magic altogether," Nero said.

"Or just immune to direct attacks." Delta stretched out her fingers.

"What are you doing?" Nero demanded.

"You'll see." Shifting magic sparkled on Delta's fingers.

"I don't think this is a good idea," I said.

"Then it's a good thing I don't care what you think," Delta snapped at me.

She slithered her magic toward the key. The artifact

flickered, then shifted into a white feather. Delta's victorious simper was short-lived. The feather turned back into a key. It slammed her spell into her, changing her into a feather. A red cocoon swallowed up Delta's feather body.

Her plan hadn't been a bad one, turning the key into something that then floated toward her, but Ronan's wards were too clever.

"Our spells just bounce off it," Siri said. "We can't bring the key to us."

"If we can't bring the key to us, we need to go to it," Arius said.

Siri and Arius exchanged hard looks, then they both sprinted toward the key with inhuman speed. Just as fast, they bounced off the invisible barrier that surrounded the key. As they shot backward through the air, a cocoon swallowed each of them.

General Spellsmiter stepped up to the key, careful not to get too close. He grabbed a handful of dust off the floor and tossed it lightly. The dusty particles revealed the form of the invisible magic barrier. It was about a foot in diameter, with the key at dead center.

I waited, but nothing more happened. General Spellsmiter's dust hadn't set off the key's protective measures.

Because the dust is mundane, not magical, I realized.

Only magic or magical beings triggered the shield around the key. It actually made a lot of sense. When Ronan had designed the shield, he'd realized that any threat to his key would come from a magical source. The more magic someone had, the more the shield reacted. Ronan had turned our strengths into weaknesses.

The anti-magic shield made it pretty much impossible to get close to the key, but there had to be a way around it.

There had to be a trick. Everything had a weakness. I just had to figure out what it was.

Leila hit the barrier with elemental magic. She should have known better. Andrin had tried that and failed. But as Leila cast her spell, she ran straight at Harker. She grabbed him by the shoulders and threw him at the backfiring spell. A cocoon slid over his body.

Clever.

The force of throwing Harker caused Leila to stumble. General Spellsmiter grabbed her before she could regain her balance and hurled her overhead toward the barrier. A cocoon claimed her and spat her to the ground. Her body hit the floor with a thump, dust swirling up around her.

While General Spellsmiter's attention was focused on Leila, Colonel Fireswift blasted him with a psychic spell. General Spellsmiter hit the barrier, vengeance burning in his eyes as the cocoon consumed his body.

My competition was dropping like flies. I didn't make a move one way or the other. Nor did Nyx. She didn't attack anyone. She made sure no one got close enough to attack her, but besides that, she simply stood and watched. When I met her eyes, I realized she'd come to the same conclusion as I had: wait it out, allowing the others to fight amongst themselves, as she developed a strategy to defeat the barrier.

But what was the right solution? How was I supposed to get past a barrier that blocked and countered all magic?

It hit me. The solution was so simple, it was almost laughable. Ronan had turned our strengths into weaknesses. I had to flip that around. I had to turn my weaknesses into strengths. The key to getting past his wards was to not have any magic at all.

I watched the few remaining competitors. Jace was

fighting his father. Nero was fighting Nyx. This was my chance, while the others were distracted.

I grabbed the potion ingredients I kept in my pouches. I had to make a potion that removed all my magic, a potion just like the one Ronan had given me and Nero before dropping us into the City of Ashes. But how did I make such a potion?

I'd recently read through an ancient book of potions, one my sister Bella had bought from a disreputable dealer who'd likely stolen it. Inside that book, I'd found a magic-nullifying spell. I struggled to remember the ingredients and instructions.

Vampire blood to neutralize Vampire's Kiss. Witch's Root to cancel out Witch's Cauldron. Five petals from the siren rose to silence Siren's Song. Dragon Gold, a glittery powder, to counteract Dragon's Storm. The wolfsbane flower to nullify Shifter's Shadow. The hair of a psychic to negate Psychic's Spell. The lacy white Fairy's Breath flower blossom to subdue Fairy's Touch.

I started mixing my potion into a slim cup I'd taken out of my pouch. All the while, I kept one eye on my competitors, just in case they decided to stop fighting their current opponents and instead come after me.

The next ingredient was angel juice, a pale golden goo squeezed from an angel's pimple. Since angels' perfect skin rarely broke out, the goo was extremely rare and exorbitantly expensive. It was also highly magical.

Then there were the ghost tears, collected from a telepath directly after a vision. The more powerful the vision, the more potent the tears. The tears were also very expensive.

I had all the ingredients in my potions pouch. That was a perk of being at the Legion: we got top pick of magical substances. Finally, a catalyst was required to ignite the potion. I dipped a drop of Nectar into the cup. It was the diluted kind Legion soldiers used at parties to unwind, but it should be potent enough for this potion. At least I hoped it was.

I swirled the potion around a final time, then took a sip. Nothing happened. Maybe I just needed to give it time to take effect. I put a stopper in the vial and tucked it into my jacket for later. The recipe had warned of the consequences of taking too much, but my magic was weird. I might need more.

Magic slammed into me. I turned to see that Nyx had been the one to launch the spell at me. The look in her eyes told me that I had guessed right about Ronan's ward—and Nyx had just come to the same solution. She unleashed a series of spells at me.

The potion was starting to work, albeit really slowly. I still had my magical resistance. That was a good thing in this case, considering that I wasn't nearly fast enough to dodge all of Nyx's spells. She was bombarding me from every side. There was no way to run, so I just had to endure. That was much easier with magic than without it.

The spells slammed into me like a meteor shower. I'd be lying if I said it didn't hurt. It hurt a lot. I barely stayed on my feet.

I could feel the potion's weight on me, stripping me of my magic. I had to strike back at Nyx before my magic was completely gone. I shot several psychic spells at Nyx, trying to drive her back. To my surprise, they slammed her down—and she didn't get back up. How could that be, that I'd knocked out the First Angel? She was a demigod, and my potion was blocking most of my magic.

My mind went back to the moment that I'd read the

potion recipe in that book. *A Potion for Nullifying Light Magic,* the title had read. It wasn't the same potion the gods used to strip away magic. Theirs neutralized all magic. This potion had only blocked my light magic.

Which meant my dark magic was still working. I'd hit Nyx with pure dark magic. That was why it had knocked her out. Angels were weak against dark magic.

Gods, I really was a weapon.

No, I couldn't think about that. It would only cripple me. Emotional turmoil was poison to my mental defenses. Keeping telepaths out of my mind required fortitude and focus.

Nero was currently engaged in a three-way battle against Jace and Colonel Fireswift. No one was paying any attention to me. They must not have seen me knock out Nyx, or seen my potion either.

I looked at the key behind the invisible barrier. Was this even going to work? The potion hadn't stripped away all of my magic. Maybe Ronan's wards only sensed and reacted to light magic. It was possible. After all, this was a challenge set up for us, soldiers of light magic.

But could I really afford to risk it?

There's no risk without gain, Faris's words echoed inside my head.

I pulled my potion out of my jacket and considered it. Bella's spell book hadn't specified how to block dark magic, but if Nectar was the catalyst for light magic, then Venom must be the catalyst for dark magic. If only I'd had some Venom on me. Alternately, I could just give the potion to Colonel Fireswift. He was on my team after all. Yes, that was what I'd do.

I didn't make it far. Jace knocked me back with psychic punches. Without my light magic to resist his, I flew back much further than I should have. His magic hit me again, flinging the potion out of my hand. He caught the vial, uncapped it, and emptied the contents; at the same time, he ran at the key.

Unlike with me, the potion worked immediately on him. He went right through the barrier as though it weren't even there. Then he grabbed the key, claiming it for himself.

CHAPTER 28

THE GOD'S PRISONER

Jace had won the gods' final challenge. The magic shield around the key collapsed and exploded into a fiery show, like a firework bursting in the night sky. Magic flashed through the room, dissolving the cocoons.

"That was dirty, stealing my potion," I told Jace as the soldiers formerly trapped inside the cocoons rose to their feet, once again conscious.

If the fireworks hadn't been obvious enough, this was a definitive sign that the challenge was now over.

"You've taught me a few things," Jace told me.

"I didn't think you were listening."

"I would be a fool to ignore you when you're constantly coming out on top."

"When you're the underdog, you have nowhere to go but up."

"That would be the perfect angel name for you, Pierce: Underdog."

"Somehow I doubt the Legion would approve. The

name Underdog doesn't exactly instill fear in the hearts of our enemies."

"Unlike Pandora," he chuckled.

I nodded in agreement. "Yes, everyone fears the Queen of Chaos, the Legion's Interrogators most of all."

I glanced back at Colonel Fireswift, who was closing in behind me like death's henchman. Unlike his son, he certainly didn't look amused by my statement. Still, he was glaring at his son more than at me, probably because he expected proper decorum from the son of an angel, especially his own. His steely glare promised more torture in the name of training lay in Jace's future.

Jace didn't meet his father's eyes, nor the threats burning in them. Instead, he looked down at the artifact he held. "A key." He flipped over the gold key in his hands. "I wonder what it unlocks."

The key began to glow, its light pulsing out. It lit up the dark cavern—but only in one direction. A tentacle of gold light spread out before us, stretching down a long hallway.

We followed the trail of lights past paintings and statues. Gradually, the dusty dirt floor gave way to a dusty concrete floor. Then dusty concrete yielded to dusty bricks. Further down the trail, the dust was gone, revealing glossy tiles. Every step felt like it brought us further into the light, closer to civilization.

Then the hallway ended abruptly at a solid brick wall.

"There has to be a keyhole somewhere." Jace brushed his hand across the bricks.

His key glowed in his other hand, its magic light shining onto the wall. Reacting to the key's magic, the bricks slid aside to reveal a dark space. It was so dark, the shadows so deep, that I couldn't even tell how big it was.

The space could have been tiny, or it could have been an endless abyss.

A rustling, shifting sound whispered inside the dark space.

"There's something moving inside," Jace said.

"Not something," Nero said beside me. "Someone."

Metal clinked. The key's light flickered off a hint of silver. Recognizing the outline of chains, I moved in for a closer look. I cast a light ball spell. It bobbed in the air before me, slowly gliding into the dark space. As it illuminated the area, I saw it was hardly larger than the prisoner chained up inside of it.

For one exciting moment, I thought that I'd found the poor prisoner from my visions, but the person in the dark space was not a woman. He was a man. His clothes were tattered, his skin filthy. Blue feathers drooped weakly from his limp wings.

"An angel," I gasped.

"A dark angel." Nero pointed out the tattoo on the prisoner's chest, the symbol of the Dark Force. It consisted of the nine signs of magic—vampire, witch, siren, elemental, shifter, telekinetic, fairy, angel, ghost—all surrounded by the emblem of hell.

This was Ronan's secret, that he was keeping a dark angel chained up in his dungeon? That wasn't exactly out of the ordinary, not for the Lord of the Legion, whose angel forces battled hell's dark angels.

Cuts marred the dark angel's body. Dried blood marked the spots where old wounds had healed. It was everywhere, crumbling off him like rust. He stared out of the darkness with haunted blue eyes.

"Leon," Nyx gasped, pushing past us to reach the prison cell.

She looked more surprised than I had ever seen her. Anger quickly trailed that surprise, consuming it. Soon that anger was all that burned in her eyes.

"Who is Leon?" I asked Nero as Nyx took a closer look at the dark angel.

"He is the First Betrayer."

I'd heard that title. "The first angel that the demons converted to their side."

Nero nodded. "He was the first dark angel on Earth, the beginning of their Earthly army. In the early days of the Legion, Leon was part of Nyx's inner circle. He was one of her first angels, one of the people that she trusted most of all. And then he betrayed her."

"Then why does she look so upset that he is being held prisoner?"

"Leon wasn't just her trusted soldier. Before she was with Ronan, he was her lover," Nero explained.

Nyx emerged from the cell and stormed down the hall, shouting out, "Ronan! Show yourself! Explain this!"

Ronan appeared in the hallway, right in front of her. Gods did not tolerate being summoned or shouted at, but he didn't look ready to punish Nyx. Instead, he looked guilty, like he'd been caught in the act.

"When did you capture him?" Nyx demanded.

"I did not capture him. Damiel found him and delivered him to me before revealing himself to us."

So that was the real reason Ronan hadn't punished Damiel. Damiel had delivered the Legion's First Betrayer to him, the one who'd hurt Nyx, the one who'd betrayed her and the Legion. Including Ronan, the Lord of the Legion. This prisoner was worth more to Ronan than Damiel's head. A whole lot more.

I had to hand it to Damiel; he sure was devious. He

hadn't revealed himself empty-handed. He'd come bearing gifts. Damiel must have wanted something from Ronan. Otherwise, he would have continued hiding. But what was it he wanted from Ronan? Did he believe he could use Ronan to find the Guardians and Cadence?

Whatever Damiel's reasons, the same time that he'd revealed he was still alive, he had also reminded Ronan of how useful he was, how good at tracking he was, how resourceful. All this time, Damiel had been answering to Ronan, not Nyx. Neither Ronan nor Damiel had told Nyx about Leon's capture.

The look on Nyx's face said she'd just figured *that* out too. She'd realized Damiel wasn't really her angel to command; he was Ronan's angel. Nyx's face was an even mix of hurt and pissed off as all hell.

"We agreed there would be no secrets, Ronan," she growled.

"It was necessary," the god replied. "Leon knows things. And your feelings for him would have complicated matters if you'd known he was here."

"He betrayed me most of all. I no longer have feelings for him."

"We both know that's not true, Nyx. You are half-human. You lived as a human for years. You can't help but feel empathy."

"I am also half-god." Her voice sizzled with fury. "And I lived with the gods even longer than with humans."

"You taught Leon well, Nyx. Too well. Extracting his secrets was not easy."

"And you didn't think I was up to the task? That I would falter?"

He frowned. "Quite the contrary. I knew you were up to it. I knew that you would do anything to protect us, the

Legion, and the Earth. I also knew that doing 'anything' would hurt you. Because you do still care about him, Nyx. I didn't hide him from you because I thought you weren't up to the task. I hid him from you because I wanted to spare you the pain of hurting someone you care about."

Nyx glowered at him, and the walls shook. "You should have let me make that choice."

I recognized the way Ronan was looking at Nyx, like he would do anything to protect her, to keep her happy—body, mind, and soul. He was completely devoted to her. And I got it. I understood that he wanted to save Nyx the pain of torturing someone she still cared about, despite Leon's betrayal. He was right; she would hurt Leon because she saw it as her duty. She would bottle her feelings to do what she thought was right. But that didn't mean those feelings weren't still there.

I could also understand Nyx's side because I'd been in her shoes before. Like a god—or like an angel—Ronan always thought he knew what was best for everyone. He protected Nyx without asking if she even wanted to be protected. He just decided for her, never giving her a choice. In Nyx's place, I would have been mad at Ronan too—and yet touched at the same time. To be in a relationship with an angel or god was to be torn by opposing emotions. Happy and sad. Grateful and furious. I had felt this way with Nero many times before.

Ronan reached toward her. "Nyx—"

"No, Ronan," she cut him off. "Not now. I just…can't. I can't talk to you right now." Then she stormed off, disappearing into thin air as she walked, demonstrating yet another godly power she possessed.

The walls shook, and this time it wasn't from Nyx's anger. Ronan cast a magic window before him. It showed a view of a castle, presumably the one we were currently inside. An army of dark angels and Dark Force soldiers had us surrounded.

Two female demons moved to the front of the army, clad in gold armor. Each of them held a gigantic magic sword in her hand. One of those demons was Sonja, goddess of the Dark Force. The other looked very much like Sonja, except her hair was pale blonde, not dark.

In fact, she looked identical to the demon from Faris's memories, Sonja's sister Grace. It seemed my mother had finally come calling.

CHAPTER 29

DEMON SISTERS

In fact, the dark dungeon wasn't deep below Ronan's castle; it was inside a windowless concrete tower high above all the others. We descended the spiraling staircase to a wide balcony that was even big enough to hold seven Legion soldiers, six angels, and the God of War. From there, I looked down upon the demon's army at our doorstep.

"So this is where all the demons' forces disappeared to when they fled the last battle, Faris," said Ronan. "They left to march on us here."

Faris suddenly appeared beside Ronan. "So it would seem," he said, his face hard.

The demons had abandoned the battle and come here. But why? What was so special about this castle that they'd risk bringing their fatigued army here?

Faris's eyes panned across the enormous army below. "Sonja has come for Leon."

"I know," Ronan said. "But how did she know he was here?"

"Her spies are everywhere." Faris's voice cut like steel.

If Faris hadn't revealed Ronan's secret in front of everyone, that spy wouldn't have been able to tell the demons that Leon was here. From the way Ronan was glaring at Faris, he was thinking the same exact thing.

"Sonja came personally to rescue her dark angel," Faris said. "Did you extract everything of usefulness from him?"

"We were thorough," Ronan told him.

A calculating gleam burned in Faris's eyes as he considered the demons' army.

"You're thinking of throwing Leon to them," Ronan said.

"If you have indeed extracted his secrets, he's no longer of any use to us."

Ronan frowned.

"You can't make every decision based on Nyx's wishes," Faris told him. "It's bad enough that she rules your heart. No need for her to rule your head too."

"I don't expect you to understand, Faris. You've never cared for anyone but yourself."

"And it's kept me out of trouble."

"Not always," Ronan countered. "You had to have sex with a demon? Really? How the hell did that happen?"

I perked up, trying to catch every word that had anything to do with Faris and Grace—anything to understand the twisted series of events that had led to my birth.

Faris shrugged. "Even I get bored sometimes."

Boredom? Really? I'd been conceived because Faris had been bored one day, so he decided he'd alleviate that by doing something completely outrageous and screw a demon. Obviously, he had to upstage his brother who'd slept with a mortal. I was sorely tempted to punch Faris in the face.

"Eternity is a long time to hold my attention," Faris

told Ronan. "We all experimented once or twice over the millennia. Or have you forgotten you and Meda? And you and Maya? Both sisters. You playboy." Faris tsk-tsked. "Does Nyx know?"

"Firstly, that was centuries ago, long before Nyx was born," Ronan ground out. "And secondly, you very well know that Nyx knows, otherwise you would have exposed it all in this little game of yours."

There wasn't a hint of remorse on Faris's face. "As I said, I get bored sometimes."

"No, this training, this game of yours, wasn't about boredom," Ronan shot back. "It was too calculated. And my response will be equally calculated." His gaze shifted to the demons' army. It hadn't moved since we'd stepped onto the balcony. What were they waiting for? "Just as soon as we're done with them."

"I'm looking forward to it," Faris said, grinning.

I wasn't sure if he was referring to Ronan's retaliation or to fighting the demons' army.

"Have you sent for reinforcements?" Ronan asked him.

"Why should I? This is your world, and you have an army."

"An army to protect the Earth, which it's doing right now. You are the God of Heaven's Army, and this is a demon attack outside of Earth. Don't make me throw *you* to the demon army, Faris. They'll probably find you tastier than Leon."

Faris sighed. "Relax. My soldiers are on their way. In about five minutes, they will close in on the demons from behind, and then we'll have a little fun with them."

Down below, at the front of the demons' army, Sonja lifted her arm in the air. Magic fireworks shot up.

"Sonja is summoning us," Ronan told Faris.

"So she is. How adorable that she thinks I obey a demon's summons."

"Don't tell me that you bedded her too."

"No," Faris laughed. "Definitely not. To even contemplate such a thing, I would have to be more bored than I could possibly imagine."

Fireworks shot up again.

"Ava is summoning us now," Ronan said.

"Ava?" I asked.

"Sonja's sister, the Demon of Hell's Army," Ronan told me.

So the demon beside Sonja was Ava, not Grace.

"Oh," I said. "She looks just like…"

"Like Grace," Ronan finished. "Yes, the resemblance is remarkable. Ava and Grace are sisters."

I wasn't sure if I was disappointed that my mother wasn't here, or if I was happy about it. After all, my father wasn't all that stellar, and I sure didn't hold high hopes for my other parent.

"Twin sisters," Ronan added. "Ava the Demon of Hell's Army. And Grace the Demon of the Faith."

"And their big sister Sonja, the Demon of the Dark Force. The demon sister triad." Faris made a face. "The three sisters are even more trouble together than Meda and Maya."

"I doubt Meda and Maya will be making trouble for you anytime soon," Ronan said drily. "You took care of that by putting a rift between them."

"You say it like you wouldn't do exactly the same thing if you had the chance."

Ronan cleared his throat. That wasn't a denial. "Let's get back to the matter at hand."

"Of course," agreed Faris. "Let's go parley with the Demon of the Dark Force and the Demon of Hell's Army."

"Parley," Ronan repeated, frowning. "Don't use that word. Ever. In fact, after seeing that little memory of yours, I don't think I ever need to hear it again."

Faris laughed. It was an eerie, disturbing laugh, one that made goosebumps prickle up across my skin. If any monsters had been present, they'd have run for cover.

"Ava has a demon soldier by her side," Ronan said. "And Sonja has a dark angel by hers."

"They always did love accessories." Faris looked around. "Where is Nyx? Don't tell me she is still pouting."

"She is going to kick your ass when she finds out you said she was pouting," Ronan told him. "You know that, don't you?"

"Who's going to tell her?" Faris asked with a sardonic smile. "Last time I checked, you two weren't speaking."

A scowl etched Ronan's face.

Wow, Faris really was an asshole. I hoped it wasn't genetic—or contagious.

Faris waved Nero over. "Windstriker, you're with Ronan."

Nero was Nyx's second at the Legion, so the choice made sense.

There were no godly soldiers here. Faris would have to pick an angel. The problem was Ava had a demon soldier by her side. Gods trumped angels, and so did demons. Not having a godly soldier at his side would make him look weak.

Faris's gaze fell on me. "Pierce, you're with me."

"Me?" I gasped.

Colonel Fireswift protested, "Her?"

"You heard me," Faris snapped. "Now go. Over the edge."

Faris and Ronan stepped over the balcony, flying down on their wings. Nero glanced at me before he jumped off too. He looked like he wanted to help me, but he couldn't. Even though I had no wings of my own, I had to get down there all by myself. Appearances were everything when you were marching out to meet an invading force. I had to show I was strong in front of the demons.

Faris had picked me for a reason, likely because Sonja knew what I was: half-god, half-demon. That unusual magic cocktail trumped angel when it came to showing off your weapons. It seemed the result of this whole *parley* hinged on me. If I didn't demonstrate how badass I was, the demon army would sense weakness and attack.

So I jumped over the edge. I didn't use any spells to slow my fall. I trusted in my origins, in my blood.

I am strong.

I kept repeating those three small words silently to myself on the very long way down to the ground. I used the words as a shield against the temptation to cast my magic and cushion my fall. I dropped like a stone, panic boiling in my stomach, my breath catching as I sped toward the inevitable collision with the ground.

I'd like to say that those three words and my unwavering determination were all that I needed, that the landing didn't hurt at all. But that would have been a lie. It hurt. Of course it hurt. But the Nectar and Venom had fortified my body, making it strong, resilient. Instead of shattering me completely, the impact broke only a few small bones in my feet. The breaks weren't so big that I couldn't walk. Well, sort of. The hard part was not limping

—or whimpering in pain as each step delivered a fresh dose of agony up my legs, exploding inside my nervous system.

I walked beside Faris. Nero walked beside Ronan. And together we faced Sonja, Ava, their escorts, and the enormous army at their back.

Sonja's sparkling green-blue eyes, the color of blue fir trees, zeroed in on me. A calculating smirk curled her lips, one that quite honestly scared the hell out of me. The Demon of the Dark Force had held me prisoner for days. She'd tested me, tortured me, and pumped my body full of Venom. If she got hold of me again, she'd pick up right where she'd left off.

Beside Sonja, Ava was looking at me with something bordering on amazement. "This is the one?"

Sonja nodded, her two high black pigtails jingling with strands of gems. Today, she really looked like a gothic high school girl. Well, at least from the neck up. The rest of her was clad in gold armor that shone like a pulsing star.

"I've never seen anything like her," Ava commented, her gaze panning up and down my body.

"You will," Sonja said. "Soon enough."

She looked at me like she wanted to finish what she'd started in her fortress, pumping me full of Nectar and Venom until she maxed out my magic. And then she planned to breed me to create more balanced light-and-dark beings for her army. According to Faris's memory, that plan went back over two decades, before I'd even been born. Sonja had wanted me from the moment she'd learned of my conception.

Well, Sonja wouldn't be getting her way if I had anything to say about it. I was not an animal, a lab rat, to be experimented on.

"Are you lost, ladies?" Faris said smoothly. "We'd be happy to show you the way back to hell."

"Charming as always, Faris." Ava brushed her long blonde hair off her shoulder, hair so like Grace's, so like my own.

Honestly, I was surprised no one had made the physical comparison yet, that no one had identified me as the offspring born from Faris and Grace.

Sonja shifted her weight, her armor clinking. "You know why we are here."

"You have come for the traitor, Leon Ironfist," Ronan said.

"Leon Hellfire," Sonja corrected him.

That was presumably Leon's dark angel name, the one he'd taken on when he'd defected to the Dark Force.

"Hand him over, and there will be no reason to crush that pretty armor of yours." Sonja's eyes slid over the bronze symbols on Ronan's dark armor.

"Truth be told, we have no further use for the traitor," Faris said.

"But you don't intend to release him anyway." Ava's tone was pleasant, her eyes burning with menace.

Faris hit the demon sisters with a dazzling smile. "I'm sure you understand. After all, what precedent would that set?"

His smile was so bright that it seemed to sparkle. That was his siren magic at work. Clearly, he didn't only wield Siren's Song with force; he could weave the spell smoothly as well. In fact, he almost came across as downright charming right now. Was he trying to seduce Ava like he had Grace, or was he just intrigued by their similarities? You know, because he was 'bored'.

"What precedent would it set?" Ava repeated gruffly,

not drawn into his charms. "The precedent of you turning things around and thinking with your brain for once."

"Faris acting reasonable?" Sonja laughed. "The Immortals will return first."

"You're hardly in a position to dispense judgment, sweetheart," Faris told her.

Sonja flashed him her bright, vicious teeth.

"Well, isn't this fun." Ava planted her gloved hands on her hips. "Let me be blunt, gentlemen. You have no more than a few paltry soldiers guarding your castle. Our forces consist of demons and dark angels, soldiers numbering in the hundreds. Surrender Leon to us now, or be destroyed." Her smile was every bit as charming as Faris's. "The choice is yours."

A ring of magic flashed around the demons' army. Faris's newly arrived forces closed in on them from behind, cutting them off. His soldiers' numbers were easily double those of the demons.

"Ava, if you're going to make a threat, at least make sure you're holding the right cards to follow through," Faris said, his smile brighter than ever.

Ava and Sonja looked back at Faris's army with obvious annoyance as they did a mental count of the soldiers.

"Let me be blunt, Ava," Faris said. "Our forces outnumber yours twofold. This is your chance to walk away. Or be destroyed." His smile was decidedly more threatening than charming now. "The choice is yours."

Sonja's brow crinkled.

Ava just looked resigned. "Move out," she told the demon soldier beside her. "We're leaving."

The soldier motioned to the troops, who began to withdraw.

Ava nodded at Faris. "Until next time."

"May next time be your last time," he replied.

Ava shot him a haughty look, then she and Sonja marched off with their retreating army.

"You're letting them go?" Ronan said in surprise as he watched the demons leave.

"We only outnumber them two to one," replied Faris. "If we fought, I am sure we would win. But we would also suffer heavy losses."

"I know that. I'm just surprised that *you* know it too. You were never shy about suffering heavy losses if the other side suffered heavier losses."

"Times have changed," Faris declared. "Right now, we need to conserve our forces for the battles to come. Those battles will decide the course of the immortal war. We need to be smart so we can outlast the demons."

Faris and Ronan walked back to the castle. Nero and I followed behind them.

"Are you all right?" Nero asked me quietly.

"Several bones in both my feet are broken."

During that whole really long parley with the demons, I'd resisted grinding my teeth, as well as screaming out in pain.

"I know," Nero said, his hands brushing against me.

His healing magic poured down my legs, absorbing into them. His power warmed me, healing my breaks and soothing my pain.

"Thanks. But you knew?" I frowned as we continued walking. "I thought I was hiding the pain well."

"You were. You looked very ferocious."

"That was on account of my stoic silence. I made sure to keep my mouth shut, even though I was itching to comment on Sonja's ridiculous hairdo."

"A wise choice," he said. "Smarting off to the enemy does detract somewhat from your ferocity."

"See, I figured that. Hence the no talking."

"You should try it more often," he told me.

"Very funny, General."

He looked pretty damn smitten with his own cleverness.

"It's over. The trials are over," I sighed with relief.

"Not quite," Ronan said, turning around.

We'd just entered the lower hall of the castle. All the other Legion teams were here. Even Nyx was back.

Dread twisted and coiled in my stomach. We'd gone through seven challenges. We were done. We *had* to be done. There couldn't be any more trials left.

Or could there? I supposed the gods could keep throwing challenges at us indefinitely.

"It's not over," Ronan said. "Because the gods' council must still decide who will be made the Legion's next angel. And which angel will receive a new gift of magic."

CHAPTER 30

SANCTUARY

"The gods will now convene to discuss your performance in the challenges. We will decide which of you we'll make an angel—and which angel will receive new powers," Valora declared when we were all back in the gods' audience chamber.

Unfortunately, we'd had to return the gods' items. I really could have used a few immortal artifacts in my possession. Given my track record, I was due to be thrown into calamity again next week at the latest.

As the gods disappeared behind the closed doors of their meeting room, we all waited in the audience chamber. There weren't even any snacks this time, nothing more satisfying than the joy of our collective shared company.

Colonel Fireswift and General Spellsmiter were closely watching me—and each other—like they were competing to see which one of them could break me first. Colonel Silvertongue looked at me like she was going to make another go at compelling me. Delta, on the other hand, appeared to be contemplating when and where she'd catch me alone and unawares, so she could stab me through with her sword. And Jace was trying to catch my eye, so I'd go speak to him. He wanted to know why I hadn't leveled up. He wanted answers. I didn't know what to say to him.

Most everyone else was watching me with more curiosity than disdain, which was a decided step up from just an hour ago. I guessed they wanted to know why Faris had chosen me to stand with him on the battlefield.

I couldn't be here. There were too many questions whose answers inevitably ended in my death. It was just all too much.

I left the room. I was heading toward the garden entrance when I saw Athan coming through those very doors. If I went past him, he'd drop more cryptic hints and uninvited pearls of wisdom in my lap. I couldn't handle any more of that right now.

So I detoured to the nearest staircase. The stairs ended one floor up, in a small open room with angled beams across the top. It kind of looked like an attic space, but the castle was many floors higher than this room.

I heard the quiet hum of voices, filtering in past a cross section of beams at the back of the room. Peering through the web of thickly-woven wooden bars, I saw the fractured slivers of seven people. The gods. It seemed that this room was hanging partially over their meeting chamber.

I backed up, away from the peephole into the gods' private conference. I didn't need to hear what they were saying. That would just plunge me deeper into their drama. I'd come here in search of a sanctuary, to be alone, to put some distance between me and everything that was going on.

I was sitting here, crosslegged, trying to clear my mind and find some inner peace, when I heard light footsteps coming up the stairs. Someone had found me. I hoped it wasn't Athan or Colonel Fireswift or General Spellsmiter. Or anyone actually, for that matter.

But it was only Nero. "Hiding from the world, Pandora?"

"From the universe actually," I sighed as he crouched down beside me.

For a while, we simply sat there side-by-side on the wood-planked floor, not talking, simply enjoying each other's company.

"How long do you think the gods' discussions will last?" I finally said.

"If you're curious, you could take a look." His eyes flickered toward the peephole into the gods' meeting chamber.

"Not even tempting."

He chuckled. "It's hard to say how long their meeting will take. It depends."

"On whether they can stop bickering long enough to actually discuss the matter?"

"Yes, there is that," he agreed. "But even under normal circumstances, the gods' council sessions can last a long time."

"What exactly is normal?" I laughed. "When we're not in a constant state of war? When everyone isn't trying to stab their own allies in the back?"

"When a topic is especially heated, when the gods all have strong opposing opinions, the session can go on for days," he said. "Or even years."

"I wonder if they'll let us go home in the meantime."

"Doubtful," he said. "This isn't simply about rewarding excellent performance. It's also about critiquing unsatisfactory performance. Before the gods let any of us go anywhere, they must first agree that none of us will be punished."

"If I scrape through this without being punished, I'll consider that a miracle. The gods don't particularly appreciate my methods."

"Perhaps not, but some of them will stand up for you," he said. "Only out of their own best interests, of course, but it will help you just the same."

"You sound awfully certain of that."

"Yes."

"How can you be so sure?" I asked him.

"Experience." A devious spark twinkled in his eyes. "Centuries of being always right."

I snorted. "Thank you. I needed a little humor to brighten my mood."

"I am completely serious, Pandora."

I smirked at him. "Oh, I know you are."

Nero's hand caressed my cheek, brushing lightly across my lips. "You have such a beautiful smile."

Though his touch was soft, it was backed by a megaton of magic. My whole body, wound up by stress and worry and far too many battles, quivered in appreciation. My fangs burned inside my mouth.

"Sorry." I covered my mouth as my fangs descended. "How embarrassing."

It had been a long time—like my early days of the Legion long—since they'd come out on their own, not controlled by my will.

Nero took my hand, peeling it off my mouth. "Don't be embarrassed or sorry, Leda."

As he spoke, his wings unfolded from his back. The glossy dark feathers of black, blue, and green were so beautiful that I couldn't resist touching them. So I didn't resist.

I stroked my hand over his wings. They were as soft as silk. Nero's magic burned through them, pulsing through my fingers.

I leaned into him, my mouth kissing his skin, my fangs caressing his pulse. Each throbbing beat invited me to bite him.

What was I doing? This was a public place. Sure, no one else was here right now, but it was far from private. There wasn't even a door. Anyone could just walk up here at any point.

But I really didn't care about that. I cared only about Nero.

He looked at me, his eyes burning. "Don't expect to get away with that." He kissed me softly on the lips.

"Get away with what?"

"With touching my wings and not following through."

Smiling coyly, I traced the tip of my finger across the bridge of his wings.

Nero's arms folded around me, holding me tightly to him. His hand slid the braid off my shoulder, baring my neck as his mouth dipped to my throat.

"I don't think we're supposed to be doing this in the gods' attic," I whispered.

"Pandora, I'm disappointed in you. I thought you relished in breaking all the rules."

Heat scorched my cheeks. "Usually."

Nero chuckled, a deep and decadent sound, like dark chocolate poured over cherries. "Always."

He moved in closer, his huge body casting a shadow over me. His wings extended wide.

I rose and scooted back. He followed, matching my movements.

"What's gotten into you?" I smiled.

The look on his face shot an electrifying jolt of lust through me.

"The challenges are over." He stepped toward me again, a step as soft as a rose petal and as forceful as a bolt of lightning. "We are no longer on opposing sides."

I smirked at him. "But it was so much fun being on opposing sides."

"You stole from me, Leda. And you tormented me far too much."

I'd run out of space to retreat. His hand was on my back, catching me as I stumbled over a big box. Storage? I had a fleeting thought—wondering what the gods could be storing up here in their loft—before Nero distracted me once more.

"As I recall, you did a fair amount of tormenting yourself," I said.

Nero chuckled deep in his throat. It was the growl of a predator who knew he had his prey cornered—and there was nothing I could do about it.

My heart skipped as his hands plunged down my back, rounding my butt. "Stop that."

A sexy smile lit up his face. "Stop what?" His right hand settled on my hip.

"I'm not going to have sex with you in the gods' attic," I told him.

His left hand set down lightly on my other hip. "You are mistaken."

"I am never mistaken."

"Your angelic demeanor is delicious," he purred. "Sweet with just the right touch of arrogance." He spoke like he was describing a dessert.

Despite my vocal protests, my body had other ideas. I peeled off his jacket and unzipped the shirt below, leaving him in only his pants. I traced my finger down his chest, following the hard ridges of his abdomen, sliding lower and lower… His muscles contracted, tensing at my touch.

"Tsk, tsk, General." I sucked on his lower lip. "You're out of control."

"You make me forget what control is," he said, his voice tolling with impatience.

He slipped my jacket off of me, one sleeve at a time, and tossed it to the ground. Then, with calculated slowness, he relieved me of all my clothes, all except my underwear. His hand slid up the inside of my thigh, as soft as velvet.

I squirmed beneath him. *Please.* I willed him to remove my panties, to thrust inside of me and satiate that hunger that had plagued me for days. It had started as a dull throb, building up every time I saw him, until it was so intense that I felt I might explode.

Nero out of control? No, *I* was the one out of control. I vaguely recalled that the gods were meeting in the room below us, but I couldn't scrounge together enough propriety to give a shit. I just wanted Nero. Now.

His breath kissed my skin, every breath intoxicating my senses. I moved, clutching his back, trying to pull him to me. He pushed me down and pinned my legs beneath his knees. His hands closed around my wrists and held me there.

"Nero," I whimpered, shaking with denied desire.

He pulled off my panties and slid them down my legs. "The moment I walked into the Crystal Falls gym and saw you, I knew I wouldn't be able to follow Nyx's orders." He grabbed my hips, flipping me around. "I went to your room that night, not to chastise you, but to seduce you."

His words trickled like hot honey down the back of my neck.

"And then the gods came," I gasped.

"Yes, then the gods came. Do you know how hard it's been to be so close to you all these days, Leda?"

His hand slipped between my legs, the touch of his fingers so hot that I couldn't stand it. I shook, biting back the moan blossoming on my lips.

His hand lifted from me, his finger brushing against my mouth. "Shh, my love."

My back arched, my legs spreading wider as my bottom lifted. Nero's hand traced down my spine and rounded my butt to slide between my legs. His fingers teased my slick, swollen lips, even as his other hand stroked my mouth. I could smell myself on his fingers and it made me crazy. I bit his finger. A drop of his sweet blood touched my tongue. It slid down my throat like pure ecstasy, stoking the wild fire raging inside of me. His blood and mine merged into one. My pulse pounded and my body shook, craving a release from this delicious torment.

I moaned softly. "Nero, if you don't stop playing around, I swear I'm going to tie you down and have my way with you."

"I thought you weren't going to have sex with me in the gods' attic," he whispered in my ear.

"I've changed my mind," I said huskily.

His eyes burned with promises of dark pleasures. "That's all I needed to hear."

His gentle, teasing touch turned hungry. He grabbed my hips, turning me around to face him as he set me onto his lap. My legs straddled his body.

I screamed as he thrust inside of me. I tilted my hips, taking him fully into me. He thrust again, rough and forceful—so hard that I shook from head to toe. He filled all of me—his body, his blood, his desire. And his love. They all mixed with mine, becoming something more, something greater than we each were alone. We moved together as one, in perfect sync.

Nero completed me like no one could, body and soul. There was an empty longing inside of me, growing each day, that space that only he could fill. I never wanted anyone else.

"Nero," I gasped.

His eyes met mine, so much fierce love in them that I almost cried.

"Colonel Fireswift and General Spellsmiter are each vying to recruit me," I said. "When this is all over, when we're back home, the Legion is going to test my magic."

He gripped me to him in a protective embrace. He knew what that meant just as well as I did.

"Nyx knows what I am," I said. "She won't tell anyone. She knows that if she does, the gods will find out about me, and then she'll lose her secret weapon. But if she finds my magic is compatible with someone else at the Legion—"

Nero kissed me roughly, swallowing my words. "I won't lose you, Leda."

"But if the Legion—"

"They can try all they want, but they will not take you from me. Do you hear me? You're mine, and I'm yours." He set his hands on my cheeks, dropping his forehead to mine. "There's no going back for me, don't you see? I've fallen too deeply in love with you. The rest doesn't matter. It will only ever be the two of us, now and forever."

Tears stung my eyes. "I feel the same way."

I knew right then and there that if the Legion tried to

pair either of us off with someone else, we would fight back. We wouldn't let that happen.

"I won't allow them take you from me," he promised me, conviction ringing in every syllable. "Not ever."

He moved hard inside of me, my body shuddering with every savage stroke.

"You are my Leda. My Pandora."

Rapture collided with euphoria, cascading, drowning me in delicious waves of bliss. It consumed me—it consumed us together. We were one. No one in heaven or hell or any of the realms would ever break us apart.

Nero wrapped his arms around me. His wings closed over my body like a shield. I rested my head against his chest, listening to his heart beat, feeling him breathe, the gentle rhythmic rise and fall of his chest beneath me. At the same time, it grounded me and made me soar.

This old attic wasn't the sanctuary that I'd sought, a place away from the world. Nero was my sanctuary. He was the one I'd always run to.

We might have lain there for minutes or hours. I couldn't tell. The world around us had melted away. Time had lost all meaning. There was only the eternity that stretched out before us.

The gods' bell toned. Voices whispered in the hall below.

"The gods' council has reached a decision." Valora's words pierced the walls and ceilings and floors, as though they weren't even there. "We've decided which soldier we are making an angel."

CHAPTER 31

JUDGMENT

"How long did the gods convene in their meeting chamber?" I asked Nero as we put our clothes back on.

"Under an hour," he said.

"That was fast. I wonder what that says about our chances of being punished."

"We shall soon see," he said practically, his face that of a seasoned soldier.

When we entered the audience chamber, everyone's eyes were on the gods. If anyone had noticed our tardy arrival, they didn't comment on it.

"As soldiers in the Legion of Angels, you are given many gifts of magic. In exchange, you are all sworn to serve the gods for the eternity of your immortal lives," Valora said. "Any personal sacrifices you make are for the greater good, so that the Earth and its people remain safe and happy under our rule. You must often put your personal feelings aside, ignoring the discomfort of working with colleagues you don't like. To be a Legion soldier is to sacrifice personal ambition and vanity."

It was a very rehearsed speech, one the gods had given countless times before. And I wasn't a fan of it. I was a firm believer that you could hold on to personal choice while serving the greater good. The two ideas didn't have to be mutually exclusive. As I'd told the gods the first time I'd stood in their hall, I had every intention of having my cake and eating it too. Otherwise, what was the point of having a cake at all? What was the point of life if it wasn't enjoyable?

Besides, Valora's speech rang very ironic after all the gods' personal drama and secrets we'd just seen play out.

"We have selected the Legion's next angel," Faris said, rising from his throne. "Jace Fireswift performed consistently throughout this training, demonstrating the qualities of an angel."

I wasn't surprised that the gods had chosen Jace. He'd won the key in the last challenge. Also, as far as most of the gods knew, he'd wielded an immortal weapon to kill a demon.

Logically, I couldn't really be disappointed anyway. Even in the unlikely event that the gods had picked me, it would have put me in a bind. Nectar alone didn't level me up anymore. Everyone would definitely notice when I didn't sprout wings as an angel should.

But I wasn't feeling particularly logical right now. The competitive side of me bucked at the idea that I'd been passed up. Yeah, I was definitely disappointed and annoyed—and all for foolishly vain reasons. I felt the sting of not being picked, of my talents not being recognized, and it quite honestly sucked.

The Legion soldiers gathered in front of Jace. Their lips offered him congratulations on his promotion, but their eyes burned with jealous fury. I was suddenly embarrassed that I'd ever felt anything but happiness for my friend. I didn't want to be like the others, who'd let hate into their hearts.

"So, you won our little contest," I said to Jace. The Legion brats had all already uttered their false congratulations and rushed off to other parts of the room. "You will be an angel first."

"If I survive," Jace replied, paling. He looked genuinely worried.

I patted him on the back. "You will survive. Of all of us, the gods chose you because they thought you would make the best angel."

"They should have chosen you. The magic-blocking potion was your idea."

"Their decision wasn't about the potion alone. It was about everything that's happened since the training began. I am too renegade, too wild for them to reward me."

"I saw you drink the potion, Leda," he whispered. "It was a good potion. It worked immediately on me. But it didn't work on you."

A question burned in his eyes. He was trying to figure out how a potion could affect me and him differently. In many ways, Jace really was his father's son, ever the Interrogator.

"The potion did work on me," I told him. "It just worked too slowly. It works differently on everyone—for some people faster, for others slower." I shrugged. "I don't think I made it potent enough."

"There was nothing wrong with the potion." He looked at me, a crinkle forming between his brows. "There's something wrong with you."

"People have been telling me that all my life," I laughed.

"Your magic isn't like ours," Jace pressed on, unamused. "That's why the potion didn't really work on you. And that's why you can't heal yourself. You never leveled up. The Nectar didn't work on you because your magic is different. But why is it different?"

He was too clever, too observant. All this time, I'd been worrying about Colonel Fireswift figuring out something was off about my magic, but I should have been worrying about Jace. Colonel Fireswift didn't know me, and he didn't understand me. Jace did. He knew how I thought and how I acted. Since he understood me, he knew when something was wrong.

I couldn't tell Jace the whole truth, that I was half god and half demon. That secret was dangerous to both me and him. I had to settle for a half truth.

"When Sonja held me prisoner, she did things to me," I said.

"What kinds of things?"

"She injected me with Venom. She mixed dark magic into my light magic."

Jace blinked in surprise. "Then you should be dead—or have gone insane like General Wardbreaker did."

"Yeah, I know. But I'm not dead. And I'm not any crazier than I've ever been." I winked at him.

"Leda—"

"Sonja injected me with Venom several times. The pain was…almost unbearable." I winced at the memory. "But she managed to balance my light and dark magics."

"So when you used magic against Nyx back in Ronan's castle…"

"It was dark magic," I said. "The magic-blocking potion worked, just as I'd made it. It blocked all my light magic, but *only* my light magic."

Jace didn't say anything. He just watched me like I was a ticking time bomb.

"You can't tell anyone," I said quietly.

"Who would I tell?" he laughed helplessly.

"Your father." I shrugged. "The gods."

"I meant what I said earlier, Leda. You are my friend. And it's not your fault that Sonja did this to you."

I wondered what he would say if he knew the full truth, that my magic was both light and dark at my core. I should tell him—and yet I shouldn't tell him. I shouldn't burden him. As an angel, he would have new responsibilities, many more things to worry about than keeping my overflowing cup of secrets.

Jace set his hand on my shoulder. "I have your back, Pierce. Always. Just remember that."

As he walked off, I got the feeling that he realized there was more to my story—and he was inviting me to share it. If only I could.

I looked across the room. The dynamics had changed considerably since I'd first arrived in the gods' hall. Nyx and Ronan weren't even speaking to each other anymore. Neither were Maya and Meda. Valora was mad at Zarion. *Everyone* was mad at Faris. A lot of strife had been sown during these challenges. Only Aleris still looked completely comfortable.

The gods' bell toned, then Faris declared. "The gods have decided that, based on his performance in the challenges, the angel Colonel Fireswift will be gifted new magic. He will be promoted to an archangel."

It seemed Faris was rewarding Colonel Fireswift's loyalty—and securing it further. His promotion would have been an easy sell to the gods. Colonel Fireswift acted as an angel should. He was obedient, efficient, and dignified. Not to mention brutal. He embodied everything Valora's speech had praised in an angel, in a soldier of the Legion.

Like Jace, everyone lined up to offer Colonel Fireswift their congratulations. Even Nero said the words, but his eyes screamed his true feelings about the head of the Interrogators.

"Congratulations on your promotion," I told Colonel Fireswift when I reached him.

"You are partly responsible for my promotion." He said it like he was accusing me of a crime, and yet…

"Was that an olive branch, Colonel?"

After all, gruffness was just his way. Gratitude was not in his vocabulary.

"I don't believe in olive branches," he declared.

"Just grenades."

He grunted. "Indeed."

"Well, I will take your olive branch masquerading as a grenade."

"You are incorrigible."

"Some people would call that sticking to my guns," I pointed out.

"This isn't thanks. I cannot thank you for your inappropriate, undignified, and often downright dirty behavior. But I do recognize that there is a place in the Legion for you, a way your bizarre methods can be used."

"Well, I do just love being used."

"I can give your purposeless existence meaning, purpose. Direction," he told me.

I sighed. "I think I preferred it when you were trying to kill me, not recruit me."

"I will be watching you closely, Leda Pierce."

"Join the club," I muttered as he walked away.

I joined Nero by the buffet table. Platters of food had appeared on it sometime during my conversation with Colonel Fireswift.

"What a week," I commented, grabbing a plate and filling it with cupcakes. You knew the end was in sight when sweets had replaced performance-enhancing shakes on the gods' buffet table. "It seems like no one's getting along anymore."

Nero opened his mouth to speak, but the gods' bell rang before he could say anything. When we got out of here, that damn bell was one of many things I would definitely not be missing.

"Jace Fireswift, step forward," Ronan declared.

He held a glass-and-gold goblet in his hands. Pale silver liquid, almost white, sparkled inside of it. That was the Nectar that would make Jace an angel.

Ronan didn't bother with the usual flowery speeches heard at Legion promotion ceremonies. By now, we all knew the lines by heart anyway. He merely handed Jace the Nectar goblet and waited. We all waited. His face hard, determined, Jace lifted the goblet to his lips and drank.

He fell to the ground. For one terrifying moment, I thought my friend was dead, but he rose again. Wings spread from his back, a beautiful tapestry of bright blue and white feathers with a dusting of silver swirls. His wings were so light, so bright.

Jace stepped forward, looking both weaker and stronger at the same time. The Nectar had drained and rejuvenated him. A silver halo shone around his body, lighting him up as though a spotlight shone on him. Magic uncurled from him, bursting and snapping. It was the volatile magic of a new angel.

"I present to you our newest angel, Jace Angelblood," Ronan declared.

The gods' servants came around with champagne glasses. One of the glasses was pushed into my hand. It seemed toasting to the Legion's new angel was not optional. In this case, I didn't mind. Jace was my friend, and I would have toasted to him even of my own free will.

After we'd all drunk, Faris said, "And lift your glasses to Colonel Fireswift, who will soon be facing the trials to become an archangel."

A new glass appeared in my hand. The second drink went down a bit harder. Even after all we'd been through together, I still wasn't the biggest fan of Colonel Fireswift. The liquid even burned a little. I suspected they'd laced the fruity alcoholic drinks with Nectar.

"Have the gods changed the archangel trials since your promotion?" I whispered to Nero as Colonel Fireswift pretended to look gracious and humble.

"Unlikely," replied Nero. "The gods bask in tradition. The archangel trials have been this way for too long. The location shifts, but the driving purpose remains the same."

"To sacrifice what is most important to you, to weaken your ties to your loved ones and strengthen them to the Legion," I said softly. "To prove your unfailing loyalty. But which person is most important to Colonel Fireswift? Jace?"

"His wife," Nero told me. "Despite the man Fireswift is, he does love his wife, perhaps even more than he loves his legacy."

"That's almost romantic."

"And the gods wouldn't make Jace an angel just to immediately kill him off," Nero said.

"We have to warn Jace," I told him. "His mother will

die. This doesn't just affect Colonel Fireswift. It will hurt Jace too."

"We can't warn either of them. It's forbidden. The gods weren't happy we tricked our way out of my trials. We survived only because Faris was trying to use us to expose his brother's secret. If we warn Colonel Fireswift or his son, the consequences will be dire for both us and them."

"We can't just do nothing." My voice shook. "What the gods are doing is wrong. It's barbaric."

Emotion choked up my throat. My mind was swimming, floating. I didn't even hear what Nero replied. I started walking. Something was drawing me forward, something important.

I was running now. I had to get there. I had to help her.

I slammed into Athan. "Sorry," I muttered, stumbling back.

He set something in my hands. Aleris's glasses.

I blinked. "Didn't I give those back to the gods?" My mind was foggy. I couldn't quite remember anymore.

"Put them over your eyes," Athan told me.

"No, I'm sure I gave back the glasses. Aleris took them."

"Put them over your eyes," Athan said again.

I drunkenly lifted up the glasses. Something was compelling me to look through them. No, not compelling. This was not Siren's Song. It was something else entirely, something I couldn't resist. It pulled at my heart, not at my magic.

Out of control, my mind scrambling for answers, I moved the glasses closer to my eyes. When they were mere inches from my face, I just stopped.

"Look," Athan said. "And see."

I looked at my hands. They were blurry, moving.

No, that wasn't right. It wasn't my hands that were shaking. It was everything. My vision had gone weird. Everything shifted in front of my eyes, rewinding. I was seeing time in reverse.

I stood in the gods' audience chamber. We were all drinking to Colonel Fireswift.

Rewind a few seconds.

Athan was standing beside me. He'd handed me the glass.

Rewind again.

I drank at Jace's promotion ceremony. Athan had handed me that glass too.

I snapped back to the present. "You drugged me," I said groggily to Athan.

Athan held the glasses in front of my eyes. I didn't even try to stop him. For some reason, I didn't want to. I had to help her. Her? Her who?

Visions crashed into me, bombarding my mind. Everything was flashing past so fast.

A woman pounded on the bars of her prison cell. I knew that woman. One of the gods was holding her, hurting her.

The nightmare that had been plaguing me for days now solidified, the holes in the vision closing, forming a complete picture at last.

I felt everything the woman felt—her pain and shock and absolute terror. Her feelings and senses and memories seemed to live inside the glasses, like they were part of them. And my magic had awakened them.

The glasses had sat on Aleris desk the day his warriors had brought the woman to him in chains. Aleris! He was the one who'd captured her. He was the one holding her prisoner even now.

I ran, not seeing anything, only sensing the trail of magic that pulled me toward the woman.

She was close. I could feel it.

Magic splashed against my skin. I vaguely remembered the feeling. It happened whenever I passed through a magic mirror.

I was in a different world? The thought barely processed. I had to keep moving. I had to save her. She was screaming. She was in pain.

I kept running, following the twisting hallways.

People were shouting. Arguing.

My hands clutched prison bars, ripping them open. A woman was crouched in the corner, covered in filth, shaking. Fear rocked her body.

The bubble popped. Blurred outlines grew solid once more. I was standing in a dungeon, just outside a prison cell. The woman from my nightmares was there.

So were all the gods. They had me surrounded. And they didn't look happy.

"How did you break into my realm?" Aleris demanded of me. "The way was warded."

My head was spinning. I tried to talk, but the words fizzled out on my tongue.

"So this is your secret, Aleris. Your *sin*," Zarion hissed.

A cool smile twisted Faris's lips. "You are not above reproach after all, it would seem."

"I have not invited you here," Aleris said, his composure cracking. "Any of you."

"She is an Everlasting," Meda said, gazing upon the woman in the cell. "You have been holding an Everlasting woman prisoner, Aleris." Her voice shook with anger. "There are lines even we do not cross."

Athan was in the prison cell, helping the woman to her feet.

"Who is she?" Valora asked.

"My sister," Athan said.

Faris's eyes hardened. "Aleris, I'd wondered how an Everlasting could owe you a favor. They are so reclusive," he said. "But Athan didn't owe you anything. You captured his sister and held her ransom."

That was why Athan had spent the whole training trying to help me, to lead me along the way to finding his sister. He'd needed me. He hadn't known where she was being held. Only Aleris's glasses did. And only I could read that memory.

But why me? What made this memory different from all the others we'd seen exposed?

"You used her to force Athan to reveal the artifacts imprinted with the memories of our biggest secrets," Valora said, her lips drawing together in disgust. "She is of Immortal blood, Aleris. Sacred blood. You didn't just cross the line; you defiled it."

"It is a terrible crime to harm someone of holy blood. Especially this woman, someone with great magic but no offensive spells, no way to protect herself," Faris told Aleris, clearly enjoying his unexpected revenge. "She and Athan are at the same time greatly powerful and completely powerless."

That explained why she'd been unable to escape Aleris's warriors or free herself.

The gods continued to lay their reprimands thickly on Aleris, but their voices were fading out. Dizziness was dragging me under. Something was happening. Everything had gone very crisp, so crisp that I couldn't keep my eyes open. It was all too sharp, too bright, too much.

I grabbed for the wall to catch my fall, but my hand broke right through the bricks, crumbling them. I stumbled, barely maintaining my balance. I gaped at the sizable hole I'd put in the wall. I opened my hand, and stone crumbs spilled through my fingers, sprinkling to the ground. Athan stood beside me, his arm folded over his sister.

"What the hell did you do to me?" I demanded of him.

The gods weren't paying me any mind. They were all focused on criticizing Aleris for what he'd done.

"Your magic wasn't powerful enough to find her," Athan whispered to me.

"*What* did you do to me?" I repeated, my voice cracking with anger and fear.

Your magic wasn't powerful enough to find her, he said again, in my mind this time. *So I leveled it up. I gave you a double dose of Nectar and Venom. I made you an angel, Leda.*

That was the last thing I heard before I collapsed to the ground and passed out.

CHAPTER 32

THE ANGEL

I opened my eyes and saw Nero.

"What happened?" I asked groggily, sitting up in bed.

"What happened is you are an angel." His voice was soft, even gentle. He was looking at me like I might explode—or shatter before his eyes.

"I'm fine," I assured him, taking a deep breath.

Athan had told me he'd made me an angel, but Nero's words made it more real.

Nero was tracking every twitch of my body, every flicker of my eyes. "We are still trying to figure out how that happened."

"Athan happened," I told him. "He said he needed me to wield Aleris's glasses, to read the memories imprinted there…to find his sister."

It all clicked. Athan's sister was a descendent of the original Immortals. That meant her magic was both light and dark too. And so the memories her magic imprinted were mixed light and dark magic. All the other imprinted memories we'd seen during the challenges had come from people with only light magic. Legion soldiers with potent light magic had used the glasses to expose those memories off the immortal artifacts.

Athan had needed me to expose the memories his sister's light-dark magic had imprinted on the artifact. No one else had the right magic to do it.

"Leda," Nero said after I'd shared my revelation. "Aleris's glasses, an immortal artifact, exposed the memories from other immortal artifacts. That is the glasses' power. And it's one of your powers too. You didn't use an immortal artifact to expose the memories from the glasses. You only used your own magic."

He was right.

"Just like I saw memories imprinted on the weapons of heaven and hell back in the Lost City last year," I said. "Athan must have known what happened there. He knew I had this power. That's why he needed my magic to find his sister. But I couldn't fully read his sister's memories off the glasses. They came to me as only dreams, fragmented sounds and images. I couldn't find exactly where she was."

"You needed more magic to fully expose the memories. More light magic and more dark magic," Nero said. "So Athan leveled up both. He gave you a double dose of Nectar and Venom to make you an angel and a dark angel."

"It's all so unreal," I said, hugging my knees. "A few days ago, I couldn't level up at all. And now I'm an angel." I looked around the bedroom. It was *our* bedroom. "We're back in New York."

"I thought a familiar place would help you," he said.

As I rose to my feet, my pulse quickened. "Help me do what?"

"Help you stay calm and recover."

"I'm fine," I assured him, even as fear suddenly and inexplicably sparked inside of me. The lamp on the nightstand exploded, and I cringed.

"Don't worry about it." Nero took my hand, leading me out of the bedroom, away from the lamp I'd blown up.

Unfortunately, there were even more things to blow up in the living room, including some pretty expensive antiques Nero had collected over the centuries. Thinking about that only made me more nervous. I was a roller-coaster of emotions. One of the paintings wobbled on the wall. I slammed my eyelids shut and tried to concentrate on not freaking out.

"That's your new magic at work," Nero told me. "It's one of the less fun side effects of gaining angel magic. Becoming an angel has boosted all your magic across the board, but it's also put your emotions into high gear."

Something tickled my back, perhaps my boosted senses picking up a particle of dust. But when I glanced behind me, I didn't find dust. I found wings. *My* wings.

I brushed my fingers along the soft feathers, fear melting away to wonder. My wings were almost entirely white, except for the last few inches, which dripped vibrant color. Before my eyes, the bright red-orange tips turned pink.

"Just like my hair," I commented.

My hair changed color with my mood too. Sometimes, it even changed depending on what kind of magic I was using at the moment. I wondered if my wings were the same.

I cast a cloud of snowflakes overhead, and my wings indeed changed from white-and-pink to bright azure blue.

"They are beautiful." Nero's gaze slid across my wings.

"As I knew they would be when you became an angel." His expression was guarded.

"What's wrong?" I asked.

"Faris is coming here."

"When?"

Magic flashed, and then the God of Heaven's Army was standing in the apartment, directly in front of me.

"Now." Faris stepped toward me. "Hello, daughter."

My pulse jumped, my throat tightened. All hope that Faris wasn't my father died. Having him say it made it all so real. I was his daughter. Shit.

"Well?" Faris's voice grew impatient. "Don't you have anything to say?"

Nero was gone. I glanced around, but I couldn't find him.

"What did you do with Nero?" I demanded.

Faris scowled at me. "This isn't the welcome I'd had in mind."

I planted my hands on my hips. "So I shouldn't have cancelled the parade in your honor?"

"Irreverent as always. Your new wings haven't cured you of that." His irritated magic popped and snapped at me.

My magic snapped back.

"Your precious archangel is fine." He shot me a hard glare laden with threat. "Now control your magic. It's most unruly."

I ignored him. "Why did you send Nero away?"

Nero tethered me. He would always look out for me, stand by me. When he was here, I was never alone. Faris had uprooted that tether.

"I wanted to have a private chat with my daughter." He set his hand over mine.

I was alone with him. Vulnerable. I jumped back, the burning need to find a weapon—and preferably stab Faris with it—flooding me. But I had no weapons on my body. I was wearing only a tank top and shorts, no pouches or belts or holsters.

Then I remembered my magic. *That* was my weapon.

A psychic blast punched out from my body, pushing Faris away.

He was back beside me all too fast. "Good." He nodded. "Very good. Your magic has blossomed nicely." He said it like he was talking about a weapon that was assembling well.

"Stay away from me," I growled at him.

Faris kept coming. He was too close.

I ran to the opposite side of the room. I was there in a flash. I'd never moved so fast in my life. My new angel magic really had super-charged all of my abilities.

My heart was pounding. I was so afraid—no, make that terrified. The magic boosts were cool, but the emotional turbulence of being an angel so wasn't worth it. Not that I had a choice. It was already too late for me.

Proving what a stellar father he was, Faris told me without delay or pity, "The emotional turbulence will be even worse when you become a deity."

"You read my mind."

"Yes."

"I don't like it."

"Your wild emotions have dissolved your mental defenses," he said. "With sufficient training, by properly honing your magic, your moods should settle down in a few days. I can help you with that." He reached out.

I sneered at his hand. "You've done quite enough already," I snapped.

"I had nothing to do with Athan's ploy to use your magic to find his sister. Unfortunately," he laughed. "It was a marvelous plan. Aleris was quite beside himself when you ripped the bandage off the scarred remains of his morality."

"I wasn't referring to Athan's ploy."

"I know what you mean, daughter." Faris said 'daughter' like he said 'gun' or 'sword'.

I swallowed hard. "I have questions."

"Of course you do," Faris replied smugly.

"Will you expose me?"

"What do you think?"

"Before Aleris revealed your secret, exposing me would have meant exposing yourself too," I said. "But now the gods know about your affair with a demon, so you might throw me under the bus to save yourself, using me, your 'weapon', as a bargaining chip."

"Now, that's a thought."

"But I don't think you will," I continued. "Not because you care about me, of course. It's because you plan to use me against the demons and probably against the other gods as well."

"No one can wield the immortal artifacts like you can. So fully. So completely," he said. I could practically see the birth of a million machinations sparkling in his eyes like stars.

"You intended to create a balanced person with light and dark magic. That's why you had an affair with Grace. This was your plan all along, to forge a living weapon out of light and dark magic. Just like Meda is doing."

"Meda is trying to add dark magic to a person with light magic, using the Guardians' faulty methods," Faris said. "Even if she succeeds, those soldiers will never be the same as you. They'll never be truly balanced, never as perfectly powerful as the original Immortals. Meda's work is a graft, a hack if you will. You are something else entirely, Leda. You are special."

When he used the word 'special', he didn't mean I was a special person to him, or he cared for me at all. No, he said it like I was a one-of-a-kind weapon he couldn't wait to unleash on an unsuspecting enemy.

"*I* was your endgame," I realized.

His brows peaked.

"You planned to turn all the gods against one another, and then, while they were fighting amongst themselves, use my magic to wipe them out," I told him.

"A fascinating idea."

"How much does Grace know of your plans?" I asked him.

I could not imagine the demon entering a relationship with Faris on an emotional whim. She had to have her own reasons.

"What does it matter?" he said.

"It matters to me. I want to know."

He scowled at me in disapproval. "That is a child's answer."

"If you don't want to deal with children, don't father them."

"Don't be impudent with me. I am your father and your god."

"I grew up without a father," I barked back. "And you aren't the only god in town."

"I am the only god who matters as far as you're concerned. You will do as I command."

"Or what?" I threw the words in his face. "I'm grounded?"

"Or I will capture the people you love most and torture them, starting with your foster sisters."

Nope, Faris certainly wouldn't be winning any father-of-the-year awards.

"Thankfully, I have far greater aspirations than trivial vanity awards," he said.

"Stop. Reading. My. Mind," I ground out.

"Block your thoughts better."

Easier said than done. My emotions were completely out of control. It was like puberty all over again, times about a thousand. If I'd known that was what becoming an angel meant, I might not have pushed myself so hard to get here.

"You really must control your thoughts," Faris told me. "It simply won't do for any god, demon, or angel in your vicinity to pluck my plans from your mind."

"I'm trying," I growled. "I don't like people reading my mind, you know."

"Try harder. Anger is no substitute for discipline."

His words only made me angrier. In response, my wings, which had finally disappeared, burst out of my back again. Magic crackled across the now-red feathers. My wings absorbed my bleeding emotions, my anger evaporating as the feathers turned white, lightly dusted with gold and silver. My mind calmed.

"Good," Faris said, nodding. "Better to show your wings than to show your thoughts."

"Of all the gods, *you* had to be my father," I growled in frustration.

"In time, you will come to realize how lucky you are."

Wow. Now, I'd known the gods were arrogant, but Faris took that arrogance to whole new heights.

"So I'm supposed to thank you for creating me as a

weapon?" I demanded. "A weapon you plan to use against your enemies—enemies who would destroy me for what I can do, or use me for what I can do."

"Don't be so melodramatic," he said coolly. "When I'm through with you, no one will be able to kill you. For centuries, I have trained gods to be soldiers. There is no one better suited to train you, to ensure your survival."

Faris only cared about my survival because I wasn't any good to him dead. If I was dead, he couldn't use me as a weapon.

"We are all weapons," he told me.

Damn it. My mental defenses couldn't hold together for more than two seconds. I wasn't hiding my thoughts at all right now.

"Indeed you're not," said Faris. "We'll have to keep you isolated for a while, until you regain control of your thoughts."

I feared that isolation equaled a prison cell.

"Stop panicking. It's very distracting," Faris chided me. "I'm not locking you up. I can't train you very well if you are trapped inside a prison cell."

"What if I don't want you to train me?"

"Would you prefer Valora or Aleris?" His mouth cut a hard smile. "Or perhaps Sonja?"

I cringed.

"That's what I thought," he said.

"Who knows that I'm an angel now?" I asked him.

"At least everyone who was standing outside the prison cell when you collapsed in a magnificent explosion of light and sound, your magic and wings bursting from you like a giant lotus blossom."

Great. I always did put on too much of a show—even when unconscious, it seemed.

"I've told the other gods that Athan put Nectar into your glass, using you to expose Aleris's secret in the glasses, the memory of his sister being captured," Faris told me.

"That memory required light and dark angel magic to expose," I replied. "My magic."

"They believe you saw Aleris's memories, memories imprinted on the glasses with light magic. Athan hasn't corrected their misconceptions. It seems the Everlasting feels some sense of loyalty to you." Faris gave his hand a dismissive wave, like he didn't understand why Athan would want to protect me. "There have been so many secrets exposed over the last week. In time, Aleris's secret will bleed into the rest. No one will investigate you if you stick to the story: Athan, trusting in your incorrigible habit of feeling compassion, slipped you Nectar. He knew that when the visions hit you, you'd not stop until you found his sister. Even fear of Aleris wouldn't stop you as it would stop others. This is the story the gods heard. And it is the story you will confirm the next time you see them."

"What makes you think I'll play along?"

"Because the other gods would kill you if they knew the truth. As much as you like to play the rebel, you like to live even more," Faris told me. "And you want your loved ones to live, don't you? Nero Windstriker, for instance."

Anger flared inside my heart—and on my hands. "You will not hurt him."

"So protective," Faris laughed. "Especially considering the circumstances."

Circumstances? What circumstances? No, I wasn't playing along.

"You're trying to bait me," I said.

"Am I?" Faris walked to the window, looking out on the city. "You think you can trust Nero Windstriker?" He glanced back at me. "Then ask him why he interviewed you the day you came to this office to join the Legion of Angels. Ask him why he oversaw your training. Or did you think it's common for an angel, the head of a Legion office and a large territory, to concern himself with a lowly initiate?"

I opened my mouth to rebuff his words, but that protest died on my lips. Honestly, it *was* strange that Nero had overseen my initiation training. I'd been too enamored with him to see it back then, but now that Faris pointed it out, I couldn't deny that he had a point.

"There is much more going on here than you know, child," Faris told me. "And Nero Windstriker is entrenched neck deep in it all."

AUTHOR'S NOTE

If you want to be notified when I have a new release, head on over to my website to sign up for my mailing list at http://www.ellasummers.com/newsletter. Your e-mail address will never be shared, and you can unsubscribe at any time.

If you enjoyed *Fairy's Touch*, I'd really appreciate if you could spread the word. One of the best ways of doing that is by leaving a review wherever you purchased this book. Thank you for your invaluable support!

Angel's Flight, the eighth book in the *Legion of Angels* series, is now available.

ABOUT THE AUTHOR

Ella Summers has been writing stories for as long as she could read; she's been coming up with tall tales even longer than that. One of her early year masterpieces was a story about a pigtailed princess and her dragon sidekick. Nowadays, she still writes fantasy. She likes books with lots of action, adventure, and romance. When she is not busy writing or spending time with her two young children, she makes the world safe by fighting robots.

Ella is the *USA Today*, *Wall Street Journal*, and International Bestselling Author of the paranormal and fantasy series *Legion of Angels*, *Immortal Legacy*, *Dragon Born*, and *Sorcery & Science*.

www.ellasummers.com